BURNING TOWER

BENJAMIN ASHWOOD BOOK 5

AC COBBLE

Cobble Publishing LLC

CONTENTS

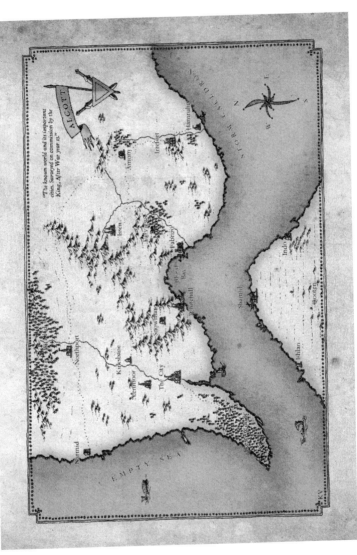

1

AKEW WOODS

Bright sunlight sparkled on the water, surrounding the town of Akew Woods with a shimmering backdrop like a thousand candles burning through an azure curtain. A salty breath of air blew away the verdurous scent of moss and forest. Below them, an inviting, hard-packed dirt road led between the forest and the town. The gates were open, and already groups of travelers were departing, heading into the forest.

Before they entered the town, Ben and Amelie wanted to scout out the surrounding terrain. From near the quarry where they'd camped, it was impossible to see more than fifty paces through the forest in any direction. Their first journey over the road had been in the dark of night, and they'd been rushing to avoid the Sanctuary's men. Now, on the rock- and moss-covered peninsula that cradled Akew Woods, in the light of day, they could get a better view.

Ben followed Amelie to the top of a bluff that rose above the protective horn of the harbor. From their perch, they looked down on the town and the empty, endless expanse of water beyond it. The Empty Sea, Ben had heard the sailors call it. The description seemed apt. On the horizon, he thought he spied a sail, but it could have been the crest of a rogue wave. The rest of the vista was only rich, royal blue, the water barely discernable from the sky.

The other way, over the bluff to the east, the coastline stretched into the distance. The bluffs continued for leagues, unbroken, until they faded into the early morning mist. Sheer cliffs dropped straight down to ragged surf. Atop the cliffs were verdant green forests.

Amelie scrambled up a moss-covered rock and peered at the town below them.

"It looks peaceful in the morning sun," she remarked.

Ben nodded, eyeing the dozen children in the distance that scampered amongst the rocks outside of the gates, playing an unruly version of tag.

Ben and Amelie's shadows stretched out in front of them, elongated by the sun rising at their backs. Ben waved his hand and smiled as his shadow mimicked him. Glancing at Amelie out of the corner of his eye, his shadow made a playful but rude motion in her direction.

She sighed dramatically. "You are a child."

Ben grinned and turned back to the east, stepping close to the edge of the bluff. He felt a trill in his heart as he looked down the sheer rock face. Two or three hundred paces straight down and then a narrow, sandy beach studded by giant hunks of rock that had fallen from the cliff over the years. The waves, unimpeded for hundreds of leagues across the South Sea, pounded relentlessly against the rocks. The air was heavy with humidity and salt.

Far below, a huge culvert extended out of the cliff. Been leaned over, looking closer to examine it. It was the size of a wagon and jutted just four paces out from the rock.

As Ben was looking down, the winds shifted, and a blast of sea air whipped up into his face, followed by a foul wave of utter filth. He stumbled back, gagging. His eyes watered and he felt his stomach churning.

"I think the town's sewers empty out there," mentioned Amelie, mirth lacing her voice.

He leaned over, hands on his knees, spitting on the mossy rocks of the bluff, trying to stop himself from retching. Amelie couldn't contain her laughter and plopped down next to him.

"You should have seen your face," she crowed, tears leaking down her cheeks. "It was like someone told Rhys that ale doesn't exist anymore."

"Why would they do that?" complained Ben, reaching for his water skin, hoping to rinse the taste of the filth of Akew Woods from his mouth.

"Better on the far side of the bluff than in the harbor," responded Amelie. "Remember? We swam through that."

Swishing water in his mouth and spitting it back out, Ben shook his head. Away from the cliff, the sea air flowed over him without the taint of sewage. Hesitantly, he breathed in deeply, letting the scent of the salt and moss fill his lungs.

"When you're ready, I'm starving," remarked Amelie. "It's about time for breakfast."

Ben groaned and then scrambled to his feet. He'd be hearing about this for weeks. He knew it.

IN THE EARLY MORNING, the town of Akew Woods showed few signs of the frantic revelry that had come to an end just bells before. The wildest taverns were empty except for a few patrons who hadn't made it out the doors before collapsing in drunken slumber. The gambling dens were quiet, and the only activity at the bawdy houses were heavily made up girls and boys drinking kaf in small groups starting the day, or more likely, finishing up for the night.

Instead of the boisterous crowd like the night they'd snuck through town, the streets were now filled with people going about their day, running the same errands they did anywhere in the world. Akew Woods was a wild town but a wealthy one. The pirates brought in loot, spent it, and made the merchants rich. The merchants and their families put the money to use buying from local craftsmen and continued the cycle of prosperity. The veins of commerce pumped with the blood of coin in Akew Woods.

Feeling better and enjoying the early bustle in the streets, Ben followed Amelie's lead. They poked their heads into several open taverns, but they were either littered with drunks or serving unfamiliar dishes. After their time in the South Continent, Amelie said she wanted something that reminded her of home.

Finally, halfway down to the harbor, they smelled sizzling bacon and baking bread coming from a clean-looking inn. Ben peeked in the window and saw it was mostly empty, just half a dozen locals filling one table.

Amelie frowned. "My father always said to never patronize a tavern that is empty because it might be empty for good reason."

Ben scratched at a mouth-shaped scar on his arm and stared through the open window. He eyed a plate a serving woman was setting on the table. Fluffy eggs, thick-sliced bacon, and fragrant bread. One of the locals picked up a small pot and poured a steaming mug of kaf.

"Let's risk it," Ben suggested, his mouth watering.

Amelie grinned, and they stepped inside. In addition to the half-dozen locals at one table, the place was filled with bustling serving women. To Ben's eye, it appeared they were working harder at appearing busy than actually being busy. One of the women directed them to an open bench and took their order.

After she left, Ben turned to Amelie. "So, a hearty breakfast then to the market to gather supplies?"

Amelie nodded. "We could be done by midday and then hike

back to camp. I think we could make it back before dusk. Or, we could take our time, spend the night in town, and leave early tomorrow."

"A night in town might be nice," murmured Ben.

"I know what you're thinking," responded Amelie.

"And?" inquired Ben, scooting closer to her on the bench. "You're the one who mentioned staying the night. What are you thinking about?"

Amelie played coy for a few moments and then relented. "A few drinks then we share a comfortable bed. We may not get a chance to enjoy civilization for a bit, so it'd be a shame not to take advantage."

Ben grinned, but before he could reply, the serving woman was back with a pot of kaf, two mugs, and two heaping plates of food. She expertly unloaded the items from her tray, and Ben inhaled deeply, soaking up the smell of the bacon and bread.

"That was quick," complimented Amelie.

The woman nodded and then gestured around the room. "Full staff in the kitchen, but no one is here to cook for."

"Why is that?" inquired Amelie. "If you don't mind me asking. Your prices seem fair, and the food smells good."

The woman grinned. "The prices are fair, and the food is good. Reason no one is here is because all the rooms upstairs are booked. Most of our breakfast custom is folks who stay overnight. A week ago, sixty foreigners rented out the entire inn. Paid in advance, believe it or not. Haven't seen 'em for two days though. That's why no one is here for breakfast. I guess Ole Meece is making his money on the rooms being booked and thinks he's savin' coin by not having to feed 'em. These people are not even using all the rooms! Paid for every bed in the house and told Meece to keep them empty. Stupid waste of coin if you ask me, paying for those rooms and not staying in 'em. Fool and his money, though, right?"

"Yeah, right," agreed Ben, shooting a look at Amelie. "You said sixty foreigners, and they've all been gone for two days? That sounds mighty strange."

"Aye, they've been gone," asserted the woman. "The cute shaggy-haired one left three days ago. Then, two days ago, all of a sudden, the whole bunch started pouring outta here. They were geared up like they was dressed for war, but no one knows who they were going to fight. Nothing happened in town, and no travelers have seen 'em on the roads."

"Shaggy-haired one?" asked Amelie quietly.

"He was a delicious little morsel, let me tell you," proclaimed the woman, leaning toward Amelie. "He was young for me, but I wouldn'ta minded bedding him anyway if I'd had the chance. He may have been some highborn, though. All those soldiers snapped to attention every time he walked in. Probably best not to mess with that type, but a girl can dream. It woulda been a fun night, right?"

Amelie nodded wordlessly.

"Where did he go?" asked Ben, drawing the serving woman's attention back.

The woman shrugged. "The forest road, I reckon. Never heard any discussion of getting passage on a ship, and there's nowhere else to go."

"Thanks," murmured Ben.

The woman scurried off when an elderly bald man poked his head out of the kitchen. She busied herself pretending to wipe down a table. Three other serving women were swishing brooms or filling up the basins below the oil lamps. The women were hoping to not be sent home and miss an easy day of pay, guessed Ben.

"She said they still have the rooms," whispered Amelie. "Sounds like no one has been up there for two days."

Ben nodded and bent to his meal.

"Ben," prodded Amelie. "She mentioned a shaggy-haired young man. Said he left three days ago."

"I know, I know," he responded around a mouthful of bread. "You're thinking the young man she mentioned has to be Milo. I agree, but let's deal with what's upstairs first."

They ate quickly, trying to enjoy their first decent meal since they left Shamiil. When they finished the food, Ben refilled his kaf mug and sat back. His gaze bounced around the room, watching the serving women scurry about. He observed the bald man, who must be Old Meece, constantly poke his head out and study the customers.

At the far end of the room, near the kitchens, an open stairwell led upstairs to where the boarding rooms would be. With the common room devoid of patrons and filled with serving staff who had nothing to do, there would be no way to make it up those stairs without being spotted.

"Maybe we can just walk up and they won't say anything?" suggested Amelie.

Ben shook his head. "She said the foreigners rented every room in this place. If they see strangers walking up those stairs, they're going to want to know why."

She grunted and fell silent for several moments before offering, "Late at night, no one may be watching."

Again, Ben shook his head. "This is Akew Woods. Night is when the town comes alive. There'll be more people here after sunset than there are now. Remember, it was after midnight when we first came through, and the streets were packed."

Amelie frowned.

"You think we can just leave it alone then?" she asked.

Ben sighed and set down his mug. "We can't. What if the wyvern fire staff is in her room?"

"You're right," admitted Amelie. "It could be there. Even if it's not, this is too good of an opportunity to pass up. There's no telling what she could have in her room and what we could learn from it. If not the stairs, how do we get in, though?"

"Let's walk outside and see what we can see," suggested Ben.

They finished quickly, sprinkled some copper coins on the table, and then meandered outside. ~~Ben ducke~~d behind a vegetable seller's stall and pulled Amelie close. He peered around the edge of the stall, furtively studying the inn.

"No one is watching us, and there's no one we need to hide from in this town," said Amelie. "If anything, skulking about is likely to draw someone's attention."

Ben flushed and took Amelie's hand, strolling down the street and then turning the corner to walk into the empty wagon yard behind the inn. The yard was dominated by a hulking, burnt-out stone stable. The structure was intact, but it was clear that days before, a fire had blazed inside.

"Rhys was telling the truth," observed Amelie, sounding surprised.

Ben grunted in agreement and studied the rest of the area.

The wagon yard was a flat, muddy space bordered by the back of the inn on two sides, the burnt-out stable on another, and a head-high fence on the fourth side. Barrels were stacked against the inn, and other supplies which must have been salvaged from the burning stable were stacked against the fence. By the empty hulk of the stable was a massive pile of hay. A delivery to replace what was consumed in the fire, guessed Ben. A wheelbarrow sat beside it, but apparently no one had gotten the energy the move the wagon load inside.

Ben jumped up to peer over the fence and saw that it shielded an open-air tavern. A sea of tables and benches were braced by a small stage and a row of ale and wine kegs.

"That place will be packed as soon as the sun sets," mused Ben.

Amelie nodded and pointed to a balcony behind the stage. "Anyone up there can see every detail in this yard."

They circled the muddy yard one more time, looking for inspiration.

Finally, Ben admitted, "This is probably the quietest the yard ever gets. If we're going to do anything, now is the time."

"What do you think, just climb up the side of the building and sneak in?" questioned Amelie.

"That's what we usually do," agreed Ben.

"Do you think it's strange we have a usual way of breaking into buildings?" asked Amelie.

Ben shrugged and then sauntered over to the barrels against the side of the building. He knelt and boosted Amelie up. She scampered higher until she was standing on the tallest barrel. With a short jump, she reached a window on the second floor and gripped the sill, hanging in the air until she set her feet against the rough mortar of the wall.

Ben, looking up at her, tapped the hunting knife on his belt. "Need this to jimmy the latch open?"

Amelie glanced down at him and wiggled her fingers. She set her hand against the wooden slats of the shutters and there was an audible pop. The shutters swung open, and Amelie hauled herself higher, disappearing inside the darkened window.

Grumbling, Ben awkwardly climbed the barrels, reached up, grasped the sill, and then wiggled through the open window. Once inside, he turned and pushed the shutters closed.

A soft glow emanated from Amelie's palm. She raised it high, illuminating the simple room. Two beds, a small table, a cloak rack, and a wardrobe. Both beds were unmade, heavy cloaks hung on the rack, and a pair of distressingly worn boots sat in one corner.

They opened the wardrobe and found travel packs and a few sets of clothing. The place looked exactly like a room should look when two soldiers were leaving behind gear to go on a day-long excursion.

"They expected to slaughter us quickly," remarked Amelie coldly.

Ben grunted. "They had Eldred."

There was nothing more to find in the room, so they crossed cautiously to the door. Ben eased it open and peeked outside into

9

the empty hallway. It was dim, lit only by small windows at either end. He slunk out into the hall and edged over to the open stairwell. Peering around the corner, he saw the common room below was just like they left it.

He tiptoed back to Amelie and leaned close, whispering, "As long as we stay away from the stairs, no one should spot us. No one has any reason to come up here, but a creaking floorboard could give us away. We should do this as quickly as we can without rushing and making an inadvertent sound."

Amelie nodded and padded to the door across from the one they exited. The door was locked.

Ben reached for his hunting knife again, but Amelie rolled her eyes at him and magically popped the latch open. Smirking, she led the way into the next room. It was much the same as the first. Standard issue gear for military men, a few personal effects, and nothing of interest to Ben and Amelie.

"We're wasting our time on the soldier's rooms," she whispered. "We need to find Eldred's."

Ben nodded tersely and pointed down the hall. The dark mage would have taken the best room, which he figured would be on the corner.

Amelie led the way, stepping carefully to avoid creaking boards or stomps loud enough to be heard downstairs. As they approached the door, she held out a hand cautioning Ben.

He stayed close behind her and gasped as a series of glowing runes materialized along the door frame. Pulsating orange and yellow, the arcane script bled menace.

"I'll take that knife now," said Amelie.

Ben passed it over and watched as she knelt to scrape the steel tip into the wood near the bottom of the door. Slowly, the glow of the runes began to fade as the stored power leaked out of the ward.

"Glad I watched Towaal and Gunther do that so many times," remarked Amelie as she passed the knife back to Ben.

He slid the steel blade into his belt sheath and held his breath as Amelie popped open the latch and pushed on the door. They stood in the threshold, peering into the dim room. Amelie raised her palm and directed a weak light around the space. No more runes flared to life, no stabbing pain, no violent explosions. They stepped inside.

Ben jumped when he saw a white, porcelain mask sitting on a small table between the beds, but on closer inspection, it looked like it could have been a spare.

"Where does she get these made?" asked Ben. "Is there a creepy mask maker in the City that you know of? I don't recall seeing one."

"It looks safe," muttered Amelie, ignoring him and peering down at the mask. "I don't think this is magical at all."

"I wonder why she needed two of them?" asked Ben.

Amelie didn't answer. She turned and began to examine the rest of the room. Ben looked around, not seeing any obvious threats but afraid to touch anything.

The room was like the others, but neither bed appeared slept in. Aside from the mask, there were no personal effects or mementos scattered around like they'd seen in the soldier's chambers. It was neat and tidy. Disappointingly to Ben, they didn't see the wyvern fire staff sitting out where they could take it and leave.

After a brief moment pawing through a mundane cloak on the rack and peeking under the beds, Ben and Amelie turned to each other and then glanced at the wardrobe.

"If there's anything in here, it will be in there," said Amelie nervously.

She crossed to the wardrobe and held out a hand, sensing for wards.

Nothing happened.

She shrugged and pulled open the door, shining the light from her hand inside.

Ben gasped.

The light flickered out from Amelie's palm.

"Harden your wi—" she started to yell, but she didn't finish. The world erupted in light.

~

BEN BLINKED.

Above him, brilliant blue stretched across his entire field of his vision, interrupted only by a handful of small, puffy white clouds. His body tingled like the entire thing had fallen asleep and was just now waking back up. He heard faint sounds as if from under water, and he smelled something that tickled his nose. It was smoke, he decided dreamily, a lot of smoke.

He blinked again and shifted, fighting the tingling in his body. He felt something poking him and turned his head to see yellow pieces of straw. He was lying on a bed of hay. He blinked a third time, and awareness crashed back in. He realized just how strange it was he was on a pile of hay. The sound came again, muffled and weak. It sounded like, like, someone yelling. He raised his head and looked around. Down near his boots, he found where the smoke was coming from.

The pile of hay was on fire.

A jolt of panic shot through his body, forcing him from his stupor. He was lying on a giant pile of hay, and it was on fire! He fought to sit up, scrambling to pull his boots back from the licking tongues of flame. He glanced around wildly. Beside him, he saw someone's legs thrashing. The rest of the body was stuck in the hay pile. The legs were kicking frantically, evidently also sensing the growing heat of the flame.

"Oh, damn."

Ben scrambled across the hay, ignoring the scorching burn when he placed his hand down in the center of the quickly growing fire. He tackled the two legs and set his feet, the heat of the flame singeing his calves. He yanked with all of his might.

Ben and Amelie tumbled down the burning stack of hay and landed hard in the muddy wagon yard. Amelie, spitting out dust and straw, scrambled back on her hands and knees, cursing loudly. In front of them, the flames licked higher. In moments, the entire stack of hay went up, burning hot and fast. Shouts of alarm and a ringing bell intruded on Ben's awareness and he glanced over his shoulder. The inn behind them was gone.

"Oh, damn," he muttered again.

Amelie followed his look and her face lost all of its color. "We have to go," she croaked.

Burning pieces of thatch floated through the air. Chunks of mortar and stone were scattered around the yard, and a few timbers still stuck up, skewed drunkenly where the inn once stood. The entire structure had been blown to bits.

Men began to stream into the area, carrying buckets and blankets, dousing the nearby buildings, protecting them from the floating, burning debris from the inn. Next to Ben and Amelie, the pile of straw burned merrily, safely leaning against the already torched stone structure of the stables.

"Not again!" came a shout from the bucket brigade.

Ben and Amelie scrambled to their feet and staggered away. Several people called out to offer assistance, but Ben waved them off. In the initial confusion of the blast, they were seen as victims instead of instigators.

"If-If we hadn't hardened our will…" stammered Amelie.

Ben squeezed her arm tightly.

"Oh, the people downstairs," she quaked. She stumbled, and Ben barely caught her.

"Here, young man," said a middle-aged woman who broke off from the crowd around the former inn. "Sit her down here."

The woman kindly but firmly took ahold of both Ben and

Amelie and directed them to sit beside the wall of a neighboring building.

"Wait here, dears. I'll get ya some water," she insisted.

Ben leaned back, his head bouncing against the stone wall. Everything sounded like it was coming through a woolen blanket, and his shoulder ached from where he must have landed on it. He patted himself, searching for additional injuries, but to his amazement, he seemed whole.

"What did we do?" moaned Amelie, tears streaking her cheeks.

"I-I don't know," mumbled Ben. "We can talk about it, but not here. Not where anyone can hear us."

Amelie's head fell into her hands, and Ben let her sit in silence. It was clear what they'd done now that he had time to consider it. They'd triggered some trap left by Eldred, and it'd blown up her room and the entire inn with it. By hardening their will, they'd survived the magical blast but had been thrown through the air. He didn't want to think about the luck they'd used up by landing in a pile of hay instead of smashing against the side of a stone building. He suspected anyone nearby who hadn't hardened their will had survived the explosion just as well as the inn, meaning they hadn't.

As he was thinking it, Ben saw the bystanders find the first body. The first of many, he realized, his gut clenching like a fist. He closed his eyes, and his chin dropped to his chest. He drew a deep breath and then slowly let it out. He breathed deeply, over and over, trying to center his thoughts like Towaal had taught him. When he felt like he was beginning to get himself under control, he opened his eyes.

He was staring down into the mud, and there, between his legs, lay a palm-sized copper amulet. On it was the face of a young woman. She was smiling at him. The amulet was hanging from half of a charred leather thong.

"There ya are. Here. Drink this," he heard.

Ben put his hand over the amulet and slid it into a pocket in his britches. He looked up and saw the woman who'd sat them down kneeling next to Amelie. She was holding a glass flagon of water. The woman fortunately mistook Amelie's shock as a reaction to getting caught in the blast instead of a reaction to causing the blast.

Wordlessly, Amelie sipped the water. The woman offered it to Ben next, and he found he was incredibly thirsty.

"What happened?" she asked.

Ben shook his head. "There was an explosion right next to us. It sent us flying. I-I'd prefer not to talk about it yet if that's okay. My mind is still reeling."

"Of course, dear, of course." The woman stood and looked around. "Tha men are getting the fire sorted, and tha constables will figure out what happened. In tha meantime, please, come rest at my inn. It's just across the way from here, and it's nice and quiet this time'a day. I've seen men act like you after a fight. They call it post trauma, or something. It helps to take a quiet moment and gather your thoughts. Please, come with me."

Ben grunted and staggered to his feet. The woman's inn was better than the muddy stable yard. He bent down and pulled Amelie up. The woman smiled at them and started pushing her way through the crowd that was forming to gawk at the destroyed building.

Amelie shot Ben a glance, distrust evident in her gaze, but he merely shrugged. He supposed it was possible this woman had some ulterior motive for bringing them with her, but they had to get away. Walking with a local seemed like a good idea at the moment. Being the only strangers standing around a strange and deadly occurrence was rarely a good idea in Ben's experience.

True to the woman's word, she led them to an inn just a block away from the explosion. Hanging above the door was a rusted metal sign featuring five peaks, the center peak rising twice the height of the other four.

"A mountain?" wondered Ben.

The woman shook her head. "Tha Goblin's Finger. You'll have more fun in here than anywhere else in Akew Woods. That's our promise."

"Goblin," said Amelie. "Like in the stories?"

"Goblins ain't just a story, girl," chided the woman. "They're out there in the dark places of the world. Nasty bastards they are, but you don't have to worry about that in here. Though, I have to admit, we got more than our share of bastards, and being nasty is our stock and trade."

The woman turned and laughed loudly as she led them through the doorway. As soon as they entered, a bevy of scantily clad serving women swarmed closer, all speaking on top of each other.

"What was it, Kate?"

"Wagon crash? I told you it'd be nothing more'na couple wagons got loose."

"An attack! We're under attack! I said that scallywag was telling the truth. He's coming to murder us all!"

The last woman let out a high-pitched shriek and took off running toward the back of the tavern. The shock of her reaction silenced the rest of them.

Kate, evidently the woman who'd taken them in, held up a calming hand. "Tha Broken Wing exploded."

Another round of squeals and wails. At the tables in the tavern, two score of unsavory-looking men watched either amused or too fogged by drink to care. None of them were stirring to see what the fuss outside was about.

"It looks'ta be some freak accident," continued Kate. "There was fire, but it's under control. Tha constables are there now, and they'll get it sorted. It's not an attack, or, well, whatever it was, they'll get it sorted."

"An explosion?" asked one heavily made-up woman.

Ben discreetly steered his gaze away from the copious

cleavage the woman had on display. He smirked when, out of the corner of his eye, he saw Amelie was transfixed on her, making little effort to hide her amazement at how much skin the woman revealed.

The nearly naked woman and their host paid them no mind. They were used to such attention, guessed Ben, as he studied the rest of the room. Without a doubt, it was more of a bawdy house than an inn. Amelie appeared to be the only woman in the room who didn't work there.

"I don't know, Marie. The building's just not there. I guess it went up in a burst of flame real quick like. These two were right beside it, but they can't talk yet. Let's settle 'em down, and maybe later they can tell us what they saw. Give it a bell, and we'll prolly find out more'n those useless sack constables will."

Kate, their host, turned to them and steered them to an empty table away from the other patrons in the tavern.

"More water?" she asked.

"Ale," croaked Ben. "If you have it."

The woman smiled. "That we do, son, that we do."

"Wine," requested Amelie.

Kate smiled at them and whisked off to get their drinks.

As soon as she was out of earshot, Amelie glanced at Ben. "We killed them, Ben. A dozen, two dozen, I don't even know. The entire staff of that place and their customers."

Ben shook his head. "We didn't, Amelie. Eldred did."

She opened her mouth to argue, but he cut her short.

"Amelie, if not us, someone else would have opened that wardrobe. Sooner or later, that explosion was going to happen no matter what. We got caught in the middle of it, but Eldred blew that building up. Eldred killed those people."

She frowned at him.

"Believe me," muttered Ben. "I've torn myself apart over plenty of our decisions, but we can't shoulder this one. That... thing is what did it. I only wish we could kill her again."

As soon as he said it, Ben paused.

"You saw it too," remarked Amelie quietly.

He sighed. "I did."

Kate returned with their drinks, but after one look at their faces, she scurried away again. Ben took a deep pull, finishing a third of the tankard in the first gulp.

"What the hell was that thing?" asked Amelie.

Ben grimaced. "Maybe we did kill her again. The extra mask, that desiccated body…"

He shuddered, recalling the horror that had flashed through him when they'd opened the wardrobe and saw what appeared to be a dried up husk of a dead woman. Its eyes had flared with a cruel red light. The next thing he remembered, he was blinking at the sky on top of a burning haystack.

"If there are more of them…" said Amelie.

They sat silently for a long moment, sipping on their drinks, thinking.

"If there are more of them," finished Ben, "then we have work to do."

"How would we even know?" wondered Amelie, a sick sense of dread lacing her voice. "If they're, ah, manufacturing these things, there could be, I don't know, a lot of them."

"The Veil knows," answered Ben.

Amelie tilted her wine up and finished it. "You're right. That's one more reason to track that woman down and put a stop to her."

Ben finished his ale and waved to Kate to bring another round. It was early morning still, but he figured anytime you were startled by an undead corpse that quickly exploded in your face, it was okay to drink before noon.

"There's one other thing," mentioned Ben.

He slipped the copper amulet out of his cloak and placed it on the table, cupping his hand over it to hide it from the rest of the room. Amelie frowned at it and then touched it with a finger. She flipped it over, and Ben was startled to see a second face.

"They look sort of like the faces that stand on the gates of the Sanctuary," she hissed.

"First Mages," said Ben slowly. "Whatever that means."

"Where did you find this?" queried Amelie.

"Right below me when we sat down in that wagon yard, sitting in the mud," responded Ben. "It's like I was supposed to find it."

"Something to do with the First Mages?" asked Amelie.

Ben shrugged.

"Rhys knows more than he's said," declared Amelie. "I think it's time we ask him. With the Alliance and the Coalition, The Veil and Avril, and the demon army, we can't afford to have another enemy out there."

"Maybe they're not enemies," offered Ben. "Maybe they could be allies. If I was supposed to find that..."

"Even more reason to talk to Rhys."

Amelie pushed the amulet toward Ben, but he shook his head.

"You keep it. You're the one who knows about magic," he said, wiggling his fingers at her.

"Just a quarter bell away from a trauma and already you're promising the girl some magic?"

Ben jumped. Their host Kate had appeared over his shoulder and was winking at him.

"M-Magic?" stammered Ben.

"Come on, son." Kate wiggled her fingers lasciviously. "What kinda inn do you think you're in? You ain't the first, and I'd bet a kettle full'a gold you ain't gonna be the last to wiggle his fingers at this little sweet. Am I right, girl?"

Amelie blushed furiously.

"That's, ah, that's not what I meant," mumbled Ben.

"Doesn't feel half as good as you think it does," quipped Kate. She leaned in conspiringly to Amelie. "I won't spoil your secret, girl, but here's a piece of free advice from a woman who don't give nothin' away for free. You tell him what you like and make him keep workin' til you get it. He'll do it, girl. He'll do whatever you want him to and beg to do it again. Men are lapdogs when you decide you want to be the master."

Kate winked and flounced away again, calling out to one of her girls and swinging her hips in a saucy roll.

"I, ah…" Ben tried to muddle through an explanation.

"I know what kind of magic you were talking about," responded Amelie with a grin.

They settled down and started to talk through their next moves. The explosion was an unwelcome surprise. Stumbling across a corpse with a second creepy porcelain mask nearby was an even worse one, but after discussing it, they realized it changed nothing about what they needed to do. They still had to get supplies and return to Rhys and Towaal in the forest. Once Rhys healed, they would make their way through the wilderness and to the City.

If Milo had left three days before them and had gone down the forest road like the serving woman suggested, then the City was the only place he could go. It dovetailed with everything they suspected about him so far. He was an agent of the Veil, and since they hadn't found the wyvern fire staff in Eldred's room or on her body, then Milo must have it. Their first order of business was still to find him and the staff.

"Eldred's body," said Amelie. "What do you call the dead body when it's, well, previously dead?"

Ben sipped his ale and shook his head. "I hope we don't run into so many of those things that we have to come up with a term."

More relaxed, Ben ordered a third round. Kate, sensing they'd gotten over the shock of the explosion, sidled up again.

"You sweethearts ready to talk?" she purred.

Amelie smiled at her. "We're ready, but I guess there's really not much to tell. We ate breakfast at the inn, what did you say it was? The Broken Wing? Well, we got to chatting about some things and decided to take a walk. We were walking out back of the inn, looking for a place with a little privacy…"

Kate's lips curled into a smile, and Amelie winked at her. Ben flushed.

"And then, well, I don't know what happened," said Amelie. "I think I blacked out for a moment. When I came to, I was buried in a burning pile of straw, and the inn was gone."

Kate turned to Ben.

"Yeah, that's about it," he claimed. "Maybe they were storing some volatile oils in the place? I've heard castles have that stuff for sieges. Or grain silos can go off like fireworks when they're full of dust and someone lights a fire. Could blow up like that, maybe."

Kate frowned. "I don't think so. There's nowhere for grain dust to be floating around the inn like that, and why would they have that much oil?"

Ben shrugged. He and Amelie fell silent.

"You didn't see anyone?" pressed Kate.

"Not after we went around back. Inside, there were the serving women and what looked like some locals eating. No one that looked strange to me. No one I think would have caused an explosion like that."

Kate sighed, unable to hide her disappointment at missing out on some unique gossip or a lead on what happened. She scooted back her chair and stood. "You two rest up. About midday, this place starts to get a little wild. You're welcome to stay, but I'm not sure it's your kinda tavern."

Ben nodded. Then, something behind the woman caught his eye. He leaned over, peering around her. She turned, following his gaze, and Amelie looked as well.

"Black Bart," muttered Amelie.

Ben grunted. She was right. Hanging above a sputtering fire

and heavy mantel was a painted portrait of the pirate, the one they'd killed after he tried to betray them outside of Kirksbane. Below Black Bart's portrait on the mantel was a slender, curved dagger.

"You know Bartholomew?" exclaimed Kate.

"We've… met him," admitted Ben.

Kate beamed at them. "The patron of this inn. Without his gold, none of it woulda been possible."

"Patron?" questioned Amelie. "He, ah, didn't seem the generous type when we met him. No offense."

Kate grinned and sat back down, waving to her girls to bring another round.

"He was the meanest son of a bitch I ever met," confirmed Kate. "Lotta fun, though. I felt a bit bad about it afterward, to be honest. Never did get a chance to apologize."

"Apologize for what?" asked Amelie.

"His eye!" exclaimed Kate with a broad grin.

"You're the hoo— the girl who stabbed out his eye?" asked Ben incredulously.

Kate beamed at him.

"He told us he killed you," mentioned Amelie. She evidently realized they were venturing into offensive territory and scrambled to add, "Well, maybe we heard wrong."

Kate leaned back and cackled loudly. "I'm sure you heard it right, girl. That awful bastard nearly did kill me. Of course, I nearly killed him too when I put that dagger into his skull."

Ben blinked at her, confused. One of her girls swung by with their drinks and Kate tipped hers up, gulping it down in three long swallows.

"Ah, grog. Terrible shit, truth be told, but it always reminds me of my days at sea. Wasn't much longer after that when I met Black Bart for the first time. He was young, full of vinegar, and his soul was already soaked in blood, treachery, and deceit. My kinda man. He sailed into town and made straight for the Pink

Cavern. That's the tavern I worked at then. He offered silver for the best girl in the house. I pushed aside all tha other hussies and told him I only took gold. Wasn't true, but he was drunk as hell and had a coin purse fatter than he knew what to do with. We became a thing after that. He'd sail off, plunder some sorry ass town or take down a slow-moving merchant cog and then he'd come back and hole up a couple days with me."

Amelie tilted up her drink as well.

Kate continued, "I was younger then and a bit wild, to be honest."

Ben nodded, trying to imagine a wilder version of Kate.

"Well, one time, we were on the backside of a three-day bender. Durhang, shine root, grog... I didn't know what was up or what was down. At some point, I guess I got a bit outta my mind and I thought Bart had offended me somehow, don't even remember how now, but I put that there dagger straight into his face, catching him in the eye. He went down howling, screeching like one o'them monkeys the westerners bring. It brought in the house muscle, but they sure as hell weren't going to throw out Bart or me. I was their gold goose, and he was the best customer. I had 'em stick a hot poker in his eye socket to stop the bleeding. Then, I blew him another cloud'a durhang and sliced off a hunk of shine root. He started feeling better after a couple bells, and we went at it for another three days. I don't think I slept that entire damn week!"

Ben swallowed his ale, wide-eyed and amazed. He believed every word the woman was saying.

"Well, after that," said Kate, "Bart got word of some Ishalneese merchant fleeing the emperor's wrath. Man was supposed to be packing a ship full'a gold, silver, statues, tapestries, and all that fancy junk highborn like. My man Bart couldn't let a prize like that go unplundered. I was glad. He'd worn me out, let me tell you. Worn like I'd never been. I took a break and went to see my mam and pap. When I came back, there was no word of Bart.

Weeks passed. Then months. Never heard of him sacking another town, taking another ship. Everyone assumed they'd been caught in a storm or foundered on some hidden rocks they were too drunk to avoid. I knew it had to be the worst. Bart left a chest full'a gold, though, which no one else knew about. It's how I bought this tavern and hired my first girls. Been in business since."

Ben tingled from the three ales he'd drank. He tried to keep a smile off his face as he listened. Kate was some kind of storyteller.

"Course," drawled Kate. She leaned forward. "Now you tellin' me Black Bart is alive?"

Ben scratched his head and looked at Amelie. She was looking at him.

"He, uh, was alive," offered Ben lamely.

Kate's eyes narrowed.

"I know you!" exclaimed a man. He pushed a girl off his lap and staggered to his feet.

A sparse beard graced his chin. His long hair was pulled back into a thick ponytail behind his head. His shirt was unbuttoned to his navel, and his pants bulged from where he must have been enjoying the girl squirming on his lap. He saw them looking and glanced down.

"I can explain that," he slurred.

"Dale," scolded Kate, "you drunk ass. Go back to Jenna. I'm tryin' ta have a conversation here."

"No, Kate," insisted the man. "I know that girl."

Ben, Amelie, and Kate all looked at the man skeptically.

"You've known a lot of girls," allowed Kate, "but I don't think this one is the type you know."

"Really," claimed the man. He swayed slightly like he was on a ship, but he wasn't. "Man named Tomas hired me back when I was livin' in the City. Said he wanted to meet some cutthroats. I took him to meet some right here in Akew Woods. 'Fore we left the City, though, I met him at a big government building. Lots of officials. Fancy stuff. Important place."

The man hitched up his belt, belched, and stared drunkenly at Amelie.

"And?" queried Kate.

The man's story wasn't making any sense to the bawdy house owner, but a sinking sensation was settling in Ben's stomach. Surreptitiously, his hand dropped to the hilt of his sword.

"And what?" asked the man, obliviously adjusting the crotch of this trousers.

Behind him, the girl he was with pawed at him. "Come on, Dale. I been up all night with you. We gonna go upstairs or what?"

The man shook his head, apparently trying to clear the fog of drink.

"That girl's a highborn," he declared. "The place where I met the man Tomas, this girl was there. I saw her through a window. They told me she was the heir to some eastern throne. Issen or Irrefort, I think."

Ben glanced at Amelie. Her face was tight, and one hand was gripping the hilt of her rapier. The other was stuffed in her belt pouch where she kept her magical catalysts. The patrons in the bar were going to get a nasty surprise if they thought she was merely some pampered lord's daughter.

"Lady Amelie," boomed a new voice.

Amelie's head whipped around to stare at the new speaker.

A tall, red-haired man stood up from his table. He had a beard stretching to his navel and was as wide as he was tall. A giant battle-axe rested against his chair. His forearms were covered in scars, and his torso was covered in a strange jerkin formed of brown-green scales.

"Who's Lady Amelie?" slurred Dale.

Kate's eyes went wide, and she discreetly shuffled closer to Ben and Amelie. "I don't want any trouble here, Musaaf."

The huge red-headed man picked up his battle-axe. Behind him, a dozen more men stood, reaching for weapons. "Lord Gregor of Issen has a daughter named Amelie. Seems our girl here answers to the same name."

Dale's voice dropped, and a cold tension crept into the room. "Musaaf, you know I respect you and your men, but I saw her first. This Lady Amy is mine."

Musaaf snorted, derisively eyeing Dale. "You and who else, Dale? Why don't you run upstairs with Jenna and see if you still got enough man in you to get it up for her. We'll take this from here."

Behind Dale, a score of drunken sailors staggered to their feet.

A shaven-headed man wearing black leather britches and a knee-length, purple velvet coat stood up. His coat was open, revealing a shirtless chest covered in green tattoos.

"Dale's on my crew now," snarled the purple-coated man.

The men behind Musaaf tensed, white-knuckled hands gripping their weapons.

"Zane, didn't you learn your lesson back in Ashraff?" snapped Musaaf. "From what I recall, you were enslaved and left to die in the fighting pits."

The purple-coated man grinned and slipped both hands underneath his coat and behind his back. When he pulled them out, he was wearing two dark steel gauntlets. They were covered in razor-sharp spikes and tipped with four brutal looking claws.

Ben gasped as the gauntlets pulsed with bright green runes.

Musaaf hefted his battle-axe. "Going to take more than fancy gimmicks to get outta here with that lady, Zane. We're not walking away from that kinda ransom."

Zane, the purple-coated pirate, merely grinned broadly and clicked his gauntlets together, causing bright green sparks to sizzle between them.

Kate turned and whispered to Ben and Amelie, "You should probably run."

Ben noticed her girls had already slunk away, along with half the other patrons in the tavern. The other half were either standing with weapons in hand or were staring drunk and confused at the men around them.

Suddenly, the fireplace burst with an ear-shattering crack. Decades worth of soot billowed into the room. Ben grabbed Amelie's hand and ran.

Screams and the clash of battle rang out behind them.

2

THE DEEP FOREST

"You did what?" exclaimed Towaal.

Ben shrugged uncomfortably.

"You said Musaaf and Zane?" croaked Rhys. The rogue was slouched against a fallen log, clutching the hilt of a long knife nervously.

Amelie coughed discreetly and appeared to be studying a nearby tree. She didn't meet Ben's eyes when he looked to her for help.

"We didn't do anything!" exclaimed Ben. "They recognized Amelie and started fighting on their own. We didn't even talk to them."

"I was talking about before," remarked Towaal with a heavy sigh. "When you triggered Eldred's trap and blew up the inn, likely killing a dozen people in the process and nearly burning down the entire town."

"It would have blown up anyway," declared Ben. "We were just unlucky to be the ones to trigger the trap. It could have happened to anyone."

"I thought you said you climbed the side of the building and broke in?" queried Towaal.

Ben pursed his lips, struggling to come up with a reasonable explanation for that bit.

"Musaaf and Zane?" interrupted Rhys.

"I think those were the names," murmured Amelie. "Do you know them?"

Rhys snorted and then explained, "They are two of the bloodiest pirate captains on the seas. They were both brought up under the vicious Black Bart. Once he disappeared, they set off on their own and have left a decade of rape and pillaging in their wake. Ironically, we could probably turn those two in for more gold than they would have gotten from you, Amelie."

"Black Bart?" said Amelie. "Did we not tell you about…"

"Well, they didn't take us," interjected Ben, motioning hastily to quiet Amelie. He'd had enough explaining for the day. "We'll just move on. Problem solved."

"We'd better move quickly," grumbled Rhys. "You managed to catch the attention of two ruthless pirate captains. Whichever one comes out of that fight walking isn't likely to forget about you, Amelie. They'll come for us, and we can't be sitting here when they arrive."

"Are you healthy enough to travel?" questioned Ben.

Rhys looked back at him blankly and then finally answered, "I'm certainly not healthy enough to fight a crew of pirates."

Ben winced. Towaal shook her head in disappointment.

"I can continue to pour energy into you from the healing disc, Rhys," she offered. "There will be a price to pay later."

The rogue nodded. "Do it. Let's get a few days away from here at least. Then, we can rest. It's possible the pirates won't follow us into the woods."

"It's possible," acknowledged Towaal. She didn't sound hopeful.

~

THE NEXT MORNING, they broke camp and ventured into the forest. Near the edges closest to Akew Woods, the trees were young and slender. They'd been logged to support the town's needs, but by midday, the trunks grew thicker, the overhanging pine boughs heavier, and the scent of the sea faded to the smell of pine.

The road was wide enough for a single wagon and packed hard. There weren't many travelers to Akew Woods, but there were some, and they had been using the lonely track for generations. There were no turns, no cut-outs, nothing but the solitary road and the quiet forest around it.

They moved slowly. Rhys had received an additional boost from Lady Towaal's healing, but the energy she imparted could only do so much. The rogue's body needed time to recover, and they didn't have it. He hobbled along, barely lifting his feet as he moved at half-walking speed. It gave Ben plenty of time to study the woods around them.

"A serious logging operation could make a fortune here," he muttered, eyeing a soaring pine. He guessed it'd take three of them to link arms and circle the thing.

"What do you know about logging?" asked Amelie.

Ben stared back at her.

She frowned and a flush crept into her face. "Oh, right."

Ben gestured around them. "You went to Farview and Murdoch's Waystation. You saw the distance it takes to move timber to market. We benefit from the Callach River, but it's a serious endeavor. Here, with a quick wagon train, they would be to Akew Woods in less than a day. Those ships could sail anywhere along the coast."

"Maybe the wood is too heavy to ship," offered Amelie.

Ben shook his head. He was thinking about Whitehall and Fabrizo. Even Shamiil or the City. None of them had nearly as much quality timber available as what the party was walking through. Surely, a savvy merchant could transport it cheap enough to earn a healthy profit.

"It's almost like they don't cut wood more than a day away from town," speculated Ben.

"They don't," confirmed Rhys from behind them.

Ben glanced back and saw Rhys struggling to keep pace.

"Let's take a break," suggested Ben.

A momentary flash of relief crossed the rogue's face and he plopped down on the side of the road, landing on a soft bed of fallen pine needles. He unhooked his water skin and took a sip.

"We'll be fine on the road," he advised, "but these woods aren't friendly to strangers. We should stay as close to the track as we can."

Ben glanced around them. The woods seemed peaceful. They reminded him of home. There was nothing more threatening in view than a quick-footed red squirrel, which scampered across the road in front of them.

"Is it a magic wood?" asked Amelie. "Like in the story of the Goblin Forest? Meredith's mother used to tell us that tale when we were little."

"It's not a magic wood," interjected Towaal, "and there are no goblins here, at least that I know of. There are people who live in this forest, though. Hermits, I suppose you could say. They're tribal and fiercely territorial. They allow people access to the road because they need trade as much as anyone, but off the road, they can be dangerous."

Ben frowned. "The sailors mentioned hill tribes, I think, and I recall in the City people said there were bandits or something out here."

"Not bandits," corrected Rhys. "The tribes couldn't care less about wealth. As Towaal said, it's about territory and ensuring that no one encroaches on theirs. That's why there isn't any logging here. You venture too deep and chop down a tree, someone is going to show up."

Ben kicked a pinecone out of his way and asked Rhys, "So, these tribes live in villages around here? We haven't seen any roads."

Towaal answered, "No one knows exactly where they live."

"The Sanctuary is within a few days' walk of the northern edge of the forest," objected Amelie. "How is it that no one knows anything about these people?"

"There are dangers in these woods for anyone," replied Towaal solemnly, "but it is even more so for people with talent. Even on the road, mages have been known to pass into these woods and never exit. Members of the Sanctuary never travel this way now. Too many mages have been lost."

"That sounds like a magical forest to me," insisted Amelie.

"Mages avoided Qooten too," reminded Ben. "There was nothing magical there, just Dirhadji. Could it be that these tribal people are related somehow?"

Towaal shrugged.

"This doesn't make sense," said Amelie, frustration lacing her voice. "If there was something or someone in this forest attacking mages, the Veil would have done something about it. This forest is nearly on her doorstep!"

"The women who have worn the veil rarely start a fight they cannot win," advised Rhys. "They are plotters, strategists. Like anyone, they are afraid of the unknown or someone bigger and meaner than them. Whatever is in this forest that represents a threat to mages never comes out. If you were the Veil, would you send your people in here or live and let live?"

Amelie grunted.

Ben, frowning, kicked another pinecone. "If this place is so dangerous for mages, should we be worried that we're going to spend the next month hiking through it? We didn't gather enough supplies to get us all the way to the City. We're going to have to hunt and forage at some point."

"Yes," responded Towaal. "We should be worried, but Milo

went through here, and if there is any chance we can catch him, we have to try."

~

THEY CAMPED a few leagues from where they had started, half a day's journey at best, but Rhys was flagging, and darkness fell early underneath the trees. Ben collected an armful of fallen branches and placed them above a pile of pine needles. With a snap of her finger, Amelie shot a spark into the pile, and the fire blazed alight.

"You're pretty handy," acknowledged Ben.

Amelie grinned.

Towaal sat eyeing Rhys from across the fire. The rogue seemed to have fallen asleep, leaning against his pack. "If those pirates come for us, we're not going to outrun them at this rate."

Ben nodded. Even with Towaal's healing, the rogue was in no shape for serious travel.

"What do you suggest?" asked Amelie. "An ambush?"

Towaal shook her head. "They didn't catch us today, and it's possible they aren't following us at all. Who knows? They could have all killed each other in that tavern, or maybe they thought you fled to the sea. Setting an ambush could be a massive waste of time, time which we can't afford to lose more of. Besides, if they do catch us, they'll be in for a surprise."

Towaal snapped her fingers like Amelie had earlier and sent a bright orange spark flying around their campsite. "A handful of mundane attackers isn't something we need to be overly concerned with," declared the mage.

Ben laughed. "I guess after dealing with the Purple and Eldred, I've gotten used to worrying about mages."

"A mage isn't invincible, as you've seen," responded Towaal, "but unless they catch me sleeping, I can easily handle a small group of men who haven't trained hardening their will."

"We'll set a watch then," decided Ben. "We can put out the fire and place someone thirty or forty paces back on the road. If anyone is coming this way, that should be time to wake the others and get ready for them. Guarding the camp, starting fires, you mages are nice to have around."

"We are," agreed Amelie. "Now, you had better make yourself useful to us and cook our dinner."

"You can take the lady out of the castle," mumbled Ben under his breath as he scooted over to his pack to scrounge through the limited supplies they'd brought with them.

"What was that?" questioned Amelie.

He grinned at her. "Just looking for those sausages."

Both Amelie and Towaal snorted. Smiling to himself, Ben set about making dinner.

After they ate, he doused the fire and volunteered for the first watch. The night was pleasant. A breeze stirred the pine trees above him, and it was warm enough that he felt comfortable with his cloak opened wide to allow access to the hilt of his longsword.

Somewhere, a few days ahead of them, Milo had followed this same road. Behind them, a gang of pirates may or may not be following them. In the woods lurked vicious tribes capable of making a mage disappear. Despite that, Ben was comfortable alone in the dark. The forest reminded him of home, and before the demon attacked, he never had reason to be worried in Farview. The sounds of night birds and the hoot of an owl were the only things that intruded on the rustling of the pine needles. He knew that if anyone was stalking through the woods, the forest critters would go silent. That, more than hearing men moving, would serve as adequate warning.

But as the bells passed, the forest remained alive, and by the time the moon was high overhead, Ben had neither heard nor seen any signs of pirates or tribal warriors. He made his way back to the camp and shook Lady Towaal awake.

Her eyes snapped open and reflected the dim moonlight back at him.

"All quiet," he whispered.

She nodded and rolled to her feet, shaking out her dress and then vanishing into the dark within a dozen strides. Ben curled next to Amelie and quickly feel deeply asleep.

THE CHIRPING of birds woke him in the morning.

Their fire was cold ash. Around it, Rhys and Lady Towaal slumbered. Amelie's bedroll was empty, and Ben surmised she must be down the road still on watch. Pre-dawn light barely broke through the pine canopy above him.

Ben quietly slid out of his bedroll, taking care to not wake Rhys. They'd spared the rogue a watch last night and hoped to give him as much rest as possible before they began hiking again. They risked overextending the man and making his recovery worse, but none of them thought staying close to Akew Woods and the pirates was a better idea.

Ben stalked out of the camp and down the road, moving silently until he saw Amelie's back. She was sitting on a log that some previous traveler had dragged to the side of the road. Ben grinned when he saw her reach down and pinch her arm, trying to keep herself awake. He paused, thinking about sneaking close and surprising her. Then, he remembered the spark she'd created to start the fire the night before. Instead of sneaking up, he called out.

She turned and stood, stretching her arms high above her head and yawning.

"I could use some of that kaf you like so much," she said.

He nodded. "Me too. Next time, before we run from a pirate battle, let's make sure to pick some up."

She grinned.

"Towaal and Rhys are still sleeping," he added.

"Sit with me then," she said, reclaiming her spot on the log and patting the bark next to her.

Ben joined her and smiled when she scooted close and rested her head on his shoulder. They sat, enjoying the peaceful quiet of the forest until they heard stirring behind them. They returned to camp and found Rhys and Towaal moving about.

THROUGHOUT THE DAY, they hiked deeper into the forest, leaving all trace of the sea and Akew Woods behind them. They didn't see another traveler all morning, but Ben could tell that somewhere in front of them, there was a short wagon train. Even he could easily spot the wheel marks left in the soil. He tried to guess how far ahead they were, but he was fooling himself. There had been no rain since they had landed in Alcott, so the tracks could be a bell old or a week old.

"Check the spoor," advised Rhys, pointing to a foul lump of animal waste in the middle of the track. "Stick your finger in it and see how deep you have to go to find warmth. Each knuckle is roughly equivalent to a day."

Ben eyed his friend suspiciously. "Really?"

Rhys shrugged. "It could be true. You don't have anything else to do for a month, so you might as well try it out. If we catch up to the wagons, we'll see if I'm right."

Ben grunted.

They kept walking for several long moments. Then, Ben remarked, "I need to hunt. Someone has to find fresh game, and you need to conserve whatever energy you can."

"Amelie will do it," interjected Towaal.

Both Ben and Amelie looked to her.

"I, ah, I've never really hunted," mentioned Amelie. "I'm not sure I'd know what to do."

"Ben can show you where to find the animals," allowed Towaal, "but when you do find one, you need to bring it down."

Amelie glanced down at her rapier. "I don't think that's going to work very well."

Towaal sighed and glanced toward the sky. She snapped her fingers. Again, a spark flew out in front of her. It shot like an arrow and then hooked right before fizzling out harmlessly two dozen paces away.

"The bigger the animal, the bigger jolt you're going to need to give them," advised Towaal. "The energy you used to start our fire last night may stun a mouse. A deer or a hog is going to take a significantly bigger blast. Start practicing now, every day, and by the time we reach the City, you could be more effective than some of the members of the Sanctuary."

Amelie stared open-mouthed at the mage.

"What you found in Eldred's room, girl, if there are more of those things, you have to be prepared. At full strength and with time to prepare, the four of us nearly failed to defeat her. We can't let that happen again. All of us, we need to be ready."

"What should I do?" asked Ben.

"When Amelie isn't flicking sparks at fauna, she'll throw them at you."

Ben blinked.

Towaal snapped at him, and a thumbnail-sized spark flew out, striking him in the chest. The spark sent a shiver down his spine, and he stumbled back, but Towaal hadn't put any real power into it.

"Akew Woods made me realize something," said Towaal. "We're going to the City and plan to take on the Veil and her minions. By the time we get there, they may have access to an incredible weapon that even Gunther was afraid of. Two days ago, you ran from a room full of pirates. That was smart. We should avoid unnecessary conflicts, but we can't always run away.

We have to push ourselves harder than we ever did before. If we don't…"

They kept walking, booted feet falling softly on the dirt road.

Finally, Rhys let out a groan and declared, "I need a drink."

BEN AND AMELIE squatted next to each other, peering silently through the foliage at a creek two dozen paces away.

They had crossed it on the road and then followed it into the wood until Ben spied a shallow bank covered in hoof prints. The creek was a watering hole frequented by deer. He and Amelie had found cover and settled down to wait until one of the animals turned up. When one did, Amelie would stun or kill it. If all went well, before nightfall, they'd have the carcass back to the road and could put it on a spit over the fire Towaal and Rhys were tending.

They'd been waiting a bell already, and Ben was starting to get bored. He knew they needed to be silent and that the fresh meat would be worth it, but sitting still just a hands-length from Amelie was driving him mad.

Slowly, he snaked his hand out and placed it on the small of her back. She ignored him, entirely focused on watching the creek. Bit by bit, Ben's hand slid lower, past the small of her back, down to her rear. Just as slowly, Amelie's head turned until she was looking at him. Not appreciatively.

Ben coughed quietly and brushed his hand on her. Leaning close, he whispered, "Some big bug was crawling on you. I was just knocking it off."

She held his gaze before responding just as quietly, "Good. I'd hate to have to squish it."

Ben sighed and turned his gaze back to the stream. He waited impatiently for another bell until a soft snort broke the silence of the forest. A deer, just barely grown, stepped into the clear space near the bank of the stream.

Amelie, eyes boring into the animal, raised a hand.

Ben knew with her other hand she'd been steadily rubbing two balls of wool together. The wool helped her build a charge, which she would direct and pour energy into. The deer stepped closer, and Amelie flung her hand forward.

A sharp crackle burst out of her hand. Unlike the tiny sparks she'd been playing with earlier, this was a finger-wide flash of lightning. It streaked across the clearing, burning an after-image into Ben's vision, and snapped when it hit the deer's side. The unsuspecting animal was thrown into the air and flung back a dozen paces before it crashed into a tree.

Ben leapt to his feet and charged forward, drawing his sword and preparing to kill the unfortunate beast, but as he reached it, he saw he didn't have to. They'd thought Amelie's attack would merely stun it, but a fist-sized burn was seared into the animal's side. Smoke drifted off the carcass. Its short hairs stood on end, and unless Ben was mistaken, the deer was now partially cooked.

Amelie stumbled up to him, weaving like she'd had half a dozen mugs of wine.

"Oh," she gasped, clutching her head.

"I think that was a little too much," suggested Ben.

Amelie blinked at him blearily, and Ben sighed. He bent and grabbed the hoofs of the deer. With a grunt, he jerked the corpse up and slung it onto his back, front and back legs straddling his neck and gripped tightly in his hands. It weighed more than he wanted to carry alone, but Amelie wasn't going to be helping just yet.

THE NEXT MORNING, Ben carved shanks of smoked venison and wrapped them carefully before stuffing the meat in his pack. They'd been losing time with Rhys needing to rest and pausing to hunt, but with a heavy load of fresh meat, he hoped they could make a decent travel day.

Rhys was stretching and grumbling, clearly exhausted, but at least he was on his feet and moving around. Ben had worried that even the light hiking would be too much for the man after so recently recovering from a near death, well, death, experience.

Amelie had recovered from overextending herself the day before and was talking to Towaal about the bolt of energy she'd struck the deer with.

"If we're in a fight, then the only concern with doing too much is that you'll leave yourself vulnerable," explained Towaal. "If more enemies are expected to arrive, for example, or it's a full-scale battle, you need to conserve your strength to face any new threats. If we're facing a small party or a swarm of demons, and we have no reason to anticipate more of them, then give them everything you've got. It's better to punch too hard and get the job done than not hard enough and leave your opponent still standing. Think back to what I unleashed at Snowmar Station. I may have been effective with half the energy I released, but at the time, it was more important to ensure I got them all than to hold back and conserve my strength."

Amelie pushed back her hair, tying it in a loose ponytail. She responded, "For hunting, though, what I did was excessive."

Towaal nodded. "True, you don't want to fry your dinner before you cook it, but we're not worried about you becoming an adequate hunter. We're worried about you standing toe-to-toe with a mage from the Sanctuary. You have natural strength. You just need practice extending it. For now, think of it as using a ballista to hunt instead of a bow and arrow."

"If needed, I can take care of the hunting," offered Ben. "You can practice on a rock or something."

Amelie set her hands on her hips and turned to face him. "Do you recall when you went hunting after we fled Northport?"

Ben frowned. So much had happened since then. He remembered it was freezing cold, and he'd fashioned a spear out of a stick, and he'd... He flushed.

"That's right," declared Amelie. "You missed. Let me handle the hunting, Master Ashwood, and you can wash the dishes."

Grumbling under his breath, Ben hoisted his pack onto his back. It was three or four times heavier than everyone else's, but he was stronger, and they were recovering. He hoped everyone recalled he had the extra load when it actually came time to wash the dishes.

Rhys, whistling tunelessly, shuffled forward and started slowly marching down the pine needle-covered road. Ben's eyes narrowed suspiciously, and he followed his friend.

As the sun rose above them, they saw a few travelers headed in the opposite direction, one long wagon train, and several groups of adventures. They steered to the side of the road when they passed someone. Other than brisk nods, they didn't communicate. The merchants in the wagon train seemed determined to make good time, and the adventurers looked like the type to seek quick fortune on the deck of a ship ransacking another ship. They didn't pass anyone they were interested in sharing a camp with.

"Should we ask someone if they've seen Milo?" wondered Ben.

"That's not a bad idea," admitted Rhys. "A young man, alone on this road would be a bit unusual. Certainly, someone would remember it. That'd give us a feeling for how far ahead of us he is."

"We'll ask the next group that doesn't look like future pirates," decided Ben.

Over the next bell, clouds crawled across the narrow gap in the pine-needle canopy above them. Heavy, grey skies threw the forest into a dark gloom. Thunder rolled through the tree trunks, and Ben glanced at his companions. Rhys was shuffling along, breathing heavy. Towaal and Amelie seemed fine, but Ben decided there wasn't any point in pressing on through a thunderstorm. They were days behind Milo already, and at the speed they were hiking, they weren't going to catch him. The former apprentice was young and fit. He could be moving twice as fast as they were.

"Let's find somewhere to stop," suggested Ben.

"I can keep going," asserted Rhys.

"Let's take it easy now," said Ben, "and then we can push hard later. We have a month in this forest. There's no reason to exhaust ourselves in the first two days."

"You're the leader," said Rhys with a wink.

Ben rolled his eyes and glanced behind them as another wave of thunder crashed overhead.

"If we are going to stop," suggested Rhys, "let's find a place quickly."

Half a bell later, they huddled three hundred paces off the road under a rocky hill. Above them on the hill, a stout boulder served as a water break and sent rivulets of rain water to either side of their camp. Thick layers of pine needles kept most of the rain off, though steady drips fell down in some spots.

Ben had attempted to collect enough wood to start a fire, but the pathetic pile he'd assembled that was dry enough to light would burn out in a bell. He stared at it and then decided it was better to wait until later in case they really needed it.

All around them, the pine boughs sagged, heavy with the moisture, and the falling water formed a curtain that cut visibility in half. They agreed to stay in the relatively dry hollow below the hill and wait until the storm blew over before traveling again. In the heavy rain, they'd make even worse time than they had so far. So, they relaxed, talking quietly, leaning against packs, and tugging cloaks tight as fat drops of water snuck through the pine and plonked around them.

Down near the road, Ben thought he saw motion, but it was

difficult to tell if a party was moving along, or if it was his imagination.

"Does it look like someone is down there?" he asked Rhys.

The rogue, who had been breathing deeply with his eyes shut, grumbled, turned his head, and glanced at where Ben was looking.

"I don't know," he said.

"If they're out in a storm like this, they may need help," said Ben.

Rhys kept watching and finally responded, "I think it is someone, but they're moving away from Akew Woods. If they needed help, that's where they'd go. Besides, what are we going to do, offer them the comfort of our camp?"

Ben grinned and glanced around the camp, if it could be called that. The four of them were sprawled out by their packs. In the middle, they'd set out some of the smoked venison and hard travel biscuits. Hardly a feast worth sharing. They had plenty of water, though, thought Ben wryly as he eyed the rivulets that ran beside them. The streams were quickly turning into tiny rivers in the pounding rain.

"It could be the pirates," mentioned Amelie.

Ben sighed and sat back. He watched the motion until it disappeared down the road. Then, he followed the rogue's lead and let his eyes sag shut. The afternoon passed uneventfully, and Ben drifted in and out of sleep. He woke to a steady drip of water that miraculously broke through the pine bough ceiling and landed directly on his forehead. Cursing and wiping the water away, he sat up.

Towaal and Amelie appeared to be asleep, but Rhys was awake and puffing on his pipe.

"I've been thinking," remarked the rogue seriously. "I'm worried you didn't secure enough drink to get us through this forest."

"We had to leave in a hurry," Ben reminded him.

Rhys exhaled a cloud of blue smoke. "Priorities, Ben. Priorities."

Ben glanced around the forest. The rain had stopped, but water still fell from the tree branches around them. It was nearly full dark.

"What time is it?" he asked Rhys.

"A bell or two until sunset. Well, if we could see the sun, I mean."

Ben nodded and got up. He started arranging their supplies as best he could into a more proper camp. In the damp, it wouldn't be comfortable, but there was no sense leaving their spot for just a bell of hiking.

THE NEXT MORNING, the skies had cleared, and the birds were chirping again. Rhys and Amelie were feeling healthy enough to run through a few of the Ohm sequences prior to breakfast. Ben followed the rogue's lead, letting the flowing motions relax the tension in his body. It gave him a sense he was doing something, even though they'd barely made it a day and a half walk from Akew Woods.

"Focus on centering yourself while you're moving," suggested Towaal. "Hardening your will is another skill that we're going to need when we get to the City."

"You think we'll have to confront more mages?" asked Amelie. "I thought you said we couldn't win a fight against the Sanctuary."

"Certainly not against all of them," acknowledged Towaal. "A direct battle near the City would be close to suicide. It would draw the mages like flies to spoiled meat, but sooner or later, we're going to have to deal with the Veil. It's a solid bet there will be others who try to stop us."

Ben frowned. Towaal was right. They couldn't risk a direct

confrontation, but what she'd left unsaid was that they didn't have a plan to do anything else.

As if reading his thoughts, Rhys said, "We'll come up with something."

While the sun was still hidden behind the trees, they trudged through the damp forest to the road. The track was hard-packed dirt, so it was passable, but their feet slipped and slid on the slick surface.

"This is going to be a long day," groaned Ben.

Amelie nodded grimly.

They had to keep going, though. They'd already delayed too much. Ignoring the fat drops that still dripped from the trees onto his head, Ben led them down the path ever deeper into the forest.

They hiked two more bells before Rhys called out, "Hold."

Ben paused, thinking his friend needed a rest, but instead, the rogue was glancing around suspiciously.

"What is it?" asked Ben.

"The forest has gotten quiet," remarked Rhys.

Ben frowned as the rogue walked a dozen paces in front of them, his eyes scanning the surface of the road. Ben glanced behind them, but for hundreds of paces, the road was straight and clear. If anything was coming that way, it was too far off to have quieted the animals in the forest.

"Look," said Rhys, pointing down at the mud.

Ben joined Rhys and saw a rut that a wagon wheel had dug on the soft edge of the road.

"There's no water puddled in it," explained Rhys. "This was made after the rain."

Ben sighed with relief. "A wagon, maybe the same one we've been following. Nothing to worry about then."

Rhys shrugged and stood back up. "Nothing I can see but something about this feels wrong."

Ben started leading them down the road again. He loosened

his sword in the sheath just in case. It was foolish to ignore the rogue's instincts.

"Should we far-see ahead?" asked Amelie after a hundred paces.

"We wouldn't be able to see anything," answered Towaal. "You'd be looking at the tops of pine trees and not much else."

"We don't need to," added Rhys. He pointed ahead.

Ben's eyes followed the gesture and he felt a tremble of dismay. Barely visible, another two hundred paces away, was a boot. That was something to worry about. They quickened their pace, but when they reached the boot, there was no owner to go with it.

"That's strange," said Amelie.

Rhys was kneeling near the boot. Ben stepped beside him and saw a footprint pressed into the soil. Beyond it, a boot print then another footprint were spaced far apart like the owner was running.

"Nothing is ever easy, is it?" grumbled Ben.

"The group that passed us yesterday in the storm didn't have a wagon, did they?" asked Amelie.

Ben and Rhys shared a glance and shrugged.

"Let's keep going," suggested Ben. "We'll find what we find. Like Towaal said, if we think we're going to face the Veil, we can't keep running from everything that makes us jump."

"We shouldn't walk into ambushes either," complained Rhys, but he drew his longsword and followed Ben down the road. He didn't have to follow him long.

Ahead, hidden by a pile of fallen pine, was a carriage. It was on the side of the road near a bend as if it had been traveling too fast and had careened over the slick surface and crashed. Fifty paces short was a body, one foot missing a boot. Two more bodies lay beside the carriage.

They quickly investigated the scene and saw that the three dead men were together. A lord and his footmen, it appeared.

One of them wore fine clothing, and the other two wore livery. Everything of value had been removed. There was no luggage or weapons. The carriage itself was wrecked, one of the wheels cracked where it had impacted a fallen tree. Whatever animal had pulled it was missing.

"Bandits?" asked Amelie, peering inside the open door of the carriage. "The ones I've heard of would have made more effort to hide their work, but this forest is lawless. Maybe they simply don't care if this was found."

"It could be," muttered Rhys. "Even out here where no one will hunt them, they should still be concerned about warning other potential victims. Maybe the wagon was too difficult to move into the woods and hide?" He paused. "It looks as though they chased the carriage from behind, though, and I would expect bandits to set an ambush. Why run after a quickly moving vehicle if you don't have to?"

"Pirates," stated Ben. "It's the men we saw in Akew Woods. They know Amelie is highborn, so an unmarked carriage would fit right into how they might think she would be traveling."

"Look at this," said Towaal. She was squatting by the rear of the carriage. The back wheel was smashed. Four parallel marks marred the wood next to the damage.

Ben glanced at Amelie. "The pirate Zane had some sort of claw, didn't he?"

She nodded tersely.

Towaal was still squatting by the carriage. She traced a finger along the scars in the wood, and orange flames stirred in the wake of her gesture.

"This isn't good," she murmured.

Ben frowned as the flames blackened the seasoned wood.

"That claw did have some sort of glow to it," said Ben. "We didn't see it in action, but I believe it was mage-wrought."

Towaal glanced at him. "You didn't think that was worth mentioning?"

He scratched his head and didn't reply.

Rhys was examining the wheel marks where the carriage had slid off the road.

"This thing didn't crash because they were going too fast," he said. "It was thrown to the side of the road. Look here. This impression suddenly stops and then a score of paces later comes down hard. Something rocked the carriage and knocked it into the air."

Ben looked around the forest nervously. All was quiet.

Towaal stood and began pacing around the carriage, peering at it, glancing at the bodies. Finally, she admitted, "I know I said we shouldn't run away from conflict, but we don't know what these pirates are capable of. Clearly, they have access to more powerful weapons than grappling hooks and cutlasses. If such violent men are able to hold onto such dangerous weapons, they may be able to harden their will or have other devices that could harm us. These are not your typical pirates."

"That's what I've been saying," muttered Rhys.

"What do you suggest?" asked Ben, ignoring his friend.

"It's your decision," said Towaal, "but the undergrowth in this forest is thin. There are rocks, gullies, and other obstructions the road avoids, but at least near here, the terrain is gentle. We could move several hundred paces away from the road and still make reasonably good time. It's a risk to venture off the road, but…"

Ben looked at Amelie.

"We made good time when we traveled cross country after fleeing the Sanctuary," she said.

Ben nodded. "We'll move into the forest four or five hundred paces, hopefully that's not deep enough to be dangerous. I don't think we'll catch up to Milo at our pace anyway, so we have no reason to risk a fight with these pirates. Unlike our battle with Eldred, there is nothing to gain from defeating them."

They readjusted their packs, made one last look up and down the road, and then hiked into the forest. The ground was soft from the previous day's rain, and it sloped gently up from the road, but underneath the pines, the space was clear. Ben found himself moving just as quickly as they had on the road. They walked far enough that the trees obscured the carriage. Then, they turned north.

"We may have to head back to the road if we run into a big creek, but this is easy travelling," remarked Ben.

"It's not bad," agreed Amelie.

As they hiked, Ben couldn't help but think of all of the horror stories they'd heard about the violent tribes in Akew Woods. So far, they hadn't encountered anyone in the forest. It was a pleasant place, and while the thick trees would prevent serious farming, the woods teemed with animals, and there was plenty of access to clean water. The forest was more livable than many of the places they'd recently seen settlements, and that was what worried him. If there were no truth to the rumors, then certainly people would live within the forest.

They made it to the end of the day without incident and found a comfortable place to camp. After finding the scene at the carriage, none of them argued about setting a watch schedule. Rhys volunteered to take the first one, but Ben insisted the rogue spend one more day resting. Instead, he took the first shift and watched over his companions as they slept. Around them, things remained peaceful, but a sense of creeping dread was growing.

After his watch, Ben slept fitfully and was half-surprised when by morning, nothing had happened. All of them felt it. They scarfed down a quick breakfast and watched as a pair of squirrels chased each other up a tree.

"The animals don't feel anything," remarked Ben.

Amelie opened her mouth to speak and then stopped cold. She shot up and looked down the hill toward the road.

Towaal set aside the bowl she'd been eating breakfast out of and stood as well.

"T-That pulse," stammered Amelie. "Did you feel it?"

Towaal nodded. "We should pack our things and begin moving."

"What was it?" asked Amelie.

"Someone is questing," explained Towaal, stooping to shake the rest of her oatmeal out of her bowl. She stuffed it in her pack without cleaning it further. "It's a powerful form of sensing, similar to delving for water or minerals. I believe in this case, they were questing for life forces."

"I've heard of mages questing but only for strictly limited purposes. On a large scale, it's not practical, is it?" asked Rhys, moving quickly to gather his equipment.

The rogue glanced regretfully at the small fire they'd started and then kicked a shower of dirt over it. Without spending a quarter bell burying the fire and smoothing the earth, it would be obvious someone camped there.

"Within a couple of hundred paces of us, there must be hundreds of living creatures," Rhys added. "A questing like that would return so much information it would overwhelm the questor. At least, that's what I've been told."

Towaal grunted and strapped her pack closed. "You and I have been alive a long time, and we've learned a lot in those years, but now, I'm starting to think half of what we learned was wrong."

They all finished breaking camp and hitched their packs on their backs. Without needing to say it, they started moving, angling north, deeper into the forest.

Towaal continued talking while they walked. "A year ago, I didn't think any real male mages existed. I would have told you wyvern fire was a myth, that mages like Gunther and Jasper couldn't be real, and that the Veil had Alcott's best interest at heart. There's more to this world than I ever expected, even after hundreds of years of exploring. Who knows. Maybe we'll see a wyvern next."

Ben grunted. Wyverns. That was one story he was certain would remain that, just a story.

Towaal continued, "To your point, Rhys, could a talented questor sort out our life forces from the thousands of animals they would have caught in that net? I'm not going to wait and find out."

A bell passed with no breaks. Then, Amelie gasped, and Towaal's face fell.

"It happened again?" queried Ben.

"It felt closer," stated Amelie.

Towaal didn't speak, but she picked up her pace.

Every bell, another jolt would shoot through Towaal and Amelie, and after every time, they would start walking faster. For the midday meal, they only paused long enough to dig food out of the packs and continued to walk, eating as they went.

Ben's skin was crawling, running from something he couldn't see and couldn't feel. He didn't doubt the mage's urgency, though. Even Rhys was starting to get jumpy, twitching at every animal call or rustling branch. They marched in silence, afraid their voices could give away their location.

As darkness fell across the forest, Ben risked speaking. "We should stop and rest."

Towaal shook her head. "The questing is coming closer. They're catching up to us. If we stop, they'll be on us in our sleep."

Ben hooked a thumb at Rhys. "I'm not sure how far he'll make it. If we stumble across these pirates, we'll need him ready to fight."

"I can hear you," muttered Rhys.

The rogue was huffing and puffing, exhausted from the all-day hike. It was obvious already he wouldn't be much use in a fight. With rest, though, Ben thought he could recover enough to help.

"We have to keep going," declared Amelie. "Ben, whatever is behind us is powerful. We don't want to tangle with them if we don't have to. In the dark, we may be able to lose them. If they keep following us through the night, then we'll have to deal with it. There's no reason to force that confrontation, though."

"That makes sense," acknowledged Ben. "Onward we go."

They trudged deeper into the forest, at least a league from the road now and angling northward. If they could lose their pursuers and turn back to the road, Ben figured they'd only lose half a day from the excursion. If they could lose their pursuers.

A bell later, Ben saw from Amelie's reaction that another pulse must have happened.

"It feels like there is a pattern to it," she mused.

Darkness fell, and they stumbled onward, choosing not to light a torch or use magical means to see where they were going. Light at night in the dark forest would be a beacon to anyone nearby. Instead, they crashed into low-hanging tree branches and tried to avoid walking straight into one of the thick trunks. Ben stumbled over more rocks than he cared to count. He could only hope their pursuers weren't close enough to hear their bumbling.

"That one was quicker," said Amelie suddenly. "I'm sure there is a pattern."

"A pattern that is getting more complicated as they go," added Towaal. "It's almost as if... they're communicating something with these pulses. A code, maybe?"

A quarter bell later, the mages felt another one.

"It could be communication," agreed Amelie, "but what would they be saying?"

"Our location and extrapolating the direction we're traveling," suggested Rhys. "What else?"

"Good guess," called a voice from the darkness ahead of them.

Ben's party stopped. Light bloomed from Towaal's hand, illuminating over a dozen armed men scattered in a half circle amongst the trees.

"A mage," hissed one of the men.

The leader, the purple-coated pirate Zane, shouted his man down. "Of course they have a mage. The lady fled the Sanctuary, you idiot!" He turned to face Towaal. "You planning to take the pretty girl back behind your white walls, mage? I'm afraid we had something similar in mind."

"You are right. I am a mage," growled Towaal. "Now that we have agreed on that, do you really think this is a good idea?"

Zane stuck his hands behind his back. Just like Ben had seen before, when he pulled them out, his hands were encased in two, glowing and spiked gauntlets. The pirate captain rolled his bald head on his thick neck and showed his teeth. Broken stubs shined in the mage-light.

Rhys drew his longsword and let the silver runes sparkle to life. Ben drew his sword as well, regretting that he'd lost the mage-wrought blade.

"Everyone has fancy tricks," cackled Zane.

Clicks sounded on both sides of Ben's party. His eyes darted back and forth. He saw six crossbowmen with squat, sturdy-looking crossbows, all cocked and aimed at his friends.

"It's clear you don't intend to fight us," said Towaal. "Otherwise, you wouldn't have called out. You would have ambushed us and let the chips fall. Let's dispense with the games. Tell me, what do you want?"

The pirate Zane laughed maniacally. Ben realized with a shudder the teeth weren't broken. They were sharpened.

The pirate raised his gauntlets. "I just wanted you to provide some light for my men to shoot by."

Towaal's light flicked out, and the crossbows thrummed.

Ben flailed back, hoping the man aiming a bolt at him didn't guess which way he ducked. A cry went out as someone was hit, but he couldn't tell who it was, his friends or a pirate caught in the cross fire. There was no time to wonder as a swarm of angry pirates closed on him in the darkness.

He sensed footsteps coming fast and swung his longsword wildly, hoping just to make contact so he could figure out where his attacker was. He felt the blade hit something coming at him, something hard. He heard the crunch of bone and smiled to himself. The man must have been coming low, ready to slam into Ben. Instead, he'd caught the edge of the longsword with his face.

Ben wasn't prepared for the next one, though, and a heavy body crashed into him, throwing him to the ground. Sprawled on his back, he gripped his sword and waved it viciously where he thought his attacker had been, but the weapon didn't hit anyone.

Then, a dozen steps away, two pirates suddenly burst into flames, illuminating the clearing in the stomach-churning light of burning bodies.

Ben saw a pirate right next to him, the man who must have tackled him, and kicked out with his foot, catching the man's knee, surprising him and sending the man sprawling.

Ben scrambled to his feet just in time. Backlit by their burning counterparts, two more of the villains closed. They carried cutlasses, common weapons amongst seafaring types because they were light. Sailors were rarely stupid enough to wear heavy armor in the middle of the ocean, so a heavier blade wasn't necessary. The blades weren't designed to stand against a longsword in skilled hands, though.

Acting quickly, Ben thrust at the closest man, the tip of his longsword aiming for the man's stomach. The pirate deftly parried the stroke, sliding it to the side. Ben continued his momentum and let the blade follow the course the pirate put it on, right into his companion's chest.

The second man gave a startled grunt when the sharp tip of steel pierced his torso. It ended in a gurgle as the blade penetrated deeper and found his heart.

"Thanks," Ben muttered to the first man before slamming his elbow into the pirate's startled, heavily tattooed face.

The pirate stumbled back, and Ben grimaced. The man was enough of a scrapper that he didn't drop his weapon. This wasn't going to be easy.

Behind him, one of the burning men fell to the ground and

rolled frantically across the damp earth, extinguishing the flames on him. The second burning man wasn't so fortunate. He fell onto his back, the flames licking hungrily at his melting flesh.

Ben's friends still stood, along with a dozen pirates. Their leader, Zane, was grinning broadly in the light of his burning crewmen. He clicked his gauntlets together, and sickly green power flowed over the claws and spikes.

Rhys stepped toward the man, his longsword glowing silver, but his shoulders were slumped, and it was evident the still-recovering rogue was not expecting to win the fight. Towaal's hands blazed alight with orange fire, and she pulled back, preparing to launch a fist-sized ball of flame at the pirate.

A thump sounded behind them, and an instant later, Ben was flung to the turf like a giant had just kicked him.

"Nice try, mage," snarled Zane. "You think I was stupid enough to follow a runaway from the Sanctuary without bringing my own magic user?"

Ben, lying on his side stunned, saw a tall woman step into the flickering light. She wore plain clothing and her hair was tied back into a severe bun behind her head. Her face was twisted in disgust.

"Lady Agwaa," Towaal groaned. She raised her hands and then blinked, frustration evident with her every movement.

"What did you do?" exclaimed Amelie.

"Nice to see you again, Karina," the woman remarked coolly. "You are feeling a little spell I picked up in the west after that witch Coatney banished me from the Sanctuary. Your strength should return sufficiently within a few moments." The woman looked to Zane. "Kill them both now before that happens."

"We need the girl," growled Zane.

"The girl is a mage, you fool," snapped the woman. "Even a runaway is too dangerous to leave alive. You cannot control her long enough to deliver her to a buyer alive. She's still worth a fortune if she's dead."

Zane raised his gauntlets. "Do not challenge my leadership, Agwaa! You will be with us the entire way, and I trust you will keep her under control, or sedate her. I don't care. Just do it!"

A flash of cool blue light came streaking out of the darkness and flashed in front of Zane. It clashed against the man's gauntlets in a burst of green sparks. The armor was split, and the pirate's hands severed. Ben watched in astonishment as green-lit blood spurted from Zane's wrists.

Stumbling, Zane turned. Beside him, a man stood, illuminated by the blue glow of his weapon. He was a hand taller than Ben and his head was shaved bare. He was shirtless, and the soft glow from his blade lit his muscular chest in sharp relief. He had baggy trousers and no fear about facing a dozen pirates and a former mage of the Sanctuary. On his chest hung a copper amulet.

Zane collapsed in front of him.

"The agreement is that travelers stay on the road," the man remarked, nudging the pirate's body with his foot. "Failure to follow the agreement is punishable by death. Violence and expending your will in this forest are also punishable by death."

The pirates, understanding a fight to the death better than anyone, attacked.

Ben watched in awe as the man danced through the pack of assailants. He was fluid like Saala but quick and brutal like Rhys. In the space of several heartbeats, Ben observed the man was a better swordsman than both. He blew through the pirates like a cyclone, felling them with ease.

"This is not good," mumbled Rhys, shuffling to stand beside Ben. As they watched, the last of the pirates fell before the man's glowing blade.

Ben looked at where Lady Agwaa had been standing and saw she was gone.

"The amulet, Ben," hissed Amelie, looking at the man's chest.

Understanding struck him, and Ben dove for Amelie's pack, ripping it open and frantically riffling through her clothing, trying to find the copper amulet they'd found in Akew Woods after Eldred's trap had gone off.

The mysterious newcomer stepped toward Ben's party, his sword raised, no trace of the pirate's blood on the glowing steel.

Suddenly, Ben's hand closed around the copper disc, and he tore it out of the pack, dangling it from its leather thong so the man could see it. The newcomer paused his advance, staring at the slowly twirling disc. He cut his eyes to where Agwaa had fled.

"I will be back," he stated calmly. "Stay here, and we will talk."

The man padded silently into the dark trees, the lack of light not seeming to be a problem as the glow from his blade winked out.

Exhaling a burst of breath, Amelie asked, "Who was that, and what just happened?"

"I have no idea," responded Towaal slowly.

3

THE VILLAGE

"WHERE DID YOU GET THAT?" ASKED A VOICE.

Ben tried to locate its source, but the man remained within the darkness of the forest. Ben and his companions were huddled around a small fire. They'd started it half a bell after the man had left and had been tending it for a bell after that. They'd moved several score paces away from where the fight had taken place to avoid the stench of burning bodies.

"You've been gone a while," remarked Rhys, puffing on his pipe.

"The woman was faster than she appeared," responded the voice from a different point outside of the light of their fire.

Ben breathed deeply, trying to remain calm. They'd decided that whoever the man was, he was extremely powerful and not worth fighting unless they had to. So, instead of preparing for battle, they'd made dinner.

"Would you like something to eat?" asked Towaal. "Venison, taken just yesterday."

"I do not eat meat," answered the man.

Ben shivered. The swordsman was circling them as silently as a ghost.

"The copper amulet you showed me," said the man, "show it to me again."

Ben picked it up off the ground beside him and raised it.

Like a striking viper, the man stepped out of the darkness and snatched the amulet out of Ben's grasp before he could react.

"Hey!" he shouted, but a warning look from Rhys kept him seated.

Rhys was right. If the man had wanted to attack, he could have sliced Ben's head off as easily as he took the amulet. Whoever he was and whatever his intentions, he wasn't spoiling for a fight either. At least, not yet.

"This is real," murmured the man.

"Uh, thanks," responded Ben.

"Where did you get this?"

The shirtless man began circling them again, staying at the edge of the firelight, the copper amulet in one hand, his sword in the other. The blade glowed subtly now, not the blaze it had been earlier, but it wasn't dark either. Ben wasn't sure if that was a good sign of a bad one.

"I found it," answered Ben.

The man paused behind Lady Towaal and then moved again. He studied each of them, waiting for Ben to elaborate. Finally, Rhys had enough.

"This is ridiculous!" barked the rogue. "We were chased off the road by those pirates, and yes, we fought them, breaking your rules, but what do you expect us to do? We did our absolute best to avoid the situation. I'm happy to talk if you want to talk or fight if we have to fight, but I'm not going to sit here any longer like I'm part of some silly children's game. I keep expecting you to tap me on the head and start running around the circle."

The man paused, a far off look in his eye. They waited for a moment. Then, Amelie guessed what was happening.

"You're communicating through a thought meld," she stated. "What are you saying? You don't even know who we are."

The man gripped the thong holding the copper amulet. "I know enough."

"What do you know of the First Mages?" asked Towaal, eyeing the amulet.

The man's eyes snapped back to the group. "That knowledge has been lost to the Sanctuary," he claimed. "What do you know of them?"

"As far as I know, it still is lost to the Sanctuary," responded Towaal. "I'm no longer part of the Sanctuary, though. You would know that if you paused to speak with us."

"What do you know of the First Mages?" asked the man again.

Towaal raised an eyebrow. "I believe I asked my question first."

The man was circling again, slow step by slow step, his blade always at the ready. Amelie was studying him and the copper amulets, one around his neck, one hanging from his fist. The fire-light reflected off of them dully. The tension was rising in Ben. He was sure the man was about to make a move to attack. He didn't seem the type that was willing to live and let live.

"They're keys," guessed Amelie.

Again, the man paused, staring at her. His body tensed. Then, the faraway look returned.

Ben and his friends glanced at each other, nervousness painted on their faces. The man had easily cut down the dozen pirates and the mage, Lady Agwaa. His sword was clearly mage-wrought, he knew Lady Towaal was a mage and displayed no fear, and he was standing, weapon in hand, and they were seated. If it came to a fight, Ben wasn't sure they'd win it, and if they did, he knew not all of them would survive.

Suddenly, the man's blade winked out. Ben could only see a flickering reflection of their campfire on the blade as if it was made of glass. The man slid the weapon into a loop on his belt and hung their copper amulet around his neck next to the other. "Come with me. Then, you will talk."

Everyone looked to Ben.

He grunted. "I don't suppose we have time to finish supper first?"

THEY FOLLOWED the man through the dark forest, lit again by Lady Towaal's glowing palm. The man didn't repeat his claim that it was a death sentence. He had merely looked away when her hand flickered alight.

"His boss called us in," whispered Amelie to Ben. "Apparently, we've piqued someone's curiosity."

Ben gripped his longsword, watching the bare, muscular back of the swordsman. Towaal followed behind him, and the light of her hand cast the swordsman's shadow large on the foliage ahead. The man led them through the forest like it was his bedroom, easily avoiding low branches and protruding roots. Ben wondered if he could see in the dark.

"If he's not the boss..." muttered Ben before trailing off.

A quarter bell later, they stopped. In front of them, Ben saw a wall of rock that rose from the side of a steep hill. Towaal gasped, and Amelie took a step forward. Ben frowned. It looked like the same rock they'd seen jutting out of the forest everywhere.

The man turned and eyed the two women. "You understand?"

They both nodded.

"I will go first. Follow closely behind. Do not try to run, or I will come find you. You won't get the opportunity to explain yourselves again."

"We will follow," agreed Amelie.

Ben watched in confusion as the man strode up to the rock. Then, he gasped as the swordsman vanished into the surface of the stone.

"A light shield!"

"Are we sure this is a good idea?" asked Rhys. The rogue,

normally filled with confidence, was nervously gripping his weapon.

"Don't you want to know what's on the other side?" asked Towaal.

"Not really," mumbled Rhys.

No one said anything.

"Maybe a little," the rogue admitted.

"We don't have much choice," stated Ben. "Besides, it can't be anything more dangerous than where we are actually trying to go."

Without further word, Ben strode confidently forward, walking straight into a stone wall and falling back on his rear.

Amelie coughed, her fist held over her mouth, trying to suppress her laughter. "The opening is a pace to the left," she remarked after getting herself under control.

"I'll follow right after you," muttered Ben, scrambling to his feet.

Amelie winked, and then, she stepped into the rock.

Ben hurried after her and immediately crashed into her back, sending them both stumbling forward. He looked around wildly and saw they were in a dimly lit chamber. A handful of lights set in the walls glowed softly, illuminating a large, stone-arched room. Next to the lights were flat places the size of wagon doors surrounded by finely-etched runes.

Ben turned and looked behind them. There was an arch with a flat space in it, looking out into the forest. Rhys and Towaal were on the other side, walking toward them. The runes glowed pale green. Ben and Amelie shuffled out of the way to avoid another collision as their friends stepped into the arch.

Towaal stopped as soon as she entered the chamber. She stared open-mouthed at their surroundings. Ben snapped his mouth shut when he realized her expression of amazement was identical to his.

"What is this place?" she whispered.

"I'll let the Elders answer that," responded their guide.

He touched one of the amulets around his neck, and the green runes flickered out. The doorway to the forest coalesced into a blank stone wall. The man gestured for them to follow and led them to a mundane set of stairs. It was the only opening in the room now that the doorway they'd entered through had closed.

"What are those?" wondered Ben, waving his hand to take in the room and the series of stone arches. "Little rifts?"

Towaal shook her head no but didn't give an answer.

The stairs went straight up two flights and took them into the middle of a small village. In the dark of night, it was difficult to tell, but there appeared to be several dozen stone buildings with brown thatch roofs. Glowing stones lit some of the windows but many of them were dark.

Their guide led them confidently through the quiet village toward the largest building Ben could see. It was like the others, simple stone construction, but the sky above it was clear of the pine canopy. Ben could see it extended the size of Farview's village green. The roof rose three stories above them, but there were no windows, just one large, double door lit on either side by the same lights they'd seen in the underground chamber. Instead of taking them into the building though, their guide turned and took them to a smaller structure beside it. Without speaking, he ducked inside.

Ben glanced around and met his companion's eyes. It was evident none of them understood what this place was. It was also clear it was much too late to turn back now. Ben entered first and found himself in a small, but comfortable home.

An elderly man was stoking a fire against one wall, and their guide had set down the confiscated copper amulet and moved to stand against the opposite wall, his back to the bare stone, his hand resting lightly on his translucent sword. The old man, apparently satisfied the fire was throwing off sufficient warmth, moved to the table and the amulet.

"I apologize," rasped the old man. "This late in the evening, these old bones feel the cold more than they used to."

He settled in a chair at the end of the table and toyed with the amulet with one hand while the other stroked his long, white whiskers.

"Please, be seated," he offered.

Ben shrugged and took a chair across from the man. His friends sat around him. Their guide stayed against the wall, watching over the old man protectively.

"We make these keys here in the village," stated the old man. "We make them for our own use, and they are very rare. There was only one I was aware of that was not in our possession. I thank you for returning it."

Ben scratched at the scar on his forearm and then offered, "Happy to be of assistance."

The old man smiled at him. "How did you come by this, young man?"

"I'm willing to tell you," answered Ben. "We've been offering to share our story with your swordsman, but he won't answer any of our questions. Before I tell you where we got the amulet, let's both share, why don't you start with who you are and what is this place?"

The swordsman stirred, but Ben ignored him. His gaze remained fixed on the old man in front of him. The man's eyes had dropped to the amulet. He appeared lost in thought. Finally, he looked up.

"You are right. We do have secrets that we do not share with outsiders," he admitted. "Many of them, I believe, for good reason. There are some things that do not need to be known. Some things are too dangerous in the wrong hands. That's what we do here, protect those secrets. We are guardians, you could say, of information that I hope will someday be used by its appropriate owner."

The man sat forward, and suddenly the years seemed to fade

away. His eyes blazed with awareness and he pinned Ben with his gaze.

"That is why it concerns me when it seems people know more than they should, when they know secrets that I have spent my life trying to hide. I think to myself, how have they learned this information, or how did they obtain this object, and how do I ensure no one else does what they have done?"

The man's eyes didn't move to the swordsman, but Ben felt the looming threat in the room. It was clear what he meant. The man was either telling the truth, or he was lying. Uncomfortably, Ben was reminded of the Purple, and that group's deceit about ancient secrets and the greater good. He gambled and hoped they hadn't run into two ancient evil cabals in a row.

"The amulet was recovered when we set off a trap left by an undead mage, one who had been unnaturally sustained through death magic. The same magic was used by the Society of the Burning Hand long ago. We didn't create that monster, but we stopped her. Are those the types of things you are worried are too dangerous? Because, from my perspective, we were the ones who actually did something about it. The undead mage passed through your forest and had this object of yours, and you did nothing."

"You found the amulet on the mage?" asked the old man.

"W-Well, not on her..." stammered Ben. "She didn't have it with her. It was luck, honestly, that we came across it when we were attempting to search her room. We didn't know she had it or that it even existed. Until this evening, we didn't even know what it did."

"Luck," said the man, frowning down at the amulet. "What may appear to be luck is occasionally something else. There are unseen forces in this world, and part of our role is to ensure they stay that way, unseen and untapped by those who would seek to use them for evil. If this object wanted to be found by you..."

Ben blinked at the man, uncertain of how to respond.

The man looked back to Ben. "Where did you battle this undead mage?"

"Just outside of Akew Woods," answered Ben. "A few short days' hike from here. She came from the City, though. Right down the same road we were walking on."

"Akew Woods is several weeks' walk from here," replied the old man offhandedly. "The forest is laced with wards. So are the typical seafaring paths outside of Akew Woods. There is no way someone could pass without us knowing. We found you, didn't we?"

"I bet those wards are set to catch travelers on the road," remarked Amelie. "Ones like us, who aren't trying to avoid detection."

The old man glanced at her. She met his eyes and then looked down at the amulet. The old man's eyes widened, and he placed a hand on the object.

The swordsman rumbled behind him. "Impossible! No one outside of this village knows the use of the keys! Even if they did learn how to activate the nodes, there are wards around most of them."

Ben snorted. "You can say it's impossible all you want, but we had that amulet, didn't we?"

The swordsman's mouth opened to argue, but a raised hand from the old man stopped him.

"It has been years since I've checked the wards myself. Is this possible? If someone were to use the nodes, could they pass undetected through our forest from the City to Akew Woods?"

The muscular swordsman's shoulders rolled. He admitted, "I don't know. Jonji would know. He is the one who monitors the magical barriers now."

"Ask him," instructed the man. "Instruct him to go check personally. Then, if he finds it is possible, the wards must be laid again. If another key is lost, we cannot be caught unawares. Go now. We cannot delay."

The swordsman looked at Ben and his friends, clearly reluctant to leave the old man unattended.

"I will be fine."

With an irritated grunt, the swordsman ducked out of the house.

"Not the friendly type, is he?" asked Rhys dryly.

The old man eyed the rogue. "You seem familiar to me."

Rhys shrugged. The old man kept his eyes on the rogue, but Rhys stayed silent.

Finally, the whitebeard turned back to the rest of Ben's companions. "Tell me more about the undead mage."

"Tell us why you have amulets embossed with images of a First Mage that activate these nodes of yours," challenged Ben. "We saw dozens of those gates below in the chamber. What do you do with them?"

"First Mage?" asked the old man. He leaned forward, resting his elbows on the table. He looked anything but relaxed. Ben was certain he was about to ask them how they knew about the First Mages. Then suddenly, the old man's mouth snapped shut. Thin, bloodless lips disappeared beneath his bushy beard. He sat back and sighed.

"I'm not used to having a discussion with anyone," admitted the old man. "The people here do as I ask, and it's been a long, long time since I was in a real argument. I'm afraid I've been going about this wrong. As long as I stay adversarial, you have no reason to share with me, do you?"

Ben eyed the man suspiciously.

"So," continued the man. "I will share some of our secrets, and then maybe you will openly share with me. We can talk honestly and then decide what to do about our unusual predicament."

Ben raised an eyebrow.

"In over one hundred years," explained the man. "We have not allowed an outsider to see this village and then leave. That's the predicament. I don't expect you want to stay with us, do you?"

~

THE OLD MAN offered them a mug of ale, and the tension in the room noticeably dropped. Ben lifted his mug, the foam threatening to spill over the side, and took a tentative sip. Sharp, bitter flavor filled his mouth. The hops tasted like the pine trees around them, like fragrant spruce and earthy loam.

"You mentioned Society of the Burning Hand and the First Mages," said the old man. "Before I begin, help me know where to start. How much do you know about these groups?"

Ben raised a hand. "Maybe you should start from the beginning."

The old man smirked. "Where every tale should start, I suppose."

He sipped at his ale and glanced at his fire, watching the flames slowly consume the logs he'd placed there.

"Long ago, man first discovered the ability to manipulate energy."

Ben shared a look with Amelie, and they both leaned forward, hanging on the old man's every word.

"The world wasn't like we know it now," continued the man, his voice rasping with age. "There were villages where cities stand. Conflicts were resolved with minimal bloodshed, and the rare times it came to it, war was only between tribes quarreling over hunting grounds, rather than power over their fellow man. People did not travel except when necessary to find new food or water sources. Trade was barter because no one had yet invented monetary exchange. Wealth was measured in a tribe's sources of food and security from outside threats. The view of the world was simpler, more primal then."

"And better," whispered Amelie.

The old man smiled. "Better in some ways but not others."

The door opened, and the swordsman returned. Now, he was wearing a loose tunic. He no longer looked like a bloodthirsty warrior, but he hadn't lost the deadly grace of a natural predator. The old man ignored him and continued telling his story.

"Man's understanding of the world was simplistic, and there was nothing like what we consider science today, only knowledge gained through direct experience. But, there were some men and women who were able to see deeper than their fellows, to make connections outside of what they could see or touch. They understood things that were beyond the rest of men. These men and women had an intuitive understanding of how things worked. Over time, they began to travel, to explore the world, to seek knowledge. They asked questions that no one else was curious about. These men and women were strange in their time, but with the knowledge they began to obtain, they could be helpful anywhere they went. They ran into each other and started to disseminate their knowledge to others. At some point, true understanding took place. Disparate pieces were fit together, and a complete picture began to emerge. They found the 'whys' at the heart of our natural world and sensed the energy that surrounds us all. For some like myself, it's hard to imagine a world so full of ignorance, but that's what it was like then. Before long, though, changing the world for better or worse, these men and women began to manipulate this new-found energy using their wills."

"How many years ago was this?" inquired Rhys.

The old man shrugged his thin shoulders. "I do not know. I doubt anyone does. There are no written records from that time, only the faintly recalled memories of those who lived then. And to my knowledge, only one still does. If he recalls dates, years, millennia, he has not shared those memories anywhere we've been able to find."

"Long before the darkness then," surmised Rhys. Speaking to himself, he muttered, "So that was not the original catalyst."

"The darkness," murmured the old man. He studied Rhys. "I am not what I used to be. I should have seen it before. You are long-lived. Nearly as old as myself. It's been centuries since I've meet another from our era."

Behind the old man, the swordsman gasped. His hand was on the hilt of his blade in an instant. It glowed brightly, but before he could draw it, the old man snapped, "Hold."

Rhys smiled bitterly. "I've been around. When I was a young man, though, I was only interested in the blade, women, and drink. I have no knowledge of the things you are discussing. It wasn't until long after the darkness that I had my first experience with someone extending their will."

"First Mages came before the darkness," confirmed the old man, getting back to his monologue. "Many years before, I believe, though, I'm not sure there was ever a definition of what it took to be known as a First Mage. That is a conceit of history, labelling something long after the fact. Merely being alive and learning to manipulate energy before the ones who came after, I suppose, is a good enough definition for me. It was after the darkness when the societies formed and mages as we know them came into being. Lines were drawn, allegiances were made, and power became something to hoard. Previously, it had been something that was natural and available to all."

"My memories are... fuzzy sometimes," said Rhys. "I find it difficult to recall details and specifics from my youth. The First Mages were a story, then, told to explain the origin of magic."

The old man shook his head. "The First Mages were never merely a story, but they are not the origin of magic either. The energy is there, always has been there. They just figured out how to use it before the rest of us."

Rhys sat back, the ale mug in his hands forgotten.

"You are right in a sense. The darkness did mark a pivotal point. Before that point," continued the man, "knowledge was obtained for its own sake. The First Mages thirsted for that knowledge. They gathered and disseminated information freely and with little regard for how it would be used. The manipulation of energy, magic, was rarely used in battle then. Why would it be? There was no wealth like we think of today. The world was a wide open, largely unpopulated place. There was nothing to fight over, frankly."

"Some suspect that the First Mages burrowed too deep and uncovered places that should have been left undisturbed. Whether they caused it themselves, or whether it just happened, the arrival of the dark forces changed our world permanently. Mankind, for the first time ever, found a true enemy, a real reason to fight. Demons, goblins, wyverns, and others began to appear."

Silently, the swordsman circled the room, refilling everyone's ale mugs. Ben barely noticed him.

"Also, for the first time, it was not merely seekers of knowledge who became interested in manipulating energy. Many flocked to what the First Mages had to offer. They were taught, much as before, uninhibited and unrestrained. As you can imagine, using energy as a weapon was a paramount concern all of a sudden. People studied and formed groups based on their interests. They specialized in areas, and in some cases went further than the First Mages had themselves. Society of the Burning Hand, the Sanctuary, the Purple, and many others. They responded to the threat of darkness differently, but they all responded. It wasn't until years later that the knowledge of man was turned to truly nefarious purposes. By then, the First Mages had begun to step back from the world, to retreat into far off places, or, they were killed."

"These societies," asked Towaal. "They were founded by the First Mages?"

The old man shook his head. "No, they were founded by the ones who came after. The First Mages never had much use for organizations and structure. It is why they disliked the modern world that came to be after the dark forces were pushed back. It's why they fled or were unable to survive."

"Who could kill a First Mage?" asked Ben.

The old man shrugged. "Like today's mages, they did not all specialize in combat. In fact, I'm told some of them were quite unconvinced for the need to defend themselves. Others did study combat, and they were viewed as threats by the next generation. The Society of the Burning Hand, for example, had little interest in their branch of death magic existing outside of the cabal they formed. They hunted and destroyed their tutors. Anyone with knowledge of their skills was a threat, and by then, people had begun to seek power for the sake of power. The world had changed."

"I am sorry to be rude," said Amelie, "but what does this have to do with you? If all of the First Mages are dead, then why are your protecting their secrets?"

The swordsman in the corner laughed.

The old man crossed his arms with a grin. "Not the normal Sanctuary fare, are you?"

"I left there," responded Amelie abashedly, "a turn of the seasons ago, but it seems like a lifetime."

"Life passes quickly when you are young," acknowledged the old man. "To answer your question, it has everything to do with us. The First Mages are almost all gone now, but their legacy remains. Their knowledge continues in the individuals who followed them. Their will, in some cases, was so strong that it remained as well. A swirl of force, unseen and largely unnoticed. Not untouchable, though, for those who understand what it is. Like any energy, the will of the strongest First Mages is there and available. We retain that will. We ensure it is there for the last First Mage to use and no one else. That repository of power, and the knowledge associated with it, is what we protect here."

Ben glanced around and saw Towaal with her jaw hanging open. Rhys had a sickly look on his face like he'd just swallowed his own boot. Amelie's face was contorted, confusion battling with incredulity.

"How?" whispered Towaal.

"How does it exist, or how can it be used?" answered the old man with a smile. "How it can be used, of course, is our secret. How it exists is because the First Mages, over millennia, refined their will into a force in and of itself. The First Mage's last great trick, you could say. Some have claimed they did it to provide a layer of protection for the people who came after them, and some say it was a barrier to the forces of evil that they knew were arising. The truth, I think, is that they did it unintentionally. Some actions are so great the echoes last for a long time. The power is not what it was a thousand years ago, but it is not gone either. In time, our leader will return, and all we have protected will be there for him."

"Your leader?" inquired Ben. "I thought you…"

"There is one First Mage we know of who still lives," said the old man. "He will lead the guardians when he chooses. I am merely minding things until he returns."

"The copper faces on the gates," muttered Ben. "What about those? They are First Mages, right? That's not very secret."

The old man nodded. "The glyphs. Many, even those who have the faces on their own gates like the Sanctuary, do not understand what they are doing. The Veil understood, in the past. I cannot tell you what the current Veil is aware of. The faces are a call for protection. They invite the will of the First Mages to a place. If the artificer was skilled enough, the glyph may trap the First Mage's power there, allowing it to be invoked by those who know how. In some cases, like that wall in front of the Sanctuary, the power flows through, sustaining the structure, charging the defenses. It's why they haven't had to do maintenance in over a thousand years, though my guess is that most of the mages, despite their claims of careful study and observation, don't ever wonder about that. Their negligence and lack of curiosity is what allows us to do nothing about it."

A low whistle escaped Rhys' teeth.

The old man nodded. "When done by someone with sufficient skill and knowledge, the glyph of the First Mages contains immense power. It is not to be trifled with, but fortunately, we've been effective at our work."

"Gunther claimed the one in the Purple's fortress was real," said Ben, turning to his companions. "Remember, the face hung there after he smashed the door with his hammer?"

Now, it was the old man's turn at incredulity.

"You know Gunther? The Gunther?" exclaimed the old man, bolting to his feet. "When did you see him? Do you know where he is now?"

Ben looked at the old man.

"Gunther is a friend of ours," Ben responded slowly. "I am sorry, but I will not tell you where he is. I appreciate you sharing, but we still have a long way to go before I give out information about my friends."

The swordsman shifted. Ben expected the man to be gripping the hilt of his sword, but instead, he had one hand on the side of his head, and he was staring back at Ben in what looked like either awe or terror.

The old man frowned and then collapsed back into his chair. "Gunther is lost to us. For two moons now, we have been unable to sense him. He has not joined the hall, but it feels like he should have. The other elders look to me for understanding. I am the oldest, but I have no answers. This has not happened before. If you know what is going on, please tell me. It is... important to us."

"I am sorry, but I do not think he would be pleased if we told you," said Ben quietly.

Moments passed in silence.

Then, the swordsman spoke up, startling all of them. "Three years ago, someone began burrowing new node gates indiscriminately. Holes were left into the void, similar to the way a rift works. The dark forces have found them and have begun to walk the lines. Our barriers are insufficient to stop them. They are far more attuned to the lines than we are. Gunther was our last hope. We sent word, but he has not responded. I will not lie. It has been longer than my lifetime since he wanted anything to do with us, but we remain hopeful. Without him, the dark forces will travel unimpeded through the nodes. It is only a matter of time, and they will overrun all of us. Our work will have been for naught if we cannot close the remaining rifts."

"The nodes are like the rifts," asked Amelie, "but instead of to a demon world, they transverse our world?"

The swordsman nodded confirmation.

"Gunther would know what to do about this, but we do not," admitted the old man.

Amelie looked to Ben, then said, "An offshoot of the Purple, based on the South Continent, opened a new rift three years ago. Or maybe it was a node. I'm not sure they understood what it was they were doing, and I certainly don't. They were able to move it anywhere in our world, but only demons could pass through. Maybe that is what caused the disruption here?"

"The Purple opened a rift?" exclaimed the old man. "It must be destroyed immediately!"

"Already done," responded Ben. He paused and then added, "You guys really need to get out more."

"Do you believe him?" asked Amelie.

Ben shrugged. "No reason not to, I guess."

They were watching the sun creep over a distant mountain range. The first shards of light stabbed between the jagged passes, painting the bare rock in vivid oranges, yellows, and pinks.

"Yesterday, we could barely see a hill through the trees," observed Amelie.

Ben nodded agreement.

She continued, asking the obvious question, "Where do you think we are?"

They sat quietly while Ben pondered.

"Two, maybe three weeks north of Akew Woods," he said. "Two weeks short of the City, I'd guess."

"How do you know?" wondered Amelie.

"I don't know," admitted Ben, "but on the map, the peninsula that Akew Woods sits on has a few peaks about two-thirds of the way up. We're higher in elevation than we were yesterday. The air's colder and thinner but not as cool as I'd expect this time of year further north. In Farview, in early autumn, we'd be bundled up in our cloaks right now. Where we are is not the important question, though."

"What is, then?" asked Amelie, looking at him out of the corner of her eye.

"What are we going to do?" responded Ben. "We saw what that swordsman is capable of, and I'm certain the old man is a mage. Who knows how many others are in this place. I don't think we can fight our way out of here. We can ask to leave peacefully, of course, but what if they say no? I think that man was entirely serious when he said he keeps his secrets at any cost."

It was Amelie's turn to frown. She looked behind them, at the stone and thatch village that climbed the hill, two score buildings, mostly houses, but a few larger structures as well. There were no walls, no guards, no watchtowers to spy incoming marauders or escaping witnesses to their power. They didn't need that. The guardians of the First Mages had laid a network of wards all around the forest.

Ben and Amelie didn't speak about it because they didn't have to. On the way up the road, neither Amelie nor Towaal had sensed wards or even a hint of magic. For generations, no one in the Sanctuary detected the tripwires the guardians had left. If they couldn't sense the wards, then they'd be stumbling blindly. If they fled, Ben knew in his gut the guardians would be able to find them. The question was, if it came to a fight, could they win?

He was afraid he knew the answer.

Ben sighed and turned back to the vista before them. They were sitting at the base of the village, perched on a flat shelf of rock that overlooked a narrow valley. Ben guessed there was a sizeable stream below them. Across the valley was a pine-covered ridge just like the one they sat on and beyond that, to the north, jagged mountain peaks. Walking away would be easy. No one was watching them, but if they fled, what would they gain?

"You carry that sword like you know how to use it," remarked a calm voice from behind them.

Ben turned, struggling to mask his surprise that someone snuck up on them. The swordsman was standing next to a slender girl.

"We didn't get a chance to introduce ourselves last night. My name is Adrick Morgan," said the man. "This is Prem."

"Benjamin Ashwood. Everyone just calls me Ben, and this is Amelie."

"The elder asked me to tell you that the things we discussed last night should remain between us," said the swordsman. "There are those in this village who will not leave you alone if they learn what you shared with us."

"Keeping secrets from your own people?" asked Ben.

Adrick Morgan shifted his weight and shrugged. "Perhaps. Do you care to spar?

Ben shared a look with Amelie and clambered to his feet. He reached down a hand and helped her up. "Why not?"

The swordsman gave Ben a quick nod and turned to lead them back into the village.

"Do you sword fight also?" asked the girl, glancing at Amelie's rapier.

Amelie shrugged. "Not well."

The girl smiled. "Maybe we should practice then."

She pushed back a light cloak to reveal two long knives strapped to her sides. The weapons were the length of Ben's forearm, and judging by the width of the sheath, they'd be narrow and sharp. Nothing that would hold up against a heavy blade, but something about the way the girl carried herself made Ben suspect she knew what she was doing.

She had an undyed, thin linen cloak. It covered baggy trousers similar to Adrick's, and she wore a strange, tight tunic underneath. Her hair was pulled back and tied behind her head, and her cheeks were covered in scattered freckles. Ben pegged her a good five years younger than he and Amelie, but he reminded himself the Lady Avril appeared younger too. With mages, anything was possible.

"It's been a while since I've practiced the blade," admitted Amelie.

"Good," remarked the girl. "Then it's time you did it again."

The girl gave a quick bow and then stepped quickly to follow Adrick. He led them to a small, dirt clearing. It was flanked by benches, a water trough, and racks of practice weapons.

"There is not much to do here except roam the forest, so we spar," explained the girl.

Adrick slipped his sword belt off and hefted a wooden practice sword.

"Do not worry," he said to Ben. "I gather these from the western edge of the forest south of Narmid. It's bamboo. Hollow and light. It won't have the same weight as your blade, but it won't hurt when I strike you."

"Or when I strike you," challenged Ben.

His heart wasn't in the banter, though. His eyes were locked on the man's weapon. The previous night, he hadn't seen it in good light. Now that he did, he was confused. The thing appeared to be fashioned of a thin sheet of glass or crystal. Ben could see the bench it was resting against through the blade. The sword was without question mage-wrought, but it was like nothing Ben had seen before. If he hadn't seen it in action, he would have thought it would shatter the moment it struck steel.

"Let's watch for a bit if that is okay," suggested Prem to Amelie. "It is rare to see my father spar with an outsider. I am curious how he fares."

Ben grunted. Her father. After seeing the man single-handedly take down Zane's pirates without breaking a sweat, he had no doubt how the man would fare.

"Here," said Adrick, interrupting Ben's thoughts. He tossed a practice weapon Ben's way.

Ben smoothly snatched it out of the air and then fumbled to unbuckle his own sword belt with one hand while holding the practice sword in the other.

Adrick waited patiently. When Ben cleared his belt and set his feet, the swordsman attacked. He came quickly, his bamboo sword whistling through the air like a swarm of angry hornets.

Ben stumbled back, trying to adjust to the man's speed. Barely perceptibly, Adrick slowed, and Ben settled into a rhythm. He was scrambling on defense, but Adrick didn't press the attack. Instead, he kept up a constant barrage, forcing Ben to stretch to defend each new tactic the man threw at him.

Ben had learned against Saala and was used to sparring with Rhys. They were quick, but nothing like this man. And while Ben had learned forms from Saala, Black Bart, the guards at Whitehall, and the rogue, none of them were like Adrick's movements. Instead of set forms, the swordsman seemed to whirl with unseen currents of wind or as if he could sense Ben's movements before Ben made them. He moved ahead of Ben, his blade going where Ben was going, his feet stepping away from Ben's strikes before Ben started them. In moments, Ben had accumulated several painful welts on his sides where the bamboo blade had smacked against him.

"Hold," he gasped.

Adrick paused mid-swing.

Ben stripped off his shirt, ignoring the early morning chill in the air. Adrick grinned and tossed his shirt aside as well. Ben looked at Amelie and tried to ignore her admiring the swordsman's chiseled physique. In the light of the day, the man looked even more impressive than he had in the firelight the night before.

Removing his shirt wasn't to put on a show for the girls, though. It was to give Ben time to think. The swordsman was relentless and quicker than anyone Ben had faced, but the man wasn't invulnerable. Ben smiled to himself and then tried a thrust at Adrick's midsection. As expected, the swordsman brushed it aside and settled into an attack.

Parrying, Ben laid down a predictable defensive pattern, avoiding most of Adrick's blows and keeping his practice blade constantly in motion.

Suddenly, Ben's eyes widened, and his mouth dropped open in shock. Concerned, Adrick glanced over his shoulder where Rhys was taking a place on a bench to watch. Ben's bamboo sword smacked meatily against the man's muscled chest, and the swordsman jumped back, his weapon rising and a smile curling on his face.

"Sorry for the cheap shot," apologized Ben.

Adrick chuckled. "I haven't had someone try a trick like that on me in fifty years. It's good you did and a reminder that I need to be aware of more than just your blade. In a real fight, anything can happen, and you have to be ready."

Behind, Ben heard Prem whispering to Amelie. "What'd he do?"

"A dirty trick," responded Amelie. "He learned from the best."

Ben didn't hear any of the rest of the conversation because Adrick swarmed back at him, the bamboo practice blade whipping at his head. Ben dodged under it, slashed a counter attack which was deflected, and then retreated back out of reach.

As he and Adrick danced across the clearing, out of the corner of his eye, he saw Amelie and Prem squaring off as well. The young girl was just as quick as her father, and she used her two practice long knives with incredible precision. Amelie looked to be getting the worst of it, but Ben didn't have time to observe their match. It was taking everything he had to avoid getting beaten like a dusty carpet during spring cleaning.

For a bell, they sparred before finally, Adrick held up a hand to pause.

Ben stopped, breathing ragged gasps of air. His torso was covered in raised red welts, but he was pleased to see half a dozen of them on the swordsman. The man was a blademaster and then some. Even when he wasn't moving full speed, striking him was a victory in and of itself.

"You are quite skilled, Ben," claimed Adrick. "Maybe we will spar again. Soon, though, I believe you must meet with the council of elders. They have been discussing what to do with you this morning."

Prem and Amelie came to stand beside them, and the girl offered a tentative smile. Ben did not feel the warmth. It was impossible to ignore the ominous implications of the council meeting.

Sparring with Adrick had taught Ben one valuable lesson, though. They wouldn't be able to fight their way out of the place. The swordsman alone was formidable. Maybe the best Ben had ever faced. Better than Rhys or Saala, certainly. Ben would pay good gold to see Adrick and Lord Jason face off. If the other guardians trained with the swordsman, it was a safe assumption they'd be skilled as well. There was no way Ben and his friends could fight a village of them.

Rhys came sauntering up, a sense of preparedness marking his every movement. It reminded Ben of the Rhys of old, before Northport, when the rogue had been ready anytime, anywhere. Hopefully, today, he wouldn't need to be.

Adrick nodded a goodbye and disappeared amongst the houses in the village.

"Have you eaten? If not, I can find something for you," offered Prem.

Ben's stomach grumbled and he was reminded that he hadn't had breakfast that morning. As soon as dawn had broken, he and Amelie had walked to the rock overlooking the valley. A bell of hard sword practice had stirred his appetite into ravenous hunger.

The girls grinned at the sound, and Ben flushed.

"That would be wonderful," responded Amelie.

"Come with me then," said Prem.

She took them to a squat stone house and led them around to the back. A wooden pergola arched over a table and chairs. Wrist-thick vines grew up the wooden structure and draped the seating area in cool shade.

"It's a bit late in the year to eat outside," admitted Prem, "but after sparring, I like to feel the breeze."

"Outside is good," murmured Amelie. She was glancing around the village. They'd have an excellent view of it while they ate.

"Great. I'll be right back then," said Prem.

Ben, Amelie, and Rhys sat and studied their surroundings. The village was quiet, with only half of the buildings showing any signs of life. The other structures were well-maintained, though, with fresh thatch on the roofs and windows tightly shuttered. Several of the houses had small gardens near them, and from somewhere, Ben heard the comfortable sound of animals. Pigs and goats, he thought. A rooster had woken them at dawn, so there were unseen chickens stalking the village as well.

He nudged Amelie and pointed to where Lady Towaal was slipping between houses. The mage was clearly snooping, but no one made a move to stop her. The houses that were occupied had doors and windows opened wide. The ones that didn't seem occupied were tightly shut. Nearly all of the larger buildings were closed and dark, and at least while they watched her, Towaal wasn't bold enough to try entering any of those.

The people were dressed simply and, for the most part, ignored the presence of strangers. Whatever other secrets they concealed were buried deeper than the surface of the village. From what Ben could see, the place was a small but prosperous settlement, well maintained by its residents.

Prem returned with a wide, wooden platter heaped with sausages, cheese, and bread.

"The bread isn't fresh, but it's better than nothing," she said with a grin. "Hold on. I'll be back with water and wine. You do drink wine?"

Amelie nodded. "Sometimes."

Ben snorted and she shot him a glare. Rhys grinned broadly but miraculously held his tongue. They tore into the stack of sausages and cheese while Prem ducked inside to get the wine. Surreptitiously, Ben kept glancing around the village while they ate. It was strangely quiet outside of the sounds of the animals.

"You're wondering where everyone is?" guessed Prem when she returned.

Ben finished chewing a bite of tangy, white cheese and admitted, "It does seem strange. It feels like more people should be around. There are so many shuttered houses, but they look well-maintained."

"Less than half of us are here now," murmured Prem.

"Where are the others?" queried Amelie. She quickly added, "If that is okay to tell me."

Prem grimaced and pushed a hunk of sausage around on the platter. "That is no secret. They are fighting the dark forces."

Ben blinked. "The dark forces, like, demons?"

The girl nodded. "Demons, goblins, whatever comes at them. There is a place on the northwestern edge of this forest where the space between our worlds is thin. The creatures come through there, and we must meet them."

"Like the rift in the Wilds!" exclaimed Ben.

"Yes," agreed the girl, giving Ben a surprised look. "Like the rift in the Wilds. That rift is gone, though, somehow destroyed. It left our forest, the one in the east, and the tunnel across the Empty Sea as the vulnerable locations in this world. If those rifts could be closed, it would be a great victory, but with the node lines weakened, it is a huge risk now. We must hold our position or the dark forces could enter the nodes and travel all over this continent. It would be utter chaos."

"Node lines?" wondered Ben.

Prem gave him a tight-lipped smile, and he understood that was venturing into a forbidden topic.

"You're like the hunters in the Wilds," speculated Amelie.

The girl picked at her food. "What we do is similar."

"If this battle is so important, why are you and Adrick Morgan here?" asked Ben. "He's the best swordsman I've ever seen. If he were to face the demons, surely he'd make a difference."

"He wants to go, but he must stay." A bittersweet smile twisted Prem's lips. She paused and then looked around the village to see if anyone was near. "Maybe I shouldn't say this, but he is required to be here. Without him, the Elder would fail, and much of our magic would be lost."

"I don't understand," said Amelie.

"My father is strong, full of life. The Elder is weak, at the end of his," explained Prem. "The Elder uses my father as a source of life to sustain himself, like a crutch. If my father was to travel too far from him, the Elder will lose the connection."

"Why doesn't the Elder go to the front line then?" wondered Ben.

"He will," said Prem, "when the end comes."

∾

AFTER THEY ATE, Ben, Amelie, and Rhys left to find Towaal. They gathered her and huddled together inside the building where they'd spent the night.

"Find anything out?" asked Ben as they settled in the room.

"I found more questions than I did answers," muttered Towaal. "How about you?"

"We sparred with the swordsman Adrick and his daughter," explained Amelie. She related everything they'd found out from the two of them.

"Everything we've been told checks out with everything I was able to discover walking around," stated Towaal.

"Which, is a bit shocking for a group that prides itself on so much secrecy," declared Rhys.

Ben smirked. "They don't think we'll leave."

Rhys cracked his knuckles.

"You saw me spar with that man," reminded Ben. "If there are more like him, we wouldn't get far, and let's not forget whatever mages they have who were able to set wards in the forest that Towaal and Amelie couldn't sense."

Towaal nodded grimly. "The old man is powerful, and elsewhere in this village, I sensed strength like I have rarely felt. I do not think fighting our way out is a viable option."

"Can they really be stronger than Eldred?" wondered Rhys, his fingers absentmindedly toying with his long knives. "With proper planning, we defeated her. These people have to sleep sometime."

Towaal sat back in her chair and shook her head. "I estimate there are over three hundred people living in this village. Dozens of them may have talent, not to mention their martial skills."

"We're not fighting them," stated Ben, trying to bring the discussion to an end.

"What do we do then?" challenged Rhys. "You want us to wait

until they decide to slaughter us? You saw what that man did to the pirates. He didn't even give them a chance to speak."

"These people are worried about ancient secrets and old powers getting out into the world," responded Ben, meeting his friends' eyes. "They're worried, just like we are about Eldred and what the Veil did to her. They're fighting the dark forces, just like we are. They want to find out what happened to Gunther, just like we do. I think there's a lot they could help us with, and maybe we can convince them that we could return the favor."

Amelie smiled. "We need to give them a reason to need us."

"Exactly," said Ben.

"Do you have any ideas of how we do that?" inquired Towaal.

"The things these people have been trying to prevent are happening right now out in the world," answered Ben. "Let's tell them about it. We can tell them that the demons are swarming uncontrollably. Tell them the Veil and Avril are awakening ancient evils, and that if we don't act, the Veil will get the wyvern fire staff. If they mean what they say about helping Alcott, then they have no choice but to help us."

"There are some uncomfortable details we may want to avoid," suggested Towaal.

"They don't need to know everything," Ben agreed, "but we should tell them enough to know we aren't the enemy."

"Are you sure we aren't their enemy?" asked Rhys.

Ben shrugged.

WITH THE DECISION MADE, they left the house to find the council of elders. It wasn't difficult. It was the one building with a guard out front.

The man looked like a jealous cousin of Adrick Morgan and he cemented the notion in Ben's head when he growled as they approached. "I heard you sparred with the Lightblade. How did that go?"

Ben blinked at him.

"Adrick Morgan, the Lightblade," said the man. "I heard he bested you in the practice yard."

"He did," Ben responded, laughing. He hooked a thumb toward Rhys. "He's been training me for a year now, but I'm nowhere close to where I want to be. At least I got a few more strikes in on Adrick than I normally do when I spar this one."

The guard frowned, and Rhys winked at him.

"We'd like to speak to the elders," said Amelie.

The guard drew his shoulders back and puffed out his chest. "The elders are in council and aren't to be disturbed. They'll let you know when they make a decision."

"To kill us or not?" snapped Rhys.

The guard glared back at the rogue.

"No problem," said Ben. He turned to go and then over his shoulder mentioned, "By the way, can you let them know that a wyvern fire staff is on its way to the Sanctuary? I haven't seen it in use myself, but I'm told that it has the ability to destroy an entire city."

The man blinked at him but did not move to go inside.

"I'm sure the Veil only has altruistic plans for it, and it was merely a coincidence the undead mage she sent after us was using one of your node keys to move through your forest unde-tected. Probably nothing to worry about. If the elders decide to kill us, I'm sure they'll be able to learn about these things from the next group of strangers who arrive in this village, assuming the Veil doesn't get here first with her wyvern fire, of course."

Ben started to lead his friends away when the guard finally climbed over his ego and thought better about keeping those bits of information from the elders.

"Hold here while I go inside," he barked. "I'll tell the elders what you said. You stay there!"

Ben smiled pleasantly at the man. "Of course."

Moments later, the man returned and beckoned them inside.

They were led into an open, circular room, which made Ben wonder how they fit it inside the square building. The walls were covered in chalk drawings of strange symbols. They appeared to have been wiped away and redrawn over and over again, or maybe, refined as the mages in the council studied them. The roof was stone, fashioned into a dome which rose far above their heads. There were no windows, no openings, save a small hole at the top.

The council was half a dozen people, all men and all ancient appearing. They dressed the same as the rest of the village, and to Ben's eye, there was nothing to tell their status except for their apparent age, which he guessed didn't tell the half of it. The oldest of the men, the one they'd met the night before, spoke first.

"I'm told you know of wyvern fire. That is banned knowledge and is punishable by death."

"Isn't everything?" jested Ben. The elders on the council didn't laugh, so he continued, "We do know of wyvern fire, but our knowledge isn't your problem. Your problem is what will someone do with wyvern fire. Right now, a young man is approaching the City with a staff that generates the stuff. He's intending to give it to the Veil. She could be back here in two weeks with the device. Will your wards protect you from that kind of power?"

"Our safety is not your concern," responded the elder crisply.

Ben snorted. "It's not your safety I'm warning you about. If you were to be vaporized by wyvern fire, who will watch over the power of the First Mages?"

Around the table, the elders shuffled.

"Without your support, who will fight the dark forces?" pressed Ben. "The Veil already turned down the opportunity to meet them in the Wilds. I doubt she'll be any more open to the idea in this forest."

The old man frowned at him.

Ben kept talking, not letting the elders have a chance to interrupt. "All of the banned knowledge you are worried about us knowing is actually being used in the world outside of this forest. You don't need to be concerned about what could happen. You need to be concerned about what is happening right now!"

"You want us to let you go?" asked one of the elders slowly. The man had a bald pate and bushy white eyebrows that threatened to hide his eyes.

Ben blinked at him, unsure if it was a serious question.

"Of course they want to leave, Faeger," answered the eldest, the one they'd met the night before.

Adrick, surprising Ben who hadn't seen him, stepped out of shadows against one wall. "This young man with the staff, you say he is in the forest?"

"He left several days before us. I'd guess he's halfway through the woods now."

Adrick turned to the council. "Let me go. I will find this boy and stop him. I'll recover the staff and bring it here."

The old man shook his head. "Even you cannot stand alone against wyvern fire. In the old days, when it was first used, the only way to bring down a mage who could call it was to work as a team. The heat is such that it can only be directed in a very narrow funnel, or it will destroy the person using it. An attack must come from multiple fronts, preventing the wielder from turning the flame against all of the attackers."

"Prem and I—" started Adrick.

The old man held up his hand. "You would sacrifice your daughter or yourself? The fire cannot be directed in two directions at once, but certainly, it will be used on one of the attackers."

Grim-faced, Adrick shuffled his feet nervously. "We will do what we must."

"No, I think there is a better way," declared the old man. He turned back to Ben. "You are certain this staff can call wyvern fire? Have you seen it used?"

"I am certain," declared Ben, skirting the truth. "It was recovered from the Purple's fortress on the South Continent."

The old man frowned at Ben.

"The staff is real," continued Ben, "but it is only part of the threat. The Veil is using death magic to raise undead mages. The former Veil, Lady Avril, is still alive and plotting. The demons are swarming in the north, overtaking towns and wreaking havoc. The Alliance and the Coalition are gearing for an intercontinental war. You can sit here in your quiet village, pretending you are saving the world, but you're hiding from the real threats. Every moment you delay us only increases the risk of complete disaster. If you don't let us leave, before long, there may not be anyone left to keep your secrets from."

Blank-faced, the old man studied Ben.

Ben started to wonder if he'd gone too far. Moments passed, and Ben shifted uneasily.

The swordsman, Adrick Morgan, cleared his throat.

The old man shot him a warning look and then turned to address his fellow elders.

"The boy is right," he admitted.

Several voices spoke up in protest, but the old man cut them off with a glare.

"It's been too long since we've left our forest," he rasped. "Our mission is to retain the knowledge and power of the First Mages, to keep it safe for when it's required, to ensure that it does not fall into the wrong hands, but how do we know it's safe? How do we know it is not already in the wrong hands and our actions are only allowing it to spread further?"

Around the table, wrinkled, old men muttered under their breath and eyed each other uncomfortably.

"Many of you are old enough to remember a time before we founded this village," continued the elder. "A time when there was more than one First Mage, when our role was to find and remove dangerous knowledge from the world. We were thorough, we believed, and then we retreated into our shell. It may be time to venture out again, to find threats and protect against them. What is our purpose if we do not do this?"

One by one, the elders murmured assent. They weren't happy about it, Ben could see, but they couldn't argue with the logic.

"There is one more thing," said the man slowly. Sorrow fell over him like a shadow. "It is time. We must close the rift."

No one spoke.

"I will not force you," whispered the elder, his voice barely audible in the silent room.

Finally, one of the others spoke. "We hoped it would never arrive, but we knew this day was coming. We will do as you ask. We will help you close the rift."

The old man turned to Ben. "Go and rest. We must prepare. Tomorrow, you will come with us and assist. When the job is finished, no one will stop you from going on your way."

Ben swallowed, unsure of what he was agreeing to but happy they would be let go. "Ah, okay. We'll do it."

THE REST OF THE DAY, the village was a beehive of activity. The remaining warriors girded themselves for battle, the mages prepared whatever they felt necessary, but Ben and his friends were largely ignored.

In the evening, Prem came and found them. "I'm guessing no one has fed you yet?" she asked.

"We have some supplies left," responded Amelie.

"With what is coming tomorrow," responded Prem, "you'll need a hot meal. Come to my house. I will make something."

"Where is your father?" asked Ben.

"He is with the elders," answered Prem. She looked over her

shoulder at the group. "They have much to discuss about tomorrow and what comes after."

"What will come after?" asked Amelie.

"We do not know," replied Prem.

"I've been wondering," said Ben. "Why does your father have to stay here to serve as a source of life for the elder? There are many people in this village. Can no one else do it?"

The girl shook her head. "It requires a unique connection, like father and son."

"Ah," remarked Ben.

"Or grandfather and granddaughter?" asked Amelie.

The girl smiled at her. "That could work as well, but my father would never allow it. Despite what it may seem to you, he has visions of me leaving here and starting a life and a family elsewhere. He wants me to leave someday, but I do not know if that will come to pass." She waved her hands around the village. "As you can tell, there are few here in my generation, and it is rare that any fresh blood arrives. There are many amongst the guardians who have lost interest or the ability to have children. From what I have seen, the ones who could be interested in children are not interested in their neighbors in that way. Romance is one thing even the elders have not tried to impose on the rest of the guardians. Every moon, we lose more people at the rift, but there are no younglings to replace them. I'm the last living member of this village to be born here. I fear if I were to leave, then who will be left to carry on?"

"Hold on," interjected Ben. "You've never left this village?"

"I've never left the forest," admitted the girl. With a sigh, she continued, "Nearly one hundred years and I've always been the baby, the one they would not let out of their sight. My father insists I shall leave when the time is right, but where will I go? The City is the closest settlement to us. I am told it can be dangerous for our people."

She shrugged and then opened the door to her home. Ben met

Amelie's eyes as they stepped inside. One hundred years, the girl had said, and she was the youngest one.

"Make yourselves comfortable," continued Prem. "I have more of the wine if you like. I grow the grapes on the vines behind the house. My father and I are the only ones who drink it."

"That would be lovely," murmured Amelie. Behind the girl's back, she mouthed, 'One hundred years' to Ben.

He nodded. The girl, if she could be called that, was five times older than him. She was older than his father, and his father, and probably his father.

4

HOLD BACK THE DARKNESS

Dawn rose on the village, and Ben and his friends joined Adrick and Prem in a stream of armed men and women heading toward the underground chamber that served as the hub of the node gates.

"How do people pass through without being harmed?" asked Ben. "I thought that the energy given off by transporting through a rift would be fatal for a person."

"Traveling through a rift likely would be fatal to a person," agreed Adrick. "I've never done it myself, of course. The nodes are similar but different. Instead of burrowing through the fabric of space, we are riding along top of it."

Ben frowned.

"If that doesn't make sense, you should hear the elder explain it," muttered Adrick. "Think about it this way, there are established currents of energy constantly running through our world and what exists outside of our world. They are invisible, but they do exist. When using the node gates, we are slipping into the current of these streams and following them on their natural journey."

"Like a boat on a river," suggested Amelie.

Adrick smiled. "Yes, something like that. Riding the current is relatively safe if you are in a waterway that you are familiar with. The rifts are different, though. A rift does not follow a current of energy. It blazes its own trail. It tunnels through space, which is incredibly disruptive, and throws off massive amounts of violent power. Getting hit with that force would likely kill you, as you said."

"So, can these nodes be made to go anywhere?" asked Ben.

"Thinking about saving yourself some walking once this is over?" asked Adrick.

Ben shrugged.

"In theory, the gateways could be opened in many places. The lines of power are everywhere, but they do not always intersect with where you would want to go. Our cavern is a hub, and many lines intersect there. That is why we built the village in this location. Away from a hub, a gate could be opened, but finding the proper direction would be difficult. There are some devices the First Mages created which we are able to link with our hub using the First Mage's trapped energy, but we've lost the knowledge to create more of them."

"The real problem isn't our convenience," said Prem, who had come up behind them. "It is that the dark forces are able to use the rifts and the node gates. They're more attuned to it than humans are. And worse, while a rift can be sealed, the node gates are merely entries into currents of power that exist outside of our influence. We can close the door, but beyond the door, the road is still there."

"But then a rift..." mumbled Ben, trying to understand.

"A rift is like a hole in a wall. If it's there, you could pass through, but when it's not there, there is no hole, just wall. Nothing to even attempt entering."

They made it to the stairs that led down into the chamber and Adrick paused.

"A few years ago, the fabric of space was shaken. Someone,

somehow, was burrowing new rifts. We didn't know it at the time, but we now suspect it was this offshoot of the Purple you told us about. It disrupted things, and we found it more and more difficult to close the node gates. To continue the door metaphor, because it's the most logical way we can describe this, it was like the doorway shifted, and there is a gap now. The dark forces have been able to worm their way through that gap and make use of the node gates. They could travel anywhere in this forest and to some places outside in the blink of an eye."

Ben swallowed.

"That," finished Adrick, "is why we have to close the rift gate. We do not have the resources to keep the dark forces bottled up and also venture out into the broader world."

"Could the creatures appear elsewhere and use the node gates?" asked Ben as he followed Adrick down the stairs into the chamber.

"Possibly," confirmed Adrick, "but in a moment, you'll see why we are particularly worried about this situation."

In the chamber, a steady stream of guardians was passing through an open node gate. Two-thirds of the population, Ben had heard. A minimal force was left behind in case anyone stumbled across the settlement, but they were anticipating all hands would be needed to close the rift once and for all.

Ben stepped through the opening and gasped.

They were standing on a stone stairway set high on a ridge. In front of them, a narrow valley extended a quarter league, forming a box canyon with steep, rock sides. A huge cliff rose to block the end, and at the base of the cliff, loomed the dark maw of a cave.

"That's the rift, in there," said Prem.

She started down the stairs, and Ben and his friends followed. At the base of the ridge was an encampment made up of half a dozen permanent structures and a dozen long tents. In front of the camp was a stout stone wall that spanned the width of the canyon. Three watchtowers anchored the wall, and above it on the ridge was another platform studded with compact siege weapons. They were small enough to have fit through the node gate, realized Ben. In the wall, there was no opening, no way to pass the barrier except climbing over it.

"Damn," whispered Rhys.

Ben followed the rogue's gaze beyond the fortifications and swallowed. The entire length of the valley was covered in debris. It was littered with the wreckage of war. Shattered weapons, armor, and bodies lay like a grisly carpet for a quarter league. The mud was dark, nearly black, stained with the blood of the fallen.

"The mages send fire every few days along the length of the valley to burn the dead," said Adrick grimly. "It keeps the smell and pestilence at bay. It's not a good sign that so much filth is out there now. They're saving their strength for combat."

"I've never seen anything like this," murmured Towaal.

Adrick chuckled mirthlessly. "This valley has been a battle-field off and on for the last seven hundred years. In the last three years, excursions from the dark forces have grown more common. In the last few months, it's been every night. The demons are running out of doorways to use into our realm. Every night and into the morning, we stop them here. In the past, we could have months or even a year with no sightings of the dark ones, but now, the war is never-ending."

Ben grimaced, eyeing the torn earth and the heaps of the dead.

"It's everything we can do to maintain our line, to use our superior skill to turn back the tide of evil. With what you've told us, staying still is no longer enough. We hoped this was merely a bad run, and the pressure would ease. We know now that is not the case. Because this is one of the last open rifts, the pressure will never ease, until we close the rift."

They made it to the platform with the siege weaponry, and

Ben eyed the catapults and ballistae there. There were well-made, well-used weapons of war. Stacks of ammunition lay behind them, and the half-dozen men and women minding the platform eyed the new arrivals grimly. They knew what it meant, Ben guessed, seeing the elders arrive in force. They knew the old man would only be there for one reason.

"If you can close the rift," asked Ben, "then why haven't you done it already? Why fight this never-ending battle if you don't have to?"

"There is a cost to continuing the fight," answered Adrick, "and there is a cost to stopping it. Closing the rift will not be cheap. It is the cost that the council has debated for the last three years, the sacrifice they will have to make that's stopped them. They have debated it endlessly, but now, our hand is forced, and my father has made his decision. We cannot defend one of the last remaining rifts in Alcott."

"The cost?" asked Amelie.

Adrick didn't answer, but after a long moment of silence, Prem finally did. "Closing the rift will take incredible power. If done sloppily, it will cause a massive explosion. Containing the release will take everything the council has. To do it safely, they will have to do it from within."

"I... I don't understand," said Ben.

"To close the rift," explained Prem, "the council and most of our magic users must go inside, and they won't be coming back out."

BEN and his friends followed Prem and found a relatively comfortable place in the encampment.

"The elders will prepare the spell the rest of today and most of the night. When night falls, expect the dark ones to issue forth and attack. When the sun comes back up, hopefully, we have won. We'll escort the mages to the cave in the light of morning. Once they enter, they'll be on their own."

"We can rest until then?" asked Ben.

"Rest until tonight," advised Prem. "At night, you'll need to be ready. You've faced the dark ones?"

"We've faced plenty of demons before," responded Ben, sitting down on a rickety camp chair.

"Demons, goblins, and even wyverns have come through," said Prem. "There's no way to predict which of the creatures will arrive. We have no idea if they are sent or are merely in the area and are attracted to the life forces on this side of the rift. No one has been to the other side, of course, so no one knows what their society is like. If there is one."

Ben crashed to the floor, the camp chair collapsing underneath of him.

"What was that you said?" squeaked Amelie.

"We can't predict—"

"Wyverns!" exclaimed Ben from the floor.

Even Rhys looked a little pale. He coughed nervously. "It did sound like you said wyverns. Goblins and wyverns. No one has seen goblins on Alcott in decades, and wyverns in, I don't know, millennia..."

The girl looked at them blankly. "Yes, wyverns. They are rare, but we do face them here. Small ones usually. This rift is natural, which, according to the mages, makes it easier for the dark forces to use. Wyverns and goblins, they only cross at natural openings. Demons, being lower species like animals, can cross through any opening."

Ben picked himself up slowly. His friends were left speechless.

Prem, apparently taking their stunned silence as a lack of questions, stood and said, "I'm going to go find some friends that have been out here the last several weeks. I will be back before evening."

After she left, Rhys blurted, "Are you kidding me? What else do we need to show that this isn't a good idea? When the sun goes down, instead of standing on that wall, we should be heading the other way!"

Ben could only shake his head, still stunned.

"Wyverns!" cried Rhys.

"It's too late to leave," remarked Towaal, "but even if it wasn't, getting these people's help is worth whatever we have to go through tonight and tomorrow."

Rhys snorted incredulously.

"Milo was a few days ahead of us," reminded Towaal. "At our pace, we never would have caught him before he made it to the Sanctuary. With these nodes, we can pop out in front of him. It's probably how Eldred made it to Akew Woods so far before us. There is still plenty of time to stop Milo if these people can help us find a gate near the City. Rhys, we can head him off and recover the staff before he meets the Veil."

Rhys opened his mouth to respond, but Towaal interjected. "Also, I saw what Adrick is capable of, and you told me about him sparring with Ben. That's an ally we can't afford to turn down if we want to face the demons, the Veil, Avril, the Alliance, and the Coalition. Rhys, whatever the risk, it's worth it."

The rogue's mouth snapped shut, and he crossed his arms across his chest. "Wyverns, Karina. She said there were wyverns."

THE REST of the day passed in restless tension. Eventually, too nervous to sleep, Ben decided to explore the encampment and the walls. He took Amelie with him, but Rhys remained behind sulking. Towaal meandered further up the slope, planning to lurk around the mage's tent and see if she could learn anything.

Ben didn't blame Rhys for being upset, but Towaal was right. No matter the risk, they had too much to gain from assisting Adrick and his people. A two-week jump on Milo and the guardian's help recovering the staff. Without those advantages, the Veil would get the staff before them, and there was nothing they could do to prevent it.

The others in the encampment and on the wall largely ignored them. Certainly, they knew who the strangers were, but Ben guessed since strangers were normally cut down before explaining themselves, no one considered it worth becoming friends.

Finally, they saw Prem at the top of one of the watchtowers. She was leaning casually against the railing and gesturing at the war-torn field in front of her. She noticed Ben and Amelie and waved for them to come up.

With nothing better to do, Ben ascended the narrow ladder into the wooden tower. It stood three stories above the field below and offered a slightly worse view of the landscape than the side of the hill near the node gate.

"Frand, Ignice, meet Ben and Amelie," said Prem.

Ben nodded to the two men.

They were wearing tightly woven chainmail shirts, conical helmets, and thick leather gauntlets studded with steel spikes. Two huge, kite-shaped shields rested against the wall next to bows and baskets full of arrows. One of the men had a massive two-handed sword next to him and a shorter sword at his hip. The other was resting his hands on a heavy-looking mace and carried two falchions on his back. Both men had a number of long daggers stuffed into their boots, hung on their belts, and a belt on the floor contained half-a-dozen knives that could be used for throwing.

Ben self-consciously placed a hand on the hilt of his longsword.

"Don't worry," grinned Prem. She tapped her long knives. "Frand and Ignice get a little nervous if they're not carrying enough steel to start their own arms shop. I think all that steel must be compensating for something."

The two men grunted. They had identical cinnamon-colored beards and looked to be about the same build. Brothers, Ben was pretty sure.

"Girl," claimed Frand, "if you get surrounded by a pack of goblins, you're gonna wish you had a steel shirt too. Those little darts and arrows they shoot don't seem like much til one of 'em catches you in the eye or a dozen of the damn things get stuck in your back. Nasty way to go, that, stabbed to death by a buncha little pricks no bigger than your finger."

"Buncha little pricks," replied Prem, fighting to hide a smile. "That's what Tabby said about you two. It did sound horrible."

Frand rolled his eyes.

"If Tabby wasn't happy with what she was gettin'," claimed Ingice, "she wouldn'ta followed us here, would she? She'd be sittin' back at the village with you, weaving baskets or whatever it is you do to bide your time."

Prem slipped her knives out of the sheath and spun them slowly, one in each hand. She looked meaningfully below the brother's belts and then made a quick slash with each blade before sliding them back out of sight. Now, it was the brothers who hid smiles.

Ben took the chance to ask a question that had been bugging him since they'd first understood what they faced. "Wyverns and goblins, I've heard about them in stories, but everywhere I've been, people think they're just that, stories. Are there really wyverns and goblins that come out of that cave?"

Frand rubbed his beard. "Naw, goblins and wyverns are real as anything else I've ever seen. Keep watchin', and you'll see some of 'em soon enough."

The man pointed to the sun, which just beginning to touch the ridge to the west.

"Once it's full dark, they'll come across. Been coming harder and faster since that rift was destroyed up north. Every night for, what, Ignice, two or three months now?"

Ignice shrugged, his chainmail rattling with the motion, "Four, I think. Hard to remember. The days are blurring together now. I can't remember the last time we had a night off."

"What are they like?" wondered Ben.

"I don't know the stories you've been told," answered Frand, "but goblins are probably just like you'd expect 'em to be. Little short things, maybe halfway up your chest. Thin, like the scrawniest demons, but they don't have any of the strength and little of the quickness. They're smarter, I guess. They don't have the same animal brain demons do. Don't have a human one either, though. They can fashion simple clothing and weapons, but the quality is poor as shit. No talent for harnessing their will, fortunately."

"They're blue, and in our atmosphere, they glow," added Ignice.

"Really?" asked Amelie.

The warrior nodded. "Some of our mages have explained why, but I wasn't listening. Goblins are weak, and at night they can't sneak up on you, so as long as you know what you're doing with that rapier, a single one shouldn't give you much trouble. The problem is, you ain't ever gonna see just one of 'em. They travel in packs. Could be a score come through that rift. Could be a hundred. In the last few months, it's been more than that. We've seen, what, maybe five hundred of them at once?"

Ben's eyes bulged. No matter how weak the things were, five hundred enemies was something to worry about.

"They're not what you really gotta worry about, though," advised Frand.

Ben fought a groan.

"Wyverns, now," continued Frand, "those are bad business."

Ignice nodded. "They're small when they come through the rift here, not like the ones they had to deal with in old times, but a small wyvern isn't exactly small, you know? Thirty, forty paces long. Sharp teeth, big claws, that kind of thing. Stronger than an arch-demon and smarter too. Smarter than even the goblins, though, they don't have hands to create any tools. Just brutal strength and cunning."

"Do they…" Ben swallowed. "Do they breathe fire?"

Frand snorted. "Nah, not that I ever seen." He paused. "Damn, man, that'd be scary as hell. You think I'd be standing here if there was some forty-pace long lizard that was gonna come out that rift and shoot fire at me?"

Ignice banged on his shield and then his helmet. "This stuff is steel, man. You know what happens when steel gets hot?"

"Just relating what I heard in the stories," muttered Ben. He was torn between being glad he wasn't going to have to face some fire-breathing creature of myth, and being disappointed that part of the stories wasn't true.

"So, what happens when darkness falls?" asked Amelie.

"Depends on the night," answered Frand. "Usually, within a bell or two, we'll see something poking out of the cave. Probably a few goblins but occasionally the demons get over-eager and come right at us. The goblins aren't quite so… enthusiastic, I would say. They gather their numbers before they'll charge at us. It's best to hold the wall and let 'em come where the artillery can pick 'em off, but sometimes, they get clever, and we have to sally out and bust up whatever formation they're in."

"That's strange they adjust their tactics," said Ben.

"Not by much," clarified Frand. "Just like there are arch-demons, there are leaders amongst the goblins. Whichever one is biggest and meanest, I suppose. Like human commanders, some are better than others. Sometimes, something seems to be controlling the demons, but other times they act like any swarm you'd see. They're hungry and they come straight at you."

"When the horn blows," added Ignice, "it's beginning."

Ben stood, staring out at the battle-torn canyon below the watchtower.

"Before then," remarked Prem, "we should get some sleep. The watchers here have shifts, but we've been up all day. Come true night, we need to be ready."

Ben and Amelie thanked the warriors for their time and shimmied down the ladder, following Prem back to the encampment. They filled in Rhys and Towaal on what they'd learned, including about the wyverns, which caused a great deal of grumbling from Rhys. Then, they laid down to rest.

~

A SONOROUS BOOM snapped Ben out of his slumber. In the dim light of the tent they'd commandeered, he saw Amelie's eyes shining back at him.

"Survive tonight. Help get the elders into that cave tomorrow. Then, we're off to the City."

"Yeah," mumbled Ben, rubbing his eyes, trying to squish the sleep out of them. "No problem."

"Come with me," called Prem from the flap of the tent.

Ben's friends gathered the little gear they'd brought with them and followed the girl into the early night. Along the wall, braziers blazed with magical fire. It pulsed an angry red, but Ben was assured when Rhys commented, "Smart. The red light will spare some of your night vision. You should be able to see what is happening in the field, and then still see them when they get close."

The towers on top of the walls remained dark. In the red glow from below, Ben could see silhouettes moving atop them, but he guessed they didn't want to completely expose archers or any mages who could be up high. Some of the demons would be able to fly, and he certainly wouldn't want to be sitting in a tower as a target for a wyvern.

Prem took them down the wall, weaving between men and women who strapped on gear and made their last preparations before battle. Finally, they found themselves at the base of the watchtower Ben and Amelie had climbed earlier in the day.

"I hope this is okay," said Prem.

Ben shrugged. "One spot is as good as any."

"What do you see?" Prem called up to the watchtower.

"Goblins," said a voice from above. Ben thought it was the warrior Frand. "A dozen or so poked their heads out and then vanished back inside."

"Just a dozen," said Ben, a grin splitting his face. They had a small army lining the walls, a contingent of mages, and siege equipment above. A dozen goblins would be nothing. He started to think this might be fun.

"Yeah, a bad sign," continued the voice. "That's a lotta scouts. They went back inside to muster their forces. My guess, at least two hundred of the baddies. We'll do what we can with the arrows but looks like we're going to have to get our swords bloody tonight, boys and girls."

"Huzzzah!" called a man from the other side of the tower.

Ben's grin slipped off his face.

Nervous moments passed as they stared out over the darkened field. At night, they couldn't see much of the debris from previous battles, but the red flames of the braziers along the wall lent what they could see an evil aspect. Broken hafts of polearms, shattered helmets, and lumps which Ben was certain were corpses. Goblin, demon, or human, it was still awful to see them fallen.

Slowly, Ben noticed a pale blue glow began to suffuse the mouth of the cave. It was a quarter league away, and down on the wall, Ben couldn't see details, but he didn't need to. A mass of shapes, moving restlessly, began to march out onto the field of battle.

"Bunched up like that," murmured Rhys, "they'll get hammered by the artillery."

"They're smarter than demons but not by much," stated Prem.

"The archers will wreak havoc on them before they get to us. Most nights I've been out here, we just watch while they get torn up by the ranged weapons. You've always got to be ready, though, because if they get up here and slip by, it's an unbelievable pain to track them down in the woods. A few times, they've made it to the node gate and gotten through. Fortunately not in numbers, but let me tell you, waking up in the morning to a goblin smashing through your door is no fun."

"Were people hurt?" asked Ben.

"Not that time," responded Prem. "Everyone in the village is an expert in their craft. I told you I'm the youngest. You don't make your first century in the forest without learning how to fight one way or the other. People die on the walls, though. Five hundred goblins, a wyvern, there's no easy way to stop that kind of force. If a pack of them were to get through a gate to somewhere else, well, most people aren't prepared for that kind of thing."

The blue glow crept closer and a quarter bell passed before Ben could make out individual shapes within the mass. A hundred, at least, with more strung out in a loose line leading all the way back to the cave. Ben clenched his fist around the hilt of his longsword.

"Mind the sides of the canyon," shouted a voice from a watchtower down the wall. "I've got movement."

"Demons," hissed Prem. "That many goblins and demons as well. It's going to be a rough one tonight."

At the other end of the wall, another shout went up. "Got 'em on the north side. Demons. Dozens at least."

A thump sounded behind them, and an object whistled overhead. It flew out into the darkness and crashed down in the center of the goblin horde, sending them flying like jacks.

"One advantage of holding the same wall night after night," said Ignice from above. "Artillery men know exactly when to shoot."

"Why don't the goblins know to spread out?" wondered Amelie.

"Not many of 'em make it back alive," responded the warrior. "They're pretty relentless when they attack. There's a hatred inside of them, and they'll sacrifice themselves to take one of us. I've seen 'em flee, though, when it's just one or two. I wonder if their leaders back on the other side give 'em time to explain themselves."

"Explain themselves?" wondered Ben. "They speak?"

"Not that you can understand," answered Ignice, "but they communicate with each other."

"It's a ploy," declared Rhys. "They're drawing the fire of the heavy weapons while the demons move up the sides in darkness."

"It's not our first time facing these things," reminded Frand dryly.

Just then, another thump. This time, a burning bale lofted above them, soaring toward the south side of the box canyon.

"Nice," admitted Rhys. "Let the demons draw close. Then, prick them with the archers."

"Keep watching, old man," called Frand. "We'll teach you a thing or two."

The thumps of the catapults and the twang of the ballistae sounded over and over. In the black field in front of them, angry howls, cries of pain, and a steady, rhythmic thumping drifted back as the goblins marched closer. From the watchtower, a bow string snapped, and the archers joined the fight.

Ben glanced at his companions and saw Amelie's tight look. Despite the damage the artillery was causing and what the archers would do, it was becoming obvious that some of the goblin horde would make it to the wall. In the field, there had to be three hundred of them.

"The cave," shouted someone from the darkness.

Ben's heart sank. The mouth of the cave was glowing blue again. Another wave of goblins was amassing.

"Don't worry," called Frand. He grunted, and his bow string snapped. "We've got plenty of ammunition. The plan is to use it all tonight and then finish this come dawn."

The sound of close combat sprung up from the south end of the wall. Some of the demons had made it through the arrows. Snarls, shouts, and pained shrieks. It was nerve-wracking listening to the fight in the dark when he couldn't see it, but Ben judged the guardians were competently handling the creatures that climbed up the wall. He didn't hear any cries that sounded like a dying man.

"Center of the field," screamed a man from a watchtower. "Center of the field, hit it with everything you've got!"

Behind them on the artillery platform, someone else shouted, straining to be heard over the growing sounds of battle. "What are you talking about?"

"Center of the field! Wyvern. There's a bloody wyvern coming behind those goblins."

"Just drawing the fire," groaned Rhys. "They've planned this."

The rogue drew his blade, and Ben slid his out as well.

A pale blue glow sprang into light by his side, and Ben jumped, thinking a goblin had somehow snuck up on him, but the light showed the muscled physique of Adrick Morgan.

Lit bales of flame flashed overhead, falling behind the goblins now as the artillery men scrambled to adjust their range and find where the wyvern was passing. The flames flickered two hundred paces away, and Ben couldn't see a damn thing.

He glanced at Amelie and hissed, "What are we looking at? All I see is the glow from those goblins."

"The mages are enhancing the sight of the warriors," replied Amelie, peering hard into the darkness. "Though, with half of these people, I can't tell if they're a mage or a soldier. Some of them may be enhancing their own sight."

Ben grunted.

"I, ah, I think we have a problem," called Frand. "There's… well, there's more than one of them."

"Damnit. There's more than one of them!" yelled Ignice, screaming back toward the artillery platform.

"There's never been more than one wyvern to cross at a time!" exclaimed Prem. "You must be seeing something else. More demons maybe?"

"I don't know," said Frand. "It looked big."

Shouts of alarm were going up around the other towers.

"You sure this was worth it?" whispered Rhys in Ben's ear.

Ben tried to ignore the man and the sinking sensation in the pit of his stomach.

"They can sense magic," said Adrick calmly, raising his voice to be heard in the tower and down the wall. "The wyverns will come for the elders and the spell they're fashioning. Like demons feed on lifeblood, wyverns feed on magic. The preparation the elders are doing is like a feast laid out for them. They've probably never sensed anything like it."

"Where are the elders?" asked Ben. "Is someone protecting them?"

"They're right behind us on the ridge."

"Oh," responded Ben. "Damn."

THE ARCHERS above them on the watchtower started furiously firing arrows at the approaching horde of goblins. A hundred and fifty paces out, the creatures scattered, evidently realizing the people on the wall had seen the wyverns coming behind them. Ben's stomach churned with the realization that they had only been in formation as a ruse.

The artillery thumped from the platform on the ridge, but the engineers were aiming wildly into the darkness. The wyverns gave away no glow like the goblins, and even with enhanced magical sight, it was clear the defenders were having difficulty spotting them.

A clawed hand slammed down on the stone battlement in front of Ben. Without thinking, he twirled his longsword and slashed down with the blade, severing the hand and causing a horrific howl as its owner lost its grip and went plummeting off the wall.

"Demons in the center. Look alive," shouted Frand from the watchtower.

"Thanks," muttered Amelie, taking Ben's side. She held her rapier ready, but he knew that's not how she intended to enter the fight. Amelie and the other mages would now be focused on the wyverns, directing everything they could at the big beasts. Towaal took Ben's other side and raised her hands, static beginning to form between her fingers.

"Leave the wyverns to us," instructed Towaal.

"Wyverns consume magic!" shouted Adrick. "Whatever you do, do not direct a single thread of energy at one of those. You'll only make it stronger! Haven't you faced these things before?"

Towaal blinked at him, her face a mask of confusion in the crimson light from the braziers.

Rhys, his sword glowing silver, asked the obvious, "So, how do we fight them?"

"Steel and guts," barked Adrick. He turned, and his sword flicked out over the battlement, taking another demon in the neck and severing its head. The blue glow of his blade illuminated a surprised look on the demon's face.

"They're getting sneaky," he muttered. To Rhys, he instructed, "You can use that weapon on a wyvern. Their hides are as stiff as chainmail, so the mage-wrought blade helps. Just don't release the sword's power. You'll be feeding the damn things we're supposed to be fighting."

Rhys nodded tersely. The time for discussion was coming to an end. All along the wall, demons were trying to sneak over the battlements. Having the creatures behind them when the goblins attempted to scale the structure would be a deadly combination, not to mention whatever it was the wyverns were planning to do.

Ben stepped to the edge of the battlement, peering down in the ruddy red glow from the mage-light to see if he could tell what was below them. A sharp-taloned claw swung at his face, and a demon scrambled up the wall after him.

"A dozen of them," he yelled, "right below us."

A heavy creature hauled itself into view, and Amelie launched a crackling ball of flame at its face. Yellow and red burst out around its head, and it went flying back into the darkness, only to be replaced by half a dozen of its peers. Ben and Rhys fell on them, longswords stabbing, trying to keep the creatures off the wall. Gnashing teeth and grasping claws were met by uncaring steel.

Out of the corner of his eye, Ben saw two of the beasts clambering up the side of the watchtower. Frand and Ignice wouldn't be able to see them coming! Then, the blue glow of Adrick's blade burst into life, and the swordsman tiptoed along the battlement, shearing the creatures off like they were unwelcome barnacles on the underside of a ship. A black hand shot up and grasped at his foot, but in a blue blur, his blade swept down and cleaved through the hand's owner.

"Ben," shouted Amelie, drawing his attention to three demons that had scrambled onto the wall and were pressing back two guardians. Behind the trio of demons, more were crawling into the gap in the defense.

"Go, I've got this," shouted Rhys over the snarls of the creatures in front of him. He rushed past Amelie and Lady Towaal.

They were conserving most of their energy for if the mundane defenses broke. All along the wall, the village's mages would be doing the same, watching the battle, waiting for the right moment to add their might to the defense.

Ben swung his Venmoor steel longsword and caught a demon

that was squirming through a crenellation in the battlement, the tip of the blade cracking the creature's skull, and it fell where it was, lodged in the stone gap. He then fell on the backs of the beasts that had made it onto the wall, stabbing his blade into one's side, jerking the weapon out, and spinning to take another in the back of the neck.

The man and woman who'd been struggling with the creatures surged forward and pinned the remaining demon between the two of them. A spear lanced into the beast's torso. Then, an axe fell on its head.

"Sorry," gasped the man. "I'm a carpenter, not a warrior. We were holding his flank."

Ben glanced at the stone walkway and saw the body of a man, his entrails strewn in a grisly arc around him. A heavy falchion lay in his outstretched hand.

"Watch mine now," growled Ben.

He turned to meet the next wave of demons and nearly lost an eye when a jagged stick struck him in the head. It smacked a glancing blow against his forehead, snapping his head back and throwing him off balance. The sharp point of the stick dug a painful gash into the flesh above his eyebrow, but the indirect blow didn't have the force to crack his skull.

"Goblin arrows," came a shout from somewhere down the wall.

In the dark, they were impossible to see, but as Ben was preparing to find a shield and duck behind it, the next wave of arrows burst into a shower of sparks in the air. The mages were igniting the things, keeping the deadly darts off the swordsmen. Twinkling, white lights and the acrid scent of burnt tin washed over the wall.

A demon lunged at him, and Ben ducked, a powerful arm whistling over his head. He stood, swinging up with his sword, catching the creature in the abdomen, and cleaving it from midsection to throat. A spray of blood, black in the red mage-light, flew up in the air. Through the spray, Ben saw a glowing blue hand slap down on the battlement. An ugly face dragged into view behind it. The goblin looked like someone had smashed it in the face with a frying pan repeatedly. Its eyes were set too close together, its nose was nothing more than a flat stub, and thick lips parted to reveal over-large, rotted teeth.

"At least it's easy to see these bastards when they come," muttered the carpenter. He stepped past Ben and jabbed his spear into the goblin's face. With a muted grunt, it fell back.

Beyond the wall, the air was filled with a menacing blue glow. A hook clattered over the wall to Ben's left. Then, a rickety ladder smacked against the wall to the right.

Ben swung at the hook, severing the rough rope that was attached to it and trailing a line of sparks across the stone where his blade scraped along. He raced to the ladder and set his shoulder against it, intending to push the thing back.

A fist holding a jagged metal short sword thrust through two steps in the ladder, aimed at Ben's head. He scrambled back and swept up with his sword, catching the blade and snapping the poor-quality metal in two when it cracked against the side of the ladder. A goblin glared at him in consternation. Ben kicked it in the face.

His boot smashed through a wooden rung and caught the goblin in the chin. It went flying back, gripping tightly to the ladder. A chorus of wails and screams brought a grim smile to Ben's face as he imagined a line of the goblins falling away, but he knew the fall from the wall wasn't high enough to seriously injure most of them.

With the momentary respite, Ben saw Rhys jerking his blade out of a dead demon. Amelie and Towaal crouched at the back of the wall, hands raised and ready should the defenders fail. The girl Prem was nowhere to be seen until three goblins came running around from the other side of the watchtower.

She dropped right on top of them, her boots landing solidly

on one creature's head and her long knives plunging into the other two. She rode the first body down and then casually stooped to draw a blade across its neck. Ben didn't even have time to think about rushing to her aid. She twirled her knives in her hands and winked at him.

"Watch out!" screamed Frand from the watchtower.

An instant later, the tower exploded in a shower of broken boards and shattered timbers. Ben lost sight of Frand and Ignice as he ducked a hurtling chunk of wood the size of his leg. A thunderous roar split the night as a wyvern announced itself.

The creature loomed high above the wall, its powerful forelegs on the battlement. Ben cringed as he realized its hind legs must be on the ground two stories below. The thing's head was the size of a wagon, and its mouth hinged open, displaying arm-length fangs. It looked able to swallow a person, and then, it did.

One of the guardians rushed it, a spear held ready. The creature struck, fast as a snake, and chomped down on the man. He disappeared inside its gullet as the beast swallowed him whole.

"What does it need those teeth for?" wondered Rhys.

Ben looked at the rogue and then groaned as his friend shot forward, his blade lashing at the wyvern. Rhys caught it on the leg and jumped away. It didn't seem to notice his attack, and Ben couldn't see if the rogue had even marked it.

Towaal and Amelie ran past them, heading away from the wyvern, panic painting their faces, their magic useless against the giant lizard.

Ben sighed and ran toward the monster.

A goblin came out of nowhere, and Ben skidded to a halt, narrowly avoiding a rusty blade that flashed in front of him. He swung his sword down, catching the blade and knocking it from the goblin's hands. He reversed his motion and pounded the hilt of his longsword into the creature's skull. It absorbed the blow and lashed out with the back of its hand, catching Ben on the cheek.

His head snapped to the side, and the goblin grasped his neck with both of its hands. Its mouth opened wide, and it tried to drag Ben closer. He was too close to use his longsword effectively, but he yanked out his hunting knife with his left hand and slammed it up, catching the goblin in the chin and forcing the steel into its brain. Its blue glow winked out, and Ben shoved the body away.

Three more of them smashed into him, knocking him off balance, and he fell to his knees. Between the goblins, he saw the wyvern thrash around, a pair of villagers vanishing over the wall when the huge lizard caught them with its horns and flung them away.

Ben, anger firing him, swung his blade with all of his might, catching the three goblins on the legs and tumbling them all into a pile on the wall. They struggled, unable to stand, and Ben pounced on them, stabbing down over and over again until they stopped moving and their blue skin flickered dark.

The stone of the wall shivered, and Ben looked up to see the wyvern crawling over it. Its long, scale-covered body dragged, shattering stone and leaving a trail of broken mortar and bodies in its wake.

"It's going for the mages!" called a voice from the other side.

Rhys was scrambling up the hill alongside the beast, dashing forward to strike at the wyvern's head and then leaping away. It snapped at him, but it was intent on climbing higher. Rhys and the other warriors swarming around it were merely distractions.

Ben, still on the wall, saw its foreleg step onto the hillside, its scales reflecting the red mage-light, but behind its leg, there was a dull patch. It looked like leather instead of shining scales. Ben gambled and charged.

At a full sprint, he set his foot on the back of the wall and launched himself into the air. He grasped his longsword with both hands and with the weight of his entire body behind it, aimed the tip of his sword at the dull patch behind the wyvern's foreleg. The sword punched into the creature, and Ben's body pounded against the weapon. The blade was the nail, he was the hammer. He felt his ribs crack as the cross guard of the sword slammed into him, but the sword pierced the thick skin of the wyvern, sliding deep.

Ben fell back, splayed on the dirt of the hill, and the creature twisted, snapping with its jaws where his blade was stuck in its side. Only his fall saved him from getting chomped in two. The wyvern lifted its head and roared. The earth seemed to shake, and Ben's ears howled with sharp pain.

Then, Adrick flew into view, and his blade, unlit and invisible in the night, whipped across the wyvern's exposed throat. The creature's powerful roar warbled into a pained gurgle, and a fountain of blood poured out of the gaping wound in its neck. It took one more step, wavered, and then fell.

A cheer went up as the guardians realized the monster had been killed, but it was drowned out by two enraged calls from the field. Two more wyverns, Ben realized, his heart sinking. Two more of them and they had just seen their companion get cut down. They sounded angry about it.

Ben lay on his side, pain radiating from broken ribs.

TOWAAL KNELT BY BEN, a warm tingle creeping into his ribcage.

Rhys was by the wyvern, both hands gripping Ben's longsword, a boot placed on the creature as he struggled to draw the weapon out. Finally, with a sickening sucking sound, the steel slid free.

"Thanks," gasped Ben.

"You're going to be sore," advised Towaal.

"Better than a broken rib," responded Ben.

"You ready, Rhys?" asked the mage.

The rogue stumbled over, Ben's longsword held in front of him, dripping with viscous blood from the wyvern.

"As ready as I can be."

"Ready for what?" asked Ben, rolling to his side and slowly clambering to his knees, feeling the tenderness in his side where Towaal's healing hadn't completely mended his injury.

"This," said Towaal.

A blaze of lightning burst from her hands, skipping across the stones and leaping into racing, glowing blue figures. The goblins wailed as the electrical charge ripped through them.

"You'll draw the wyverns!" called Ben.

"Exactly," responded Towaal. "Better they come for us than the elders."

"Good idea," muttered Adrick. The swordsman was pacing along the hillside, his eyes boring into the blackness beyond the wall.

Unsure if it was really a good idea, Ben rubbed at his sore ribs and eyed the swordsman. Adrick had lost his shirt again, and his muscled chest was painted in blood. None of it his, Ben guessed.

Amelie came to stand beside Towaal and released her power as well, a blaze of white hot flame that she directed along the top of the battlement, scorching anything foolish enough to poke its head up.

"You're getting good at that," murmured Ben.

"You know what they say about practice," responded Amelie through gritted teeth.

"Wyverns are vulnerable on their underbellies, necks, and behind the legs," said Adrick. "Don't waste your time on the backs. There's a pace of hide protecting them there and your sword can't reach deep enough to do damage. The heads are just as tough unless you're able to reach an eye or inside the mouth."

"Inside the mouth," scoffed Ben. "Why would you strike inside its mouth?"

"Wait until one is about to close its jaws on you," said Adrick. "Then you can decide whether you want to strike or not."

Ben grunted.

Rhys gestured for Ben to fan out beside him. "You take one and we get the other?" the rogue called to Adrick.

"Fair enough," responded the swordsman, stepping to the side and flicking his blade to clear it of the thick, sticky wyvern blood.

"What's the plan, Rhys?" asked Ben as he joined the rogue.

The man opened his mouth to respond but was interrupted by a battle-cry from a dozen charging goblins. The rogue's longsword blazed alight. Trailing silver smoke, he attacked and carved a swath through the front ranks of the creatures.

Ben raced after him, striking to the side and hacking through the goblin's flimsy weapons and armor. Behind the first wave, more of the creatures started clambering over the wreckage of the watchtower.

"This could get ugly," called Rhys, still churning forward into the mass of enemies.

Ben followed behind, struggling to protect the rogue's back.

Then, the wall beneath his feet erupted, and Ben went flying into the air, tumbling against the side of the hill. He covered his head with his hands as stone and mortar from the wall rained around him. A goblin smacked into the earth next to him.

Ben opened one eye, seeing the thing's startled expression. Suddenly, Ben was sprayed in the face with a shower of blood and viscera as the goblin's head was popped like a ripe grape under a heavy stone. The giant block embedded in the hillside, and Ben rolled to his back, searching the dark sky for more inbound masonry.

A brutal roar stirred Ben's clothes, He looked between his feet at where the wall was, blinking to clear his eyes of sticky blood. Luckily, he saw his sword had fallen next to him, sticking straight up, the tip sunk in the damp soil. Unluckily, a giant wyvern, twice the size of the first one, had just crushed a hole in the wall and was stalking closer, looming over Ben like a small, scale-covered castle. The beast's body soared above his head, and its rear leg crushed another section of wall as it stomped onto the hill.

Ben had an opening to its soft underbelly, but it rose two man-heights above him. He wouldn't be able to reach it even by jumping and extending his sword. Out of the corner of his eye, he saw Rhys, blood streaming down the side of his face, hacking madly at the thing's leg. It didn't do any good. The wyvern lifted its foot and struck at the rogue, catching him with a glancing blow on the shoulder and flinging him a dozen paces away.

A swarm of guardians ran close and launched spears at it, but the sharp points either bounced off harmlessly or barely stuck into the thick hide. The spears then fell out as the wyvern moved again.

Ben looked for Adrick, figuring the swordsman was their best bet, but the man was nowhere to be seen. A second wyvern was causing havoc a hundred paces away.

Suddenly, the wyvern above Ben ducked to the side.

A heavy bolt from a ballista flew by, hitting nothing but air before vanishing into the black field beyond the shattered wall. With a surge, the wyvern scrambled up the hill, moving faster than Ben imagined a creature that size could, and with a swipe of its massive claws, it smashed through the staged artillery, splintering the equipment and mauling the men who'd been operating it.

Ben scrambled to his feet and charged up the hill, running underneath the wyvern's body, falling to his knees, and struggling higher on the steep hill. The wyvern paused to snap its jaws, cutting short an injured man's screams.

Ben knew that two hundred paces past the artillery platform was a large, circular tent filled with mages. There, the elders were preparing the spell they planned to use to close the rift once and for all. The elders would be helpless against the creature. Anything they tried against it would only make it stronger.

Skidding and slipping, Ben climbed higher. He passed the creature's forelegs and ducked as its head swung, snapping shut on another hapless victim. Ben pulled his sword back, but the head swung away, and the neck rose out of his reach. He cursed and started running up the hill again.

The artillery platform was a mess of crumbled masonry and broken wood. Ben jumped over a busted catapult arm and looked around wildly for anything he could use. Above him, he felt the wyvern lurch to the side again. He tried not to hear the crunch of crumpling steel and the snap of broken bones.

At the back of the platform, undisturbed, he saw a pile of ballista bolts. The shafts were as thick as his arm and as long as he was tall. They were tipped with a broad, wicked iron blade. With enough force, the thing could punch through the hull of a ship or even a wyvern's hide.

He scrambled toward the bolts, sliding his sword into the sheath and hurtling over broken machinery from the siege weapons. Behind him, he heard the wyvern roar and then a boom as it took a step forward. He had moments at best.

Ben slid on his knees, skidding across the stone to come to a stop next to the bolts. Grabbing one, he turned and fell. The thing was as heavy as he was. Grunting, Ben summoned an inner strength that only surfaced in the heat of battle. His heart pumping, he hauled the bolt up and settled it on his shoulder. He struggled to his feet, turning, and saw the wyvern looking directly at him. Two, emerald-green eyes burned with a light of their own. Ben swallowed. One shot. One chance. If he could fling the ballista bolt into one of those eyes, maybe, just maybe, it'd have enough force to reach the creature's brain. Grimly, he set his feet and prepared to run forward and chuck the bolt.

Then, the eyes vanished.

The mouth opened wide, showing huge, bone-white teeth. They reflected the crimson mage-light, or maybe, they were crimson with the blood of the slaughtered. It didn't really matter.

It was enough to send a shudder down Ben's spine and a realization about what Adrick had said earlier. When all you saw was an open maw, go for the back of the throat.

Ben hooked one hand around the butt of the bolt and the other on the shaft to steady it. One, two, three running steps and he hurled the weapon with all of his might. It flew almost ten paces, then clattered heavily down on the stone, skidding a little further before stopping halfway to the wyvern.

"Damn," said Ben, crestfallen.

The wyvern twitched. Then, its mouth snapped shut. Ben, a score of paces away, watched its eyes wobble and then focus on him. The emerald-green fire faded. Tacky, thick blood dripped out of the creature's mouth and nostrils. The beast stretched to its full height, swayed, and slowly, like a tree falling over in the forest, toppled. The impact jarred the ground, and Ben fell to his knees. He stared at the dead wyvern, confused.

Amelie came pelting around it.

"Ben, what'd you do?" she exclaimed.

"I, ah..." He looked at the ballista bolt lying harmlessly on the ground. "I don't know. I didn't do anything. I tried to..."

Towaal arrived as well, glancing at Ben and then at the dead wyvern.

Shouts of alarm knocked him out of his stupor and Ben peered down the hill to see a glowing blue wave crest over the demolished wall below them. The goblins were swerving around the corpse of the third wyvern, advancing toward the hill. Adrick must have been successful, saw Ben.

"There are still more of them," Amelie groaned.

"Hundreds more, but the wyverns are dead," remarked Towaal. She raised her hands, crackling bits of energy flying between her fingers. "I see no reason to conserve any more energy. Shall we engage?"

THEY STARTED DOWN THE HILL, joining a throng of guardians who streamed toward the wall. Three wyverns vanquished, a victory that would go down in history—if anyone survived to tell it. Below them, goblins had made the wall and were forcing the defenders back. Shadows darted through the wave of blue. Ben realized there were demons down there as well, moving amongst the goblins.

The red mage-light from the braziers began to wink out.

"The goblins are extinguishing the lights!" exclaimed Amelie.

"The demons will be invisible," warned Ben.

Towaal raised her arms and above them, and a soft glow suffused the sky.

"I can't hold it long," she said through gritted teeth. "I used most of what I had to draw the wyverns. Swing fast."

Ben drew his blade and started a slow jog down the dark hill, afraid to move too quickly or he'd end up tripping and tumbling to the feet of one of the goblins. Amelie, rapier in one hand, the other smoking with heat, followed in his wake. Rhys came from around the side of the wyvern's corpse and joined them. With the lizard dead, his blade sparkled with silvery smoke. The swordsman Adrick arrived as well. His weapon pulsed with blue power, shimmering in the dark night.

"Nice work," remarked Rhys.

"It was easy," responded the swordsman. "The thing was distracted by something. I just had to walk up and stick my blade in."

Prem appeared beside Amelie. "Glad to see you're still with us."

Amelie didn't respond. She was focused ahead.

The swordsman, Adrick Morgan, had finished three wyverns. Ben didn't have time to consider it. He was a dozen paces from the closest goblins and broke into a run, Amelie, Rhys, Prem, and Adrick flanking him. The goblins were forcing the guardians back along the wall, but they weren't prepared for the storm of steel that hit their center.

Ben plowed into two of the goblins, using his size advantage to trample them. He lashed out at one with his longsword and stomped on the head of the other. Beyond the first two, he put his shoulder into the side of a third one of the light-weight creatures and shoved with everything he had, tossing it into a mass of its fellows, knocking half a dozen more over like lawn bowling pins.

With at least two hundred of the monsters on the wall in front of them, it was about creating a maximum shock and pushing them back, giving himself and his companions room to slice the things up.

A spear darted at him, and Ben dodged back but not quick enough to stop the point from snagging on his shoulder, puncturing his flesh but not incapacitating him.

Prem skipped around him and whipped a long knife across the attacking goblin's throat. She reversed her grip on the knife in her other hand and plunged it into a second goblin's side. The creature, looking the other direction, didn't have a chance to defend itself. The simple leather armor it was wearing did nothing to stop the razor-sharp tip of her knife. Adrick, a dozen paces away, swirled through the goblin ranks like a terrible wind. His blade, blurred by the blue glow of the goblins, flashed through them invisibly, leaving dark geysers of blood in its wake. Rhys chopped down a goblin and then slid his longsword into the back of a demon which had latched onto a fallen guardian.

Around Ben's companions, the goblins scrambled away, their simple hunger overcome by an even more powerful emotion. Fear.

Ben, ignoring the sting in his shoulder and wiping a trickle of blood off his forehead where the arrow had struck him earlier, waded back in. Beside him, Amelie pounded the hilt of her rapier into the face of one of the goblins. Another, thinking it had an opening, came close to grapple with her. She slapped it with an open hand, and it went back screaming, angry orange flames licking where she'd struck it.

Ben grinned, easily parrying two spears out of the way with one stroke and then bringing his blade back, slashing through both the spears' owners with a single blow. It was easy, the goblins were small and weak, like fighting children. Ben swung down and decapitated one of the creatures. Its body fell away, but its head remained stuck, teeth fastened on the face of a fallen villager it had been gnawing on.

Maybe not like any children he'd want to bounce on his knee, corrected Ben.

With the arrival of Ben and his companions, and mostly Adrick, he admitted, the guardians rallied. The goblins were broken into smaller and smaller knots of survivors. Within half a bell, the creatures were surrounded and slaughtered, no match for the superior strength, skill, and weapons of the humans.

The blue glow vanished, fallen goblin by fallen goblin, but Ben realized with a start that he could still see. He glanced back and saw the pale, yellow light from the sun rising from behind the ridge. It was morning. They'd fought all night. He slumped, exhausted, forearms resting against a remaining section of the battlement. In the still-dark field below, half a dozen goblins retreated toward the cave. The rest of them lay dead.

"Well fought," remarked Adrick.

Ben glanced at the swordsman. He was shirtless in the cool morning air, his chest glistening with sweat where it wasn't covered in dark blood.

"Thanks," muttered Ben. "We're not done, though, are we?"

Adrick nodded. "Not yet."

Ben's head fell down onto his crossed arms.

"I'm told it was you who held the interest of the largest wyvern when I struck it, and I saw you attack the first one. I'm impressed with you, Benjamin."

Ben raised his head. "You can call me Ben."

"Without even a mage-wrought blade, you displayed a courage that is rare in this world."

"Rare in your world, maybe," retorted Ben. "You have an important fight here, I can see that, but it's not the only fight. We've been battling the dark forces as well and worse. Our companions have faced odds longer than this, and some of them have made the ultimate sacrifice. When I know what is out there, what choice do I have?"

"There is always a choice," responded Adrick. "Instead of fighting and risking yourself, you could hide or run away. That's what the mages of the Sanctuary are doing, isn't it? Hiding behind their walls, not venturing out to face the true threats in the world."

"Hiding is not something I'm inclined to do," Ben responded. He paused, thinking, and then plunged ahead. "What will you do when this rift is closed? Will you face the darkness in the world or hide in the forest?"

Adrick grunted and turned from Ben. He didn't respond.

Shouts rang out on the ridge behind them. Ben turned and saw a procession of villagers making their way toward the wall. The mages. Two dozen of them, the elders and a score of younger ones as well, nearly every talented man or woman in the village. From what Ben heard, they had already said goodbye to their friends and family.

"That's courage," remarked Ben.

"On that, we agree," responded Adrick.

The swordsman turned and called up and down the wall, rallying the warriors to form at the base of the structure where the wyverns had breached it. Amelie and Prem joined Ben, and they climbed down to meet the others.

"Why do we need the warriors?" asked Amelie. "Didn't we kill all of the dark forces last night?"

"We don't know what's in that cave," answered Prem. "No one's ever been in there."

~

THE LIGHT of the sun was peeking over the ridge, and Ben tried to ignore what it showed him. He tried to ignore what he was stepping on. Goblins and demons lay like a thick, squishy carpet below the wall. The stench of their death was impossible to ignore. Bodies were torn apart, viscera splattered everywhere. Blood puddled in ankle-deep pools at the bottom of the pile. Ben grimaced and tried to step over a particularly disgusting corpse of a goblin. He winced as he nearly set his foot down on a human hand that poked out from under the pile.

"Do they bury the dead humans?" asked Amelie.

"No," said Prem, pinching her nose between her fingers. "They're burned, just like the dark forces. The risk of disease is too high to go rooting through these piles."

"People's friends, family," murmured Amelie.

Prem shrugged. "There's nothing to be done about it."

Three-dozen paces from the wall, the corpses thinned out, and it was possible to walk without stepping on one. Before them, a quarter league of devastated landscape spread out until it met the towering cliff at the end of the canyon. From the ground, Ben couldn't see the cave, but he knew it was there.

One hundred guardians spread out across the field, the warriors taking point, the mages walking in a cluster behind them. Ben and his friends walked with the warriors. Shattered ammunition from siege weapons was strewn near demolished bodies, goblins and demons, thousands of them.

"This was just from the last few weeks when they didn't spare the energy to burn them," said Amelie, shaking her head.

"Why do they come?" wondered Ben.

"One of the mages explained it to me," said Towaal. "Their world has very limited life that these creatures are able to feed upon. The wyverns consume our magic, somehow using a practitioner as a funnel for pure energy. The demons consume our lifeblood, and the goblins eat our flesh. The guardians believe there may be other sources of sustenance for the dark forces at home, but in our world, they survive off of us. You saw through the Purple's rift, their world is dead. They've stripped it bare. There's no sense of conservation. Our farmers, they water the earth and fertilize it. Human farmers swap crops to ensure they don't suck all the nutrients from the soil. The dark forces do nothing like that. They only consume. They only know hunger. The dark forces are drawn to the abundant life in our world like you would be drawn to a well-laid buffet after years of deprivation. They can't help themselves. They're driven to come here and feast."

They trudged on until the cliff rose in front of them. Near the cliff, the ground was soft from countless feet pounding over it every night, but there were no bodies. Those were clustered closer to the wall, where the siege weapons and archers could reach.

"Beware of anything coming out of there," yelled Adrick, his voice drifting over the quiet field. "If we drew the wyverns last night, it's possible they may sense us again. They could come for the magic."

Ben gripped his sword, but he didn't draw it. There was nothing but mud between them and the cave. Above it, pale gray granite soared into the sky, the cave loomed in the cliff face like an open mouth. Inky black filled the maw, impenetrable by the morning sun. One hundred paces away, the group stopped and clustered together.

"Do you sense anything?" Rhys asked Towaal.

She shrugged, eyes fixed on the cave.

Adrick turned to the elders. "Shall we precede you, or..." The man trailed off, clearly unsure how to suggest the elders go in alone.

"There is nothing you can do to assist once we begin," responded the old man, Adrick's father.

Ben frowned. They had never learned his name.

Wordlessly, the old man shuffled forward. Around him, the rest of the mages walked as well, all of them marching slowly toward the cave. From the warriors, several others peeled off. Mages who had martial skills, guessed Ben. A dozen of them, total, only a handful of mages staying behind. Adrick stepped up to join them, but the old man shook his head.

"You will be needed here, son."

Thick muscles tensed. "I may be needed in the cave."

"When we are gone, it will be your responsibility to lead those who remain. The rift will no longer be a threat, but the secrets we hold will be. You must protect the knowledge we've acquired and protect the world from the threats it poses. The mission remains even after this rift is closed."

Adrick bowed his head and stepped back.

The mages continued toward the cave, reluctant to enter, or in the case of some of the elders, it may have been the fastest they could move.

Ben leaned to Amelie and whispered, "Do you think they're up to it?"

She shrugged. "Strength of will and strength of body are not the same thing. They've been preparing since yesterday. This will not take long."

The cluster of mages entered the cave and vanished inside the darkness. Moments passed quietly. Then, people began to stir.

"How do we know if they're successful?" whispered Ben.

Towaal opened her mouth to respond, but a loud snap silenced her. Above the cave, the granite split, a crack running from the roof of the cave to the top of the cliff. A shower of rock fell down, and a rumbling shudder boomed so loud that Ben almost lost his balance.

"Back up!" yelled Towaal.

No one needed much encouragement. They stumbled away from the cliff, the ground leaping and jolting as earthshattering concussions rocked them. Ben watched in horror as the cliff began to crumble, showers of rock dust falling first, and then larger and larger chunks of gray granite. He didn't wait to see any more. He and everyone else turned and fled.

Rocks bounced down around them, thudding into the mud or into people. A few villagers fell, but they were grabbed by their friends and pulled clear. In the space of a couple of dozen heartbeats, they'd made it out of the fall area and turned to watch the cliff collapse into a giant pile of tumbled rock. A cloud of dust billowed out, and Ben covered his mouth and eyes, feeling the air blow by him, moved by the impact of the falling rock.

As quickly as it started, it was over. The villagers, stunned and dismayed, stared at the collapsed cliff. A war they had been fighting for centuries was over, but they'd lost a third of their population to finish it. The rift was closed, shutting one of the last remaining openings for the dark forces to enter the world of man, but the oldest, most respected members of the guardians had to die to do it.

5

―――――

HALL OF THE MAGES

THE VILLAGE WAS A SOMBER PLACE WHEN THEY RETURNED THROUGH the node gate. Ben guessed there had been three hundred villagers before. Now, there were two hundred. A hundred bodies lay in the morning sun on the other side of the gate, unburied, rotting in the open or buried under the cliff. Ben and his friends returned to the house they'd been in the day before, what seemed like weeks before, and sat around a small table.

"What should we do?" asked Amelie.

"Leave," remarked Rhys dryly. "Today, everyone is thinking about what happened. Tomorrow, they'll be back to protecting their secrets. The mages are gone, but I don't think we want to fight past that man Adrick Morgan to get out of here. Did you see him last night? If he wants to, he could stop us."

"The elder said we would be allowed to leave," argued Ben. "You think Adrick will betray that trust?"

Rhys shrugged. "You heard the last words of the elder just as clearly as I did. 'Protect our secrets'. Letting us leave doesn't exactly accomplish that. I don't know if he changed his mind or misspoke, but that's what the man said."

"If we use the node gates, we could still gain weeks on Milo," mentioned Towaal.

"You think we can sneak through?" asked Ben.

"They're unguarded, so I don't see why not," answered Towaal. She frowned. "But how would we know which one to go through? There are two dozen gates down there, and they're all marked with script I don't recognize. We could try randomly walking through them, but even if we found a gate near the City, would we even be able to tell? If it's on the edge of the forest, it may look the same as anywhere else."

"Take the gates or hike out," said Rhys. "Either way, we've got to get out of here before they decide we're a liability."

Ben rubbed at the scar on his arm and then finally responded. "We need allies."

Rhys sighed, but the rogue didn't protest.

"Adrick may try to convince us to stay here or he may try to kill us, but I spoke to him on the wall after the battle. I don't think he will hinder our mission. I think he'll understand. We might even convince him to join us. He alone could change the tide in a battle against the demons or against the Veil."

"Well," drawled Rhys, "if we're going to stick our foot in the bear trap, we may as well get on with it. No sense dragging this thing out any further than we need to."

Ben smiled at his friend. "I appreciate that."

Rhys snorted.

Ben led them out of the door and into the village. He stopped, looking around, wondering where they could find Adrick. Instead, Prem found them.

"Looking for my father?" she asked.

Ben nodded.

"Come with me."

She led them to the old man's, her grandfather's, house, the first building they'd entered in the village. She knocked on the door and pushed it open after a muffled response. Inside, they found the swordsman pouring over a set of handwritten note-books. He looked up, his face grim.

"I'm not much of a reader," he said. He gestured to the pile of tomes in front of him. "He must have written a dozen pages of notes a day. He was alive for hundreds of years! You know how much of this stuff I have to work through?"

Towaal stepped forward. "I could help you."

Adrick smiled a bitter smile. "I don't think so. Besides, aren't you here to ask if you can leave?"

Ben flushed. "Things are happening in the world. Things just as dangerous as what we faced last night. Someone has to deal with them."

Adrick sat back and met Ben's eyes. "You know when I first found you, I wanted to kill you."

Ben blinked.

"My father convinced me otherwise," continued Adrick. "Now, he's gone, and I'm in charge. The weight of that responsibility is heavier than I ever imagined. The rift is gone, the demons can no longer pass into our world through any gate on the western half of Alcott, but our core mission remains as it always has. You tell me there is death magic afoot, wyvern fire…" Adrick trailed off, frowning.

"Father, you have to let them go," stated Prem.

Ben turned in surprise.

The slender girl continued, "Whether it leaked from here or some other way, dangerous knowledge has reentered the world. Dangerous items are in the hands of people who may be ignorant enough to use them. We cannot allow it. We cannot simply hide in our forest and hope that it goes away."

Adrick winced when his daughter mentioned hiding.

Ben saw an opportunity and added his weight. "We have no interest in sharing what we've learned about you, the rift, or anything else here. What we do need to do though is continue on our mission. There is a growing threat of demons, the wyvern fire staff, the Veil, and her predecessor."

"Fine," barked Adrick. "You can go, on one condition."

Ben looked to his companions. Rhys shrugged, and Amelie nodded.

"What condition?" Ben asked.

"You take Prem with you," said Adrick.

"Take me with them?" exclaimed Prem.

Her father looked at her. "You believe in their mission, yes? Enough to try and convince me to let them go, apparently."

She nodded.

"Then, you should be a part of it."

Prem rolled her shoulders and glanced at Amelie and then back to her father. "Okay. I will go."

"They seem to be in a hurry, so I recommend you leave quickly," he responded. "Keep it quiet as not everyone in this village will agree, particularly if they learn what these people shared with me and the elders about the First Mage... I think it's best if you leave soon. The others would never defy the elders and go against their orders, but the elders are gone now. I don't know how they'll react when breaking a hundred-year old tradition is my first official decision. If the rest of the village finds out you know the First Mage, well, I don't think leaving will be an option, no matter what I say. And, Prem, take this with you."

From a pouch on the table, he shook out a silver amulet. It sparkled in the light streaming through the windows. Both Towaal and Amelie leaned forward, examining it. Ben could tell from a distance it was a face. He was certain there would be another one on the other side.

"Father," whispered Prem. "Are you sure?"

He nodded. "When the time comes, and you decide that our people are needed, use it. Before you leave, take them to the hall. Show them what we protect, and then go."

~

THEY FOLLOWED the girl out of the elder's house. She led them to the huge stone building Ben recalled from the first night. It was large enough to fit the rest of the village's buildings inside, but nothing outside gave a hint to its purpose.

Prem set a hand against each of the tall, double doors and shoved. With a creak of disuse, the doors swung inward. Light sprang up as she crossed the threshold. A soft, green glow permeated the room, reflecting off a hundred copper masks hanging against the walls and sitting on pedestals. The masks glowed from within, pulsing with barely constrained energy.

Ben gasped. Mouth hanging open, he pointed at one of the masks. He recognized it, and his friends would as well. Rhys strode to the mask and bent to examine it, his hands carefully tucked behind his back.

"I don't understand," said Towaal.

"Enrii," said Prem. She walked over and studied the mask beside Rhys. "Ah, I remember. She is hanging on the gates of the Sanctuary, isn't she? I've never been there myself, but I believe that's what I was told. I confess, I never paid much attention when the elders taught these things."

"But, what does it mean?" asked Amelie.

Prem looked back at her. "It means the Sanctuary has called for Enrii's protection. They've harnessed her power and likely infused it into grounds. There could be extra healing energies pulsing in the area, structures may be stronger or last longer, fires could burn hotter, or maybe there are some magical defenses that trigger using her power. If I recall, Enrii spent a great deal of time fashioning protective wards. That's what I would tap her energy for."

Ben glanced at Amelie. All too well, he recalled the floating discs of light that had followed them when they were fleeing the Sanctuary.

Prem shrugged and continued, "There are many things one can do if you are able to marshal the spirit of the First Mages. Their energy flows still, and usually, it is attuned to something the mage was skilled at. I'm told most of the busts out in the world are poorly done, though, and rarely harness the full power of the mage. That is a good thing."

Towaal opened her mouth and then shut it, clearly flabbergasted at what Prem was telling them.

Ben began walking through the hall, looking at the array of faces hanging there. Even he could feel the energy flowing through the place. It was a coiled spring, pulsing with expectancy, a repository containing nearly endless power.

As he moved deeper, he saw some of the masks burned brighter than others. A few were dull, merely a low sheen coming off the copper, where others sizzled with strength. At one, he held out his hand. His eyes widened to see the hairs on the back of his wrist standing up.

"Prem," said Prem with a smirk. "One of the oldest First Mages and one of the first to die. My father named me after her. I believe he thought it was a bit of a joke, but I take it as a compliment. Look at her. After all of this time, she's still strong."

Before the mask of Prem, Ben felt lightheaded, and his heart was beating uncomfortably quickly. He felt like he could float away. He moved on.

"She does that to some people," murmured Prem. "She senses their potential and strives to add her strength to it. It's what she did in life, I think, support others. You should be proud that she is showing interest in you."

"Is it, is she... sentient?" asked Ben.

Prem shook her head no.

"Ben, Lady Towaal, come look at this!" exclaimed Amelie from another side of the room.

Ben rushed to her. His heart sank when he saw what she was looking at, a large mask that didn't reflect any of the light around it. He knew the man. He'd traveled with him through the desert of Qooten and assaulted the Purple's fortress with him. Gunther.

"The last First Mage," explained Prem. "The mask was fashioned long before my time or my father's time. He still hasn't needed it after all of these years. Some day, he will pass like all of the others. Then, the mask will collect the echoes of his power. We hope to find him before he passes, though. There is so much we have accumulated over the years. Devices, knowledge, the stored power in this room. We mean to gift it to him if he ever returns to us. If they were able, many of the residents of our village would follow him, study at his feet, but I'm told he has not been back in hundreds of years."

Ben didn't respond.

Prem waited, and then finally said, "My father said you claimed to have met him. My grandfather believed you. My father was not sure at first. Most of the elders were certain you lied. How would you recognize him, though, if you haven't met him?"

"Nothing we told you was a lie," declared Ben.

Prem pursed her lips. "My father was right. If others in this village find out you have met the First Mage, they will be reluctant to let you out of their sight. They will try to keep you here or even follow you. I see now why my father urged us to leave quickly. Gunther, the First Mage, he is revered by our people. Worshipped even, though they would not admit that."

"I don't think Gunther would appreciate that," remarked Amelie.

"We should leave," said Prem. "Only my father and I know what you discussed with the council of elders, and they're all dead now. If others find out…"

They slipped through the village, walking quickly but afraid to run. Without incident, they made it to the stairwell that led into the node gate chamber, and they disappeared below ground. Prem held up the silver amulet her father had given her, and a gateway flickered to life. Through it, Ben saw pine forest.

"A day and a half from the outskirts of the City," explained Prem, hesitancy creeping into her voice. "I've never been. I'm hoping you can lead us there?"

"I've been before," responded Towaal dryly. She strode through the gate and appeared on the other side.

Ben gripped Amelie's hand. Then, he walked through as well.

6

A RAT BY ANY OTHER NAME

BIRDS CHIRPED, THE WIND RUSTLED THE BRIGHT GREEN LEAVES that surrounded them, and a chill of foreboding crept up Ben's spine.

The City. The last time they'd been there, they had to jump into the river and swim for their lives while the Sanctuary's mages lobbed fireballs at every passing vessel. Ben and his business partner, Lord Reinhold, had been set up by Lord Gulli and Lord Jason. Ben had been jumped by thugs, and Reinhold and all of his men had been slaughtered in an ambush.

In addition to that, the place was full of soaring towers and delicate bridges spanning between them. The bridges made Ben shiver just thinking about them. The rent was expensive, and most of the ale tasted like swill. There was always noise, and you could never get a good night's sleep. In short, Ben wasn't looking forward to entering the City again.

"We need a plan," declared Rhys as he walked out of the node gate.

Behind him, it flickered out and appeared to be a flat stone wall broken by an intricate array of cracks in an arched pattern.

If Ben hadn't seen the runes glowing on the other side, he would assume it was just an odd quirk of the geology of the place.

"Well," said Amelie. "First things first, we need to get inside. Once we're in, we need to set a watch for Milo, and we need to undermine the Veil, all without drawing her interest or falling into an open battle against all of the Sanctuary's mages. Above all else, though, we need to get that staff."

"Seems simple enough," remarked Ben.

Rhys snorted.

"Don't forget the demons," reminded Towaal. "There is an army of them somewhere. We need to figure out where and then figure out what to do about them."

"Oh, right," conceded Ben. "The demon army."

"Now that we're away from the village," advised Amelie, "I think it's time to check in with Jasper."

Ben nodded. "Agreed, but not here. Let's go until we can make camp and then contact him in the morning. Getting a little distance from this node gate is not a bad idea."

"Fair enough," said Amelie, glancing at Prem out of the corner of her eye. She hitched her pack and turned to the group. "Which way?"

Rhys pointed downhill. "Walk until you see the river. Then, turn and go until some mage tries to light us up with lightning or fireballs. That's when we know we've made it."

THEY CAMPED EASILY, not worried about fires or giving themselves away in such proximity to the City. It wasn't mundane guards, patrols in the woods, or bandits they were worried about. It was mages and anyone who could recognize them.

"We have a problem," Ben admitted after they'd settled down to dinner. "We're well known in the parts of the City that we want to get into, and no one who knows us is likely to be a friend. We need to sneak in and find a place we can use as a base. From there, we can scout for opportunities to stop Milo and get to the Veil."

"I'm not going back into an ale barrel," growled Rhys.

Prem looked at him curiously.

Ben shook his head. "No, not an ale barrel, but a smuggler is what we need."

"Do you know any smugglers?" asked Amelie doubtfully. "How do you even meet someone like that?"

"We know of at least one," confirmed Ben.

Amelie frowned at him. Then, understanding fell over her face. "Oh, no. Are you sure? Not him. I don't think he's very trustworthy. He'd sell us to the Sanctuary in a heartbeat, wouldn't he?"

Towaal sat forward, a chunk of hard bread forgotten in her hands. "You're not thinking…"

Rhys cracked his knuckles and laughed. "We always say we need to find allies, right? According to his Captain Martin, that little rat has been building a proper smuggling network. Ben's right. He's the one we need to talk to."

IN THE MORNING, they clustered around the thought meld, everyone sticking a finger to the smooth wood. For several moments, the device hummed softly, a gentle vibration thrumming through it. Then, Jasper spoke.

"I'm glad you contacted me. We have much to discuss."

"You have no idea," said Amelie, her thought filling Ben's head.

There was a pause. Then, Jasper suggested, "You go first."

"You are aware of the First Mages?" asked Amelie.

"I am," Jasper pulsed back through the thought meld.

"We found…" Amelie started and then paused. "Let me try something."

In Ben's mind, an image of the hall, decked in the copper faces of the First Mages, unfolded like an opening book.

"I've heard of this place," sent Jasper. "I didn't know where it was, though. I assumed it had failed and been lost to time like so much else. There were people there?"

"There is one of them with us," responded Amelie.

A sense of Prem nudged into Ben's thoughts, and he glanced at the girl. She was frowning.

"She is working with us after…" Again, Amelie paused. Then, images flicked through Ben's mind. The village, the hub for the node gates, the wall, the battle, and the mages closing the rift. "Demons, wyverns, and goblins were pouring through. It's been stopped, but many were lost."

"Ah," responded Jasper. "Closing the rift was the right decision, but it's unfortunate the price was so high. The openings between our worlds are vanishing. If we can find the last few, we could end the threat of the dark forces once and for all."

They all paused, considering that.

Jasper continued, his thoughts sounding in their heads. "Closing the rift was good, but The First Mages, like so much else from that time, should be forgotten. Gathering those memories, sustaining them, is not advisable. It's a treasure trove of secrets that anyone could stumble across and use for evil."

Prem muttered something under her breath that Ben didn't catch. He tried to ignore the girl, sure she wasn't happy about a stranger disparaging the work she had spent one hundred years doing.

"We have bigger and more immediate problems, though," said Jasper. "I was able to track down and recruit some of the wanderers who had passed through my valley over the years. We made some progress against the swarms that have ravaged the north. Three days ago, though, Northport fell. We were a few days away and couldn't arrive in time to help. From afar, we studied the aftermath."

A new image swirled into Ben's head and he gasped. The huge walls that surrounded Northport were breached, torn down in half a dozen places. Buildings were leveled, rubble strewn everywhere. The image zoomed in closer, like it was from far-seeing, and it was a knife twisting in Ben's gut. Everywhere, bodies littered the streets, torn to pieces, their lifeblood drained by their attackers.

Another image flashed, and Ben's jaw dropped open. An arch-demon, like nothing he had seen before, crouched atop Lord Rhymer's keep. Huge wings that looked like they could span the entire building shrouded its body. What Ben could see terrified him. Claws, larger than a person, stuck out from its hands. Muscle corded its body, and Ben had no doubt about how Northport's walls had been torn down. The thing looked like it had strength to tear the Citadel off the top of Whitehall and throw it halfway across the Blood Bay. As Ben watched, the creature's head tilted up, and it stared right at him, eyes burning red with hatred. The image flicked out.

"As you can imagine," thought Jasper, sounding shaken even now, "we stopped looking after that."

The group fell silent, the news of Northport's fall like a cold blanket thrown over their fire.

"The group I've assembled is formidable," continued Jasper, "but I do not think we are sufficient. That arch-demon is like nothing I have experienced. It sensed me watching it! I could feel it, like it was looking right back into my eyes."

"What can we do?" wondered Ben through the thought meld.

"There is only one thing to do," responded Jasper. "We have to find help. We need allies. We need someone or something that can stand against that monster."

"Do you think the arch-demon has talent?" asked Towaal.

"That would be unique," responded Jasper. "I've never heard

of a demon able to manipulate energy, but..." His thoughts trailed off. They'd all seen the creature look up at him. If it didn't have talent, how could it sense the far-seeing?

"Did you get the object we spoke about?" asked Ben.

"I did," responded Jasper.

A new image, one of silver, full-plate armor was revealed. Prem gasped.

"The armor from the Purple's watchtower in the Wilds. Let me tell you, getting there through these demon swarms was one of the most harrowing experiences of my life. The bards could sing about that one for ages, but, if we can make use of it, it will be worth it. I've been studying the armor. There is more to this set than I originally thought. I believe in addition to exceptional protection, it will imbue incredible speed on the wearer." His thoughts continued, sounding frustrated, "The problem is, the wearer must also power the armor. It will take strength of will and not inconsiderable strength of arm to operate it. Whoever crafted this plate mail did it for a true warrior-mage."

"So," thought Ben. "We need to find someone who can harness their will and knows how to swing a sword."

"Before you ask," responded Jasper, "I have the will, but I'd be like a slow-moving turtle. This armor weighs more than I do. None of my companions are likely to fit in it. We need someone about my height with significantly more muscle mass. While we can certainly find plenty of warriors with the physical characteristics, I don't think any of them would also have talent to harness their will."

"I know someone," responded Ben, "if we can get him to do it."

He raised his eyes from the thought meld and met Prem's gaze.

"He'll do it."

THE NEXT EVENING, they approached the outskirts of the City. They were coming in over the hills, far away from the well-traveled roads. Not because they thought someone would be watching for them, but because there was only one road that led out of Akew Woods, and the node gate was several leagues away from it.

"We're sure no one will be watching?" asked Amelie.

"If the Veil somehow got word of what happened to Eldred," answered Towaal, "she wouldn't expect us for another week or two. Even if we left the day we killed that thing, we still wouldn't be here yet."

"Edlred had a key to the node gates," reminded Ben. "The Veil must know about that, so maybe she'd know we could travel the node lines as well."

Towaal shrugged.

She was right. There was nothing they could do about that.

They crested a low hill and started down. The City spread out below them like a brilliant candle cupped in a crystal bowl. Lantern lights were springing alight on the island that housed the City proper, and around it, lights reflected back off the water and the settlements that rang the river basin. In the early evening, the roads and docks around the City were still filled with people rushing to make it inside or depart before full dark set. Thousands of people were coming and going in a steady stream. Dozens of docks stood out from the island. Scores of roads extended out like strands in a spider web. With any luck, the Sanctuary couldn't be watching all of the entry points.

Ben sighed. Looking at the expanse below, he realized it would take more than a little luck to catch Milo before he arrived. They didn't have a fraction of the manpower the Veil could command. If they could slip in unnoticed, then Milo could as well. Ben began to wonder if it was even worth trying to intercept the young man.

Rhys, seeming to read his thoughts, suggested, "We could start down the road back into the forest and meet him there."

Ben shook his head. "It is possible Milo had a node key too, or maybe he went cross country, or maybe he's traveling with mages. There are too many unknowns to try finding him in the forest. If he did get by us somehow, we'd have no way of knowing. Those woods extend for a month's walk. We could spend our lives searching in there. And as much as we need to confront Milo, we also need to begin laying the groundwork to overthrow Lady Coatney. We can't do that from the forest."

"Waiting until he's in the city is risky," advised Rhys.

Ben shrugged helplessly.

They continued down the gentle, grassy slope of the hill until they approached the outskirts of a town. Like all of the towns that surrounded the City, it had run together into one contiguous mass with the ones next to it. Whatever name it once held was lost.

"I hate to say this," started Ben, "but we need to find a rundown dive that's as far away from the main roads as we can be. A place with a busy tavern would be good. We need to find Renfro's men, and that's where they'll be."

Amelie groaned.

Prem chirped, "We're going to go to a tavern? I've never been to one."

Rhys wrapped an arm around the girl's shoulders. "I know a place near here. I think you're going to enjoy it."

"Of course he knows a place," muttered Amelie under her breath.

They followed Rhys through filthy backstreets and behind the ramshackle buildings that clung to the outskirts of the City. In the early evening, few people were about, but soon, they started to hear the din of busy streets, and Rhys led them into more populated areas.

After several blocks, he paused and whispered, "Hold on. I have an idea."

Ben frowned. The rogue's ideas could go either way.

Rhys stepped up to a meat pie seller and began negotiating with him.

Amelie caught Ben's eyes and mock-gagged, clearly not interested in meat a man on the side of the street was selling in that part of town. Ben grinned and set his back against the wall of a building. Around them, people walked about, returning from work, running last errands before dinner, heading to the taverns.

Rhys began loudly complaining to the meat pie man about making change. The vendor started barking back, and Ben was surprised to see the rogue with a fistful of gold in his hand. He was waving it angrily in the vendor's face, and the man was protesting, claiming he couldn't make change for the heavy gold coins. Finally, Rhys spun on his heel and stalked off, waving for his companions to follow. He shoved the coins into his belt pouch and Ben watched it bounce along at the end of a long thong.

"What was that about?" asked Amelie.

Rhys eyed her out of the corner of his eye. "You wanted one of those pies, I thought. The man couldn't make change."

Amelie rolled her eyes.

"You put on that show for someone specific or just fishing?" asked Ben.

The rogue winked at him and then pointed to a dark alley. Loudly, he declared, "We should find the tavern through here. Trust me. It's a short cut."

Amelie sighed skeptically and followed the rogue into the dark alley. As they entered the narrow confines between the buildings, Ben advised Prem to watch where she stepped.

"Cities are," the girl paused, sniffing at something she stepped in, "rather dirty."

"It gets better," consoled Ben. "Rhys is purposefully leading us through the worst of it."

"Why?" asked the girl.

"Fair question," responded Ben, grinning. "Just wait."

They didn't have to wait long. Rhys took several turns, leading them deeper and deeper into a warren of confusing streets and cul-de-sacs.

"The shortcut is through here somewhere. I'm sure of it," he claimed, his voice echoing in the empty streets. "We'll find somewhere to eat that can take good gold coin."

Ben casually pushed his cloak back from his longsword and let his eyes dart back and forth, checking every dark doorway, every cross street. Finally, they entered a courtyard and found a slender man waiting for them.

"Y'all lost?" he asked.

Rhys set his fists on his hips. "No, we're just, ah, turned around."

The man smiled, showing more missing teeth than whole ones. Behind them, someone cleared their throat. Ben turned to see three thugs spreading out, closing off any avenue of escape. They held a collection of heavy clubs and knives. Ben smiled, remembering the last time he'd been ambushed by a thug in an abandoned street in the City. That time, he'd been scared, worried the heavy clubs would shatter his bones and nervous for what would happen to his friends.

"It looks like you need help making change, stranger," cackled one of the men. A boy, Ben corrected. He couldn't have been more than sixteen summers.

Rhys cracked his knuckles but made no move toward his longsword or long knives.

"Don't think about drawing steel," growled another of the thugs.

"I wouldn't think of it," replied Rhys calmly, "but if you want my gold, you're going to have to come take it."

"Fine by me," snarled the first thug, and he gestured to his companions. Without word, they charged.

Ben almost felt sorry for them. Almost. He stepped forward and intercepted one of the thugs headed toward Rhys. He swept out his arm and brought it across the attacker's chest. The man flipped into the air and crashed down on the ground. Ben knelt and pounded his fist into the man's head for good measure.

He glanced up in time to see Rhys swing one of the men by his arm and then lash out with a foot, tripping the man and hurling him head first into the side of a building. An audible crack brought a wince to Ben's face, and the unfortunate man's neck twisted disturbingly to the side.

"Damnit," muttered Rhys, eyeing the corpse in dismay.

Prem was standing over another, her knives dripping with his blood.

"You didn't have to kill him," complained Rhys.

"He was trying to rob us," responded Prem, confused. "Besides, you killed yours."

Rhys nudged his first victim with his toe. "I just killed one of them. This one will wake up, I'm pretty sure."

"I left mine alive," said Ben. He looked down at the fallen man. "Sorry about this."

He pulled his water skin off his belt and unstoppered it. He dumped the contents on the unconscious thug's head.

"Wha..." spluttered the man before scrambling away from Ben.

"You tried to rob us," reminded Ben.

The man glanced around wildly, first seeing the bloody corpse by Prem, then the other that Rhys had accidentally killed by the side of the building.

"You killed them!" accused the thug.

Ben scratched at his head. He was ready for a bath, but first things first. "Like I said, you were trying to rob us."

The man rose unsteadily to his feet, feeling at his swollen temple where Ben had punched him.

"You should put some ice on that," suggested Ben, "and then, rethink your life. If you try to attack and rob someone, sometimes, they might fight back. I'm sorry your friends were killed, but they would have done worse to us for the gold in our pouches. We've got a fortune of coin and small valuables on us. It's too much to let the likes of you walk away with it."

The man glared at them balefully, memorizing their faces, Ben was sure. Then, he turned and bolted.

"That should do it," said Rhys cheerfully. "Time for a drink."

"What just happened?" wondered Prem, wiping the blood off her long knives and then sliding them into their sheaths.

"Sending a message to an old friend," said Ben. "Either he'll hear about this, or someone who knows him will."

"Or someone who knows someone who knows him," added Rhys.

"Something like that," agreed Ben. "Eventually, one of these thieves will lead us to Renfro."

FOUR BELLS LATER, they sat at an uneven table in the back of a ramshackle tavern. They'd found lodging across a narrow street, but even Rhys balked at drinking in the place once he'd smelled what passed for food.

"Quality has slipped since you've been gone," assessed Rhys as he took a deep pull from a sour mug of ale.

"I'm not sure a place like this ever carried my stuff," said Ben. He looked around. "This place is rather empty, isn't it?"

"The ale is driving everyone away," guessed Amelie.

"It's not bad after the fourth or fifth one," claimed Rhys. "It's like anything. It requires dedication, persistence…"

The rogue trailed off. The half-empty common room was

entirely empty now. A loose door banged shut as the last patron scurried away.

"How does everyone always know to leave the room before the thieves arrive?" wondered Amelie.

"This happens to you often?" questioned Prem.

"More than you'd expect," admitted Ben.

Cloaked and hooded figures began to stream into the room, edging along the walls, surrounding Ben and his companions.

"Their presentation isn't bad," observed Rhys. "They certainly brought enough guys, though, displaying a few weapons would be more menacing. With all of that fabric, this could be the clothier's guild."

"Small-time crooks," guessed Ben. "I think we're going to have to go through another layer."

"You've made a grave error," began one of the cloaked figures, his voice booming in the empty tavern.

Rhys cut him off, waving a hand to silence him.

"We're looking for someone," he interjected. "I was hoping you could help."

"We…" the figure turned and looked at a companion, spoiling the act. Then, apparently with reassurance, he turned back to Rhys. "You assaulted members of our guild, and for that, you owe us. We'll be taking your gold and your weapons now."

Rhys snorted.

"They attacked us," said Ben. "Look, let's just talk about this. Killing your men was more or less an accident, and no one else needs to die."

The thieves stirred, likely gripping weapons under the cloaks, but none of them appeared to have crossbows or anything else that would make Ben nervous. If they weren't any more skilled than the ones he and his friends fought outside, even a dozen of the thieves would be no problem. The speaker's cloak parted, and a short sword rose from within the folds of fabric.

"We should just injure them?" asked Prem, shifting to clear space to use her knives.

"We only need a few," advised Rhys. "You can kill the rest."

The rogue stood. In one smooth motion, he grabbed his chair and hurled it across the room at the cloaked speaker. The man was shocked and didn't get his sword up in time to stop the wooden chair from crashing into his face. With a surprised grunt, he went flailing to the floor.

A surge of cloaked men rushed forward, only to quickly begin retreating.

Prem had jumped onto their table, nearly toppling the fragile thing in the process, and launched herself into a crowd of the attackers. Her knives flashed. Screams and blood followed. The thieves were used to intimidation. If that didn't work, they'd bust a head in a dark alley from behind. They had no idea that the little girl had been alive for one hundred years or that she'd been training with her knives that entire time. She'd fought goblins, demons, and even wyverns. A couple of toughs in a tavern was nothing to her. Not to mention Rhys, who'd probably brawled in the first ever tavern.

Ben sighed and picked up a chair. He charged as well, laying about and smashing the thing into kindling over men's heads. When the chair was nothing more than broken sticks, he snatched an arms-length club out of one of the surprised men's hands. Their assailants were thieves who intended to harm them, but Ben felt a mild twinge of guilt that they'd lured them into this trap. He tried not to kill any of them as he whirled with the club, striking arms and legs, breaking them in two, or pounding the end of the club into midsections, sending the thieves flopping down, wheezing, breathless and unable to continue the fight. In a moment, the scuffle was over. Towaal and Amelie still sat calmly at the table.

"Nice work," complimented Amelie, clapping her hands together slowly.

Ben grinned at her. Around him, injured thieves groaned and attempted to crawl away.

"Which one of you was the leader?" asked Rhys.

Only pained moans answered him.

The rogue sighed and slipped a long knife out of the sheath. "Okay, I'll start cutting throats until there is only one left, and that one will be the leader. I don't want to harm any more of you than I have to, but there's a message I need delivered."

"Him," muttered one of the fallen men, pointing to a figure lying flat on its back.

Rhys went to stand over the purported leader and nudged him with his foot until the man awoke. He cried out, startled to see the rogue looming above him, and tried to scramble back on his heels and elbows. Rhys stomped a foot down on the man's cloak, preventing him from scooting any further away.

"Do you know Renfro?" he asked.

The man's mouth opened and closed, either unsure of the answer or unwilling to give it.

"He's small, looks like a rat," added Ben.

The man shook his head, his eyes wide with fear.

Ben sighed. "Look, you don't have to take us to him or anything like that. Just go tell him or someone that knows how to reach him that Ben is here, and we need to talk."

"Ben?" asked the thief.

"That's all," answered Ben with what he hoped was a comforting smile.

"We'll be waiting," responded Rhys.

He sat down at the table and glanced over to where Prem was still standing in a pile of dead thieves.

"Ah," added Rhys, looking back at the leader, "before you and the boys go, can you drag these bodies away? The watch may have questions if they stumble into here, and I haven't finished my ale yet."

~

TWO BELLS LATER, they followed a furtive figure through the streets. It wore a cloak like the other thieves, but this one didn't speak. It only gestured with small, glove-covered hands. Ben wondered if it was a child or maybe a woman. The figure led them to the waterfront, where the island of the City proper rose in front of them like a shining torch in the night. There was a long, narrow boat tied to an abandoned dock. In the shadows, two dozen paces away, Ben saw more cloaked figures lurking, trying to stay out of sight.

"He's got the drama down," muttered Rhys, clambering into the vessel.

The slender figure joined them after they'd all climbed in the boat. Several more shapes appeared to shove them away. They drifted into the current, and their guide pointed to a set of oars lying next to Ben. Grumbling, he took them up. Noticing the thick cloth around the oar-locks, he ducked them in the water and propelled the boat toward the City. They had no lights on their vessel, and in the dark of night, they'd be invisible on the black water. Better than attempting a bridge, decided Ben as he rowed them closer.

Silently, their guide pointed to where Ben should row, and he hauled on the oars, the small boat knifing through the water. A quarter bell and they made it under the lights of the City.

They were directed to a dim section of dock, bordered by poorly lit residential towers, boisterous taverns, and small shops that looked to be closed for the night. Ben had expected some abandoned warehouse district, but he realized as they approached that this area was even better for covert arrivals. There were enough people in the streets that movement wouldn't be unusual, but it was the kind of low-income neighborhood that had no interest in speaking to the watch. The people in these towers were more likely to listen to the authority of a dagger than the mages in the Sanctuary.

They bumped against a small, padded wharf and climbed out of the vessel. Their guide slipped around them and led them into the City.

Ben and Amelie flanked Prem. The girl's mouth hung wide open, absolutely stunned at her first view of a real city. Ben grinned at the thought of taking her to some of the nicer parts of town where the towers soared twenty or thirty stories high, with thin bridges hanging between to connect them, the sculpture gardens, the parks, and more. The City was magical in some areas. He shook his head and brought his attention back to what they were doing. They were here to challenge the Veil. There'd be no time for sightseeing, and the only magic was the stuff they were trying to avoid.

Their guide led them three blocks away from the water and ducked into a four-story flat of apartments. They walked through a narrow, dark hallway and then came out behind the building. They scurried unspeaking through an unlit courtyard and entered another building.

Inside, they found a wide-open room filled with ragged couches, battered tables, and no windows. It was lit by a handful of smoky lanterns. In the back, Ben spied another entrance shrouded by a dirty curtain. On one wall was a table set with earthenware flagons of what Ben assumed was wine or ale. Rhys went to check and poured himself one. He raised an eyebrow at Ben, who nodded back at him.

Their guide perched in one corner of the room and stayed bundled in the cloak. Not one for conversation, apparently.

Rhys took a sip and made a face at the ale. "Renfro didn't learn anything from his time with you, Ben."

Ben sipped it as well and grimaced. "Cheap hops," he explained, "or they used sewer water instead of fresh water."

Rhys blinked at him and set his mug down.

Ben grinned. "Just kidding." He paused and added, "I'm pretty sure he wouldn't do that."

They sat for half a bell under the watchful eyes of their guide before suddenly, there was movement. From the back of the building, they heard a rustling, and two huge men ducked through the curtain.

They were street brawlers, no doubt about it, at least a hand taller than Ben and twice as wide. They wore open vests to display thick slabs of muscle, and at their belts, they had iron-studded clubs and short swords. Ben couldn't help but notice, also prominently showing on their chests, were hand-sized tattoos of a rat.

Behind the bruisers, a small man entered. He wore snug black britches, a billowy white, silk shirt, and had a fine, silver rapier hanging from his hip. Ben thought about mentioning how similar the outfit was that of their former captor in Fabrizo, Casper, but he bit his tongue instead. They needed Renfro's help. Needling him about his attire wouldn't get it.

"Hello, Ben," remarked the newcomer in an outlandish accent that Ben guessed was supposed to make him sound cultured.

"Renfro," acknowledged Ben.

"You've certainly gained a flair for theater since we last saw you," remarked Rhys.

Renfro glanced at the assassin. "A few other things as well. For example, it looks like you need my help now, instead of the other way around."

"We do," agreed Ben. He eyed Renfro's companions. "I think it's best we speak in private."

Renfro pursed his lips and then turned to the two hulking body guards. "Wait outside."

"Rat," protested one of the thugs. "They took down a dozen of Booh's men, and they're still armed."

"They have no intention of hurting me, and if they did, I can take care of myself," replied Renfro. He gestured toward the cloaked figure who'd led Ben and his friends to the apartment. "Sincell will stay. You wait outside."

Grumbling, the two toughs departed.

"Let's save ourselves the embarrassment of you trying to cajole me into some plan. I pay my debts," declared Renfro as soon as the men were gone. "What do you need? Safe passage out of the City, weapons, gold, a ship?"

Ben smirked. From what he recalled, Renfro rarely paid his debts, but he certainly wasn't going to argue with him. Instead, he explained, "It's a bit more than that."

"A lot more than that," mumbled Amelie.

Renfro frowned, and their original guide, Sincell, stirred in the corner.

"We need to find someone," said Ben.

Renfro chuckled, tension flooding out of him. "Ah, that's not so bad. It takes a lot of manpower to do it proper in the City, but manpower is something I've got. I can have fifty urchins scouring this city by tomorrow. You have any clue where this person may be located? If we have a neighborhood to start in, that will speed things up, of course."

"The Sanctuary," said Towaal.

Renfro jumped. Evidently, he'd been choosing to ignore the presence of the mage.

"The person we are looking for is carrying a very powerful magical weapon they intend to give to the Veil."

In the corner of the room, Sincell fell off her stool and scrambled up, cursing. The hood had fallen back, and Ben saw a narrow-faced woman.

"The bloody Sanctuary?" she exclaimed, brushing herself off.

"Sincell," murmured Towaal. "I knew that name sounded familiar."

The woman glanced at the mage and then flushed.

"Using magic in the City is rather risky, isn't it?" Towaal asked the girl. "If the mages sense you, there's no escaping them here. Runaways tend to, well, run. There's a reason for that."

"What does she mean, 'sense you'?" asked Renfro nervously.

"Don't worry about it," grumbled Sincell, retaking her place on the stool.

Towaal snorted and turned back to Renfro.

"We need to find this person," stated Ben, directing everyone's attention back to the matter at hand. "We need to find him and capture him if possible. We need to obtain the object he is carrying, and we need to undermine and then overthrow the Veil."

Renfro stared back at him, open-mouthed.

"Did we forget that earlier, about overthrowing the Veil?" said Ben. "Sorry. We did warn you it was more than sneaking us out of the City and a few weapons."

Renfro was at a loss for words.

"Oh, and we need news as well," finished Ben. "Demons overran Northport. We need to find out what people in the City know, and I suppose what's being done north of here in places like Venmoor. After we're done on this island, we're going to have to go and face the demon army."

"Bloody hell," murmured Sincell.

7
_____

WATCHING, WAITING

THREE DAYS LATER, THEY REMAINED IN HIDING WHILE THE RAT'S urchins formed a net around the City. They were watching every bridge on the southwest side of town where Milo may enter. They were also watching the gates to the Sanctuary itself, and Renfro claimed he was checking with sources within the Sanctuary to see if they'd heard anything. Ben doubted Renfro had sources within the Sanctuary, but he had no doubt his old friend had a small army of urchins at his disposal.

Over the last few days, it had become apparent that Renfro had formed something of a fledgling thieves' guild in the City. It was ambitious and very stupid, but Ben had to admire the guts it took. The City, home to most of Alcott's mages, was not a place that had ever had an organized ring of thieves. Fear of the mages drove most sensible thieves far away, but like any large city, there was a seedy underbelly. There were pleasure houses, gambling halls, durhang dens, and down and out low-lifes who had no other choices.

The one reason Ben thought Renfro's plan may work was that his friend, the Rat as he was now known, always remained behind the curtain. Outside of a dozen of his closest associates, no one knew who he was or what he looked like. If the mages made a serious, sustained effort to hunt him down, Ben was sure they could, but with any luck, Renfro would have enough warning to get out of town. It was bold and fool-hardy, and no one else had considered the risk worth the reward. Hence, the Rat was rapidly becoming the defacto head of all of the thieves in the City.

"The trick," Renfro explained, "is knowing who to target. It's not about the volume of people you knock over or the size of an individual haul. It's about knocking over the right people. A gambling den that's selling durhang out of the back isn't going to call the watch if some of their product goes missing. A respectable merchant selling carpets, though, he'll have mages rooting through his warehouse magically searching for clues. I make sure that anyone working for me knows who they're stealing from."

"Aren't you worried you're going to upset the owners of those gambling dens?" asked Rhys. "If they're willing to sell durhang in the City, they'd also be willing to put a knife in you then dump you in the river."

Renfro grinned. "You're right. Some of them are quite dangerous. Again, it's important to know your target. If they've got enough muscle to come after us, then I've found it's easier to propose a compromise. Instead of us taking the coins ourselves, we ask for them to hand us a piece. Protection money. It's cheaper for them to shuffle a little of the loot our way instead of engaging in an underground war. Coin is the lubrication that keeps the wheels turning in the underworld. No one minds spreading a little around when they need to."

Rhys sipped his wine and didn't respond.

Ben frowned, but he didn't know enough about thieving to argue with his old friend. Instead, he took a sip of his wine as well and set back, studying the room Renfro had put them up in. They were housed in another slum-like housing complex that the Rat controlled. On the outside, it looked like it was one windstorm away from collapse, but inside, it was lined with plush carpets, sparkling crystal decanters filled with expensive wine, and tapestries that lined the walls like a second coat of paint. It was literally wealth everywhere you looked.

When they'd first seen the apartments Renfro planned to house them in, Amelie had murmured, "Good fortune does not equal good taste."

Ben couldn't agree more, but he had to admit, it was more comfortable than sleeping in whatever flea-infested inn they would have to choose to avoid anyone from the Sanctuary.

"So," said Ben finally, interrupting the silence. "You've convinced everyone to toe the line, steal from the soft targets, and all the thieves benefit? Let me guess, you get a slice of everything anyone brings in?"

Renfro, slumped in his chair with one leg slung over an overstuffed arm, grinned and nodded. "I'm fair. I have to be. Otherwise, they'd put me in that river Rhys is so fond of putting people in. Turns out, a small piece of a big enough pie is still a whole lotta pie. There's plenty for me, and like I said, people are used to sharing some of their coin to facilitate a professionally run underworld."

"It seems like a big risk," murmured Ben.

Renfro raised his goblet. "This is the best wine that gold can buy. From the hills outside of the City, unfortunately. I wish it was more exotic, but it's still the best. You can't have the success I've had without taking some risk, Ben. Did you ever think a year ago when you first met me that one day I'd be serving you this kind of wine?"

Ben couldn't help a wry smile from crossing his face. "I thought we'd turn you onto the straight and narrow."

Renfro guffawed, nearly dropping the heavy crystal goblet. "Maybe you would have, in time, but you left."

"We didn't leave," retorted Ben. "All of Reinhold's men were killed, and they were coming for Amelie next."

"You didn't even warn me," said Renfro.

Ben sensed the hurt lurking in his old friend's voice. "I tried to, Renfro, I really did. Mathias looked for you but couldn't find you. I had no choice but to get Amelie and go. After what happened, there was no way we could come back into the City. Besides, I knew you were capable of surviving on your own. Thriving, even."

"You could have left me a note," complained the thief.

"Renfro, you can't read," Ben reminded him.

The little thief laughed again, suddenly all smiles, and turned up his wine.

"What happened after we left?" asked Amelie. "How did you, well, I guess, how did you become the Rat?"

"A story for another time," declared Renfro. He crawled off the stuffed chair and stretched. "Now, I need to go check with my sources and see if they've stumbled across this boy you're looking for. Sounds like a pretty boy, the kind the urchins love to pick-pocket. I'd better make sure that instead lightening his purse, they're running back to report what they've found."

"He's dangerous," warned Ben.

Renfro waved dismissively and stomped to the door, swerving a little and bumping against the door jam on his way out.

"He still can't handle his drink," remarked Rhys after the Rat left.

Amelie crossed the room and sat down next to Ben. He could sense her frustration, that she was ready to do something, but there wasn't much they could do. The City was full of people who may recognize them, so it was safest to rely on the Rat and his urchins. If they could find Milo, then they could formulate a plan. Without even knowing whether the former apprentice was in town, it was fruitless to scheme of ways to steal the staff.

Prem, evidently feeling some of the same strain at sitting still, suggested, "Why don't we spar?"

Rhys grunted and set down his wine. He stood and cracked his knuckles. "Better than sitting around trying to figure out which wall has the tackiest decoration."

Ben shrugged and stood as well.

~

THAT NIGHT, Ben lay on a broad, rumpled bed. Amelie was at a small table across the room doing... something. He raised his head to look at her. "What are you doing over there?"

She glanced over her shoulder at him. "Getting ready for bed."

He frowned. She'd been getting ready for bed for half a bell now. They had their own room, and after so much time on the road in the company of their friends, he was ready to take advantage of the privacy, except he was in danger of drifting off to sleep.

"That Prem is pretty quick, isn't she?" he mumbled, more to keep himself awake than to have any serious conversation.

"She's been training since before your grandfather was born," reminded Amelie. "She is quick, though, and she uses those long knives like a butcher. I don't know how much you saw, but she carved those thieves up like they were already dead meat."

"Why do you think she's helping us?" asked Ben.

"She wants to do good, like us, or maybe because her father told her to?" speculated Amelie.

Ben grunted.

Amelie began humming to herself, doing something with her hair. From his back, Ben couldn't see what, but he didn't bother to get up and examine her. He'd done that the night before, and she'd shooed him off and suggested if he was that eager for a romp, he could do it by himself. He'd gone back to silently sulking and waiting for her.

"Maybe she's spying on us for her father," suggested Ben.

"Of course she is," replied Amelie. "I bet she's speaking to him every night."

"What?" exclaimed Ben, bolting upright in the bed.

Amelie looked at him in the smoky mirror that was set on the table. "A thought meld, Ben. We saw Adrick use it to contact his father, why do you think it'd be any different with his daughter?"

Ben frowned.

"Should we…" he trailed off uncertainly.

"We don't have anything to hide from her," said Amelie. "Whatever the girl sees could help our case with her father. We need him, Ben. We need him to come wear the armor Jasper recovered. We need the knowledge he can bring and the others in that village. Prem has done nothing to earn distrust. We treat her like she's one of the party, and when the time comes, I think she'll come through for us. A link to her father could be exactly what we need when we leave to face the demons."

"You're right," Ben acknowledged. He shuddered, thinking about the look in the eye of the creature that Jasper showed them. Intelligence and palpable hatred. That thing wanted nothing other than to feast on all of humanity, and Ben wasn't sure they could stop it.

"We're not facing the demons tonight," said Amelie.

She stood from the table and walked to the bed. Ben blinked. Her hair was piled loosely on top of her head, and he saw she was wearing a wispy gown that did more to emphasize her curves than hide them. Looking her up and down, Ben's throat went dry, and he felt an immediate stirring below his belt.

"I found this little thing in the wardrobe," said Amelie, a finger lifting one of the straps that kept the gown clinging precariously to her shoulders. "I can only imagine what kind of women are normally in this place, wearing this kind of thing.

You wouldn't think badly of me if I wore it to bed, though, would you?"

Ben, speechless, could only shake his head.

Amelie gave him a smile that made the half bell of waiting all worth it. Then, she pounced onto the bed. Ben reached for her, suddenly not tired at all.

WHEN BEN WOKE, he slipped out of bed while Amelie still slumbered. He tugged on his britches and shirt and stood, smiling down at her. The fact that she was there, lying naked in his bed, was something he thought he'd never get used to. A year ago, he'd been a simple brewer in a small village. Now, he couldn't believe his luck.

The apartments were quiet, but he smelled freshly brewed kaf. After so long on the road, it called to him. He stepped out of the room into the common area and stopped. At their table was the rogue mage Sincell. She was seated in front of a steaming ceramic pot that had to be the kaf. She was sipping from a small mug.

"The Rat tells me you live for this stuff," she remarked.

Ben conceded, "That and ale."

"It's a bit early for me to have an ale. Come, have some kaf," said the woman, gesturing to a chair opposite of her.

Ben settled in and poured himself a mug. The rich, earthy aroma soaked into his nostrils, dragging him to full wakefulness.

"I've been thinking about what you said," remarked Sincell as Ben tried the kaf. "Good, isn't it?"

He nodded and indicated she should continue.

"I assume you're exaggerating about these demons, but I've faced a swarm or two in my time. They're not something you can ignore. If even half of what you say is true…" She took a sip of her drink and eyed Ben over the rim of her mug.

"It's all true," assured Ben. "Why would we have any reason to lie?"

"That's what I've been thinking about the last few days. If Northport really fell, the City will know about it soon enough. What would you gain by telling us demons overran the place if they did not? It'd be such an easy lie to disprove."

Ben drank his kaf in silence, letting the woman have time to sort out her thoughts.

"I've decided you are telling the truth about that, but the five of you aren't enough to stand against an army of demons," declared Sincell. "Even with some special mage-wrought weapon that the Veil herself wants to get her hands on, it's not enough to stand against what you've been telling us about."

"I know," said Ben. "We have other allies, but even then, it is not enough."

"You need more men," said Sincell, leaning forward with her forearms resting on the table. "Well, not necessarily men, but warriors. Soldiers, armies, even mages if you can get some."

"You know anyone who wants to help?" asked Ben.

The woman sat back.

"I ran from the Sanctuary nigh twenty years ago," she said. "Didn't come back within five hundred leagues of here for fifteen of those years. I was drawn back, though, pulled by the promise of the Sanctuary."

Ben poured himself another mug of kaf and let her continue.

"It's not all bad, you know," explained Sincell. "They're capable of awful things, and I suspect you know even more about that than I do, but they're also capable of good. There are good people there. Friends of mine, mentors. People I know who wouldn't lift a finger to harm another. People who would be appalled if they knew the things you told us a few days back. That's why I came back to the City, because some of the members of the Sanctuary are the best people I know."

Ben nodded. "Lady Towaal was a mage there for, well, I don't even know how long. A long time though, for sure. Amelie was an initiate for a brief span. They had no idea what kind of machinations the Veil was up to when they were there."

Sincell, seemingly encouraged by Ben's words, continued, "I'm certain that if some of the people I know heard what you have to say, they'd run from behind those white walls just as quick as I did. Most of them went to that place to do good. Sitting on an island, safe and sound, while an army of demons storms across the continent? That's not what they signed up for."

Ben sipped at his drink. "I think you're probably right, but it's not like the Veil's inviting me to come in and do a speech in front of her mages. It's not like she'd even let us live if she knew we were here. You know that. Towaal thinks she knows some mages who would be willing to join us, but how do we get ahold of them? We've thought about writing a letter, but what if she was wrong about the person's character, or what if the letter fell into the wrong hands? We'd be cooked before we knew what was happening."

Sincell spun her mug on the table, watching the kaf swirl within it. "You need to find folks you know can keep a secret from the Veil."

Ben, sensing where the conversation was going, asked again, "You know of anyone?"

The woman smiled. "I may know a few," she answered. "There are some I see from time to time. They've kept my secret safe for the last few years, and I know they aren't satisfied with the current Veil. They have a meeting tonight. You could come talk to them if you want, and try to bring them over to your cause."

"Let me think about it," murmured Ben.

"Of course," responded Sincell. "Lady Towaal is up on the roof." The runaway mage stood and left.

Ben sat for a long moment, thinking about what she'd said. Then, he went to wake Amelie and find Towaal.

~

THAT AFTERNOON, they crept through the warrens of the City's slums. Ben hadn't realized how extensive the network was of dilapidated housing, unsavory taverns, and durhang dens.

"Anywhere that has rich people is going to have poor people," muttered Renfro as he led them from building to building, alley to alley.

They were bundled tightly in their cloaks, hoods pulled up, eyes cast down. They appeared entirely suspicious, but that wasn't an unusual look in the neighborhoods Renfro took them through. Half the people they passed didn't want to be noticed and had even less interest in noticing who was around them.

"I don't think I would like living in a city," remarked Prem.

"It's not all like this. I promise," assured Amelie.

"This isn't so bad," claimed Renfro. "There are far worse places to live, like on a farm."

"Fresh air, open space?" responded Ben. "A farm doesn't sound that terrible."

"Pre-dawn wake-up times, filthy animals, no women," retorted Renfro.

They fell silent as they scurried across a busy street, and then, they found themselves entering the lobby of a soaring tower. The space was clean but not wealthy. A far sight better than what they'd been trooping through but not so high class that anyone affiliated with the Sanctuary was likely to be staying there.

A guard at the door merely glanced at a subtle hand gesture from Renfro, and his eyes snapped back to the streets in front of the tower. They slipped by him, and Renfro led them to a tiny, narrow staircase at the back of the lobby. Ben eyed a broad, lime-stone one that they passed.

"What's wrong with that stair?" he hissed.

"Too public," answered Renfro. "All of these tall places have at least two. In case there is a fire, they've got another way out if one gets blocked. If you ask me, living in a place where you have to worry about that kind of thing is your first problem."

"I thought you liked the city," challenged Amelie. "Big cities come with big towers."

"Big cities come with basements too," declared Renfro.

He started up the narrow stairs. Ben immediately felt a creeping sense of dread. Not from any magical wards, a sixth sense about watchers, or anything like that. Instead, he found himself sandwiched between his friends in a staircase that was barely wider than his shoulders. As far as he could see, it extended up above them, story after story. It was nothing but wall and stairs, with the occasional opening into a narrow hallway when they passed another floor.

"Imagine racing twenty stories down this thing, stuck behind hundreds of people, and the place is burning above you," said Rhys.

Ben groaned.

"You can't help yourself, can you?" Amelie asked the rogue.

"Don't want our leader getting a big head," he responded.

Ben breathed deep and tried to ignore the man.

A quarter bell passed, and Ben's legs were burning with the strain of climbing stair after stair.

"Sorry about this," gasped Renfro. The little thief looked like at any moment he could lose it and go tumbling back down the stairs to the bottom. He'd never been in good shape, and Ben doubted lurking in basement lairs, drinking fine wine, and carousing had done anything to improve his constitution.

Finally, they reached the floor they were climbing to. Renfro led them into a wide-open room and flopped to the floor, his back resting against a circular column.

Ben walked across the empty floor and peered out the window. They were twenty stories above the City on the northern edge of the island. The window Ben peered out overlooked the grounds of the Sanctuary.

"It's like spying on ants," said Prem. "Wouldn't it be easier to just far-see?"

"Oh, yeah," muttered Renfro. He dug a tube out of his cloak and rolled it across the floor to them.

"Far-seeing could alert the mages to our presence," explained Towaal. "Generally, it is not intrusive, but there are centuries of wards laid over that place. It's possible they could detect us. Remember, they have the mask from the First Mages. As we discussed back in your village, they've called on power that I do not entirely understand to provide protection."

The mage bent and scooped up the tube Renfro had produced. She held it to one eye, looking out the window. Then, she flipped it around and looked again. For long moments, she studied the grounds of the Sanctuary. Finally, she passed the device to Amelie.

"This will work," Towaal said to Renfro.

"If he's able to slip in unnoticed, Milo won't be able to move around the grounds without us seeing him," said Amelie, peering at the Sanctuary below. "Once we figure out which building he's staying in, we should be able to form a plan."

"I can't believe you're going to break into that place," said Renfro.

Ben shrugged. "It worked before."

The little thief clambered to his feet. "When they catch you, make sure you forget my name."

"Of course," said Ben. He paused. "Thanks for the help, Renfro."

Renfro paused at the door to the stairwell. "You helped me when I needed it most. I couldn't live with myself if I didn't pay you back."

"You're an honorable man," said Ben.

His old friend started down the stairs without a response.

"An honorable man?" questioned Rhys once the little thief was out of earshot. "You know he steals from people for a living, right?"

Ben shrugged. "He needs to hear it. Maybe someday, he really will be."

"If you say so," responded the rogue.

"You used to kill people for a living," reminded Ben.

Rhys grunted and moved to stand beside Amelie.

"Another bell here then Towaal and I need to go speak with Sincell's mages," said Ben. "The rest of you can keep an eye on the Sanctuary. Look for anything out of the ordinary."

"Of course. You sure you don't want me to go with you to meet the mages?" asked Amelie.

Ben shook his head. "They'll be nervous, I think. The fewer of us who are there, the better. Towaal lends a certain credibility and may know some of them."

"I'm not credible?" asked Amelie with an eyebrow raised.

"You're..." Ben paused, thinking of ways to extract his foot from his mouth.

"An initiate to these women," said Towaal.

Amelie winced, and Ben shrugged.

BEN AND TOWAAL, cloaks pulled over their heads, entered the Wily Goose. It was a place Rhys would have appreciated. Dark corners filled with uncouth figures, gambling, girls, and copious amounts of ale flowing from the taps in a constant waterfall of drunkenness.

"I don't think the Veil will stumble across us in here," remarked Towaal.

"I'm not sure anyone we meet in here will be any better," said Ben, eyeing a group of unsavory-looking characters at a table nearby. He led them to a backroom where Sincell had promised a group of mages would be waiting for them. Friendly mages.

Mages who didn't want to immediately run back to the Sanctuary and turn them in, she had said. Ben put his hand on the door and breathed deeply. He glanced back at Towaal.

"I'm ready."

He pushed the door open and strode inside.

8

THE MAGES

HALF A DOZEN WOMEN SAT LOOKING AT HIM FROM THE OTHER SIDE of a table. They'd arranged themselves with their backs against the wall, facing the door. To join them, his back would be to the door. He grunted. The Sanctuary's mages would naturally put themselves at an advantage. They'd do it without thinking, he hoped. If they'd intentionally put him in a weaker position, then this meeting wasn't starting well.

"Thank you for agreeing to meet with me," he said, trying to sound confident. "Sincell tells me you are interested in talking to me."

"The girl is a runaway and I have very little interest in her claims," remarked one of the women coldly. Her face was wrinkled like old leather and her stark white hair was pulled back into a severe bun, but her eyes blazed bright blue. "I don't really care what you have to say either. I'm told…"

Towaal stepped forward and flipped back the hood of her cloak. "Still a bitch, I see. You should listen to what he says, Hadra, before judging the merit of those words. I believe you taught me something like that, once."

The woman, Hadra, threw back her head and laughed. "Still as impulsive as ever, Karina. I was sure it would be you who was with this young man, but I had to see it myself. This boy is nothing to us, but you, you have a story we want to hear. Why did you leave, Karina? Why did you betray us?"

Ben saw the other mages nodding along with Hadra. He was suddenly glad he'd insisted Towaal come along for the meeting.

Towaal smiled bitterly at the group. "Did I betray the Sanctuary, or is the Sanctuary betraying its purpose and us?"

The mages looked back at her, waiting on Hadra to respond, but the woman did not. She merely gestured to the empty chairs at the table. Towaal took one, and Ben sat beside her.

"Since I have been gone," began Towaal, "I have learned many things, things that were difficult to believe in some cases, and things that I do not think you would believe if I told you right now. I have seen horrors that I never could have imagined, and I've seen the courage it took to defeat those horrors. We've traveled from the City, to the Wilds, to Irrefort, to Qooten, to Akew Woods. I've met mages who have been alive since before the Sanctuary was formed and defeated mages who had been dead for months but kept on fighting."

Hadra's eyebrows rose. Ben suspected the woman had spent hundreds of years practicing a blank face, but she couldn't keep the look of shock out of her eyes as Towaal continued.

"One thing I suspected and have only been able to confirm recently is that the Veil herself is behind many of the ills that our world faces. Her schemes and her double-dealing have led us to a precipice. Below is chaos and death, perhaps for the entire continent. Northport has already fallen to a swarm of demons like this world has never seen. Other cities will fall as well if no one acts. On the cliff, though, is even worse in some ways. There, the Veil intends to rule over us as an immortal queen, and she may be able to do it if we don't stop her. There is a weapon which will give her power that is, literally, beyond your belief. I know, because I wouldn't have believed it either if I hadn't held the device in my hands."

In the tavern around them, the sounds of revelry bled through the walls and door, but the mages were stunned, speechless. Silence blanketed the room for a long moment.

"You've said more than we expected you to," murmured Hadra. "We-we thought you would tell us about the Veil's political machinations, her disregard for helping those she could. This is, well, I'm not sure what to make of what you've said."

"It seems fantastical, Karina," mentioned another of the women. "The Veil has gone astray, I agree, but it sounds like you are claiming she is evil. I know you were friends with her and that friendship ended badly, but calling her evil is a rather large leap, isn't it?"

Grim-faced, Towaal pulled a bag from under her cloak.

Ben looked away. He heard a thump and the gasp of indrawn breath.

"Look closely," instructed Towaal.

"What the hell are you thinking, Karina!" shouted Hadra. "Why are you walking around with something like that? That is disgusting!"

"Look closely."

Ben risked a glance and swallowed hard to keep the bile from blowing out of his gullet. He could only see the back of it, which didn't make it any more pleasant. He knew exactly what the front looked like. Instinctively, he gripped the scar on his arm, the one that had been dug into him when the undead mage Eldred had sunk her teeth into his flesh and torn off a chunk.

"Is t-that..." stammered one of the mages. "No, that is not possible."

"It is Eldred," stated Towaal.

One of the woman stood, calmly turned, shoved open the shutters that looked out the back of the tavern, and got violently sick.

"Eldred was killed when the initiate Amelie fled," muttered another mage. "She's been dead for nearly a year. I went to the woman's funeral. Where did you get this?"

"She was dead for nearly a year," agreed Towaal. "She didn't stop moving until we tore her head off a few weeks ago."

"I don't understand," admitted Hadra, a tremor of fear lacing her voice. A terrified pallor had leeched into her skin. She looked like she'd swallowed a frog. "Tell us... tell us what this is."

"I think they're ready to hear your story now, Ben."

ONCE TOWAAL PUT the head back into the magically sealed bag she'd been carrying it in, the discussion resumed and went late into the night. The women had been skeptical, but every time Ben started to feel doubt creeping in, he would lower his eyes to the bag containing Eldred's head. The mages' gaze would follow, and they couldn't help but recall the arcane runes carved into their former colleague's face and the damage that had been done to her during the final battle. To anyone with their knowledge of anatomy, it was evident that the worst of the injuries happened postmortem. With the head as an unsettling reminder and Towaal filling in with technical knowledge, Ben was able to finish his tale.

Hadra spoke first. "Avril alive after so many years? I was an initiate when she was raised to the Veil, you know. She was a schemer then. It seems nothing has changed."

The other mages murmured in response, all of them shaking their heads like they'd caught a puppy stealing the Newday roast.

Ben blinked. He'd expected them to be a bit more concerned about the army of demons that had just overthrown one of the largest cities in Alcott, or maybe that they were part of an organization led by a ruthless murderer who cared only about her own power and was about to get her hands on a legendary weapon that would make her unstoppable.

"The staff," mentioned Towaal. "That is of great concern to me, and it is something you could help us with. If the Veil obtains it and figures out how to use it, then we may have no chance to defeat her."

Hadra frowned, her lips forming into a thin line. "You are right, of course. After what she did to Eldred, I believe we can all agree Coatney is no longer fit to serve as the Veil. The process to depose her is rather complicated, though, and requires a majority of the Sanctuary's mages to agree. At any given time, a third of them are not in the City, so we'd need—"

Towaal held up a hand to stall the woman. "I don't think a vote is what the situation calls for."

"I know what you're implying, but we're not assassins, Karina," declared Hadra.

"You may not be, but she is. Do you think a vote to depose her would really work?" asked Ben. "The staff could be here in days. With that in her hands, how likely is it that the Veil would agree to step down even if all of the mages voted for it? She plotted to overthrow Avril hundreds of years ago and has been consolidating power since then. I don't think she's going to give it up that easily, certainly not because someone asks her nicely."

Hadra fell silent, but one of the other women responded, "He's right."

"I'm not comfortable with violence," murmured Hadra. "Not until we've had time to consider our options, to make sure that it truly is necessary. If we act without thinking, we're just as bad as you are accusing Coatney of being."

Ben glanced at Towaal in frustration, but instead of chiding the older mage, she stated, "We'll give you time to think. While you do, consider who else you can trust. Who else would oppose the evil that is at the heart of the Sanctuary? We do not have a lot of time, but we cannot rush into a plan tonight either. Help us figure out a way to address the threats to this world. At the least, I hope we can agree on that."

The six mages murmured assent, and with a look from Hadra, they stood to go.

"We will be in touch through the runaway," said the woman. Then, she followed her companions out of the room.

Ben sat, dumfounded. "You didn't even try to talk them into it!"

Towaal met his gaze, grim-faced. "It became apparent that they would not stoop to violence based on our words. They need to see the threat, to understand it viscerally. Apparently, Eldred's head wasn't enough. Ben, there was nothing we were going to say to convince them to battle against Milo and Coatney. We are on our own when it comes to the wyvern fire staff, as we were before, but in regards to the demons and the eventual unseating of the Veil, I believe they will come around. Now that the seed is planted, they will pay attention to what is happening. When Coatney bends or breaks the Sanctuary's rules and standards, which she will, they will have the evidence they need. They'll tell others, and when we leave to face the demons, will these women be able to sit on their hands knowing what we've shared?"

Ben eyed the mage uncertainly.

"Trust me, Ben. I have known these women for a very long while. There is a reason I left and joined you."

"I'll trust you on this," he agreed, clenching his fists and then slowly relaxing them. "Since the mages are unlikely to come around in the next few days, what do you suggest we do now?"

"Come up with a plan to find Milo and get that staff back."

9

BURNING TOWER

THE NEXT TWO DAYS WERE FILLED WITH TENSION AND BOREDOM. They squatted in the tower Renfro had found that overlooked the Sanctuary and constantly watched over the place with the spyglass. There was nothing to see, though, other than the everyday business of a large organization. The interesting stuff, like classes and experiments, happened inside and out of their view. Living quarters were placed so none of the windows were visible from the south where the City's towers were located, which Ben supposed was actually pretty sensible from an individual privacy standpoint. Still, it didn't help them. Outside of the tower, the Rat's urchins were allegedly hard at work looking for Milo, but there were no reports of him in the City.

Ben was sitting at the window, peering through the spyglass at small groups of guards and initiates strolling around the park at the northernmost tip of the island, the same place he and Amelie had jumped into the river. There was no sign of the ominous discs of light that had tracked them or the mages who had lobbed fireballs out over the water. It looked exceptionally peaceful, actually, like the people below didn't have a care in the world.

"This is the most pleasant-looking evil lair I've ever seen," grumbled Ben.

Amelie guffawed in very unladylike fashion. "Most of the people down there aren't evil, Ben."

"Tell that to the hordes of dead left in Eldred's wake."

"Towaal and I both lived there, remember?"

He grunted.

"You're not going to see the Veil standing on the lawn performing some evil ritual to bring a mage back from the dead. What we might see, though, is Milo. You should be looking for him."

Ben acknowledged that she was right, but he also couldn't help trying to find one building he recalled from that frantic night he had broken Amelie out. In the midst of the insane dash to find her and escape, he still distinctly recalled the place and the ominous sense of dread that emanated from it. It had been a low, white stucco building like all of the others, but from its closed doors and shuttered windows, a menacing red glow had pulsed steadily out. At the time, he'd never seen anything like it, but now, he knew the glow was mage-wrought. It was similar to the runes they'd seen which Towaal had labeled fatal. The building wasn't large, but the light inside was significant. That building was important. He was sure of it.

He'd discussed it with Amelie, but she wasn't familiar with the building. She thought it might be a part of a series of small laboratories and pointed them out to Ben, but he couldn't identify which one he'd seen. He'd been ready to give up and brush it aside until Amelie reminded him of who ran the laboratories at the Sanctuary. Eldred.

Whatever had been done to the former mage, Ben was certain that building had something to do with it. The sense of evil and dread hadn't been his imagination. It was real. If they'd created Eldred there, what was to stop the Veil from creating more of them? What if the mask was a sign she already had?

During the light of day, though, the Sanctuary couldn't be further from ominous, and there was no sign of the evil he suspected was taking place. Even in the autumn, the warm humidity of the City allowed flowers to bloom, grasses to grow green and wild, and trees to be covered in a thick layer of leaves. Ben continued to study the grounds of the Sanctuary, muttering to himself, until Rhys stumbled in from the stairwell.

"That bloody climb is going to kill me," groaned the rogue.

"You should just stay up here," remarked Ben.

"I know what the Sanctuary looks like," responded Rhys sarcastically.

"What are you doing here then?" asked Amelie. "That is an awfully long climb if you only came to complain."

The rogue grunted. "Renfro says he's got something suspicious, something we should look into."

"What is it?" asked Ben. "Has he found Milo?

"No, not Milo. At least, not yet. It's a tower on the eastern edge of the island. A nice place, he says. Mages keep coming and going, and he claims it's not the kind of place you'd expect to see them."

Ben lowered the spyglass and looked at his friend.

"It doesn't sound like much, I know," said Rhys, "but I spent years around here, and I agree something isn't right with this. Mages have rooms within the Sanctuary and staff to get them whatever they need. They rarely wander around the City with no purpose. If what the Rat said is accurate, something strange is going on in that place."

"So, why are they going there?" asked Amelie.

"That's the question, isn't it?" responded Rhys. "It probably has nothing to do with Milo, but I think it's worth investigating anything unusual in this town that has to do with the Sanctuary. We may have started a ball rolling with Hadra and the others, but taking the Veil down is going to take more than a handful of disgruntled mages."

"Fair enough," agreed Ben. He looked at Amelie, and she nodded.

Prem, who was lounging on the other side of the room, offered, "I can watch the gates while you're gone. No reason you have to stay here for that."

"Thanks," murmured Ben.

~

THEY MET Renfro at a small ale shop a few blocks away. It was set in the base of a broad tower, and the door faced away from the street. Ben commented on it, and Renfro explained that they weren't the only ones who wanted to avoid being in public. Ben began to wonder if Renfro's empire was as stable as his old friend said it was.

One of Renfro's big thugs was with him, and Ben spied the black ink of the rat tattoo peeking out from under his loose tunic. Stupid, thought Ben, making everyone get a rat tattoo. He'd wondered about it when he'd seen it on Martin, but seeing it on the thugs in the City made it that much more obvious. If anyone connected the tattoos to a burgeoning thieves' guild, they'd be able to hunt the Rat's minions down in no time. Renfro's ego put him at risk. It was not so different from when Ben had first met the thief. Then, his overreaching had gotten them both thrown into a cellar in Fabrizo.

"What are you thinking about?" asked Renfro.

Ben blinked at him. "Oh, nothing. Just wondering what these mages are doing, I guess."

"I have no idea what they're doing," said Renfro, "but I figured it was worth checking out. If you're going to get yourself in trouble by putting your nose in the Sanctuary's business, then you may as well put your nose in all of their business, right?"

Ben forced a grin. "Right."

Renfro and his thug led them through the City, sticking to the alleyways and passing through buildings when they could. Ben and his friends had altered their appearances as much as possible without standing out, but they were relying on the hoods of their cloaks and avoiding public areas to stay out of sight.

Finally, they made it to the tower Renfro had identified. He showed them a tavern across the way which had wide windows that were thrown open to catch a breeze in the warm, early fall air. The tower was a tall one, maybe thirty stories. Far above them, narrow bridges spanned between it and its neighbors. They swayed gently in the breeze. Ben tore his eyes away as he watched someone venture out on one carrying what looked to be far too heavy a load to manage safely so far above the ground.

"I don't know what the mages are doing here, but once I recognized the place, I knew I had to show you," said Renfro.

"What tower is this?" asked Ben.

The Rat cleared his throat and glanced at the girls out of the corner of his eye. "It's, ah, it's a place where men can meet women. They, ah…"

"Are you sure?" asked Amelie sharply.

"I'm sure."

Ben nodded, studying a group of women who exited the building with interest now. He wondered, "Mages?"

Towaal shook her head.

"How can you tell?" asked Ben.

"They're made up like trollops," mentioned Towaal dryly. "Look, that woman there has makeup caked on like someone did it with a paint brush. Mages don't age. They don't need that kind of cosmetics."

"Hadra looked pretty old," grumbled Ben.

"Hadra is old," replied Towaal. "She's probably five hundred years old. At that point, there's no reason for vanity."

"They don't look like trollops to me," argued Amelie.

"The Rat is right," agreed Rhys. "If I've seen one, I've seen a thousand. Those are ladies of the night."

"You're saying you haven't seen a thousand?" chided Amelie.

Rhys winked at her.

"I need to check into some things," muttered Renfro, staring up at the structure and the one across from it. "Lord Gulli bought this entire tower, which didn't come cheap, let me tell you. It's the biggest flop house on this island. I heard a rumor he's disappeared. He's been missing for days. If that's his place, we need to find out where he is."

"Good thinking," said Rhys, reluctantly agreeing with the little thief.

The Rat gestured for his man to lead the way, and they scurried back into the streets, moving quickly away from the tower.

"There'd better be more than prostitutes inside this place," snapped Towaal, watching another cluster of girls walk up the broad stone steps to the tower's lobby.

"Let's give it some time," suggested Rhys. "I don't think the Rat has the stones or the intelligence to pull a prank like that. If he said there were mages coming and going from here, it's because he thinks there are."

"Let's watch and see," suggested Ben. He nodded to the tavern Renfro had suggested. From its open windows, they'd have a clear view of the tower. That time of day, it was almost entirely empty. It was a perfect spot to wait inconspicuously.

Amelie sighed but followed him inside. Ben waved down a serving woman while his friends found a table by the windows. It'd look awfully strange to be camped out in a tavern and waiting for several bells without having a drink. They needed to blend in.

Several drinks later, Towaal tapped her fingers on the table and glanced out the open window. Two women, wearing plain but well-made dresses and no cosmetics, were ascending the stairs to the tower.

"Look at that," she said.

"Lady Greenfoot!" gasped Amelie. "I haven't seen her in over a year."

Ben frowned. The name sounded familiar.

"She wouldn't have stayed in Issen after it fell. The Coalition has no love for mages," said Towaal, her gaze following the women inside. "It makes sense she is in the City, but I can't tell you why she'd be going into a pleasure house."

"I knew her for years," said Amelie, her voice sounding distant and soft. "She was my tutor since I can recall having one."

"She's like any other mage of the Sanctuary now," interjected Rhys. "The Coalition knew you were here somehow. I'm not saying she's the one who told them, but someone did. Could have been the Veil or any number of other mages."

"It could have been one of my father's lackeys in Issen too," challenged Amelie.

Rhys shrugged. "We cannot trust anyone we don't know for sure is opposed to the Veil. Do you have any reason to think Greenfoot has loyalty to you and not Coatney?"

Amelie tipped up a half-full glass of wine and didn't answer.

"Renfro was right," said Ben, changing the subject. "There are mages going into that tower."

"Why would mages be frequenting a pleasure house?" wondered Rhys innocently, a mischievous sparkle in his eyes.

"Not for the same reason you would," responded Towaal crisply. "We can be sure of that, but as you say, Ben, the Rat was right. This is highly suspicious, and I think it's worth investigating further."

Ben and Rhys left to circle the tower, looking for a better vantage point or any other clues as to what may be going on inside that would attract the interest of mages. The base of the tower was as wide as the village green in Farview, and on the ground level, there were no windows, just four tall double doors that opened north, south, east, and west. Wide stairs led up to the doors, and they could see inside that the ground level was a large, open lobby. They weren't yet desperate enough to risk walking in, so they continued around until they found themselves back at the tavern.

"Nothing appears unusual from outside," reported Ben.

Amelie and Towaal looked distracted.

"What's going on?" asked Ben.

"There's something," murmured Amelie, "happening high up in that tower."

Ben raised an eyebrow.

"We can sense energy being manipulated," explained Amelie.

Ben looked to Rhys, and the rogue merely shrugged.

"For us to sense it from here, it must be an enormous effort," added Towaal.

"I don't see anything happening," said Ben, moving to the window and peering up to the top of the tower.

"Yes, and that's what is so interesting. This is far more power than Greenfoot and another mage could command on their own. There are very powerful mages up there, or several lesser ones, or maybe someone is drawing on a repository. That kind of activity would only be done for a purpose, and it's one we cannot discern."

"One we cannot discern from down here," corrected Rhys.

Towaal smiled grimly. "True enough."

"Someday," declared Ben, "we are going to come across an easy answer."

"That day is not today," said Amelie.

Rhys stood and cracked his knuckles.

"What's the…"

He trailed off and sat back down. He grabbed his ale mug and turned it up, his eyes following a new set of people ascending the stairs. Three men, all heavily armed, had falchions hanging from their sides and short spears resting on their shoulders. Knives and short swords dangled from half a dozen sheaths strapped to their bodies.

"Customers?" guessed Ben.

"No one goes that heavily armed into a whore house," said Rhys.

"What else do you have to tell us about these places?" questioned Amelie.

Rhys winked at her. "Seriously, that's the kind of place you don't bring weapons into. It's bad form in the seedy ones, and this tower looks far from seedy. It just wouldn't happen here. A place like this would turn heavily armed customers away in the blink of an eye. Their business is about staying outside of the concern of the watch, and you don't do that by getting heavily armed men drunk and aroused. That's a recipe for disaster, so you take their weapons. There are still brawls, but the bouncers can come in and quiet that down quick enough."

"What are they doing then?" asked Ben.

Rhys could only shrug.

A quarter bell later, the women shared a look.

"What?" asked Ben.

"The surge in energy has stopped," explained Amelie. "Whatever they were doing, it's done now."

Ben frowned, glancing out the window. All appeared as it had before.

Another quarter bell passed. Then, the two mages appeared at the doorway of the tower. Towaal hid her face, but Ben saw the women were paying no attention to anyone at the tavern or anywhere else for that matter. They had cold, determined expressions and strode with purpose north, toward the Sanctuary.

"How long do you think it would take to walk up to the top of that tower and then walk back down?" asked Rhys. "A quarter bell, I would guess."

Ben grunted. That was enough time for the armed men to walk up and the mages to stop what they were doing then walk back down.

"A pair of mages and a trio of heavily armed warriors all

possibly going to the same place near the top of a flophouse," said Amelie. "It sounds like the start of a joke, but for the life of me I can't think of what the punchline would be."

"Let's wait," said Ben. "We're here. We may as well see what else we can find out."

They sat patiently, watching the customers stream in and out of the tower.

"How many working girls can possibly be in that place?" wondered Amelie.

Rhys smirked. "A lot of the building is likely high-end taverns, durhang dens, private rooms, apartments for visiting dignitaries, batching facilities, that kind of thing, but you'd be surprised how many girls are in there. The City is big, obviously, but it's also a hub for trade and political maneuvering. A bunch of wealthy foreigners arrive and are told it will be a week before the Sanctuary can see them. What do you think they're going to do? They're not going to spend that week at the sculpture garden, I'll tell you that much."

Ben scooted closer to the window and looked up and down the street, not really certain what he was trying to see but knowing that just watching people come and go from the tower wasn't going to answer the questions he had bubbling in his head. He glanced up and smiled.

"Sky bridges," he said.

His friends clustered together, looking up the length of the tower. Half a dozen bridges connected to it far above their heads.

"Looking for a good time?" asked a voice behind them.

Ben spun, surprised at the voice, but a wave of relief immediately washed over him when he saw their serving woman standing at the table.

"That place costs a fortune," continued the woman. "I can send you somewhere that's half the price, and the girls are twice as good looking." She looked at Towaal and Amelie. "Girls, boys, whatever you need. There are cheaper and better places. Just mention my name, will ya? I know, I know, you're thinking I get a kick-back. Well, I do. Don't mean it ain't good advice. My sister works at the Monkey's Tail. Wouldn't let her work there if it wasn't clean, would I?"

Ben coughed.

"Another round of ales and wine, please?" asked Rhys.

The serving woman shrugged. "Just trying to save you some coin. Once you get enough drink in ya, and you want to go somewhere, let me know. The Monkey's Tail is just two blocks away."

Rhys nodded. "We'll consider it."

The woman turned to go, but Ben called out, "Hey, if this place is so expensive, what are all these sky bridges connecting to it? It seems like they'd want to keep an eye on people coming and going through the main floor, make sure they pay and all of that."

The serving woman grinned. "There's expensive, and then there's you-don't-even-want-to-know, son. Yeah, sure, they want to keep an eye on who is coming and going, but that don't mean all the patrons want to be seen. Lords, ladies, merchants, all us common folk know what they're up to, right? Knowing and seeing are different, though. If you're some fancy lord, your wife may suspect what you're up to, but if you're seen walking in the front door of that place, she has to do something about it."

"Makes sense," murmured Ben.

The woman nodded. "Lord Gulli is highborn himself, you know? It's not just some fancy moniker he took on to impress people. He was born into it. He knows how to cater to his ilk. It's why he's been so successful this last year. He's turned the Octopus into the busiest whore house in the City. That's why it's so overpriced, mind you." A call from across the room caught the serving woman's attention. "I better go 'fore these folk start pulling their own taps. I'll be back with your drinks."

"Well," remarked Rhys after the woman passed out of ear shot. "That is interesting."

Amelie looked up at the sky bridges again. "Do you think we

should try to access one of the bridges? There is one way up there. It looks like it connects to the top floor or close enough. Haven't you said, Rhys, that it's always better to go in near the top?"

"It is," confirmed the rogue.

Ben shook his head. "No, I think before we go charging in there, we should check with Renfro."

"Renfro?" asked Rhys. "You want him to make a plan?"

"He hates Gulli, and he has resources," reminded Ben. "He's the one who found the mages coming in here in the first place, remember?"

Rhys sighed. "We're never going to be rid of him, are we?"

AFTER RETURNING TO THEIR HIDEOUT, they sent word to Renfro, ate, and rested the rest of the afternoon and evening. As darkness fell on the City, the Rat and his runaway mage, Sincell, came to find them. Renfro had his two thugs as well. Ben didn't think either one ever left his old friend's side.

"My boys and I tend to avoid such high-end establishments. They always have connections to centers of power, watch commanders, lords, that kind of thing. Not the people we want to steal from," said Renfro, a smile splitting his face. "To tell you the truth, I've never even been inside, but with a chance to get back at Gulli, I've decided I should come with you. I want to help."

Ben eyed Renfro's attire skeptically. He was certainly dressed for the part. The Rat had on black trousers, a black tunic, a black cloak, black gloves, and two daggers with black wire wrapped around the hilts. He crossed the room, his black cloth boots making no sound on the thick carpets. He made to pour himself a glass of wine from their decanter but set it back down when he found it was empty.

"You need more wine," remarked Rhys, drawing a frown from Renfro.

The Rat sat down the decanter and eyed everyone else's clothing. "Do you need to change?"

"Renfro," explained Rhys. "We're going to be walking through the most populous city in Alcott. This isn't a town you can scamper along the rooftops of the towers. There are lights on every street corner and most of the windows will be lit as well. We're going to a tower that will be at peak business over the next several bells. If we want to stay hidden, we do it in plain sight by blending in. You, ah, well, you'll stand out like a sore thumb. You couldn't look more like a thief if you tried."

Renfro stared back at him blankly before finally responding, "Rhys, it's night outside. It's dark. You wear black to blend into the night. They do it in every story."

The rogue drew a breath, preparing to respond, but Ben interjected, "We didn't bring anything appropriate for skulking, Renfro. Hopefully, we can make do. I'm assuming you found a place we can observe the top of the tower? Lead on."

The Rat nodded briskly. "Yes, I'll lead the way."

Behind his back, Sincell winked at them. The thugs maintained the same stoic expressions that they always had.

In a quiet column, they made their way down the stairs and out of the seedy apartments that they were housed in. Within the decrepit structures, Renfro had lined the floors and walls with luxury. Impulse buying of expensive items that he didn't need or know how to appreciate, thought Ben.

Outside, the streets were filled with the detritus of life. Unlike other areas of town, no major effort was made to beautify this quarter. There were no parks, no statues.

"The Sanctuary doesn't spend much here, do they?" mumbled Ben, thinking about how the mages were still responsible for management of the city.

"Out of sight, out of mind," responded Rhys. "You'll never catch a mage in this neighborhood."

Towaal coughed behind them, and Ben looked over his shoulder.

Rhys snorted. "In your hundreds of years living in the City, how many times have you been on this street?"

"What'd you say?" asked the Rat from up front. "Hundreds of years?"

"Looks like these buildings have been here hundreds of years," replied Rhys quickly. "What do you think?"

"I don't know," answered Renfro. After a moment, he thought to add, "Or care."

Sincell, who surely overheard them, didn't bother to clarify the discussion for her boss. Ben began to wonder why exactly she was working for him. A mage, even a runaway one, would have plenty of opportunities to make a fortune out in the world. She had no obvious reason to be employed by a cut-rate thief master. Ben resolved to keep an eye on the woman.

They made it through the backstreets and alleys of the city without incident, except for when they crossed one major thoroughfare and spotted a knot of the Sanctuary's guards. They ducked out of sight and waited nervously as the men passed, but it was a routine patrol, and the men didn't pay any attention to their party. They were likely looking for more obvious signs of disruption like tavern brawls and thieves climbing up the outsides of buildings. They were a show of force to discourage surreptitious activities. Ben grinned, thinking about what they were intending to do.

"What?" asked Amelie.

"Nothing," he whispered back.

She raised an eyebrow.

"Since the day we fled this place, I've been itching to come back and settle the score," he said. "For months, the Veil's minions chased us from one side of this continent to the other.

Then, she had her spy Milo go with us to an entirely different continent. She sent hunters after us, mages, even an undead, uh, whatever Eldred was. For the first time, we're back on her turf, looking to strike a blow."

A smile stole onto Amelie's lips.

"When you put it like that," she said. She looked at the back of the Sanctuary's guards as they vanished down the street, "maybe this will be fun."

They started off again, weaving away from the main roads until they found themselves close to the tower, the Octopus as the barmaid had called it. Ben stared up at the soaring spire of stone, wondering why it was called that.

Instead of going straight to the tower, Renfro turned two blocks before and led them into a narrow tower nearby that housed a number of leather workers. They began to climb a tight spiral in the center, moving higher and higher. Most of the shops were closed, but the people in the ones that were open barely spared a glance at Ben and his party. They were bent over, focused on their crafts. Apprentices, guessed Ben, scrambling to finish projects after their masters had gone home for the day. It was getting late, but the stairwell in a commercial tower would be as busy as a street elsewhere.

After ten flights up, judging by the ache in Ben's calves, they took a turn and stepped out onto a narrow stone bridge. The City rose around them, a forest of towers sparkling with lit windows. It would have been beautiful if Ben wasn't squeezing his eyes shut and trying to ignore the fatal drop below them.

"At least it's a stone bridge," mentioned Amelie.

He nodded and cracked one eye open enough to follow her down the center of the path.

Sincell, evidently feeling none of Ben's fear of heights, was leaning over a chest-high rail and peering below them. Ben shuddered.

"Guard troop," she said. She looked back and saw Ben and

Amelie were venturing nowhere near the edge. "Can't you hear the boots?"

Ben concentrated and heard she was right. A company of men was marching below, their heavy military-grade boots stomping loudly on the cobblestone streets.

"Hundred of them, I'd guess," added the rogue mage.

Renfro, peering back to see why they weren't coming, called, "It has nothing to do with us."

Ben hoped the Rat was right. He breathed deeply and followed his old friend onto the bridge. Finally, they made it through the door into the next tower.

"I hope we don't have to do that again," Ben said. His heart was still racing after being so high up in the open air.

"Once or twice more," responded Renfro. "Maybe three times."

Rhys slapped Ben on the back. "You've always survived when you've fallen off things like this before, right? No reason to worry now."

Ben groaned.

"Come on," hissed Renfro. "We have four more bridges to get across before we get to where we can spy on the top of the Octopus."

FIVE BRIDGES and numerous flights of stairs later, they stood in a room with the double doors thrown wide to an open-air balcony. A waist-high balustrade blocked a twenty-five-story drop to the streets below. Just two stories down, though, was a rope-and-wooden-slat bridge. It was wide enough for three big men to walk abreast, but as they watched, it swayed gently back and forth in the steady night breeze.

"Why?" groaned Ben. "Why would you make a bridge this

high out of rope! What happened to the stone ones that we crossed below?"

"This high up," explained Rhys, "the towers sway. Not much unless it's a really strong wind but enough that you want a bridge to be able to flex with the motion. Otherwise…"

Rhys dropped his hand and whistled, lowering it until his palm smacked into his other hand. Ben winced at the slap and took an involuntary step back from the edge of the balcony.

"How did you find this apartment?" wondered Amelie.

She was looking around the room they were standing in. The walls were lined with red silk. A giant bed with luxurious gold linens sat against one wall. On the opposite wall and the ceiling were mirrors. Golden lampstands stood scattered around. Against the third wall hung a dozen whips. Black leather outfits and black iron chains were stored in a gilded, glass-doored wardrobe. Amelie was examining the whips and outfits. She gave a mischievous look back at Ben. He frowned, choose to ignore her, and turned to Renfro.

"Gerrol Gundar," answered the Rat. "Owner of the Lucky Siren gambling parlor, which takes up the four floors below us. He also owns a number of, well, downright predatory gambling halls along the water front. A gang of thieves started knocking over the places, coming in with heavy muscle, scaring off the gamblers as well as stealing whatever coin they could get their hands on. Classic smash and grab. Gerrol got in touch with me and begged for my help, so I put a stop to it."

"How'd you negotiate with the muscle?" asked Rhys.

Renfro blinked at him. "They were my guys. I just told them to stop and sent 'em somewhere else."

"How did he know they were yours?" asked Ben.

One of the Rat's thugs let out a wheeze, which sounded suspiciously like he was trying to cover a laugh.

"Know they were mine?" exclaimed Renfro. "Damn, Ben, if Gerrol ever found out that was my muscle, I'd be flying like a rock outta this tower instead of getting the use of it for the night. You'd be scraping me off the cobblestones."

The thug wheezed again, and Ben wondered if maybe it was him who'd been smashing up Gerrol's gambling dens.

"That's not important," declared Renfro. "What is important is that we have a perfect view of the top six floors of the Octopus. I've asked around, and none of those are open to the public. Either they're for more exclusive whores than even I can find out about, or it's private quarters for someone important. None of the thieves knows what happens up there."

"Someone important," murmured Towaal.

She was standing near the balustrade, eyeing the tower across from them. The clear windows at the top of the Octopus were just two hundred paces away, but all of the lights were out. They may as well have been solid stone.

"Can you send a light over there?" asked Ben.

"We could," responded Towaal. "Remember, though, something was happening up there, something that required a great deal of energy. I'm afraid the place could be warded, or maybe there is someone there in the dark, sleeping or on watch. Either way, it's too great a risk. We need to stay here until we get a view into those windows."

"At daylight, we need to be gone," declared Renfro.

"Gerrol only owes you one night?" asked Towaal. "He's a business man. I'm sure we can convince him to let us stay longer."

Renfro scratched at the back of his head and wouldn't meet Towaal's eyes. "Well, it's not exactly Gerrol I dealt with. It might have been one of his men, the manager of the gambling den. He's the one who contacted me and arranged for my help. He threw a little party tonight and is making sure Gerrol is busy. By daylight, my guy said to be gone."

"When Gerrol gets back," added Sincell, "he'll find out what happened to his guards. We should definitely be gone by then unless we want to fight our way out of this tower."

"Bloody hell, Renfro," barked Rhys. "What did you do to his guards?"

The Rat stayed silent.

"It doesn't matter," interjected Ben. "What's done is done. We have until morning."

He was seething with frustration at his old friend's risky plan, but it was too late to change, and so far, it had worked. The room was perfect for their intentions, and they had it for the night. They could observe the Octopus, see who was on the top floors, and then come up with a plan. Once they knew what was going on, he hoped an idea would materialize.

They settled down to wait, Renfro's thugs moving to watch the hallway outside of the apartment. Towaal found a chair on the balcony, and Sincell sat near but not next to the mage. Renfro lounged in a chair on the other side of Sincell, his eyes drooping shut. Rhys started rooting around through Gerrol's personal items, and Ben began to pace.

"Are you sure that is wise?" asked Ben, looking askance at Rhys as he shuffled through an ornate desk. The top was a pale pink marble, and from a certain angle, it appeared to be phallus-shaped. Probably his imagination, thought Ben.

"Renfro killed the man's guards," remarked the rogue dryly. "I don't think we can do anything more to piss him off."

Ben shrugged and resumed pacing until, on the other side of the room, he saw Amelie snap a short leather whip.

"What are you doing with that?" exclaimed Ben.

She smiled at him, but she didn't answer.

Ben flushed. Muttering to himself, he moved to stand several paces behind Towaal just inside the door to the balcony.

He asked her, "Can you feel anything?"

"No," responded Towaal. "I am not delving the tower, though, merely waiting to see what happens."

Ben settled in to wait as well. Behind them, he could hear Amelie playing with the whips and Rhys rooting through drawers and dumping their contents on the floor. In front of him, he only heard the wind. He frowned. There was something else. He moved to railing and, not resting his weight on it, looked over. Below them, crossing a bridge on the opposite side of the tower and several floors down was movement.

"What is that?" asked Sincell, joining him at the balustrade.

He shrugged. "It looks like people crossing, but they're doing it in the dark, and there's a lot of them. That isn't just one highborn trying to stay out of sight while he gets his jollies."

They watched as the dark shapes streamed across into the Octopus. Moments later, lights flickered on at the top of the tower across from them.

"Mage-light," hissed Sincell.

Towaal moved forward and knelt behind the stone railing. Their room was dark, and at two hundred paces away in the night, no one should be able to see them, but they were spying on mages. Ben ducked down as well. The companions lined the railing, peering between the stonework.

"We need Corinne's eyes for this," mumbled Amelie.

Ben nodded silently and glanced at Rhys. The rogue's eyes were trained on the tower across from them, and he appeared to be ignoring Amelie's comment.

"I can see," offered Prem, holding up the spyglass they used to look over the Sanctuary. "I knew this would come in handy."

"Tell us what's going on," said Towaal. "All I can see are shapes of people."

"There are four people inside a lit room," described Prem, peering through the tube. "One man, three women."

"Not all mages then," murmured Sincell.

"They're talking and moving about," continued Prem. "The man got a drink, but the others did not. His shirt is untucked, and he has a long, unruly mop of curly hair. He may have been sleeping. It looks like the other three are together. Two of them are hanging back, while one woman appears to be doing all of the talking. I think she's scolding the curly-haired man. She's pointing at him and gesturing. She has a plain dress on. Green. Red hair hanging to her shoulders. She looks young and pretty. A bit of cosmetics but not much although it could be freckles. She's a hand shorter than the man."

"Is she wearing jewelry?" asked Towaal quietly, her eyes squeezed tightly shut.

"Silver bracelets, I think," said Prem. "A necklace, but I can't see it well."

"How tall is she?"

Prem frowned. "It's difficult to tell, but she could be about my height."

Towaal grunted.

"You don't think…" murmured Sincell, glancing at Towaal.

"The curly-haired man disappeared, went upstairs," said Prem, her low voice droning in a constant rundown of what the people were doing.

"What does the woman's hair look like?" interjected Towaal. "You said it was red. Is it straight, curly, what else?"

"A little curly, wavy, maybe," answered Prem. She continued, unaware of the pained look on Towaal and Sincell's faces. "The woman is moving about, searching the room or possibly cleaning up, which doesn't make any sense to me. The curly-haired man is returning now. I think he changed shirts. He also has a stick or a weapon maybe. It's long, pale."

"This is not good," moaned Towaal.

"Wait. You think…" Ben trailed off as he realized what Towaal and Sincell had both already understood.

"The man gave the woman the object," continued Prem. "She's sitting down now, examining it. Her companions have come close to look as well."

Towaal appeared as if she was about to be sick.

"Do you want to have a glance?" asked Prem, finally sensing Towaal's distress.

"No," mumbled the mage. "I don't need to."

"She couldn't be foolish enough to activate it here," said Amelie, panic lacing her voice. "Even for someone as powerful as her, that's insanity."

"She's probing it," explained Towaal. "Delving into the staff."

"The staff?" asked Prem. "What staff… Oh. I thought, I thought it'd be bigger than this. This looks like it's only a pace long."

"That's it," acknowledged Ben. "It has to be."

"What the bloody hell are you all talking about?" asked Renfro. He shifted on his haunches, clearly annoyed that everyone else was aware of what was happening, and he was not.

"The wyvern fire staff," explained Ben. "They think the woman is the Veil, and she's holding the weapon we meant to retrieve."

"Oh," croaked Renfro. "Damn."

"What do we do?" demanded Amelie. "We can't let her keep it. She's outside of the walls of the Sanctuary. We have to stop her now before she takes it back with her."

"The figures below on the bridge," responded Ben. "They're the same as the guards on the street before. A hundred men, all in that tower. That can only be her guard."

"And whoever is in the room with her," mentioned Rhys. "Mages, I think we can assume. Not to mention, she's holding the damn wyvern fire staff. We can't come straight at her while she has that."

Towaal, Amelie, and Sincell suddenly turned back to look across to the tower.

"What is happening now?" barked Towaal to Prem.

"The woman handed the staff back to the man," described the guardian. "She is standing, settling a cloak around her shoulders. Her companions are sitting down, though. The man doesn't look happy, but he is holding the staff again… Okay, she's leaving now, but the others are staying. Are you sure that's the Veil?"

"I'm sure," growled Towaal. "And there is only one person that man can be."

"When the Veil and the guards depart, we're not going to get a better opportunity," stated Ben. "Whatever they are doing, they don't want it done where eyes in the Sanctuary can see it. That may change."

"Tonight," agreed Amelie. "It has to be tonight."

"Wait. What are you talking about?" asked Renfro.

"Stealth or brute force?" queried Rhys, standing and methodically adjusting his weapons.

Ben studied the lit windows across from them for a long moment before finally answering, "We wait until the Veil and her guards have plenty of time to get away, and then brute force."

A BELL LATER, they stood in a doorway, looking at a long, wood-slatted bridge that extended out over the open air between the towers. A steady breeze blew Ben's cloak to wrap around his legs before it twisted free and snapped in the wind.

Behind them, the click of coins sliding against each other punctuated the low hum of discussion and the tinkling laughter of working girls who implored their clients to bet a few more coins, take a little more risk.

The bridge led to the Octopus, where those girls would take their clients after they'd lost enough coin at the tables. They'd need strong spirits and consoling, which would cost them even more coin. Two wide bouncers huddled across the way and ducked back in the entry of the tower to avoid the cool breeze, paying little attention to Ben and his party. Ben knew that would change as soon as they stepped onto the bridge.

"The moment we get inside there, more men may come running," declared Rhys. "Getting through them probably won't be a problem. These men will be big and strong, but they'll be used to tossing out soft-bodied highborn who can't pay their bills. They won't be prepared for steel. Getting back out may be an issue. There will be enough of them that even if we did try to cut our way through, it'd take us all day to reach the bottom of the tower. By then, there's no telling what will be waiting for us."

"What do you suggest then?" asked Renfro.

Rhys shrugged. "Nothing. I'm just saying it's going to be a problem."

"Then, why are we doing this?" exclaimed the small thief. "Let's turn around while we can and come up with a real plan."

"We have a plan," said Ben, gripping the hilt of his longsword.

"What is it?" implored the Rat, his eyes wide.

"Smash our way in, get the staff, and then come up with a plan to escape. I have some ideas, but none of it matters unless we get that staff."

Renfro gave Ben a flabbergasted look and babbled incoherently. Sincell placed a hand on his shoulder and whispered in his ear, trying to calm him down.

The Rat's thugs shifted nervously, eyeing their boss, but not voicing their obvious trepidation at being involved in such a risky endeavor.

Ben tapped Rhys on the shoulder. "You go first. Use your long knives. There won't be much room to swing a longsword."

The rogue snorted. "This is not my first time assaulting a whorehouse, Ben. I know what I'm doing."

Prem slipped by Ben and took a place next to Rhys.

Ben turned to the mages. "We're going to need you, but wait until the last possible moment. Once you enter the fight, the Sanctuary could find out we're here."

"We know, Ben," assured Amelie patiently.

He looked back out to the bridge and swallowed. Rhys didn't wait for the go ahead. He and Prem stepped out and began casually strolling closer to the guards. They'd strike quickly and hopefully quietly, but they all knew it wouldn't be long before someone sounded an alarm.

Ben waited with the others, gripping the hilt of his longsword tightly.

Near the end of the bridge, Rhys raised a hand and waved to the guards at the door. They crossed their arms and glared back at him. Suddenly, Rhys struck right, and Prem swept to the left, both of them wielding their long knives and cutting down the guards before they could respond.

As soon as he saw the guards drop, Ben started across the bridge, his stomach dropping as his boots clattered across the wooden planks. The bridge swayed, and a wave of dizziness struck him, but he kept going. Stopping wasn't going to make it go by any quicker. In the doorway to the Octopus, Rhys was staring down at the two big bodies of the bouncers.

"Can we hide them?" asked Ben when he arrived.

The rogue shook his head and gestured to a hallway beyond the men. It was stone and lined with silver lanterns hanging from the ceiling. The floor was covered in a plush carpet. There was only one door at the far end.

"Can't put them anywhere in there," said Rhys, "so unless you want to toss them off the side of the bridge…"

Ben looked at Rhys grimly. "It would take at least a quarter bell for someone to walk up from the base of the tower, right? Maybe even longer if no one knew which floor the bodies came from. A quarter bell should be enough time to raid Milo's rooms."

The rogue smiled and bent to grab one of the dead men. "I like your style."

With the guards disposed of at least for the moment, they scurried down the hallway, the scent of expensive oils filling Ben's nostrils. At the far end there was a heavy wooden door studded with iron bolts and a fanciful octopus outlined in silver. The door evoked an aura of hidden mysteries and luxury, but it was also sturdy and would withstand anything short of a battering ram. There was a small window set at eye level, though, and Ben was certain someone was on the other side ready to look out.

Rhys glanced at Amelie. "You knock."

She raised an eyebrow at him.

"Tell them you're late for your shift," added Rhys. He turned to Prem. "You too, but keep your right hand behind your back. It's covered in the guard's blood."

Amelie sighed and pounded her fist on the door. Within heartbeats, the window slid open. The men and Towaal pressed their bodies against the wall near the door where hopefully they wouldn't be seen. Amelie and Prem stood in the center of the hall and smiled coyly at the face on the other side.

"You don't look like the kind of customers who come through here. What do you want?" barked a voice.

"Hi, honey, we're late for our shift. I didn't want to go in the normal way and get caught."

"You're late, huh? That is your problem, not mine."

"We got caught at a private party," purred Amelie. She shook her coin purse. "It was well worth whatever punishment the mistress hands out. I can make it worth it for you, too."

Ben heard a grunt. The man paused before snarling, "You know that's not allowed."

"Oh, of course it isn't," responded Amelie, her lips forming into an oval of mock surprise. "We could get in trouble for that kind of thing… if someone found out."

"Girl, this ain't a private hallway, and whatever you say, I'm not leaving my post."

Prem stepped close to Amelie and looped her arm around the former highborn's waist. "When we work together, we can work quickly."

She licked her lips and buried her face in Amelie's neck. There was a pause. Then, the window in the door slid shut, and Ben heard a heavy bolt being thrown. Rhys, a grin stretching from ear to ear, stepped out and kicked the door, flinging it back against the guard. They heard the man crash to the tile floor, and Rhys rushed inside. A curse sounded from further away. The rogue's boots pounded as he dashed across the room.

Ben followed a moment later and found himself in an oak-paneled room. The first guard was lying unconscious beside the door. Rhys was dragging a second body behind a desk where Ben saw they must check in patron's cloaks and weapons before they proceeded further.

"Drag that body over here before you slice his throat," instructed Rhys. "We can stash them behind the desk. It isn't much, but at a casual glance, maybe no one will notice anything amiss."

Ben grabbed the man's arms to drag him and said, "He's not our enemy, we leave him alive."

Rhys frowned, but didn't object.

"Somewhere, we need to find a stairwell that goes up," said Towaal. "I'm guessing it's at the center of the building."

"Let's go," said Ben before striding to another doorway and pulling it open.

The smell of scented oil grew stronger. It was the soft fragrance of flowers. A huge room spread out in front of him, taking up the entire width of the tower. One corner was dominated by a bar, staffed by half a dozen barmen, all dressed in spotless white. Behind them, an open doorway which Ben guessed would lead to stairs. No way they could get there without being seen.

The floor of the room was covered in low couches, silk partitions, and scantily clad women. They hovered around several dozen men who lounged alone or in small groups. The girls were feeding the men cheeses and fruits, fetching drinks, topping off water pipes, and cuddling up close to them. In the center of the room was a giant column that supported the structure and likely housed the main stairs.

"Ben," hissed Rhys. "We'd better try to blend in. Wink at the girls or something."

Amelie snorted, and Ben stared at his friend.

"I'm not sure this is a good time for jokes," he said.

"Who said it was a joke?" asked Rhys. He then pointed to the center of the room. "That's where we want to go. We need to attract as little attention as possible on the walk over."

Attempting to appear like he belonged, Ben sauntered into the room. At first, no one paid them any mind. It seemed patrons would come, find a comfortable seat, and then the girls would begin to flock. He saw them watching, judging where they would sit, and who would be the closest to their party. The women in their group got some strange looks, but Ben saw at least a few women who didn't appear to be working scattered around the room.

"Don't run," cautioned Rhys, slowing Ben's pace. With his voice pitched so the party could hear and no one else, he advised, "Don't be afraid to look at them. Keep your face blank, though, and if they start to approach, just shake your head subtly."

"You know a lot about how to act in these places," chided Amelie.

Across the room, Ben saw a pair of heavily muscled guards. His eyes scanned the space and picked out more of them. At least a dozen. He was confident he and his friends could take them, but they were on the twenty-fifth floor. If there were a dozen men per floor, this was going to get ugly.

"Damn," grumbled Rhys.

Ben followed his friend's gaze and saw the doorway leading to the stairs. It was flanked by more heavily armed guards. Fifty paces and they'd be there.

"We're going to have to fight our way through those two," whispered Rhys. "No way they will let us go upstairs without explaining ourselves."

A slender girl, clad in the flimsiest silk robe Ben had ever seen, gasped, a manicured hand covering her painted lips. Ben saw her eyes were fixed on their weapons.

"How much for the night?" Sincell quickly asked the girl. "My friends and I are looking for a party. Do you have friends here that could join us?"

The runaway mage cut her eyes to Rhys, and he nodded. He quickened his pace. The guards at the door noticed them coming twenty paces away. Ben saw one of the men frown, clearly seeing that Ben's party wasn't typical in such a place.

"Can you tell me," called Rhys, "where I can take a piss? I drank enough ale to float a boat. Gotta go make room for more, ya know? Figured you boys would get upset if I dangled it out the window."

That got them within half a dozen pace of the guards. Ben didn't wait any longer. He charged one of the men. The surprised guard didn't have time to react before Ben was on him. At a run, he smacked the palm of his hand into the man's face, throwing the man back where his head crunched loudly against the stone wall behind him.

Ben hoped he hadn't killed the man. Being a guard at a brothel shouldn't be a death sentence, but if they didn't fight their way through these men, a lot more were going to die when the Veil figured out how to activate the wyvern fire staff.

The second guard went down quickly as well when Rhys snatched a table off the floor and swept it into the side of the poor fellow's head. Behind them, shouts rang out as the other guards saw what was happening.

"Now's the time to run," urged Ben. "We'll find a defensible spot on the stairs or at a doorway and hold it. Towaal, you're with me. We're going to find Milo. Everyone else, watch our backs and keep the guards from coming up the stairs."

They charged up the stairwell, quickly leaving the public areas behind. The luxurious trappings didn't disappear, though. If anything, the area they entered was even nicer. It was also guarded by a thick steel door, a stoic copper face on it.

"It's not real," declared Prem.

Ben trusted she knew what she was talking about. He turned to the others. "Here's the spot. Can you hold this?"

"We've got it," said Rhys. "We'll keep them off your back as long as we can, but hurry."

"How do we get out of here?" complained Renfro, looking back down the stairwell.

"Don't worry. I've got an idea," declared Ben.

"What?"

"You don't want to know," insisted Ben.

The rogue slammed the door shut and slid a wrist-thick iron bar down to lock the door. A boom echoed through the stairwell, cutting off the conversation.

"Should hold for a bit, at least," murmured the rogue.

Ben heard the muffled sound of the guards racing behind them on the other side, but a dozen strong men had no chance to get through that barrier. They'd need tools or a mage.

"Go," said Amelie.

Ben nodded. Then, he and Towaal went higher. One floor up was a kitchen and what looked to be staff quarters, then a decadent reception hall, then a stunning dining room, and finally, the room they'd spied from the other tower. Milo wasn't there, but two other people were. Two women wearing well-made but simple dresses.

"Karina!" exclaimed one of them.

"Find Milo," screeched Towaal. She faced the women and raised her hands. A heartbeat later, a shower of sparks blasted against an invisible barrier. Through gritted teeth, Towaal yelled, "I can handle them. Go!"

The women were deep in the room, and the path to the stairs was open. Below, Ben heard a sharp clanging start as if someone was battering the steel door with a hammer. They weren't going to be exiting down those stairs, he realized. He ignored the dizzy spell that assailed him as his back-up plan flashed through his mind. First, he had to find Milo and get the staff.

A sharp crackle of released energy followed him up the stairs as he progressed deeper into the rooms. Apartments, he realized, and not cheap ones. Expansive rooms with views of the river, fine furniture, and high enough to catch a constant breeze. Prime real estate, as long as you didn't mind sleeping on top of a brothel. He wondered how Milo had managed to find himself in such luxurious rooms.

Ben made it up another flight of stairs and ducked his head into an open chamber. A glint of light and a blur of motion saved his life. He jumped back, and a short spear thudded into the wooden door beside his head. The steel head of the weapon was buried halfway into the wood, and the shaft vibrated with the impact. A short spear, just like Milo favored.

"Milo, give up the staff!" called Ben.

There was a pause. "Ben?"

"We know you took it, and we know you're planning to give it to the Veil," stated Ben. "You have no idea what that woman intends to do with the thing, how powerful it will make her. Milo, there is still time to stop this!"

A soft chuckle sounded from a different side of the room. Milo's voice floated out. "You have no clue, do you?"

Ben gripped his longsword, mind churning. When he'd glanced in, the room was open and dark. Milo could be anywhere inside, waiting for Ben to stick his neck out again. Taking time and talking him down wasn't an option, though. Sooner or later, the guards would break through the door below.

"So self-assured that you can make a difference, so ignorant of the world," continued Milo. "What are you going to do, Ben? I'm guessing you don't have a plan, do you? That was the most frustrating thing about traveling with your group, you know. Stumbling into one disaster after another, never understanding what was happening, and never knowing what you'd do next. Pathetic."

He's stalling, realized Ben. The longer it took to face him, the more time guards and mages would have to arrive and corner Ben and his friends. He had to act. He dove through the door, tucking his shoulder and rolling across the floor. Another spear flashed overhead and clanged against a stone wall. Ben rolled to his feet, longsword held ready.

Moonlight streamed in through the windows, the only light in the room. Milo stood, silhouetted before a window, another spear cocked to throw. It streaked toward Ben and he spun his blade, catching the side of the shaft and brushing the projectile away. Milo snatched another spear off a rack beside him. There were a dozen of the things there.

"Ah, hell," muttered Ben under his breath. "Who keeps that many spears?"

He couldn't clearly see Milo's face, but he could imagine the broad grin that would be plastered there. No sense waiting for the former apprentice to get tired of throwing spears. Ben charged, sword ready to deflect another missile.

Instead of throwing, Milo snatched a second spear and sprung at Ben, one bladed-tip jabbing, one sweeping low.

Ben parried the thrust and stepped into the blow of the second weapon, taking a strike on his leg from the wooden shaft but avoiding the steel.

Milo danced back, his arms weaving sinuously in the dim room, the steel tips of the razor-sharp blades reflecting the moonlight from the windows.

"Such a foolish quest," chided Milo. "Such a waste of time until, despite all odds, you actually stumbled across something worthwhile. Something you stupidly left lying in the open. The one device that could ensure victory for whoever found it and you fools just left it there where anyone could pick it up. No matter. You never would have had the guts to sacrifice and figure out how to use the thing. Opening a vein for ultimate power? No, Benjamin Ashwood would never do that. You'd never sacrifice someone's life to gain the full power of the weapon. That's why you can never be a real leader, you can never make the hard decisions."

Ben kept his eyes on Milo, his mind swirling, trying to process his comments. What sacrifice? Evidently, Milo knew far more about the weapon than Ben and his friends. What else did he know?

"Are you sure you aren't the one about to be sacrificed?" probed Ben. "The Veil doesn't care about you."

Milo snorted. "You don't know anything about my mother or what she cares about. It's funny, actually, how you inadvertently handed us the staff which she has been searching the world for. You think she doesn't care about me? You should have seen her face when I showed her what I'd found."

"Your mother?"

Milo fell silent, circling Ben, his spears jabbing and feinting like tongues of two venomous snakes tasting the air, waiting for the right time to strike.

Understanding spread through Ben's mind like a rising sun. Milo's mother. A person who could teach him to harness his will, to find masters to train him with weapons, who would know to send him to the Librarian in Northport, who could pay for the apartment they were standing in. Eldred's reluctance to attack once she saw Milo, his knowledge of things he shouldn't have known, it all fit together. With a flash, Ben understood why the young man was staying outside of the Sanctuary and still had the staff. The world couldn't know the Veil had a son, and there was no one else she'd trust to keep the weapon out of sight from the rest of the Sanctuary.

Without warning, the former apprentice surged toward Ben, lightning quick thrusts from his spears coming in a flurry. Ben swiped his blade back and forth, parrying the strikes. Milo wasn't committing to any of them, though. He was merely probing, waiting for a gap in Ben's defense. Then, he would put his weight behind a blow.

One of the spears came close, and Ben jumped in shock when a crackle of lightning burst out from the tip of the weapon and struck his left hand. A jolt coursed through his body, and it was all Ben could do to keep moving, stumbling back, thrashing wildly trying to keep Milo from delivering a fatal strike. The moonlight passed across the former apprentice's face, and Ben saw him smiling coldly. There wasn't a trace of fear, just pleasure. He was enjoying this.

"Didn't see that coming?" snickered Milo. "You never do, do you? You didn't see my betrayal coming, I bet. Oh, I wish I could have been there to see your faces. It would have almost been worth spending a few more bells around that insufferable Towaal just to see your dumb looks. It must have been glorious."

"You didn't stay, though, did you?" snapped Ben. "Had to run home to Mommy."

Milo twirled one spear above his head and then lashed out with it, swinging it like a whip.

Ben easily ducked under and jabbed his longsword at the young man. It caught nothing but air as Milo stepped out of reach.

"I've been training with these spears and my will for decades," said Milo. "How long have you been using that sword? Do you honestly think you can withstand me if I use my full will on you?"

"You don't want to beat me with your magic," snarled Ben. He was focusing on centering himself in case the former apprentice struck again, but if he could eliminate one threat and just have to defend against the spears, it'd help. "If you wanted to blast me with your will, you would have when I walked in the door. No, you're enjoying this too much."

Milo chuckled. "I'll admit you're right about that."

Ben attacked.

His blade met wood, and chips flew from the shaft of Milo's weapons. The former apprentice used his speed to stay out of reach, but when Ben got close, he shunted off the blows with the spears. It was an odd defensive style but effective. Ben couldn't get through the maze of wood in front of him. His attacks, though, had more strength than Milo could muster with a spear in each hand, so the strikes kept the young man off balance and retreating. Ben kept up constant pressure, and Milo couldn't find room for an attack.

Milo pursed his lips and blew. A puff of air, scalding hot and interwoven with a gout of flame, exploded in Ben's face.

His will was hardened, but the unexpected attack startled him, and he scrambled back, blinking his eyes and shaking his head. His forehead stung where the fire singed him, and he thought he might be missing his eyebrows. After a heartbeat, though, he could see again. He could see a vague form charging at him.

Furiously, Ben defended, more on instinct than any rational reaction to Milo's attack. Without thought, his blade moved in a blur, executing forms that were pure muscle memory. Gradually, his vision improved. He could see the tips of the spears again and lashed out with an attack of his own. Milo ducked and twisted, dancing across the room, a grin painted across his face.

A boom from below rocked the tower, and both Ben and Milo stumbled to their knees.

Milo, without pause, drew back and launched a spear at Ben.

Ben threw himself down to the floor, and the weapon swished overhead.

Milo placed his free hand on the floor and cartwheeled himself off the ground to his rack of weapons.

"Seriously, why do you have so many of those damn things?" snarled Ben, climbing back to his feet.

Milo only cackled in response. The tips of the spears shimmered with constrained energy, and Ben heard a hissing vibration. He knew a blow from one of those weapons might sending him flying. Shouts and more explosions drifted up from below. Whatever time they had was rapidly vanishing. The longer this fight took, the more chance for Milo's allies to arrive, assuming the curly-haired man even needed help. Ben had to act.

"Soon, your mommy will be back here to save you," remarked Ben coolly.

In the moonlight, he saw Milo's eyes flash with anger. He'd touched a nerve.

"Must be nice, seeing her when you're in trouble," continued Ben, starting to pace slowly around the room. "I'm guessing that's about the only time she sees you, when you're in trouble or when she wants something. Did it feel good when you showed her the staff, or did it make you realize she only cared about what you could give her and not about you?"

Milo charged.

Struggling to keep his breathing even, Ben kept speaking while he defended Milo's wild attack.

"Funny how she doesn't tell anyone about you," he said, "and this is a nice place she's put you in, on top of a whorehouse. It's a long way from the Sanctuary, though. Are there no apartments on this island any closer? It's like she's ashamed of you."

The spear thrusts came furiously, getting more and more erratic. Ben struggled to stay out of reach of the deadly spears, but a thrill spread through him. He was triggering the young man, making him emotional.

"All of that training with spear and will. I bet she never helped, did she? She always sent someone in her place."

Milo screamed and threw himself at Ben.

Ben, nearly instantly regretting it, made a quick decision and parried one of the spears. He stepped in and felt the tip of the other weapon pierce his thigh, sinking deep into the meat of his leg. A hard jolt of electrical charge battered against his hardened will, made more difficult by the tip of the weapon embedding in his flesh.

Ben grappled with Milo, slapping the spear away, which tugged painfully as it was jerked from his leg, but it relieved him of Milo's magical attack. He wrapped his arm around Milo's other arm, trapping the second spear in Milo's hand and on Ben's back.

A mop of shaggy hair came flying at Ben's face as Milo tried to headbutt him, but Ben ducked his head and absorbed the blow on the crown of his forehead. Pain shot through Ben's body as their heads thumped together, but he saw in Milo's face that the young man was hurt just as badly as he was.

Milo wrapped his free hand around Ben's throat. Leering in Ben's face, Milo snarled, "This is even better than stabbing you to death."

Ben opened his mouth to yell another taunt in the former apprentice's face, but he couldn't find the breath. Milo's hand tightened on his neck, and spots of light danced in Ben's vision. He snapped his mouth shut.

"What does it feel like to die?" asked Milo, one hand clutching Ben's throat, the other wrapped around Ben's back, the shaft of his spear blocking Ben's longsword.

Ben's answer came when his hunting knife buried in Milo's rib cage. He jerked it out and stabbed again, over and over. Milo staggered back. His second spear dropped, and both hands instinctively went to the gapping wounds in his side.

"Practice is one thing," growled Ben. "Experience is where you really learn."

He stepped forward and feinted with his knife at Milo's neck. The former apprentice's blood-covered hands shot up, and Ben plunged his knife into Milo's gut. He sawed with the sharp steel, cutting a hand-length hole in the young man's stomach like he was gutting a deer.

Milo collapsed to the floor, futilely trying to gather his spilled entrails. Within heartbeats, he'd be dead.

Ben looked around, but the room was empty. A training room and nothing more. The staff had to be upstairs, in Milo's private room. Ben was certain of it. He took a step to the door and crashed to the ground. His leg, forgotten in the battle fever, throbbed with exceptional pain. Ben glanced down and saw his entire left leg was painted in blood. He grunted. Time to worry about that later.

Grabbing one of Milo's spears, he levered himself up off the floor and sheathed his longsword. If he came across a skilled opponent, he was dead anyway. Hobbling with the spear clutched in both hands, Ben limped to the stairwell. Clenching his teeth, he struggled higher, a bloody footprint left on each step.

MOMENTS LATER, Ben crashed down the stairs, flailing to arrest his fall and grunting as each stone step pummeled a different part of his body. He finally reached the bottom and slid across the stone floor.

A woman looked down at him, eyes wide in confusion. Her hair was frizzed and tangled, like she'd just gotten out of bed or been subjected to a heavy electric shock. Her dress was torn, and blood leaked from one of her ears.

Ben, laying on his back, groaned and wrapped his hand around the broken shaft of the spear he'd snapped with his body when he had fallen on it. He shifted and rolled, swinging the spear up and stabbing the woman in the gut. She grunted in pain, still not comprehending what happened.

A frigid blast of air swept over Ben, and the woman was thrown against the wall, her head smacking against the stone with a spine-tingling crunch.

"Thanks," rasped Towaal. "The two of them proved more resilient than I expected."

"No problem," croaked Ben. "Uh, you think you can help me up?"

With Towaal's assistance, he clambered to his feet and rested his weight half on her, half on the intricately carved wyvern fire staff. He muttered a silent thanks that his body broke the spear and not the staff. That would have been embarrassing.

"Ready to walk twenty stories down?" asked the mage grimly, eyeing the staff but not commenting on it. "It's going to be a fight."

"I have an idea," muttered Ben. "Let's find the others."

They stumbled and fell down the stairs, Ben leaving long bloody streaks when he rubbed against the walls. He was dizzy and gasping for air. He knew he was losing too much blood, but they didn't have time to pause. He could only hope Towaal or Amelie still had strength to lend him healing energy when they made it to safety, but getting to safety was beginning to look like a smaller and smaller possibility.

Below them, they saw their friends clustered around the steel door which sealed Milo's apartments. The metal was bent in, and resounding booms and crashes sounded from the other side. Amelie was standing against it, both hands placed on the surface.

"Come up here!" shouted Ben hoarsely.

Amelie glanced over her shoulder. Ben could see sweat pouring down her face.

"This door is warded, locking it shut, but there are mages on the other side," cried Amelie. "I'm trying to hold the wards. If I leave, they'll be through in no time."

"You'd better run then," declared Ben.

"Do you have a plan?" asked Rhys. The rogue was pacing near Amelie, sword out, ready for when her strength failed and the door caved in.

"Sort of," responded Ben. "We have to hurry."

Renfro scrambled up the stairs, followed by Sincell and the two thugs he'd brought. Seeing them go made the decision for the rest of Ben's friends. With one last grunt of effort, Amelie let go of the door and ran up the stairs.

"Higher," said Ben. "One more level."

Rhys took over for Towaal, supporting Ben's weight as they hobbled upward.

"Milo?" he asked.

"He's dead," responded Ben.

They made it up to the dining room. Crystal bowls and decanters reflected the moonlight streaming in the wide windows. Ben could see the river out one side and lit windows of other tall towers out the other. He shuddered, thinking about all of the open air that lay beyond those windows.

"What are we doing here?" asked Rhys. "The Veil will send every mage she has once she realizes we took the staff."

"That and once she figures out what I did to her son," muttered Ben.

"Her son?" asked Rhys, confused.

"Her son."

Realization dawned on the rogue's face slowly. "Oh, bloody hell. We need to go."

"We are," said Ben.

Bracing himself against the wall, he swung with the staff and smashed a clasp that held a pair of windows closed. He pushed, and they swung wide, opening to the night sky. He looked down, cursed, and moved to the next casement.

"Could you use literally anything other than the wyvern fire staff for that?" pleaded Towaal.

Muttering under his breath, Ben flipped the next clasp with his hand and pushed the window open. A cool, steady breeze blew into the room, ruffling his hair and bringing the sounds of the city below them.

"B-Ben," stammered Amelie. "What are you doing?"

"Follow me," he instructed.

Ben dragged himself onto the window sill.

"What are you doing!" shrieked Amelie.

"Sorry. If I think about this, I won't be able to do it," he mumbled. Then, he pitched backward.

He fell two stories before smacking hard into the wooden slats of the bridge. He'd tried to maneuver his legs to absorb the impact, but his left one was reluctant to respond, so the shock pulsed through his entire body and he crumpled like an egg shell. Above him, he could see Rhys looking down.

"Nice," admitted the rogue. Then, he launched himself out into the air.

Watching his friend jump into the open night sky curdled Ben's stomach. Rhys, cloak flapping above him, landed three paces away in the center of the bridge, his legs flexing to drop him into a squat.

Sincell came next, landing lightly. She stood and warned, "Guards are flooding into Gerrol's tower. I tried to tell you before you jumped. Too many of them to fit in the stairwells of the Octopus, I'm guessing. Fighting our way down Gerrol's tower won't be any easier."

"We aren't going back into that one," declared Ben.

He rolled onto his belly and forced himself up, pain radiating from the wound in his leg. The rest of his body throbbed from the fall. One by one, the companions dropped from the window, landing on the shaky rope bridge. Finally, the Rat's two thugs came down last, their heavy bodies crashing into the bridge and giving Ben a momentary fright that the thing might snap in two.

"Where to next?" asked Rhys.

Above them, a guard poked his head out of the window.

"Whatever the plan," continued the rogue, looking at the doorway nervously, "it'd better be fast."

Ben turned to his companions. "Everyone, hold on tight. Really tight. Rhys, you cut the ropes."

Rhys blinked at him.

Ben wrapped his arm around one of the smaller ropes that connected the wooden slats to the thick support wires that anchored the bridge to the towers. He bent down and wedged his fingers between two boards. Seeing him, his friends dove to the sides of the bridge as well and scrambled to secure themselves.

"You've gone insane," crowed Rhys.

The guard in the window above turned and started frantically shouting to others behind him. In moments, the guards would be out the door and onto the bridge.

The rogue's longsword flared silver, and he swept it into one of the support wires. The bridge jerked, and Renfro squealed, clinging to the ropes and uttering a stream of the foulest curses Ben had ever heard.

One of the thugs snarled something unintelligible and charged Rhys, a shortsword raised above his head.

Renfro jumped in front of him, two blades appearing in his hands.

"This is insane, Rat," growled the thug, skidding to a stop.

"There are hundreds of guards in those towers," snapped Renfro. "I don't like it, but this is the only way. Grab a hold of something and prepare to fly."

"I ain't doing it boss."

"Yes you are," snarled Renfro. He took a menacing step toward the thug.

The big burly man clenched his fist around his short sword.

Rhys brought his sword down again and severed the last line on one side of the bridge. The bridge tilted alarmingly but didn't completely dump them to the side yet.

"They always said you'd get us killed," muttered the thug, barely audible over the rushing wind. "I shoulda listened."

Before any of the party could react, the thug charged and Renfro ducked, stabbing up with his knives. One of the blades caught the thug in the bicep, sinking deep, and forcing him to drop his short sword. The man's other hand slapped down and gripped Renfro by his hair.

"Ouch, let me go you son of a bitch!" growled the little thief.

The thug, madness shining from his eyes, brought his wounded arm down and bashed Renfro on the shoulder, causing him to drop one of his knives. Over and over, the thug battered the smaller man, still gripping Renfro's hair in his fist.

Ben stepped toward the combatants but the bridge swayed dangerously under his feet and his hand instinctively reached to clutch the remaining rope lead.

Renfro stabbed with his knife and caught the thug in the side, the little blade burying in the man's flesh.

Grunting, the thug stumbled back, his hand still tangled in Renfro's hair. Flailing, the thug toppled, dragging Renfro with him. He fell against the cut side of the bridge, and the rope sagged under his weight.

Renfro, panic fueling his motion, stabbed again and again at the bigger man, but he was helpless to break the iron-grip or the man's momentum.

"No!" cried Ben risking a step closer, but he was too late.

Renfro dug his small blade into the man one last time, twisting it, probing for vital organs.

"See you in hell, Rat," growled the thug, and he collapsed back, taking Renfro with him. Both of the men flipped over the cut-rope and plunged into the black of night.

"Rat!" cried Sincell.

She stepped toward where Renfro had fallen, but Amelie gripped her arm.

Suddenly, the door to the tower burst open, and a dozen guards stood in the hallway of the Octopus. At the sight of Ben and his friends, the guards started shouting to more men back inside.

Ben looped a hand through the rogue's belt, and Rhys twisted one leg around a rope.

"Time to go," said Ben.

"Get them!" snarled the leader of the soldiers.

They charged, and Rhys swung his sword.

Silver smoke blazed in its wake. The mage-wrought blade severed the two remaining support lines, cutting the bridge in two. It dropped out from underneath of them and the charging guards. Startled screams proceeded long, desperate falls as the dozen men plummeted into the darkness below.

Ben and his friends, secured to the length of bridge, flew through the air. A trill of excitement and fear rushed through Ben's veins until the bridge hit the side of Gerrol's tower with a crunch. It felt like he, quite literally, ran into a wall.

The bridge bounced off the stone and then smacked back into it again. The Rat's last thug streaked past Ben, the man's screams fading as he vanished into the dark.

Ben swallowed and tried to ignore the burn of the rope chaffing his wrist. Five paces below him, Rhys dangled from the rope wrapped around his leg. Ben had lost his grip on the man's belt when they had smashed into the tower.

"That didn't feel good," groaned the rogue, looking up at Ben.

"Three stories down, another bridge," said Ben.

Rhys looked down. "Ben," he called, "that's three stories down and a dozen paces to the side."

"It looked closer from the top of the Octopus. Got a better idea?" snapped Ben.

"You go first," insisted Rhys, his cloak hanging below him, flapping in the wind.

Steeling himself, Ben unwrapped his arm from the rope bridge. The flesh of his wrist was torn and bloody, making his hand slick. Blood leaked down his left leg from the spear wound, soaking his boot. He shuffled one foot lower and then a hand, wedging it between the slats of the wooden bridge. Supported only by his fingers and toes, he climbed down.

He risked a look at the stone bridge he was planning to jump to and immediately regretted it. There was nothing wrong with the bridge except that it hung ten stories above the streets below. If he jumped and missed, that would be the last of him. He swallowed the lump in his throat and kept climbing until he made it to the bottom of the bridge, Rhys still dangling upside down below him.

"Want me to, ah, do something?" he asked his friend.

"Don't worry about me," grumbled the rogue. "I'm just enjoying the evening."

Rhys was trying to slide his longsword into the sheath and secure it with a thong on his belt. It was made more complicated by his cloak, which kept flapping into his face. Ben felt bad, but the rogue didn't want his help. Amelie and Prem were scaling down the wooden planks above him. He felt the bridge swaying in the wind.

"I'm not sure how secure this thing is," warned Amelie. "We need to hurry."

Ben nodded and positioned himself to leap. He looked down, and a tremor wracked his body. He drew a deep breath, trying to steady himself.

"Ben, don't look down," suggested Amelie.

"Just fucking jump," growled Rhys.

Ben launched himself into the air, flying above ten stories of open air. If he missed the bridge, he knew he'd be dead.

He didn't miss. He thought he might still die, though.

His body smashed into the stone bridge like he was a raw piece of meat. His legs, the left one near worthless due to the injury Milo had given him, collapsed under his weight. His left arm absorbed most of the blow, nearly shattering as his body drove it hard into the stone. For a long moment, he lay there, stunned. Pain radiated through his being, and he wasn't sure he could move.

"How the hell did you get here?" barked a voice.

Ben turned his head and saw a chainmail-clad guard from the

Sanctuary. He must have been watching the bridges from Gerrol's tower. He evidently didn't see the broken rope bridge dangling above them. Ben could only hope that the man had been posted as a watch alone and didn't have friends with him.

The soldier had a broadsword on his side, but he hadn't drawn it yet. Ben admitted ruefully, the man didn't need to. Ben wasn't going anywhere. The guard stepped out of the tower, frowning at Ben and glancing at the tower on the other end of the bridge. Confusion clouded his face.

Rhys flew into Ben's vision and his boot thumped into the guard's head, snapping his neck. The rogue landed heavily on the man's body before tumbling off and rolling into the railing on the side of the bridge.

"Ouch," grunted Rhys.

"You should try it without something to land on," muttered Ben. He stirred, trying to find a way to get to his feet, but anyway he moved just brought sharp, stabbing pain.

Amelie down came next, landing hard and falling onto Ben, all elbows and knees. He groaned as her body slammed into him, jolting his already bruised shoulder and arm.

"Sorry," she muttered. She looked down, winced, and then placed her hands on him.

"Don't," he hissed. "The mages may sense you expending your energy."

Amelie snorted. "You don't think they know we're here? This won't make you right, but hopefully, I can reduce some of the pain so you can stand."

A warmth suffused him.

Prem thumped to the stones and tucked into a roll, smoothly ending up on one knee. Ben grumbled under his breath as the girl sprang to her feet, looking as relaxed as if she'd just rolled out of bed. Sincell floated to land next to Prem, her booted feet settling softly on the stone bridge. She wiggled her fingers at Ben and winked.

"Hey," called a voice from the tower.

Another guard was standing in the doorway.

Rhys was lurking beside it. The rogue reached over and grasped the collar of the man's chainmail. The rogue jerked the man outside and buried a knife in his neck, a hot fountain of blood poured out of the shocked soldier's throat. Rhys deposited the body on top of the first one and then tried to wipe his hand off on the man's trousers before resuming his position next to the door.

"Soon, there will be more than one of them coming out of there," warned Amelie.

Above them, shouts came over the sound of the whipping wind. Guards were at the doorway of the Octopus, pointing down and gesturing wildly. It'd be half a bell before any of them could get near Ben and his friends, but they could alert the soldiers in Gerrol's tower.

"Come on!" called Sincell.

Ben glanced up to see Lady Towaal perched on the last board of the wooden bridge. It was swaying in the breeze, and the mage seemed to be timing the movement to make her jump. At the pinnacle of a swing, the she let go.

Ben's breath caught in his throat as she floated out over the open air, seeming to drift to them on the wind.

She landed and met Ben's eyes. "I'm sorry about Renfro."

He opened his mouth to respond, but the clatter of armor inside the tower shocked them into motion. Amelie helped Ben to his feet and they started moving away from Gerrol's tower. Limping along, Ben wondered if Towaal or Sincell could have done the same trick for him and the rest of the party, slowing their fall. There was no use worrying about it now.

Ben met Sincell's gaze and saw the anguish there. She'd been loyal, even if Renfro's thugs weren't. Ben blinked his eyes, clearing them of the moisture that was growing there. The Rat was gone, and nothing was going to bring him back.

"Hundreds of guards will be right on our heels," advised Rhys, darting ahead.

Ben, not slowing, held up the wyvern fire staff. Deep in the throat of the wooden wyvern, a glow emanated.

"Ben!" exclaimed Amelie.

In front of him, Ben saw the red and orange glow of the staff reflected against the wall of the tower. The light was growing as the heat built inside the staff. The pale wood was cool to the touch, but Ben could feel heat on his face, like a door to a furnace was opening.

He paused before the entrance to the tower and let Rhys rush by. The rogue's booted foot smashed into a wooden door and burst it open, debris from a flimsy bolt skittering across the floor.

The party streamed by Ben, and then he set the tip of the wyvern fire staff onto the stone bridge. Flames leapt up, and he stepped back, covering his face from the heat. Towaal took his side, holding her arms up and placing a shield in front of them to keep the heat away.

"How are you doing this?" she hissed.

"The artificers who fashioned this weapon were too smart to allow it to be used unrestrained," explained Ben. "They set a price in blood."

Towaal looked at him, and then her eyes widened when she saw the staff. Covered in Ben's blood, the thousands of tiny runes glowed orange like the smoldering embers of a fire. Ben's blood sizzled, popped, and then slowly vanished as it was absorbed into the staff. Starting at the bottom, the liquid oozed higher, following the intricate carvings in the wood. It moved on its own, slowly running a course into the wyvern's mouth where it fed the incredible fire.

The flames Ben had set coursed down the stone bridge, the rocks fissuring and falling away into the night as the bridge was torched with the incredible heat of wyvern fire. In moments, the structure would be burned through. Already, Ben guessed it was entirely impassable.

"They've seen us use the staff," said Towaal tersely.

Ben followed her eyes and saw five tiny figures standing on an open balcony in Milo's apartment. Five women. They were staring down at Ben and his companions. Ben couldn't see any details, but he could tell none of them were wearing a green dress. The Veil's stooges, instead of the woman herself. Too bad.

"Look," said Towaal, pointing the streets below where people streamed out of the tower. "They've evacuated the tower. There will be no witnesses for what they plan to do. We have to run, Ben!"

A glow was forming around the women, streaks of light swirling, forming a brilliant cloud, and a blast of fatal energy, Ben was sure.

"Ben!" cried Towaal. "We have to run now!"

"I have another idea," he murmured.

Ben flicked the wyvern fire staff in the direction of the tower and the length of it sizzled, blood vanishing in an instant. A fist-sized fireball flew from the mouth of the wyvern, expanding as it soared across the open space. The five figures started scrambling, the glow vanishing from around them. They rushed back inside. It seemed they knew about the staff, and what it was capable of. Ben guessed they'd try to run down the stairs, but he could feel they didn't have time.

The fireball impacted the side of the tower and a concussive blast rocked the City. The top few floors of the Octopus burst into flame like a pitch-covered torch. The blast flared bright, turning the night sky into day.

Ben wavered and then slumped against the doorframe. The staff fell from his hands and the heat faded rapidly. His body limp, he slid down the wall, coming dangerously close to flopping out on the fire-blackened bridge.

"We'd better go," murmured Rhys, catching Ben and hauling him inside.

The rogue dragged Ben away from the door, and the world passed Ben like he was no longer a part of it. They raced down the stairs, darted across bridges, and fled through the network of pathways high above the streets of the City. Late at night, most of the stairs, bridges, and halls were clear of pedestrians. At every tower, there were numerous branches, numerous levels, and no way the Sanctuary's guards could cover each route.

Rhys carried Ben, and Ben could only stare straight up. He didn't have the strength to move his arms or legs or to turn his head. He was merely an observer to their flight. Towaal and Amelie took his side, sending light doses of energy into his body, infusing him with healing power, but it did nothing to shake him from his dreamlike state.

The entire way, through every open window, across every bridge, they were lit by the bright orange and red flames of the burning tower. Its light reached every corner of the City, and it wasn't until they'd made it across a bridge and out of the City proper that the glow finally dwindled and snuffed out.

10

THE ROAD

"How did you know?" asked Amelie.

Ben tossed another log into the fireplace. It was huge, towering half again as tall as he was. It was made to warm banquets, but it served the purpose just as well for he and Amelie. Ben had seen the fireplace once before, when they were last fleeing the City and had hidden on Lord Reinhold's estate. They were doing the same thing now, but instead of an open-air gazebo, they'd camped in the manor itself. Most of the furniture had been looted, and anything of real value had been stripped away, but it had a roof, walls, and most of the windows were intact.

"Come on, Ben," prodded Amelie. "How did you know?"

"Something Milo told me about sacrifice when I faced him and what I found near the staff when I collected it. I put it together then."

Amelie raised an eyebrow.

"Bodies," mumbled Ben. "They'd been experimenting with killing people and using their blood to activate the staff. Prostitutes, clients, people who wouldn't be missed or wouldn't be found. That's why they were staying in Lord Gulli's tower. That's what happened to Lord Gulli himself, actually. From the state of him, it looked like he may have been the first victim."

Amelie frowned. "Did it work?"

"I don't think so," responded Ben. "If it did, why were they still there? How were we able to steal it? No, if it had worked, the staff would have been with the Veil, or Milo would have used it against me instead of his spears. He spoke of sacrifice and said I wouldn't have the strength to do it. The bodies made me realize what he meant and that they also failed to have the strength. The key is that the user of the staff has to give themselves, their blood, to feed the weapon."

"So," said Amelie, staring at the fire, "we know how to use it now."

"We do," agreed Ben, "but at a high cost. Amelie, I nearly lost enough blood to kill me. I was able to destroy the bridge and burn the tower. In a battle, anyone using this staff is risking their lives. If you and Towaal weren't there to heal me, I wouldn't have survived."

"Still, it's a powerful weapon," insisted Amelie. "In the right circumstances, it may be what we need."

"It is powerful, too powerful," confirmed Ben. "What if that tower hadn't been evacuated. I could have killed, hundreds, maybe over a thousand people with a thought. I think Gunther was right. We shouldn't be the ones using this staff. We need someone wiser, someone who knows how to handle a weapon like this…"

At the same time, they both blurted out, "Jasper."

"Can't we just go the way you went before?" wondered Rhys.

They were sitting around the empty stone floor of the former Lord Reinhold's kitchen. There was nothing left in the pantry, but Ben had seen an apple orchard on a previous visit and had collected an armful of the ripe, red fruits. They were crunching through a pile of them as they had nothing else to eat.

"We could," said Ben, "but there was a hunter who tracked us last time and ambushed us in the woods. He used our blood somehow to find us. I don't know if the Veil or her minions would be aware we went that way, but it's possible."

"I've already obscured our blood," said Towaal. "Just like I did on the sea when we were going to the South Continent, so that's not a worry, but if they knew the hunter tracked you that way, it's highly possible they could send someone to head us off. She has the entire might of the Sanctuary's guards and mages at her disposal, and to find the staff, she'll use every bit of it."

"Can't we just use this staff to blast anyone who comes after us?" queried Sincell.

"No," snapped Prem. The girl looked to be no more than seventeen summers, but she spoke with a century worth of experience. "The staff should not be used. It shouldn't have been used last night. Every time it is activated, it will draw evil toward us. There are people out there, including the Veil, who will do anything to obtain this weapon."

"How do you know?" scoffed Sincell. "Didn't you say this is the first time you've been out of the woods?"

Prem glared at the runaway mage, but Ben held up his hand to stall them both.

"Prem is right," he said. "The Veil is not the only one we need to worry about. Avril is out there somewhere, and there's nothing she will want more than this staff."

"Avril?" asked Sincell, recognition dawning on her face.

"Avril," confirmed Ben. He brought the staff to lay it across his knees. "We use this weapon against the demons or to prevent it from falling into the wrong hands. Nothing else. The risk is too high, the power too great even if it is to save our lives. There is a man who may be able to tell us more, though. If anyone can figure out how to use this responsibly, he's the one. We'll meet up with him and go from there."

"Sensible," murmured Towaal.

"Who is this man?" pressed Sincell.

"An ally we can trust," stated Ben.

He didn't need to say more. His friends picked up on the subtext of his comment. Sincell had assisted them greatly so far, but they'd already been burned once by a spy the Veil had placed in their midst. They knew little about the woman, and the one person who may be able to tell them more had fallen to his death. For the time being, they would be careful what they said around the runaway.

"We still have to get to him," remarked Rhys.

"The river," said Amelie.

"Another barge?" asked Ben.

She shook her head. "Lord Reinhold's estate is abandoned, unclaimed. That's pretty common when a wealthy highborn dies with no apparent heir. Relatives, business partners, they spend years haggling in front of the local lords over who should have what piece of the treasure. If the ownership of the estate hasn't been settled, it's likely his boat is unclaimed as well."

"Who would sail it?" wondered Ben.

Amelie grinned. "Captain Fishbone, of course. He's probably still getting paid, and I'd bet anything he isn't far from that boat. If he's not around, we can find someone else."

"The boat and the sailor, they're probably all back in the City," mentioned Rhys.

"The last place the Veil would expect us to go," announced Amelie.

"We're nothing if not bold," said Rhys, a broad grin on his face, "and a little crazy. So, how do we get there?"

Sincell raised a hand. "I've got an idea."

THEY WAITED at Lord Reinhold's estate for two more days until Prem arrived with a flatbed wagon and a pair of scruffy-looking wagon drivers. The Rat's men, except they didn't know the Rat was dead. They did know Sincell, though, and that she was his right-hand woman, so to speak. She'd directed Prem where to find the men and what to say to enlist their help. It'd taken some quick talking on Ben's part to convince the runaway mage that Prem was the right one to go into the City first, instead of Sincell herself, but eventually, she admitted no one would know to look for Prem. All of the rest of them might be recognized by members of the Sanctuary.

Ben didn't mention that he also wanted to keep the runaway mage under his thumb. He had no reason to distrust her, but she did work for Renfro's budding thieves guild. She could make a fortune by turning in Ben, his friends, and the wyvern fire staff to the Veil. No, until they were clear of the City, they'd keep Sincell close by.

"Y'all needin' a ride?" drawled one of the drivers.

Sincell nodded to him. "A quiet one."

"We can keep ya hidden, but I'm tellin' ya, girl, tha roads be fulla patrols. They lookin' for someone." The driver eyed her steadily.

Sincell smirked. "Of course they are."

The man waited, hoping for further explanation, but he got none. Anyone who had been in the City the night they had escaped would be aware of the conflagration atop the Octopus, but the man had no reason to tie it to Sincell. Ben figured sneaking people around was the normal course of business for anyone working with Renfro. Anyone who had been working with Renfro, he corrected himself.

A wave of regret washed over him as he climbed into the wagon. Despite his questionable morals, his former friend had been loyal to the end and even knowing the odds, still helped them steal something he didn't understand. He'd paid for it with his life.

"Everywhere we go, someone dies." Ben sighed.

Amelie, who had climbed up right in front of him, overheard the comment and gripped his hand. She didn't say anything. There was nothing to say.

The second wagon driver clambered up behind them and started shifting boxes, stacking them high and blocking the end of the wagon. It would hold up to light scrutiny. For anyone who looked, it would appear to be a wagon load of kaf beans. Coming down the river road, that wouldn't be unusual. Most of the freight was transported by barge, but a merchant with a single wagon load didn't need and wouldn't want to pay for the extra space the barge offered. If they couldn't come up with a cooperative shipping agreement, they'd send their goods all the way in a wagon bed. Ben had seen enough of them on their last journey along the river road to be confident the charade would work, assuming the guards didn't stop every wagon and check them thoroughly. In case that happened, they all kept their weapons close. Outside of the City, they would still have time to escape. Inside, it'd be trouble.

The wagon rolled on, passing over the smooth, hard-packed dirt road. Canvass was pulled down tight on the top of the bed of the wagon, so they couldn't see anything, but Ben could hear the march of the ubiquitous patrols of Sanctuary guards. Like Amelie had suspected, though, the guards weren't interested in commercial vehicles that were going to the City.

The ride took a few bells but it seemed to take days. Every time they passed someone, Ben's body tensed, tugging at his barely healed wounds. His hand was locked around the hilt of his longsword. By the time they neared the City, it was so numb from the strain that he knew he'd be useless in a fight.

"Relax," whispered Rhys.

Ben tried to give his friend a smile, but he only managed to curl one corner of his mouth up. Then, the sound of the wagon wheels changed. They'd gone from hard-packed dirt to cobblestones. Ben nearly jumped out of his seat.

Amelie laid a hand on his leg, attempting to calm him, and Towaal gave him an assured nod.

He looked around the wagon bed and saw everyone was looking at him, trying to hide their amusement at his nerves. He tried to be glad someone was keeping their minds off the danger of their present situation.

"It's not any worse than jumping out of a twenty-story window, is it?" whispered Amelie.

"Now that was crazy," agreed Rhys in a low voice. "This is a Newday stroll in the park."

A grin crept onto Ben's face.

Half a bell passed, and the wagon slowed. The drivers jumped off, and Ben heard the clatter of the tailgate as they pulled it down. Boxes scraped across wood, and in a moment, they were looking out at the two drivers. Behind them was a dirty wagon yard and an even dirtier-looking tavern.

"Really?" asked Amelie, eyes raised skyward.

"We'd best hide inside until dusk," suggested Rhys, a twinkle in his eye.

IT TURNED out none of the Rat's employees knew he was dead yet, a fact that proved to be extremely helpful as they borrowed his resources. Ben felt awful, but the apparatus was in place, so there was no sense not using it.

Sincell called in the Rat's urchins, and after getting a quick description of Captain Fishbone, they spread out through the streets. A couple of toughs, more suspicious than the children, gathered close.

"Boss don't like to leave town," muttered one of the men, fingering a fileting knife at his belt.

Sincell blinked at him. "I didn't say he left town."

"Where is he then?" pressed the man.

"How the hell should I know?" snapped the runaway mage. "I work for him just like you do. He doesn't ask my permission for, well, whatever it is he does when he's not stealin'."

"Just weird," interjected another man. "Weird after what happened a few days ago that he's not around. The whole city is in disarray. We oughta be out there making a fortune right now, but no one wants to make a move without his approval. We don't know why the boss wouldn't be around, that's all. Strange, no one's seen him since that night."

"Well, I don't know where he is or what he's doing," barked Sincell, letting frustration creep into her voice.

Ben had to give the runaway mage credit. She played her role to perfection. Satisfied she wasn't any happier about the Rat's absence than they were, the toughs retreated to the bar and ordered another round.

FOUR BELLS LATER, the companions stood half a block away from the entrance to the City's private docks. It was where the well-heeled merchants and the highborn kept their craft, away from the sweating and cursing sailors that covered the public docks. It was also well guarded. The highborn didn't want the riff raff wandering around dirtying the immaculate vessels with their eyes.

Captain Fishbone was supposed to be in there, along with a skeleton crew of sailors. The urchins had found him deep in his cups in a dark corner of a seedy tavern. Apparently, Amelie was right. The man was still employed by Reinhold's estate. With no natural heir, Reinhold's property was locked in a dispute amongst the wealthier families, all trying to prove a relationship to the dead merchant banker. Ben had watched all of Reinhold's guards get slaughtered, the estate staff had fled, and only a few other members of his household remained, all stuck, collecting pay from the dead man's bank accounts, afraid to take another job and risk that pay drying up. It left men like Fishbone with nothing to do but get drunk and carouse every day.

With a little bit of quick talking from one of the Rat's more respectable-looking minions, they'd convinced the sodden Fishbone that he was needed on the vessel, and his continuing pay depended on it. Now, they had to get through the guarded gate themselves and get the sailing master to cut lines and abscond with the ship, which if he was captured, was something Fishbone would hang for.

"Force or guile?" asked Rhys.

The rogue's hand rested on one of his heavy long knives, betraying which way he'd prefer.

"Neither," said Amelie. She dug out a handful of gold from her purse. "If we pay the men off, they'll have as much to lose as us from talking. An honest bribe is the best way to cover our tracks and make sure the Veil doesn't find out we left on the water."

Rhys pouted. "You're no fun."

Ben rolled his eyes and then directed Amelie to go bribe the men. Half a dozen guards, three or four bright gold coins apiece, and a pretty face to deliver them. In moments, they were rushed through the gate, the guards looking anywhere but at them. The men would risk losing their positions when the ship was found missing, but unless it was discovered immediately, they could easily claim it was on another shift.

Ben figured it could be weeks before anyone actually realized Reinhold's vessel was gone, though. The suing heirs certainly weren't keeping up with his house.

They scurried along the dock until they saw the familiar profile of Reinhold's low-lying sloop. Sleek and fast, just what they needed for a water escape. They stalked up the gangplank and surprised Fishbone, who was swaying drunkenly and admonishing an equally drunk sailor about tying a proper knot. The captain turned, and his eyes bugged out.

"You!" he slurred.

Towaal stepped forward. "We have need of your services, Captain Fishbone."

The man spat. "It all went downhill the moment you stepped on my ship." The gruff sailor slowly scanned the rest of the party, his eyes flaring alive when they passed Ben. "You got my boss killed, you know."

"Sorry about that," mumbled Ben.

"Why the hell do you think I'd sail anywhere with you?" barked Fishbone. "Leaving this dock with this ship is a hanging offense. Letting you get away without me ain't much better. While there's breath in my body, you ain't movin' the Lord Reinhold's boat."

"Don't you mean, Captain Fishbone's boat?" inquired Ben.

The man blinked at him, not comprehending.

"We don't need the ship. We just need a ride," added Ben. "Whatever happens to this beautiful craft after that would be up to you."

"I ain't gonna dangle, son," muttered Fishbone.

Ben nodded. "Aye, returning to the City would certainly be inadvisable. Akew Woods, though, that's a town a man could enjoy living in, particularly if he owns such a nice vessel as this."

The captain stared back at Ben, his jaw clenched as he ground his teeth. Finally, he growled, "Where do you want to go?"

"North for now," said Ben.

"If we sail north, then to get to Akew Woods, I gotta sail by the City. You think I'm dumb, boy?"

"The mages may see you. They may not," allowed Ben. He gripped the hilt of his longsword. "We're sailing on this ship tonight. You can either stand behind the captain's wheel or sit down in the cargo hold. Which do you prefer?"

THEY MADE it around a bend in the river and passed out of view of the Sanctuary two bells before dawn. Fishbone had spent twenty years captaining boats in and out of the private harbor and up the river. Even with a skeleton crew, he could manage it. Even in the thick of a full-blown drunk his instincts were still sound. It wasn't until they'd made it to the river channel, and safety, that Fishbone got noisily sick over the gunwale. The captain's slightly less drunk first mate took over while Fishbone slumped down against the mast and began snoring raggedly.

Feeling safe for the first time since before they had entered the Octopus, Ben and his friends settled down to rest too, lying in an exhausted jumble on the deck of the ship.

Towaal crawled over to Ben and probed his wounds, adding another dose of healing energy.

"A few days rest on the ship will do you good," she murmured. "You'll have no permanent damage if you allow it to heal."

"Good to know," he said.

The excitement of the last few days was fading, and with it, the pace of his heart slowed. Despite the healing, the puncture Milo left in his thigh still throbbed painfully. It was almost enough to keep him awake, but not quite. His eyes drooped shut, and he laid his head down on the deck of the ship.

AMELIE WOKE him two bells later, the sun hanging barely over the horizon.

"Ben, Jasper's contacting us," she hissed.

He blinked, dragging himself into consciousness. Two bells

sleep on the wooden deck of a ship after what they'd been through wasn't enough, it seemed.

Amelie crawled around the deck, rousing Towaal and Rhys. She left Sincell and Prem sleeping. They clustered around her and placed their fingers on the thought meld.

"We're here," thought Amelie.

Without preamble, Jasper launched into it, "The demons have departed Northport. They're heading south, following the west bank of the river."

"The west bank?" wondered Ben.

"The mature ones can fly, but the bulk of the force won't cross the water," explained Jasper.

"Kirksbane," thought Amelie. "They may cross at the shallows there."

"They might," responded Jasper. "A swarm this size has to feed, though. The little towns and villages they roll over on the way south won't be enough. This arch-demon, or maybe we should call it the demon-king, as powerful as it is, will need to feed its minions if it wants to maintain control."

"Venmoor," thought Towaal.

"Exactly," responded Jasper. "It's possible they could cross at Kirksbane and travel east into the Sineook Valley, but I think it's more likely they'll continue south to Venmoor. If the city is unprepared, the demons will demolish the place. Unopposed, they'll feast and gain strength. They could then proceed further south to the City. After what we've seen and the strength the swarm may gain from Venmoor, the mages would have their hands full, and I'm not sure how that battle would go. If we don't stop them now, we may not get another chance."

"It's settled then," Ben thought. "We'll travel to Venmoor to alert them and try to gain their support. You warn who you can on the journey south. We'll meet you at Kirksbane. One way or the other, we know the demons will go through there."

"We need help," worried Jasper. "My band and I will not be sufficient."

"Be at Kirksbane," instructed Ben. "Bring the armor. We found something that may be enough to turn the tide. We'll tell you more when we meet."

A sense of determination flowed through the meld, and then it went silent. A subtle buzz that was difficult to notice while in use was obvious when the connection was severed.

"You sure about this?" asked Amelie, concern etched deeply on her face.

"We don't have a choice," responded Ben.

~

LATE THAT AFTERNOON, a three-man dinghy rowed through the shallow water to the riverbank. It was thick with bright green grass. A sailor grasped a tuft of the grass to hold them close, and the runaway mage Sincell clambered out of the boat onto shore.

"You certain we can trust her?" asked Amelie, watching from the deck of their sloop.

Ben laughed. "No, of course not."

Amelie paused and then allowed, "You're right. What choice do we have?"

Ben nodded. "Either she'll convince Hadra and her companions to meet us at Kirksbane, or she won't. Maybe the Veil will come and try to capture us and the staff. If she does, I hope she pauses to address the descending demon army while she's there."

"Coatney is power hungry and manipulative," commented Towaal, "but she's not insane. If she sees the true threat, she'll do what she can. No sense trying to take over the world if all of the people are dead and a demon-king is sitting on the throne."

"A demon-king, that's what Jasper called it, isn't it?" said Ben.

Towaal shrugged. "He was right. What else would you call

that image he sent us? It's certainly no arch-demon I've ever heard of."

Prem studied Sincell as the runaway mage wasted no time and began hiking south, along the riverbank back toward the City. The guardian turned to Ben. "She'll do what she says. She'll make an effort to enlist these mages you spoke to. Her fight is with the Veil, and stripping away some of the Veil's mages aligns with her interests. Our concern should be if she's caught. If they found out she was involved with the tower, they will be looking for her."

"Well, let's hope she doesn't get caught then. It's too bad we can't risk approaching the Veil with her. Of all of us, she's the least likely to be suspected of involvement in stealing the staff. If we could only talk to her, I wonder if we could convince Coatney of the threat the demons represent? Saala told us that was one of the two ways for a leader to gain loyalty."

Rhys slapped him on the back. "You're learning quick, but it's too late now. With the staff in our hands, there's no way Coatney will listen to us."

Ben grunted.

"Now, we've got three more days to Venmoor by my estimate," said Rhys. "This vessel wasn't looted like Reinhold's estate. Assuming Fishbone didn't drink it all himself, there should be plenty of good drink left to get us where we're going."

Ben glanced at Amelie.

"Go on," she said. "Rhys is right. You need to rest. There's nothing else to do for the next few days. Get drunk tonight, sleep it off, rest, and be ready when we make Venmoor."

11

VENMOOR

VENMOOR WAS FAMOUS FOR ITS SWORDS AND SWORDSMEN. BEN recalled from when they had passed it on the way to the City as a giant, dark smudge on the edge of the river, overshadowed by the constant billow of smoke from the smithies. His second impression did little to change the first.

Before they spied the structures of the city, they saw the tower of black smoke that arose from it. Hanging thousands of paces in the air, the column of ash tilted like it was falling over, drifting slowly in the light breeze away from the city.

The Alliance and Coalition were gearing up for war, and the weapons from Venmoor were the tools they used to make it. The smithies were working night and day. Every blacksmith who could swing a hammer would be working overtime to fashion weapons to rend the flesh of enemies. Venmoor steel was flexible and strong. It gave an edge to any warrior facing a lesser blade. The growing armies needed quality weapons, and Venmoor appeared to be hard at work crafting them.

"Fortunes are being made," remarked Captain Fishbone.

He was surly and rude, but Ben supposed they had pressed

him into stealing a ship. If he was caught, he'd be hung. If he wasn't, though, Fishbone was now a wealthy man.

Ben glanced at the sailor.

"Lord Reinhold told me an opportunity like this war only arises every few generations," continued Fishbone, spitting a sticky wad of intoxicating herbs over the side of the ship. "Could be the biggest conflict this continent has seen since the Blood Bay War. Maybe bigger. The winners will be the new highborn. Their families will live in castles and rule unchallenged, until the next one, at least."

"I've heard that in war, there are no winners," remarked Ben.

"Why do they keep fighting them, then?" barked Fishbone.

Ben shrugged.

"You're right, in a way," admitted the captain. "We're just talkin' 'bout different people. Most people who go off to fight end up dying or worse. Wives don't wait at home for long, wondering if their husband will make it back, and if he does, whether he'll be the same man that left. Nah, they move on. Businesses fail, fields go fallow, nets are untended. Everything a man has worked his life for rots and dies before he gets home. Most would rather be dead than face that. That don't mean no one wins, though, does it? Just means you and I won't win. Men like Reinhold, King Argren, Lord Jason, Lord Gulli. Those are tha folk who win. Well, half of 'em anyway. They're the ones who make the fortunes, and they're the ones who keep starting wars. They just don't fight 'em, ya know?"

"It shouldn't be like that," muttered Ben.

"Aye," agreed Fishbone. "It shouldn't, but who's gonna change the world, lad? It certainly ain't gonna be me. No, best to understand it and figure out a way to survive til tomorrow."

Fishbone stalked off, his strange rolling gait more suited to the sea than river sailing, but Ben supposed after this, maybe that is just where the man would be headed.

"He's right, in his way," remarked Rhys. He took Fishbone's

place at the railing and studied the cloud of smoke on the horizon.

"I know," said Ben, "but just because something would be difficult to change doesn't mean it shouldn't change."

"You're going to be the one to change it?" asked Rhys.

"Why not?" retorted Ben.

"Why not indeed," responded the rogue with a grin. "Come on. We'd best go get packed. Changing the world is nice, but having a fresh pair of trousers is a more immediate concern."

Ben smiled and followed his friend below deck.

THEY DROPPED anchor two hundred paces away from a sturdy-looking stone wharf. Every spot on it was taken.

"Wouldn't mind a night on the town," grumbled Fishbone, "but I suppose it's best. I need to get off this river 'afore someone comes lookin' for this vessel. Best of luck to ya."

Ben nodded, clambered over the side of the sloop, and dropped into the shore boat. They'd have to make a few trips to get them all over, but it was best they arrive that way. Unremarkable, unnoticed.

"I suggest we rest up tonight and then try to see Lord Vonn in the morning," declared Amelie when they'd all assembled at the end of the wharf. "We can warn him about the demons and ask for his help. We can spend the night figuring out a plan to approach him."

"Sounds good to me," said Ben. "Anyone know of a good place to stay in this town?"

He glanced at Rhys and Towaal, the only two who'd actually been there before.

"The Blademaster's Baby. It's a fine inn and within a few blocks of Vonn's keep. Also," added Rhys, wincing, "it's about as far from those damn smithies as you can get."

Ben nodded. Even at the docks, the constant clang of hammer on metal was ubiquitous. The blacksmiths would be at work from dawn until well after dusk. If the companions wanted any chance of real rest, staying as far away as possible was good advice.

They started up the wharf, dodging wheeled carts stacked high with wooden boxes. Ben suspected the boxes were stuffed full of weapons, traveling up to Kirksbane then through Sineook Valley to Whitehall. There, Argren would be assembling his men and preparing to march against the Coalition.

"One of Fishbone's crew told me they already opened staging grounds outside of Fabrizo," remarked Rhys, eyeing the equipment as they passed. "War is inevitable now, so Argren must have wanted to secure a landing before Jason got aggressive and moved to take it. The Alliance has the advantage on the water, but they can't win it from there. They've got to plunge the knife deep and threaten Irrefort itself."

"They'll have to move through Issen first," said Amelie grimly.

Rhys didn't respond.

Issen had been taken by the Coalition when Amelie's mother had betrayed her father and the city. They'd found out in Irrefort that Lady Selene had thrown the gates open and laid down for Lord Jason, in more ways than one. None of them thought King Argren's passage through the city would be so bloodless. Despite everything Lord Gregor and even Lady Selene had done to spare the common folk, it appeared Issen would be the site of the first major battle of the war. Hopefully the last if Ben and Amelie could do anything about it. He snorted helplessly. What could they do?

"I wonder if Saala is there," said Amelie.

Ben blinked. It'd been months since they'd seen the blademaster. "I think he went to Whitehall, didn't he?"

"That's the last we heard of him," agreed Rhys.

"He doesn't have any reason to stay in Whitehall," said Amelie.

"He doesn't have reason to go to Issen anymore either," reminded Rhys. "He spent a lot of time with your family, Amelie, but he's a sellsword. He'll go where someone is willing to pay him. It's not Issen, and I don't think he'd risk Irrefort. Maybe he would return to the City, but Argren's the one raising arms, and Argren's the one who would pay gold for a man with Saala's talent. Northport's fallen. He can't go home. Where else is there for a man like Saala? I'd bet anything he's in Whitehall now."

"Doing what, joining Argren's guard?" questioned Ben.

"If you were a lord with nearly unlimited resources and you were raising an army to go face Lord Jason, wouldn't you hire that bald bastard? He's one of the best blades on the continent, and you heard what we learned in Ooswam. The man's highborn, and he's used to nice things. He wouldn't turn down the kind of gold that Argren can offer him."

Amelie frowned but did not respond.

Rhys led them through the streets, heading deeper into town and, Ben noticed with relief, toward the other side of it from the smithies.

"Why is this place called the Blademaster's Baby?" asked Prem. "Surely there is a story behind that."

Rhys grinned. "One thing you have to learn about the world outside of your village is that tavern names don't make any sense. In fact, the loonier the name, the more likely it is to be a fun tavern."

"Why?" asked Amelie. "More drunks inside?"

Rhys winked at her.

"As long as it has tubs for bathing," said Lady Towaal.

She was waving her hand, trying to clear space in front of her of the ever-present cloud of soot that hung suspended over the city. It settled over everything, giving the place a dark, menacing aspect. Even the cobblestones below their feet were black, the soot ground into the stone.

"What's the point of bathing if you're going to be walking around in this mess the next morning?" wondered Rhys.

Towaal shook her head. "If you haven't learned by now, I'm afraid you never will."

Ben smiled, enjoying the banter. For a brief moment, he was able to let go of the tension he felt about what was coming.

~

THE BLADEMASTER'S BABY WAS, shockingly, a clean place. The food smelled decent, and the ale wasn't soured. When they entered, Ben paused to admire a team of harried-looking women keeping the common room constantly swept out.

Rhys glanced at Towaal and winked. "I have learned a few things in my years."

The mage grunted. She appeared to still be dubious about any inn the rogue would lead them to, but she didn't complain when the innkeeper began describing the clean beds, hot baths, and fresh food.

The next thing Ben noticed about the place was that it was filled with blademasters, more of the sigil-wearing men and women than he had ever seen in one location before. He couldn't decide if it was odd they were in a place named the Blademaster's Baby or if it made sense.

"College of the sword," remarked Rhys after they'd settled in. "Must be tutors there."

"What is the college of the sword?" asked Ben, his eyes fixed on a table of men. They wore dark cloaks, which were certainly practical in Venmoor. They had steel grey tunics, black boots, and black belts with black gloves tucked into them. He couldn't help but mentioning, "They look to be a cheerful bunch."

"For a fee, the college will teach you how to use a sword," explained Rhys. "In Venmoor, it's not a small fee because Venmoor has the most prestigious college in Alcott. As well as the locals, they attract a lot of the highborn sons from Whitehall, the City, and Northport."

"Half the highborn men in Whitehall have spent a few months here," added Amelie.

Rhys nodded. "It's a right of passage for young highborn boys, making a tour of the famous colleges. It's supposed to make them better rounded swordsmen. They spend time training intensively under different masters, or at least that's what they tell their wealthy parents. Most of the younglings I've encountered at the colleges spend their time drinking. Like me, I guess. But everyone knows Venmoor's college has the best blademasters doing the teaching."

"If they have several blademasters," stated Ben, "then it must be pretty good. I never realized there were so many blademasters anywhere."

Rhys snorted. "A blademaster in one of the colleges isn't like a blademaster you'd find elsewhere. They square off in organized duels. They go to blood, sometimes, but usually it's just sparring. The purpose of learning the sword is to fight with it, combat. These men treat it like exercise, like they're jumping horses or some other frivolous pastime of the wealthy."

Ben frowned, his eyes still on the table of blademasters. Before he'd left Farview, he'd dreamed of meeting a blademaster. Now, he'd met several and even sparred with a few. He found he was still intrigued, though. A sense of adventure was woven into Ben's being, and the idea of a blademaster embodied that sense.

"You want to get your sigil?" asked Rhys.

Ben blinked.

"I'm not sure we have time for that," remarked Amelie.

"What's a sigil?" asked Prem.

"Look at their scabbards," said Rhys. "See that marking, the leaf and the slash? That's the blademaster sigil. They earn it when they defeat another blademaster. It's a mark of distinction. It lets others know how talented they are."

"I don't understand," said Prem. "My father taught me that when fighting, it is always a good idea to allow your opponent to underestimate you. Alerting them that you are dangerous seems, well, it seems stupid."

Rhys grinned. "It is. Like I said, these aren't real fighters or swordsmen. They're just in the business of it. Look at it this way. Letting an opponent know you're dangerous is not a good way to win a fight, but it is a good way to win a commission from some highborn."

"Saala wore his sigil," challenged Amelie.

"Aye," agreed Rhys. "It got him a commission from your father, didn't it?"

Amelie blinked uncertainly.

"If they're in the business of it," wondered Ben, "would they go fight for anyone?"

"Like mercenaries?" inquired Rhys.

"Would they?" pressed Ben.

"I'm not sure," admitted Rhys. "They're not your typical sell-swords like that jackass Ferguson who accompanied us through the Sineook Valley. Here, in the college, they lead a pretty comfortable life. Why risk your life if you don't have to?"

"We can give them a reason," said Ben.

"What are you thinking, Ben?" asked Amelie.

"Tomorrow, let's go to the college of the sword before we see Lord Vonn."

BEN WOKE up to the clanging of bells. He sat bolt upright and dashed to the window, the dim light in the room confusing him and flashbacks of Indo running through his head. Slowly, the clanging of bells resolved into the pounding of hammers on metal, and the dim light was due to the thick cloud of soot hanging overhead, obscuring the early morning sun.

He yawned, his jaw cracking, and he stretched, working out the last of the sleep. There was no attack, no reason for alarm, just a bunch of over-eager blacksmiths at work at the crack of dawn. Behind him, Amelie stirred in the bed but didn't wake.

Ben crossed the room to a bowl of lukewarm water and splashed it on his face. They'd drank the night before. Not heavily, had been the plan. Rhys was never one to stick to a plan, though, and he'd dragged Ben and Amelie along with him.

As more hammers joined the metal chorus, Ben realized with a sinking feeling that his brewing headache wasn't going away until they left the city. All the more reason to get to it. He buckled on his longsword and quietly slipped out of the room, leaving Amelie slumbering in the bed. When she woke, she'd know where he was.

Two cups of kaf and a breakfast of runny eggs and undercooked bacon later, she'd come down, and they were ready to leave.

"How do you suggest we get the blademasters to listen to us?" asked Rhys.

The rogue was squinting and holding a hand up to his head as they stepped out of the inn. He looked torn between blocking the sunlight from his eyes or the constant clanging from his ears.

Ben grinned. It was possible, that for once, Rhys was more hungover than he was. He replied, "I've got a proposal for them."

"To hire some mercenaries?" asked Rhys. "Hiring more than one or two of them will take all the coin we've got. Convincing two of them to stand against a demon army is going to take more guts than I've got."

Ben shook his head. "We're not going there to hire anyone. I'm going there to enroll."

Rhys coughed and stumbled.

"You can play my father. Towaal can be my mother. Both proud parents coming to see me off to blademaster school."

"It's called a college of the sword," complained Rhys.

"I don't look anything like your mother," retorted Towaal more fervently.

"I take after my father," quipped Ben.

"You don't look like me either," rejoined Rhys.

"My real father," said Ben with a broad grin.

"Ben," interrupted Amelie. "What do you hope to accomplish by enrolling in this place? Surely you don't mean to stay."

"Of course not," he agreed.

"Then why enroll?" asked Amelie.

"We need them to listen to us. When we were talking last night, I had an idea. I spoke to one of those blademasters, and I think it will work."

His friends looked at him expectantly.

"To enroll, there is a test of skill, a sparring match to determine where you stand in the school. I'll beat them," declared Ben. "Whoever tests me, I'll beat them badly enough that we draw the attention of the leaders of the place. I'm sure they'll want to speak to a student who is better than their teachers. You said you thought I could beat one of them, right, Rhys?"

"It's risky," rumbled Rhys. A smile crept onto his face. "But I like it."

HALF A BELL LATER, they stood in front of a massive stone edifice. It rose four stories tall and was elevated above the street by five wide stairs. Beside the structure was a huge arena, but early in the morning, it was locked and quiet. The college itself was quiet too, just a handful of young men jogging in and out.

"They'll have admissions at set times of the year except for special cases," advised Rhys.

"How do you become a special case?" inquired Amelie as they ascended the stairwell.

"You'd best get that coin purse ready," suggested Rhys.

Amelie grimaced and complained to Ben, "This had better work."

He smiled back at her, trying to hide his nervousness. They were counting on him to defeat an instructor at one of the most prestigious colleges of the sword in Alcott. Rhys seemed confident he could do it, but it was a risk. There was a very real possibility that the day would end in embarrassment for Ben. If he failed, getting the blademasters to listen to them would become much more difficult. He rolled his neck, stretching the muscles and, he hoped, helping to clear the dull ache at the back of his skull.

At the top of the stairs, they found a colonnade that ran along the front of the building. Underneath was a series of nondescript doors. A handful of people rushed in and out, but they didn't see an obvious main entrance anywhere. Ben caught the arm of one of the young men who was heading in.

"Admissions?" he asked.

The boy eyed Ben distastefully and advised, "South end. Big open gate. Has a sign out front. It's labeled 'admissions'. Try there."

Ben chose to ignore the boy's unfriendly tone and led his friends to the south end of the building. There, as the boy suggested, they found an open gate with a small office next to it. Inside, a clerk was sitting at a desk, looking bored. Over and over, he'd flip a small dagger. He watched the little blade spin. Then, he would snag it out of the air by the hilt. It was the kind of game you could become very adept at if you spent bell after bell, day after day, with nothing to do.

"I'm here to enroll," declared Ben.

The man caught the dagger one more time and laid it on the desk.

"Fall enrollment closed four weeks ago," drawled the clerk, eyeing Ben up and down and then turning his gaze to Amelie and

Prem. Without looking back at Ben, he continued, "Winter enrollment won't start for another two months."

"I'd like a special enrollment," said Ben, suddenly nervous that a special enrollment didn't actually exist.

The man behind the desk sighed dramatically. "The fee is double if you do that."

"I understand," agreed Ben. "I've come a long way to be here. I'm told it's worth it."

The man yawned and then continued, "There's a test to see which class you're appropriate for."

"Of course," responded Ben.

"First month's tuition is due before I administer the test," claimed the man.

Ben glanced at Amelie and Towaal. Towaal frowned but dumped out a handful of coins. The man held up five fingers, and Towaal passed him five shinning, gold discs.

The man barely glanced at the remainder in the pouch, which was still a lot more coin than Ben had ever seen before he'd left Farview. He supposed that at a place like this, the man was used to highborn coming in and throwing around extra coin to get what they desired. Compared to Reinhold's wealth, for example, what Amelie and Towaal carried in their pouches was a rounding error.

The man stood, and Ben was surprised to see how graceful the motion was. He was tall, too, a hand taller than Ben. The man slipped the metal discs into a lockbox and then opened a wardrobe at the back of the office. Ben saw it was filled with wooden practice swords.

"You know what type of blade you prefer?" asked the clerk. No, more than a clerk, Ben saw. This man didn't merely collect the coins.

"Longsword," answered Ben.

"I'm a student," he said, his back to Ben. "I work this desk instead of paying tuition. That's what you were wondering, isn't it?"

The man turned and tossed Ben a wooden blade. It was chipped from use, but it felt sturdy in his hands. Ben shifted his grip, testing the weapon. He thought it was a bit light and weighted more toward the hilt than he'd prefer, but it'd get the job done.

They walked outside the small office, and the man led them a dozen steps to a wide, flagstone courtyard. It was surrounded by four stories of walkways that were filled with young men and a few young women. None of them were paying attention to what happened in the courtyard, but Ben saw everything that happened would be within view of plenty of people. He smiled to himself and glanced apologetically at the man. It turned out that for a clerk, he wasn't such a bad sort. It was unfortunate he needed to serve as a demonstration of Ben's skill.

"Just do your best," suggested the man. "No one is a blade-master on the first day. This is merely an assessment to determine which class you should be in."

"Are you a blademaster?" Ben asked.

The man chuckled. "Of course not. Ready?"

Ben discarded his cloak and actual sword and nodded at the man.

"Good luck," whispered Amelie.

The clerk closed quickly, jabbing a thrust meant to test Ben's quickness or maybe to test whether Ben could fall into the standard forms of defense. He didn't bother. Instead, Ben surged forward to meet the clerk's charge. He feinted and slashed.

The man, likely used to timid students who were nervous about proving themselves, threw his weapon up in defense, but he was too late, moving a heartbeat behind Ben. Ben's sword smashed into the side of the clerk's and the momentum carried it through to crack against the man's head. The clerk gave a startled squawk and awareness flickered out of his eyes. He flopped onto the flagstones, unconscious.

Ben stood by him, holding his practice sword confidently. At first, no one said anything. Then, a murmur of conversation started on the walkways above them. Ben glanced around the courtyard, but no one was nearby. He knelt beside the unconscious clerk and looked at the angry red welt on the side of his head. He hoped he hadn't cracked the man's skull, but he'd needed enough force behind the blow to leave him unconscious.

Around him, he heard stunned cries as people started to understand what had happened. In short time, a trio of well-dressed men came bustling out.

"What is the meaning of this?" the first one demanded. He had thinning black hair and a sprout of silver-sprinkled beard jutting from his chin. It was oiled into a sharp point. He wore baggy clothing, but Ben could see he moved confidently underneath it.

"I'm here for a special enrollment," explained Ben. "This man was testing me, but I'm afraid he's been knocked out."

The silver-bearded man blinked at Ben before asking incredulously, "What?"

A young woman, a student by Ben's guess, skittered closer.

"Master Velt, what he says is true," she said. "I watched it happen. This boy took one swing, and Joshua went down."

One of the other well-dressed men was kneeling beside the clerk, Joshua.

"He's out cold, but nothing appears to be broken," said the man. He chuckled. "I don't envy the headache he'll have when he wakes."

"Or the tongue-lashing Reginald is going to give him," barked the third man, mirth lacing his voice. "Knocked out by an incoming candidate. I don't think I've seen the like."

The first man directed the student to run and find one of the physics to drag off Joshua. Ben guessed they had plenty of those around.

"So, ah, how do I know which class I'm assigned to?" asked Ben.

The silver-bearded man turned and asked, "You have experience with the sword?"

"Some," responded Ben, hoping to be unhelpful.

"Well," huffed the man. "Our freshman class may be suitable for you."

"What was Joshua?" inquired Ben innocently. "Was he a freshman?"

"He's got a point, Velt," claimed the third man. "If he can lay out a sophomore with one stroke, then he's no freshman."

Master Velt sighed and glanced around the courtyard. The space was filling quickly as students, curious as to why the masters were hovering over an unconscious body, came to see what was happening.

"You!" barked Velt, pointed at a heavily muscled young man. "Spar with the candidate. I'll watch and assess his skill."

The young man stepped forward, brushing a lock of blond hair back from his eyes. Ben briefly wondered why he kept it so long in the first place. It seemed a terrible idea. He grinned when he heard Amelie muttering the same under her breath. The blond man took Ben's smile as an affront, though, and his chest puffed out.

"A longsword, eh?" he remarked coolly, stooping to collect Joshua's fallen blade. "A commoner's weapon but one we must learn, I suppose."

"It is common," growled Velt. "The most common weapon in Alcott."

"So we've been told," replied the blond man airily.

He stripped off his shirt and tossed it to a girl in the crowd. She flushed, appearing uncertain if she should be pleased he chose her or offended.

"Are you a freshman or a sophomore?" asked Ben.

"A senior," scoffed the blond man.

His arms were chiseled like they'd been fashioned out of stone. His neck was so thick that he reminded Ben of a bull. Strong, quick to anger, and dumb as a rock. Ben heard Rhys guffawing behind him.

"This will be easier than we thought," whispered the rogue.

"Are you ready?" Ben asked the blond man.

"I ask the questions, candidate," he snarled.

He advanced quickly, assuming an aggressive stance that Ben swore he recognized from Whitehall's guards. The man was big and clearly strong. He probably used his strength to bully the other trainees around the yard. If they were quick, they'd get in a strike here and there, but on the practice field, a man his size could take a few blows and keep coming. Ben decided to stop him quickly, and he felt a lot less guilty about it than the clerk earlier.

The blond man broke into a charge with his sword raised above his head.

Ben ducked to the side and whipped his practice sword across the man's legs. He smiled when he heard the satisfying crack of his wooden sword meeting the man's shin bones.

With a startled cry, the big man lost his footing and went flailing forward to crash down on the stone.

Ben rose and was about to jump on him, lashing down and finishing him, but the gasp of the crowd stayed his sword. Finishing it quick was one way to make a statement, but toying with the bigger man was another. He let his practice sword hover over the man's head. Then, he backed away. Out of the corner of his eye, Ben saw Master Vert purse his lips and cross his arms. The Master at least was aware Ben could have finished it easily.

The blond man struggled to his feet with a noticeable limp.

"A blow to the legs isn't fatal," he growled. "Duels here end when you land what would be a fatal strike."

"Ah," responded Ben. "I thought I just needed to knock you down. Understood."

Rage flashed in the blond's eyes, and he charged again.

Ben was slightly shocked and a little appalled that the man didn't vary his attack. The big man came just like before, sword raised above his head. He deserved what he was about to get, thought Ben. Instead of letting him finish the charge, Ben surged forward, quick as a mongoose, and rammed the point of his weapon into the man's exposed stomach. With a grunt, the air whooshed out of the blond, and he doubled over, clutching his gut and dropping his practice sword. He stumbled, wheezing painfully.

"A fatal blow?" asked Ben calmly.

He spun his wooden blade and raised it high, ready to bring it down on the blond's neck. It was almost too easy. The man was gasping and heaving, his head at the perfect level for Ben to strike and decapitate him if they were using real blades.

It was obvious the man had never been in a real fight where death was a consequence of losing. In that case, you fought through the pain, you got away, and you never let your opponent have such an easy finish.

"That's enough," declared Master Vert, holding up a hand to stop what he must know could be a crippling blow.

Ben shrugged and lowered his sword. Around the courtyard, the crowd was silent except for the pained retching of the blond man. He stumbled away from Ben and fell to his knees.

"Someone fetch Master Lloyd," said Master Vert. His voice was calm, but it carried over the silent courtyard.

"Now we're getting somewhere," muttered Rhys from behind Ben.

Ben hoped so.

"Where did you learn to spar?" asked Master Vert while they waited.

"Here and there," responded Ben. "I'm originally from a small logging town. I guess swinging the axe isn't so different from swinging a sword, is it?"

Vert frowned at him but didn't reply.

Quickly, a small knot of students came back, surrounding a man who must be Lloyd. They parted, revealing a man about Ben's size. His hair was tied back in a blond ponytail, and he moved like a stalking wolf. He wasn't as obviously strong as the big man, but he had a bounce in his step that Ben knew meant power. Ben couldn't help but notice the impression of a blade-master's sigil on the man's scabbard.

"Lloyd," growled Master Vert. "Would you be so kind as to test this candidate? It seems he's more skilled than a senior."

The newcomer took off his weapon and tossed it to one of the other masters. When he stooped to pick up the wooden practice sword, he did it with a preternatural grace, a grace Ben felt was familiar.

"Where do they get so many blonds?" wondered Rhys under his breath.

Ben tried not to roll his eyes at the rogue. He knew the hair wasn't what reminded him of something… something he couldn't quite place.

Lloyd's steel grey clothing washed out his pale features and blond hair. It wasn't his color, Ben thought. Ben's eyes drifted back to the clothing while the man did a few quick stretches, and then he gestured for the students to form into a circle around the combatants.

"So, you knocked down a senior?" the man said, a foreign accent on his lips. Foreign but familiar. Just like the man's face, it hung there like a sign, one that Ben was unable to read. "Where have you studied before, young man?"

"I did knock him down, and I've never studied anywhere. Just sparred with some friends, from time to time," responded Ben. "You are an instructor here?"

"I am," responded Lloyd. He'd begun to pace in a circle, his feet crossing and uncrossing in a smooth movement, every step filled with confidence.

Ben began to circle as well, watching Lloyd's motion, hoping to spot a weakness. They moved halfway around the circle and Lloyd passed by Ben's friends, his face crossing in front of Amelie's. Ben blinked in recognition. The blond ponytail, the wolf like grace… it hit him like a lightning bolt.

"I crossed swords with your brother once," remarked Ben. "He was much more aggressive than you."

Lloyd's foot work continued without missing a beat, but a flash in his eyes told Ben he was right.

"Where was that?" asked Lloyd coolly.

"In his home, in the east," answered Ben.

"Do you work for my brother?" asked Lloyd flatly. "If so, you've made a mistake announcing yourself. We're going to have some questions for you."

"I think you may have more questions to answer than I would, here in the heart of the Alliance," responded Ben. "I'm no friend of your brother. Are you?"

"I haven't seen him in years," murmured Lloyd. "If you're hoping to gain sympathy from me by mentioning his name or to threaten me with it, you've come to the wrong place. In fact, no matter your purpose, I think you've come to the wrong place."

The students were watching with mouths wide open. Master Vert's nostrils were flaring like a prize bull at the show. Ben could see the man was torn between wanting Lloyd to strike a quick blow and wanting Lloyd to explain what they were talking about.

Ben dropped out of his stance and stood upright. "How about we find somewhere private, and I can explain why I came here."

Lloyd stood as well and turned to the master holding his weapon. He opened his hand, and the man tossed the sword belt to him. Eyeing Ben out of the corner of his eye, Lloyd strapped it on.

"Is this meant to be a personal encounter?" he asked, his hand resting lightly on the hilt of his blade.

Ben looked to the other masters. "No, it is relevant to everyone in Venmoor."

Lloyd nodded and instructed Vert. "Gather the other blade-masters and have them come to my classroom."

Vert puffed himself up and opened his mouth to respond.

"Now, Vert," snapped Lloyd.

Master Vert spun and started off, the crowd of students parting in front of him. Lloyd followed behind, and Ben and his friends scurried after.

"He's one of the three Masters responsible for administration," explained Lloyd after Vert took a turn deeper into the college. "He's a capable sort at that. He's utterly incompetent when it comes to the blade or life and death situations." Lloyd looked over his shoulder as he led them through the open walkways of the college complex. "This is life and death, isn't it?"

"It is," assured Ben.

Lloyd eye's drifted over Towaal and then Rhys. He grunted and took them to his classroom. It was arranged like a small amphitheater with seating for one hundred on uncomfortable stone benches overlooking a dirt half-circle. Ben guessed Lloyd would demonstrate techniques while the students watched. Lloyd gestured for them to stand on the dirt practice area and he took a seat on one of the benches.

Ben and his friends stood awkwardly as men and a few women began to file in. Soon, there were about twenty of them present. Ben recognized a few from the tavern the night before, but he avoided their curious gazes.

"This is enough," declared Lloyd. "You came here to tell us something, yes? What is it?"

Ben took a deep breath and then told them about the demons. It wasn't a big impressive speech. It wasn't a rousing cry to battle. It was the facts of the situation.

"Hold on, you're telling us there is a big demon army that

overran Northport, and now they're coming south?" barked one of the men, interrupting Ben.

A big burly man, he wore his black hair in heavy curls. His hands were clenched into fists on his knees. From across the room, Ben could see they were scarred from battle. That man at least was not merely an academic swordsman.

"Uh, yes," confirmed Ben. "That is exactly what I'm saying."

"Surely you heard what happened to Northport last winter?" exclaimed Rhys. "Don't tell me you are not aware of it."

"The city held," growled the man. "The swarm was defeated, and the demons scattered across the north lands."

"That is true, in a sense," said Rhys. "The demons formed into a new swarm, though, and they've been overrunning small towns and villages, gaining strength. Just a week past, they toppled Northport. A swarm strong enough to defeat the most capable force in the west is coming south toward you. That is what we face."

"Just a bunch of undisciplined hunters up there," muttered the big, black-haired man.

"I'd stake the average hunter out of Northport against the average blademaster in this room," claimed Rhys. "They could beat you in a real fight, and you know it."

The black-haired man stood, drawing his sword.

Rhys smiled and drew his blade as well, the silver runes flaring to light and sparkling smoke boiling off the steel. Slowly, the rogue spun his sword, the shimmering smoke forming lazy circles in front of him. There was no doubt to anyone who knew what they were looking at that Rhys held a mage-wrought blade. He was putting on a show.

The blademasters saw the blade, and a collective gasp tore through the room. Whether they were fighters just for show or true killers, they knew exactly what a mage-wrought weapon was and how rare they were.

"He's provoking you," said Lloyd, his voice rising above the muttering behind him.

"Just getting your attention," said Rhys with a wink.

"Do you have a far-seeing device here?" asked Towaal.

Twenty heads turned toward her.

"If not, I can create one for you. You can see the size of the demon swarm yourselves. When you do, you'll understand what must be done to stop it. I must warn you, though, if you far-see, be prepared for what you will witness. There is what can only be described as a demon-king leading this force. It is like nothing you have seen, nothing you have ever heard of. It leads an army of thousands of demons."

"Bullshit," snapped one of the men near the back.

Lloyd held up a hand, and his companions quieted. Ben saw he was a leader of these blademasters, even if it wasn't formally acknowledged. They listened when he spoke. He was the one Ben needed to convince.

"Do not worry," said Lloyd. "I know you would not fabricate something so easy to check as the fall of Northport."

"When I met your brother," responded Ben, "he thought I was an enemy at first. We crossed swords. Then, he threw me through a glass door and nearly cut off my head. But like you, he was curious why we were there, why we had come to speak with him. We told him a story similar to what we just told you. We didn't know as many details, and Northport hadn't yet fallen, but he was wise enough to see the truth in our words. Even there, in the east, they've experienced the surge in demons. I am sure you have in Venmoor as well. There have been rumors about the creatures troubling the smaller towns, am I right?"

Lloyd rubbed his chin, his eyes locked on Ben, but he didn't speak.

"Your brother had his man Briggens bring us a special document, one that he thought would lead to a clue about how to face the demons," continued Ben. He studied Lloyd and guessed how the man felt about his brother. "If he, the Black Knife, was willing to help us, will you do less?"

The blademaster stood, a grim expression on his face. "You know how to pull a man's rope, don't you?"

"It's not a ploy," replied Ben. "There's no reason for us to speculate or doubt. Allow our mage to show you the remains of Northport. You can see for yourself what is coming to Venmoor."

"If Northport has fallen, we'd know it!" growled one of the blademasters behind Lloyd. "That kind of news would fly down the river."

"Yes, I'm sure it will," said Towaal. "How many days does it take a fast vessel to get here from Northport?"

More blademasters called out, voicing various objections, but Lloyd held up a hand.

"The name Briggens is not well known in the west," he said. His peers paused to listen to him. "And throwing you through a door is something my brother is like to do, but proving you know my brother gets you nowhere here. What do you want from us?"

"There are thousands of demons headed south on the river road. They may cross east at Kirksbane, or they may come here. Either way, we will march to face them before they have the choice." Ben paused and drew a deep breath. "There's no choice for us. We must stop them, and we need your blades to do it. We ask that you stand with us outside of Kirksbane and protect Venmoor and Alcott from the demons."

The room erupted in chaos, but Lloyd merely looked back at Ben, thinking. Finally, he held up his hand again, silencing the room. "I believe you. It's too ridiculous of a story to make up, and you'd be found out before long. Surely, though, it will take more than you five and some blademasters to meet this threat?"

Ben rolled his shoulders. "We have allies, but we need more."

Lloyd stared at them for a long moment, his eyes darting between the companions.

"What we say is the truth," said Towaal.

Lloyd grunted. "If the demons are coming to Kirksbane, and you will meet them, then I will meet them as well. If you are misleading us somehow..."

"Fair enough," said Ben, trying to hide the jolt of excitement that shot through him.

"What is next then?" asked Lloyd.

"Lord Vonn. If he wants to protect Venmoor, we believe sending men with us is the only way to do it."

"A good idea," agreed Lloyd. "I will make sure Vonn takes time to listen to what you say. I cannot promise he will send swords, but he will listen." The blademaster paused and looked at Towaal. "I presume you have a plan for this demon-king you told us about? Our blades will not be sufficient for what you've described."

"We're working on it," mumbled Ben under his breath.

"I will deal with the demon-king myself," said Towaal, bravely if not entirely accurately. "Even when it is killed, though, the swarm will number in the thousands."

"I understand," said Lloyd.

"This is madness!" exclaimed one of the other blademasters. "We cannot leave on this foolish quest. We don't know these people, and we don't have anything to do with Kirksbane. Here, this college, this is our place."

"Why did you begin to learn the sword?" asked Lloyd, turning to look at the man who had spoken. He moved back from his bench so he was standing in front of Ben and his companions. "Did you learn it to impress a woman or maybe to gain a comfortable position in the college teaching wealthy, overly entitled students? Did you take up the sword to get some exercise or to avoid some other trade your father was pushing on you?"

The blademaster was stalking back and forth like a lion ready to pounce. Ben pictured him giving lectures like that and imagined the uncomfortable benches were not necessary to keep his students awake.

"Or did you first pick up the sword because you wanted to be a hero?"

He left the comment hanging in the air, letting it settle onto the assembled blademasters and cut deep.

"Tell me again what we're up against?" asked the big black-haired man who had drawn steel earlier. He didn't appear any happier about going, but Ben guessed he didn't want to admit to being a coward in front of his friends.

THAT AFTERNOON, Lloyd and a contingent of blademasters led Ben and his friends to Lord Vonn's keep. The rest had stayed behind to mollify Master Vert and the others and recruit what senior students they were able. Shocking Ben, every one of the blademasters had agreed to come with them.

"Most of them have never been in a real battle," remarked Lloyd as he strode through the soot-blackened streets of Venmoor. "They earned their sigil here or in one of the other colleges. They've never killed someone or had someone attempt to kill them, much less participated in a full-scale battle. They have no idea what they're agreeing to. I can't vouch for their spines in front of an actual enemy, a massive demon swarm of all things, but they do have talent."

Rhys grunted.

"I recognize that sword," remarked Lloyd.

"Is that so?" asked Rhys.

Lloyd chuckled mirthlessly. "I've only been a Master here for about six years now. Prior to that, I lived at home in the east. You know my brother, so maybe you know a little bit about me, too. He's older than me, and I followed in his footsteps most of my life. Until, well, he started taking pleasure in what he... we, did. I traveled a lot back then. I ran into a wide variety of people in my line of work."

"I'm familiar with the business," admitted Rhys. "I've dabbled myself, a time or two."

"Just twice?" responded Lloyd dryly.

"You've never mentioned a brother," said one of the blademasters who accompanied them.

"No, I didn't," responded Lloyd.

He didn't explain further, and he dropped the inquiry of Rhys. Ben could see Lloyd's companions were eager to question him, but they wouldn't do it in front of strangers, strangers who apparently knew more about their friend's family than they did.

They made it to a squat stone keep. It was black, stained from the ever-present soot of Venmoor. The place looked evil to Ben, but the blademasters strolled in through the open gate like they owned the place. They made into a giant reception hall before someone stopped them.

An officious-looking man with a thin mustache was sitting at a delicate desk. On top of it was a single sheaf of parchment, a feathered pen, and an ink jar.

"Appointment?" he asked.

"No," rumbled Lloyd. "We're here to see Lord Vonn."

An eyebrow arched, and the man's lips pursed. His small mustache came together like icing on a cake of disapproval. "An appointment is required to see the lord. Shall I mark you down for some time next week?"

"Tell Lord Vonn that Lloyd is here to see him."

The small man smiled. "I will not be doing that."

"Do you know who I am?" growled the blademaster. He shifted, so the sigil on his scabbard was obvious.

The clerk merely steepled his fingers and raised his eyebrows.

Lloyd bent over, picked up the man's ink pot, and slowly dumped it onto his sheet of parchment. The man's mouth popped open in surprise.

"I don't see any appointments on here for this afternoon," growled the blademaster. "Now go. Tell him Lloyd needs to see him immediately."

"I-I will have the guards on you," stammered the clerk.

"Vonn knows who I am even if you do not. Tell him now so I don't have to explain why I mopped the floor with his clerk's face."

The little man shot up and scurried over to the guards. They appeared agitated at first, until they had a chance to see the group. The blademasters stared at them calmly, and the guards made no effort to intervene. In short order, the little clerk was scurrying off to find a higher ranking or bolder official.

"Everywhere we go, clerks are in the way," remarked Ben.

"Not your first time busting in somewhere you aren't wanted?" asked Lloyd.

"I had to knock out your clerk earlier this morning," reminded Ben.

"Fair enough," allowed the blademaster. He sighed like he wished he'd taken the opportunity to knock out Vonn's clerk.

Soon, another set of officials arrived. This set apparently had no concerns about taking the blademasters in to see the lord. They gestured for the party to follow. They were led through the public spaces of Venmoor's stark keep and then into the private quarters.

Ben couldn't help but study the furnishings as they passed, comparing it to the other enclaves of wealth that he'd been inside. It reminded him of Northport. Both cities controlled monopolies on their industries and had bountiful wealth. Neither one appeared to find a need to display it liberally, though.

Amelie studied it as well, paying particular attention to a set of tapestries that depicted some ancient battle. She could probably identify it, thought Ben, but he had no idea. It looked like any other battle to him.

"First time in a lord's castle?" Lloyd asked Amelie.

She smiled back at him. "Not quite."

When they finally found Lord Vonn, he was sitting alone at a massive oak table. In front of him, a map was spread out. A half-empty decanter of red wine anchored one side and an ornate dagger the other.

"Good," barked the lord. "I was just about to send for you. We've received terrible news."

Lloyd strode to the lord's side and glanced at the map.

"Northport has fallen?" asked the blademaster.

Vonn glanced at him. "How did you know?"

"We have our sources," claimed Lloyd, looking at Ben out of the corner of his eye.

Vonn grunted and then turned back to his map. "I'm told the size of the swarm is historic. Like nothing anyone has seen before. Obvious, I suppose. There are a number of possible routes they could go from there. East, roughly following the high road. South on the river. Even west to Narmid."

"They're coming south," stated Lloyd. "They're already on the move. They might be able to cross and head east at Kirksbane, or they'll come here. I'm afraid it's impossible to predict which they'll do, but we all know demons dislike water. Even the shallows may give them pause, which leaves Venmoor as the most likely destination."

"They're coming south?" exclaimed Vonn. "Are you sure?"

Lloyd nodded, ignoring the shuffling of Ben's party. "I am sure."

Lord Vonn flopped back into a velvet-covered chair and snatched a crystal wine glass off the table. He scrubbed at his face with his other hand.

"How can you be certain?" asked Vonn, glancing at Ben and his friends. His eyes lingered on Towaal. "Never mind. I didn't think you liked the Sanctuary over at the college, but I should have known. There is little that the mages don't stick their noses into, is there?"

Towaal inclined her head to the lord and did nothing to disabuse the man of the idea that she was from the Sanctuary. If he thought they had the Veil's blessing, it wouldn't hurt.

Lloyd cleared his throat to get the lord's attention back. "I've come to tell you that a number of us plan to march north. We'll hold a line north of Kirksbane. I'd like your support and your men. We'll need every blade we can put in the field."

Lord Vonn's lips twisted. He breathed deeply and was about to respond when the clatter of breaking crystal drew everyone's attention.

Rhys was standing at the side of the room, a broken goblet on a hutch in front of him, a full decanter of wine in his hand. "Sorry about that," the rogue mumbled.

Lord Vonn stared at him incredulously.

"We mean to leave tomorrow," interjected Ben, speaking quickly to draw the attention away from Rhys. "Based on our reports of the demon swarm's progress, we could arrive in Kirksbane three to four days before them."

"Who is this?" Vonn asked Lloyd.

Towaal spoke up before Lloyd could respond. "This is Benjamin Ashwood from near Issen. He's leading the combined forces against the demon swarm."

"And what is your name?" asked the lord.

"Lady Karina Towaal, and you know where I am from."

Lord Vonn turned up his wine glass and set it down on the table hard. He glanced at Rhys, and the rogue grinned sheepishly.

"The Sanctuary is sending support?" asked Vonn, turning back to Towaal. "I assume it's not just you."

"Of course," murmured Towaal. "There will be a contingent of mages. I was merely the first ready to leave, so I was dispatched to assist in recruiting allies. The demons are a threat to us all, and we have little time."

Vonn turned to Ben. "I hope you understand, Lord Ashwood, I cannot offer you much on such short notice. I must retain sufficient forces here to ensure order within the city. I will give you what I can, though."

"Your rangers, my lord," interjected Lloyd. "I believe those men would be best suited for this campaign."

"Good idea," replied Vonn, rubbing his chin. "I'll check with Commander Rakkash, but I believe we could muster near three hundred of his men by tomorrow. First light?"

Ben nodded, his head swimming.

"I'll send word to Whitehall as well," murmured Vonn, his eyes dropping back to the map. "If the demons are already on the move, it will be too late for Argren to intercept them, but maybe it will give his new foreign general something to do other than harass me for more weapons. If the worst happens, at least they'll be on the way."

"We have preparations to make and forces to gather at the college," said Lloyd. "We'll leave you to organize things here. First light tomorrow, outside the north gate."

"Good luck," responded Vonn, meeting Lloyd's eyes. "I think we're going to need it."

"That moved rather quickly," said Ben.

He and Amelie were preparing for bed in one of the college's spare rooms. It contained two narrow cots, and that was it. The hallway outside was loud with students bustling about, excited about the news of a giant demon swarm descending upon them. Ben thought they sounded a little cheerful about the matter, but most of the students were younger sons in highborn families or from wealthy merchant clans. They'd never faced real hardship and had no idea what was coming. Assuming Ben and his friends failed, that was. None of the youngest students would be going with them.

"We're nearing the end," said Amelie. "Things will be quick now, one way or the other. Besides, with news of Nothport's fall, the blademasters and Lord Vonn have little other choice. It doesn't take much to imagine Venmoor is the next major city in line, and Whitehall and the Sanctuary aren't rushing to defend them. Vonn knows they will have to face the demons. We just happened to arrive at the right time with a plan and allies."

Ben grunted. "Not many allies."

Amelie smiled. "We're gaining more every day."

"Do you think the Veil will come for us?" asked Ben.

Amelie shrugged. "We have the staff. I'm not sure if that means she will confront us or avoid confronting us. If she thinks we intend to use it against the demons, perhaps she will wait until the battle is over. If she thinks we'll use it against her, she'll send everything she has after us. She's been plotting for centuries, and who knows what webs she's spun."

"She could help if she came to Kirksbane," suggested Ben.

"Maybe she will, but I wouldn't count on it."

Ben stripped off his tunic and splashed water on his face and body from a small bathing basin. It wasn't as good as a bath, but it was better than nothing. He toweled himself off and turned to Amelie.

"Your bed or mine?" he asked.

"I'm not sure it matters. This may be the smallest bed I've ever slept in," she mumbled. "We've slept under bushes that were more comfortable than this."

"I think there's a reason this is the room that's open," responded Ben with a grin, "but I wasn't thinking about sleeping."

Amelie smiled at him. "Is that all you ever think about?"

Ben winked.

"You did well today," said Amelie. "We have an army now. I'm not sure it will be enough, but I'm hopeful. Hope is something we didn't have a lot of before today."

Ben's smile faded. "We have an army, Amelie, but I'm not ready for this. Towaal keeps thrusting me forward, but I've never led so much as a herd of sheep."

"You've been leading us," reminded Amelie.

"You, Rhys, and Towaal don't count," said Ben. "That's different. These are people we don't know. People who are just following orders. People who aren't going to take several months to get to know me and then decide they need to atone for their past sins like Rhys or Towaal. This is too much, too quick."

"Ben," Amelie assured, "no one is ready for this. Did Lord Vonn look like he knew what to do? You've gotten us this far, through more than anyone could have ever imagined. Have faith in yourself, Ben. It may not feel like it, but you are ready. As ready as anyone could be."

He sat silently until she put her hand on his chin and turned his face toward hers. Their lips met, and he forgot about his worries.

12

THE ROAD II

Dawn was breaking, the sun struggling to shine through the thick clouds above Venmoor's smithies. They stood beside the road, Ben kicking at the black dirt just outside of the city gates. In the distance, he could see green, but near them, everything was covered in soot.

"Good hard rain during the spring washes most of that away," remarked Lloyd. "When the wind blows, that helps too. Venmoor isn't so bad once you get used to it."

Ben glanced at the man and asked, "Why are you really here?"

Lloyd grinned. "You sold me on the demon threat. What else am I going to do, sit and wait for them to come? No, my choices were to fight or to run, and I've done enough running in my life already."

"No," said Ben. "I mean, why are you in Venmoor."

A flash of regret washed over Lloyd's face, but his tone was still light when he responded. "Thought I told you that. Had a falling out with my big brother. He's not the type you argue with and then hang around."

"Why Venmoor?" pressed Amelie, evidently sensing the blademaster wasn't ready to share more about his brother, but still hoping to prod him for information.

The blademaster stretched, his joints popping and cracking with the motion. "I figured I needed to get as far west as I could, and I sure as hell wasn't going to Akew Woods or Narmid. Northport is too cold. The City is too full of mages. Whitehall is too full of pompous fools. Where does that leave me?"

"Venmoor," replied Ben.

Lloyd nodded and then gestured toward the gate. "Finally."

"Is it a bad sign that they're half a bell late?" wondered Ben.

"Nah," replied Lloyd. "Lord Vonn is a good man and true to his word. His rangers are his best troops for this kind of work. We're lucky to have them."

Through the gates, row after row of heavily armed men streamed out. They were in a rough formation, but even Ben could tell they weren't used to it. He guessed men like these rarely traveled in such a large group. At their head was a tall man with red-orange hair. It was piled up in a top-knot, and from one hundred paces away, Ben could tell he moved like a stalking hunter.

"Commander Rakkash," he said when he got close. He offered a quick bow to Lloyd.

Lloyd inclined his head toward Ben. "That's the boss right there."

Ben held out his hand. "Ben."

Commander Rakkash took it and pumped it once. "Pleasure to be of service, my lord."

Ben flushed. "I'm not a lord."

"Sorry, general," corrected the commander.

"I, ah…" Ben closed his mouth.

What was he going to say, that he was a simple brewer from Farview? However it happened, he was leading several hundred men. He wasn't sure that qualified him as a general, but there was no point arguing it and undermining his authority with the rangers.

Instead, he asked Rakkash a question, "Lord Vonn wasn't sure how many troops could be ready on such short notice. How many were you able to assemble?"

"Three hundred and twenty-seven, sir," responded the commander.

Ben nodded and scratched the back of his head. He glanced at Rhys out of the corner of his eye.

"I think we're all here and ready to go," suggested Rhys.

"Right," said Ben. "Let's, ah, let's march."

They set off down the road, Ben at the head with Amelie and Lady Towaal, the rest of his friends, a contingent of two-score blademasters and their students, and three hundred twenty-seven of Lord Vonn's elite rangers behind them.

Ben kept his eyes ahead, afraid that if he paused or looked back, someone would ask him a question. Even in his dreams where he was a hero of great battles, a blademaster, and a skilled lover, he never was so bold as to predict this.

Benjamin Ashwood, previously of Farview, was striding to war against an army of demons. A highborn lady on one side, his girlfriend if he thought about it. A mage of the Sanctuary on the other. An assassin and drinking buddy beside her. More blademasters than he could remember the names of followed them. Plus, an actual army. It had happened so quickly he wasn't quite sure what to think.

"Sir," asked Commander Rakkash, "could you brief me on the mission? Lord Vonn only told me that we marched to face demons. A swarm unlike anything this world has seen, he said."

"Well," replied Ben slowly, "that's true."

"Are, um, are we the only ones marching?" inquired the commander, glancing around curiously.

"There are others meeting us in Kirksbane," responded Ben.

They marched another hundred paces before he admitted. "There aren't very many of them."

"Oh," said Rakkash.

"I think you'll find what they lack in numbers, they make up for in effectiveness," said Ben.

"Mages," said Rakkash, bobbing his head. "I expect you'll want them to do the bulk of the fighting, and my men will be the shield in front?"

"Yeah," answered Ben. "Something like that."

"Have your men faced demon swarms?" asked Amelie.

"They have, my lady," answered Rakkash. "Every one of them has. No one gets into the unit now without combat experience. These days, it's necessary. It has fallen on the rangers to keep the hills around Venmoor clear of the monsters. We send out squads every day. Sometimes, they find a demon, and sometimes, they don't. Sometimes, they go missing."

Amelie raised an eyebrow.

"Then we know it's a swarm," explained Rakkash. "For a swarm, I send a company. Every man that is walking behind us right now has faced demons in the field, but to be honest, it's wearing us down. I could have mustered twice as many experienced men last year."

"We understand Commander," said Ben. "That's why we're going to do what we're going to do. The rifts between our worlds are closing, but we've still got to deal with the ones that are already here. One way or the other, at Kirksbane, this fight ends."

THAT EVENING, they made camp on a flat, grassy lawn that sloped down to the Venmoor River. Ben was saved from embarrassment when Commander Rakkash gently suggested that he could see to his men while Ben and the other commanders camped separately. Ben gave a sigh of relief, caught himself, and tried to appear general-like.

"It's okay," said the commander. "I'm guessing this is the first time you've had this many men serving under you. Would have to be, how young you are. No offense."

"None taken," assured Ben. "You're right. This is my first time leading a group this large."

"We'll follow you," said Rakkash. "The blademasters are following you, which means they think you're gonna do something right. I'll be right behind them until it looks like you're going to do something stupid. Then, I won't be. Orders are orders, but I won't throw away my men's lives. Know what I mean?"

Ben chuckled. "Fair enough, commander. All I ask is that when things look scary, give us a chance to show what we can do."

"Deal," said the commander, and then he spun and marched off, checking his men's camp, hassling those who weren't moving quick enough, and offering a word of praise for those who had already squared away their sleeping space and started on dinner.

"You could learn a lot from that man," said Lloyd.

"You overheard?" asked Ben.

"I did," admitted Lloyd. "One of my less honorable habits is eavesdropping. You did right by telling him the truth. A man like that has led men to their deaths, and he knows that's what he's doing here. He'll save the ones he can, but you don't face a demon army bloodlessly. He won't listen to someone who isn't going to tell him the truth. He doesn't have time for that foolishness and won't send his men on a suicide mission."

Ben nodded.

"This isn't a suicide mission, is it?" asked Lloyd.

Ben winced. "I hope not."

Lloyd frowned and glanced around the bustling camp. No one

was near them. "You have more resources than just us, don't you?"

"Not many," admitted Ben. "It's a small group, but like I told Rakkash, give them an opportunity to show what they can do. Mages, swordsmen, all worth scores of regular soldiers. We also have some other tricks up our sleeve that we can't discuss just yet."

"Is it enough to stop a demon army?" challenged Lloyd.

"Wait until you meet my friends Jasper and Adrick," suggested Ben. "Then, you tell me."

13

KIRKSBANE

THEY FOLLOWED THE BROAD SWEEP OF THE RIVER AND BEN couldn't help but feel nostalgic for the first time he'd traveled those waters. Then, his biggest concern in life had been a drunken encounter with a bar maid and how Amelie would react. The Sanctuary had been a benevolent group of mages who rarely made themselves known in the broader world, and the Alliance and Coalition had been interesting in an abstract way. He hadn't even heard of the rift, and the thought of a legion of demons led by some sort of giant king would never have even made it into his imagination.

He shook his head. Even now, after seeing the thing, he was still having trouble grasping the enormity of the demon-king. It was massive, and it flew. Conventional weapons would be worthless against such a creature. Jasper, the group he'd recruited, Lady Towaal, maybe help from the Sanctuary. If they couldn't put a stop to the thing…

"It's getting real now, isn't it?" asked Amelie, evidently guessing at his thoughts.

He nodded. "It's been real. Impossible is the word I was thinking."

"You don't think we can stop this swarm?" asked Amelie.

"I'm not very hopeful," admitted Ben. "We have to try, but will that effort mean anything? You saw what Jasper showed us just like I did. There's nothing I can do against a monster like that."

Amelie hooked a thumb over her shoulder. "They're following you, Ben. By yourselves, you'd be right. We're like insects to that thing. Together, maybe we can stop it."

"Maybe," grumbled Ben. His eyes were down, watching the battered toes of his leather boots march along the hard-packed dirt road. He needed new boots. Sighing, he asked, "What if it's not enough? Where can we find more allies?"

"I don't know," responded Amelie, "but every time, you somehow find more supporters."

"Every time?"

"Jasper and his mages, Lloyd and his blademasters, Commander Rakkash and the rangers. We found them, didn't we?"

Ben rolled his shoulders. She was right, but he was right too. At every turn, they'd been able to recruit more allies, but it wasn't enough. They had hundreds, while the demons had thousands.

"Huh," said Amelie. "There are more of them than I thought."

Ben glanced at her and then followed her gaze. In front of them, spread across the road, were a dozen disparate figures. In their center stood a lean man with close-cropped silver hair. A smile crept onto Ben's face.

"We've been standing here for two bells, waiting to make an impression," drawled Jasper when they got close.

"Sorry," said Ben. "We slept in."

He looked down the line at Jasper's companions. They definitely made an impression. Beside Jasper was a hulking giant. He reminded Ben of Gunther, but instead of a war-hammer, the giant clutched a crossbow the size of a man. A regular-sized man, thought Ben, eyeing the giant. His hair was shorn on the sides, and a thick black shock of it rose straight up from his head. Mages Jasper had said, but the man looked every bit a warrior.

On the other side of Jasper was a blond man with a neatly trimmed beard. He wore chainmail that appeared to have more patches than it did original chain and he had two longswords strapped across his back. Next to him was a man leaning casually against a battle axe with a head was as wide as Ben, and a woman stared at them from behind a blue, silk mask. Ben was certain she was a woman because her face was about the only portion of her that was adequately covered. At the end was a slip of a girl. She wore a thick, brown cloak with the cowl pulled forward. Her lack of obvious weaponry only made her seem more dangerous. No one would travel with a group like Jasper's if they couldn't handle themselves.

"Friends of yours?" asked Lloyd. "They look dangerous."

"They are," confirmed Ben, answering both comments.

⁓

"How'd you convince two score blademasters to follow you?" asked Jasper.

"They would ask me the same thing about you," remarked Ben. "Besides, they're not all blademasters. Some of them are students."

Jasper grinned. The mage sipped his ale and let out a satisfied sigh. "Not as good as the Curve's ale, but not bad either. You know the innkeep over there, Tabor? He tells me he brews all his own ale. Really has a knack for it."

Ben coughed.

"We've heard," said Amelie, venom dripping from her voice.

Jasper looked between the two of them, confused.

Rhys, shockingly, was the one who pulled Ben out of the fire. He changed the subject.

"Did you get it?" he asked. He nodded to Prem, who sat quietly beside him. "Can you show it to her?"

Jasper eyed the guardian.

"Her father may be the one to wear it," explained Rhys. "We have something to show you as well, another item that shouldn't get into the wrong hands."

They streamed upstairs and crowded into Jasper's small room. Ben climbed up onto the bed and scooted down to make room for the others. Jasper glanced at Ben's boots resting on his pillow, and Ben offered a sheepish apology. The mage opened a battered wooden wardrobe. Inside was a shining suit of silver plate armor. The helmet had been removed to fit the thing inside, but even scrunched over, it looked impressive.

Prem let out a soft whistle. After a look at Jasper to confirm it was okay, she laid a hand on the plate.

"Mage-wrought," she murmured. "The entire set. I've never seen anything like it."

"Neither have I," admitted Jasper, "and I know a thing or two about fashioning devices. This, I believe, is entirely unique. It will imbue the wearer with exceptional speed. The metal will be nearly impervious to damage."

"You could be invincible in that," said Ben. "Could someone wearing that face this demon-king you saw?"

"The wearer will be difficult to kill," replied Jasper, "but not invincible. Think about it this way. The steel will withstand a huge amount of force, but the body within will be just as fragile as any human body. Imagine if you put a crystal glass in there and shook it violently. The glass would shatter."

Ben frowned.

"Also, we have the additional problem of needing a mage with sufficient will to activate it, and sufficient skill-at-arms to make use of it."

The mage glanced at Prem, and she nodded.

"My father," she said. "He is the one who should wear this."

"Will it fit him?" Ben asked Prem.

"I think it will," responded Prem, standing close and judging the size of the armor.

"Are you sure this man is the right one?" Jasper asked, glancing at Ben. "The armor is wasted if the wearer is—"

Ben held up a hand to stop the mage. "I've seen him fight. Her father is the right choice."

"There's something else," mentioned Jasper. "I can get this armor onto someone, but I haven't yet figured out how to get it off. When it clasps shut, it will be resistant to manipulation, and it will be sealed to prying fingers. There must be some way to remove it, of course, but it will have to be done on the inside."

"You're saying if he puts it on, my father may not be able to get it off?" worried Prem.

"I'm saying he's going to have to figure that out himself," answered Jasper.

Prem looked back at the suit of plate and began poking and prodding at it. They left her alone with her thoughts. Incredible power with an incredible risk.

Ben grimaced. The armor wasn't the only item to fall into that category. He reached under his cloak and removed the wyvern fire staff.

Jasper's eyes shot wide open.

"We didn't want to say anything over the thought meld in case someone could eavesdrop," explained Ben. "We believe the Veil will know it was us who took the staff, and surely, she will come looking for us. If Eldred could listen to our thoughts, then the Veil may be able to as well."

Tentatively, Jasper reached out and laid a finger on the staff. The runes flared to life, a sudden heat warming Ben's hands. The mage's eyes narrowed, and his hand closed around the staff.

Ben let it go, and Jasper drew it close, studying the intricate runes that covered its length. The mage sat down in the sole chair in the room and laid the staff on a rickety wooden table. He was bent over, eyes roving along the weapon, fingers tapping a staccato rhythm on the table.

"Let's give him time to study it," murmured Towaal. They followed her out into the hall and she explained, "I can feel him probing it, testing where I was afraid to go. It feels like what the Veil was doing but confident. Bringing this to Jasper was the right decision. We should give him silence and space to work with no distractions."

"Is it dangerous what he is doing?" asked Amelie, shooting a nervous glance over her shoulder.

"Of course it is," responded Towaal. "But his touch is delicate and controlled. He is a mage of exceptional ability."

"Stronger than Gunther?" wondered Ben.

"Not stronger," mused Towaal. "I can't imagine a mage stronger than Gunther. Where Gunther is a hammer, Jasper is a sharply pointed quill. Different tools for different purposes. We should not discount Jasper's strength, though. Prior to Gunther, I'd never felt any mage with the power Jasper commands."

Prem listened closely but did not comment.

They descended the stairs from the rooms and Ben saw scores of eyes rise to study them. On one side of the room were Jasper's mages, on the other the blademasters from Venmoor. The two groups had warily accepted that they were fighting the same battle, but there was still a high level of distrust between them. They were both too dangerous, figured Ben, like two angry mountain lions used to working alone but who'd agreed to track down prey together. He was glad he wasn't the prey.

Just then, Commander Rakkash entered the inn. He glanced around, looking sick to his stomach but then brightening when his gaze alighted on Ben.

"The men are bunked and settled," he declared. "We're ready for your next instructions."

Ben frowned and looked over the groups in the common room.

"Good, Rakkash. I'll want you with me, Lloyd, if you have time, and, ah…" he trailed off, unsure of any of the names in Jasper's contingent. "We, ah, we'll go north and find a suitable place to stage our defense."

The small, brown-cloaked girl stood from amongst Jasper's friends. Despite the heat in the room, she was still swaddled in the cloak, and Ben had not seen her even loosen the collar. It was a bit strange when he thought about it.

"I'll go with you," she murmured. "Jasper trusts me to speak for the others in his absence."

Ben shrugged, noticing no disagreement from the deadly array of warrior-mages behind the girl. "Let's go then."

Ben, feeling awkward, led the group through Kirksbane and out the north side of town. They followed the road along the river until they reached a bridge that passed the locks just above town. He paused there and looked around.

Commander Rakkash rubbed his chin and then offered, "If we tore down these bridges, most of those demons'll be afraid to come over the water. Some'll come, but those we can handle. Should be able to keep Kirksbane safe that way."

"Kirksbane," responded Ben, "but if the creatures bypassed us, they'd head straight for Venmoor."

Rakkash frowned.

"Do we have a good idea of what we're up against?" asked Lloyd. The blademaster was standing atop the bridge, looking down. "If we know some specifics, that will help understand what kind of defense we can mount."

"I do," remarked the girl from Jasper's contingent.

The party turned to her, and Ben scratched the scar on his arm. The girl looked to be no more than twelve summers.

"First," asked Amelie, offering a smile, "what should we call you?"

Amusement flickered across the girl's face and then disappeared.

"Elle," pipped the girl. "Follow me."

She led them off the bridge and down to the riverbank. The water swirled sluggishly in the shallows. Below them, some of the stream split off and poured into the canal that made the locks, and some flowed downstream, following the main channel all the way to the City and the South Sea.

"Still water would be best," murmured the girl, "but this is slow enough. Look closely."

Ben and the others leaned over the water and looked down. A fat fish swam by, startled by their shadows. Ben blinked and gasped. The water was changing. Instead of murky brown stirred up by the fish's swishing tail, it resolved into an overhead look at Northport, just like what Jasper had shown them. This one was hazy, though, as if seen through a filter.

"We were returning from the Wilds and used far-seeing to scout ahead," explained the girl. "That was near two weeks ago. This is what we saw."

A loud string of curses erupted, and Commander Rakkash went flailing backward to land on his bottom on the lush turf. He scrambled back on his heels and elbows, eyes wide with wild fear. "What is that!" he shouted.

Grim-faced, the others watched as the man lay panting, struggling to get control of himself.

"That," answered the girl, "is what we're up against."

They looked back at the image. It shifted, floating on the surface of the water. Elle closed her eyes and continued to project her memories. They soared above the grim scene, seeing huge packs of demons swarming outside of Northport's walls, seeing the carnage and destruction inside.

"Destroying the bridge will be a waste of time," muttered Lloyd.

The blademaster knelt on the thick grass of the riverbank. Rather than showing the fear that Rakkash had, his eyes were burning bright with anticipation.

"Oh," he murmured. "Go back a little, can you?"

Elle complied, and they were all looking at the demon-king, perched atop Rhymer's keep.

"The men will be worthless against that thing," said Lloyd.

"We will handle this creature," responded Elle. "Well, we will try to handle it. Nothing like this has ever been seen before in this world. That creature's powers are unknown. I think it's safe to assume they will be substantial."

"We have a weapon we believe may be up to the task," assured Ben.

Elle looked at him.

"Jasper is studying it now," he added.

The girl nodded. "We will need every advantage we can get."

"You'll want the swordsmen to keep the ordinary demons off your backs while the mages deal with, ah, that thing?" asked Lloyd.

Ben shrugged. "Yes, that's what I was thinking."

The blademaster stood and surveyed the terrain around them. "Water is good. The demons are afraid of it, and if we can put our backs to it, we'll prevent them from surrounding us. Height as well. Whatever it is the mages plan to do, I'm guessing visibility is our friend. Particularly if we lose the sun, we'll want to be above the creatures. A clear field where Rakkash's archers can slow them down, a gentle enough slope with enough room that my men have space to use their blades effectively…"

The leader of the blademasters continued talking, primarily to himself, and he set off, hiking north, looking for the perfect spot to make a stand.

"You convinced him, at least," said Rhys, slapping a hand on Ben's shoulder.

"I didn't do anything," protested Ben.

"You brought us together," said Elle, her eyes following Lloyd as he found a tree and scrambled up it. "Without you, Jasper may have not gathered us in time. Even if he had, we'd be alone in the

Wilds or dead outside of the walls of Northport. Without these arms men, we'd be overrun in a moment by a swarm this size." The girl turned toward Ben. "If we are successful, it will be because we combined our strengths, not because of our individual efforts. We must work as a team, and every team needs a leader."

She walked after Lloyd, who was perched on a branch, covering his eyes with one hand and looking to the north.

Ben bent down and grasped Rakkash's arm. The commander grunted when Ben hauled him up.

"Sorry," he mumbled. "I just, I-I didn't expect to see that."

"Can you prepare your men, so they don't have the same reaction?" asked Ben.

Rakkash twisted his lips. "I guess I'm going to have to. It just stunned me for a moment. I'm okay now, I think."

"Good," responded Ben. "I need you with me this afternoon. I'm going to see the lord of Kirksbane and the commander of the watch. I'm told they know you and respect both you and your rangers. We'll use that and gather as many swords and strong arms as we can."

Determination settled on Rakkash's face, and he gave Ben a grim nod.

THE NEXT MORNING, Hadra arrived with several companions in tow. She strode into their inn like she owned it, and then almost immediately fell back in shock and terror. Jasper and his dozen followers all looked up from breakfast to stare at the Sanctuary mages.

"What… what is this?" stammered Hadra.

Towaal stepped in to rescue the woman. She grabbed her arm gently and directed the Sanctuary's mages to a far corner of the room where she could explain a few things. Sincell left the group and sauntered over to Ben.

"I see you were able to make it back in good time," Ben remarked. "Did you have any problems getting out of the City?"

The runaway mage grinned. "That place is still a confused mess after what you did to the tower. Guards, mages, they're running around confused. You really kicked an anthill by taking that staff. The Veil is apoplectic."

Ben grinned. "That's one blow struck against her, then."

Sincell nodded but then grew serious. "Is that staff safe, still? I don't see it on you. You need to make sure it's well protected in case the Veil attempts to take it back."

"She's going to have to run if she wants to get here before the demons," remarked Amelie.

Sincell raised an eyebrow.

"We move out later today," explained Ben. "There's an old watchtower half a day north of here. Used to be a lookout for river bandits, I gather. It's near the water, high on a hill. The perfect spot to make our stand."

"Our stand?" asked Sincell. "You are planning to dig in to face the Sanctuary?"

"The demons," said Amelie, frowning at the runaway mage.

"The Sanctuary will have to wait," said Ben. "Nothing has changed with our plans, but we've learned that in two days, the demon swarm will be here."

THE SUN HUNG on the horizon as if reluctant to put itself to bed. It framed the squat tower of the abandoned watch station in stark black.

"Looks ominous," muttered Rakkash.

Ben frowned but didn't dispute the man's claim. He was right. The thing looked like it was out of a spooky story, a depressing back drop for facing an army of demons. Ben studied the toppled tower, wondering about it. True, river bandits were no longer as big a worry, but surely, it still made sense to maintain the thing. Instead, it looked as if it hadn't been used in a century.

Yellow and orange from the sunset glowed behind the toppled stone walls. The lone tower rose up from the structure, standing straight and tall, despite the dilapidated appearance of the rest of the building.

"We won't be sleeping under a roof tonight," griped Rhys.

"That tower may make for a good scout's nest," offered Lloyd.

"If it's stable enough," responded Rhys. After a pause, he admitted, "It looks pretty stable."

With no direction needed from Ben, the groups began to establish camps around the base of the watchtower. The Sanctuary mages and Jasper's groups settled on opposite sides of the stone structure. The blademasters camped in the shadows of the fallen wall, and Rakkash's rangers and the men the commander had helped collect from Kirksbane spread out on the gentle slope below.

Ben climbed over the waist-high pile of broken stone and mortar surrounding the abandoned watchtower and found an open courtyard inside. He looked back to his companions. "In here?"

"I've stayed in worse castles," jested Amelie as she scrambled over the fallen wall to join Ben.

Prem climbed up and jumped inside, landing lightly next to him. She studied the walls around them and then strode up to one that was still relatively intact. She faced it and declared, "This will work."

"For what?" wondered Ben.

The guardian pulled the silver amulet over her head, the one her father had given her before they had left, and she tossed it at the wall. The disc spun in the air, the image of a First Mage flashing in and out of sight. The back of the amulet struck the wall and stuck there. Lady Towaal let out a low whistle, and the stone below the amulet flashed with a pulse of green light and then fell quiet.

"Oh," breathed Ben.

Prem turned to him. "Did you think I was going to send my father a letter and get him here in two days? Back at our nexus, a new gate will have flickered into life."

"You can do that anywhere?" inquired Amelie.

"Once," answered Prem. "Now that the gate is established, the First Mage's energy is anchored to this place, creating a line between the nodes. It cannot be moved. The other guardians will see the new gate tonight, and tomorrow, they will arrive."

"How many?" asked Ben.

Prem shrugged. "As many as my father thinks he can spare."

Rhys jumped down into the courtyard. "That's a good group of men and women out there. There aren't many, but with the guardians, it's got to be just about the deadliest force assembled since the Blood Bay War."

"You think it's enough?" asked Ben.

Rhys shrugged. "More swords wouldn't hurt, but it's what you have."

They made a cold camp within the watchtower, and as darkness fell, they listened to the sounds of the men bustling about outside. Rakkash's troops and the Kirksbane watch were professional, they weren't drinking or carousing, but four hundred men outdoors trying to keep their minds off an impending battle made plenty of noise. It was nearly enough to cover the approach of Hadra.

The mage slipped into the watchtower and settled down in a shadow where the moonlight did not reach. From the darkness, she warned, "The Veil will come for you."

"How?" asked Towaal.

"I don't know," admitted the Sanctuary mage, "but I know her. Sincell told me what happened with the burning tower. Even before, there were rumors that the Veil was somehow involved.

Mages and Sanctuary guards died, and people are angry. Secrets are what we do in the Sanctuary, and everyone knows the Veil keeps hers. Everyone can look the other way when the darkness is happening somewhere else. When it happens in your city, when you can't look away from the blood, death, and fire, that is a problem. That shows a lack of control. If the Veil, with all of the resources she commands, cannot keep the City safe or hunt down those accountable, then the rank and file mages will no longer support her."

"They don't all support her now, do they?" questioned Ben. "You are here."

Hadra answered, "This is different."

"What would it take to convert more of the mages away from the Veil?" asked Towaal.

"You know the answer to that, Karina," replied Hadra grimly. "The women of the Sanctuary are powerful, important. They live in luxury behind the walls or roam the lands freely, guesting with lords, able to push around those who stand in their way with a simple thought. They've become accustomed to the privilege that being a mage of the Sanctuary grants them, and most will have no interest in changing. If the Veil fails to maintain that privilege, they will oppose her, but do not be so foolish as to think that means they will join you. No, they will oppose Coatney and put another in her place. Someone who will look out for their interests more carefully. Coatney knows that, just as well as you and I. She knows that she is allowed her diversions and her power in exchange for keeping the status quo. She will do anything to maintain that. Right now, your group is the single greatest threat to her power."

"Not the demons?" questioned Amelie.

Hadra snorted. "The demons are evil. There can be no mistaking that. If we fail, then yes, Coatney will have to face them. The mages will be united behind her against that kind of threat, though, and if anything, they would resist replacing her in a time of true crisis. No, it is only internal strife and discontent that would worry her. The kind of trouble that happens when a handful of people destroy a prominent structure in the City, flee from under the mages' noses, and start all sorts of rumors about the powerful weapon they used and possibly stole from the Sanctuary."

"You're right. They'll come for us," Ben said with a sigh.

"They may have already," remarked Hadra. "I'm not sure you could call this an army, but it is certainly a large group. I'm guessing you do not know them all?"

Ben frowned.

"The Veil may have agents amongst the ranks," suggested Hadra.

"What about the mages who came with you?" questioned Towaal. "Can we trust them?"

Hadra was nearly invisible in the shadows, but Ben could hear her helpless shrug. "I believe so, but if the Veil had any inkling of where I was going when I left... I've known these women for decades, even centuries, and I do not trust them completely. That should be a lesson to you."

"Why are you telling us this?" asked Ben.

"Because, young man, I believe you and your forces are the only organization making a serious attempt to thwart these demons. The Sanctuary and the Alliance are all sitting on their hands waiting for someone else to deal with the problem. By now, news of what happened at Northport is spreading. I still don't see any armies being raised aside from this one. Whatever games of power the mages and the lords play are inconsequential if these creatures continue to sweep through cities and feast. There were half a million people in Northport, maybe twice that many on the way to the City. If the demons feed on that many souls, I'm not sure the full force of the mages in the Sanctuary will have the strength to stop them. I don't think anyone will." Hadra stood and stepped into the moonlight. A frown cut through her taut grimace. "That is why I am here and why I warn you to watch your backs. What you are doing is beyond necessary, and we cannot risk an assassin's blade ending it. Trust no one."

The mage turned and vanished into the night. Ben looked around the circle of his friends, grim expressions barely visible.

"Assassins," muttered Ben. "One more thing to worry about."

Rhys shifted in the moonlight, and Ben glanced at him.

"Why are you looking at me?" complained the rogue.

"I-I'm not," Ben stammered. "Well, I was, but not like that."

Rhys harrumphed loudly.

"You were an assassin working for the Veil, right?" chided Amelie. "Come on. You can't act all offended now."

"None of us are perfect," grumbled Rhys.

"Rhys, what do you think about Hadra's warning?" asked Towaal seriously.

Rhys shifted in the dark. "I think she's right. The Veil won't risk coming herself. By now, she must know about the demon army, and she knows about the staff. She won't put herself at such a high risk of personal failure or death. Those outcomes are probably close to equal in her mind. But, there are only so many people she could trust with a job like recovering the staff. Despite what Hadra thinks, many of the mages would not go along with their leader secretly obtaining such a powerful device. The mages may not confront her publicly, but as every Veil knows, it's the murmurs behind closed doors that will end them. The Sanctuary may be willing to bury its head in the sand when it suits them, but they will not countenance the Veil hiding that kind of information, particularly with what will soon be a very obvious threat to their lives. What does that leave for Coatney? A blade in the night or a spy concealed somewhere within our forces. She has to strike us, or someone will strike at her. Sooner or later, we should expect an attack."

"Do you know any of the other assassins?" queried Ben.

"It doesn't work like that," responded Rhys. "There are guilds in other places, but in the Sanctuary, it is compartmentalized. Secrecy is paramount, and no one knows each other."

"So, what do we do?" questioned Prem. She was perched on a rock near the node gate she'd established.

"We wait," said Rhys. "Hadra's correct to think it is a risk, but what can we do except remain vigilant?"

"We'll set a watch schedule," declared Ben. "Even with an army around us, a skilled blade could slip through their guard. We watch each other's backs, and no one moves about alone. Rhys, anything else we should do?"

The rogue stood and began to circle their camp, looking at the walls around them. "This is a good spot. There is no way in except over the wall. With a watch, it will be difficult for anyone to sneak up on us. If it was me, I wouldn't attempt it. I'd strike when we're up and about, when we are distracted. They'll come in the day, when our attention is elsewhere, and they'll come from behind. They'll wait for you to be walking between groups or doing the necessaries. That's when you should be ready."

"That makes sense," responded Amelie.

"Bring your sword when you pee," advised Rhys.

Ben snorted, shaking his head at his friend. He moved to shake out his bedroll. Vigilance was their only defense, and with nothing else they could do that night, they settled down to sleep. Lady Towaal took the first watch, and Ben watched her pace slowly around the courtyard as his eyes drifted shut.

14

ENCROACHING DARKNESS

DAYBREAK BROUGHT A BUSTLE OF ACTIVITY. BEN HAD SLEPT restlessly, his mind churning with ideas for defense. As soon as the sun had crested the horizon, he'd grabbed a hard loaf of bread and salted ham and started making the rounds with Lady Towaal by his side.

They stopped by the Sanctuary mage's camp first and found the group of women sitting around a small fire. There was no wood, he saw, but he didn't blame them for expending a little energy when he smelled the rich scent of tea brewing. He frowned and made a note to ask Towaal and Amelie if they could brew some tea the next morning, or even better, kaf.

Hadra met his eyes but didn't mention her visit to their camp the previous night. Ben eyed the other mages suspiciously, and they ignored him. He wasn't sure if that was a sign they were secretly agents of the Veil, or if they considered him to be beneath notice.

"Tomorrow?" asked Hadra.

Ben nodded tersely. "I'll let you know if I hear differently, but yes, I believe we'll see the first demons tomorrow."

"Will we hear about a plan before then?" asked one of the other women without looking up.

Ben glared at her, but she couldn't see him. "Yes, you will."

Hadra smiled encouragingly, and Ben turned from the Sanctuary mage's camp without further comment. Lady Towaal walked beside him as they circled to where Jasper's contingent was situated.

"That's a good lesson," murmured Towaal. "Always get your information before going to see your troops. They will have questions, and as their leader, you should have answers."

"Thanks for the warning," muttered Ben.

Towaal shrugged. "Maybe it's better you learn that way."

They made it to Jasper's camp, and the spindly mage looked up at them.

"Any updates?" asked Ben.

Jasper stood and shook his head. "No. As best we can tell, they should arrive tomorrow, midday. We'll see some of the slimmer, faster ones at first. Larger, slower creatures may not show up until dusk."

"And the demon-king?"

A grimace crossed the old mage's face. "Our scans are quick so as to not draw its attention, but we haven't seen it in three days."

"Maybe it left," suggested Ben.

Elle, the little girl, still swaddled in her brown robe, snorted.

"We can always hope," said Ben.

"It didn't leave," responded Jasper. "It's out there, lurking behind or ranging further and faster than its minions can. I expect its feasting, gaining power for what is to come."

"It doesn't know we're here, does it?" worried Ben.

Jasper shrugged. "I have no idea what its abilities may be. Could it far-see like us? Maybe. Could it sense us? Maybe. It seemed to know we were looking when we first found it, remember? Is it intelligent enough to know that eventually it will meet resistance? I believe that's likely."

"We need to make a plan today if they'll arrive tomorrow. I'm going to speak with the troops. Do you want to accompany me?"

"Sure," responded Jasper. He stooped, collected his thin sword, and strapped it around his waist. "So, what is the plan?"

"I was hoping you could help with that as well," said Ben.

Jasper grinned. "I'm not a tactician, but I have seen a few battles."

"What should we do?" asked Ben.

Jasper pursed his lips in concentration. He took a moment before responding. "Well, unlike a conventional battle, we cannot just worry about the bulk of their forces. There are thousands of demons. A threat unlike any other but it may not be the biggest threat we face. The demon-king could represent just as much danger as the bulk of its army."

"You think the mages need to hold back?" queried Towaal.

"Yes," agreed Jasper. "With my group and the Sanctuary's mages, we could blow a sizable hole in the demon army. With ample preparation, we could mow down a thousand of them. With a bit of luck and a tight formation, we could eradicate almost all of them. Certainly, it'd be sufficient for the swordsmen to take over and clean up the rest."

"But the demon-king," said Ben. "If you pour everything into defeating his minions, then we'll have no defense against the leader."

"Right," said Jasper. "That thing will be impervious to mundane weapons. Even if you managed to score a blow, it could fly away from you until it heals. Even if the mages hit it hard, it may fly away faster than we can follow. By its size, I can only imagine it could cover a couple of dozen leagues in a bell or two. It will move faster than we can warn towns or cities. If we just kill its minions, Alcott will still be subject to a reign of terror unlike anything in our history. It could make the dark ages feel like a pleasant utopia. You saw it. Can you imagine that thing descending on small towns? There's nothing they could do to protect themselves. Nothing at all."

Ben shuddered, imagining the creature arriving in Farview. "You're right. No matter what, we have to kill the demon-king. Individual demons and swarms can be defeated by sufficient force of arms. Maybe the Alliance would rally and face them, or the Sanctuary could become involved, but the skill we've organized here is required to destroy the leader. Am I missing anything?"

Jasper nodded agreement, and Towaal murmured assent.

"How do we kill it?" questioned Ben.

"The staff," suggested Jasper. "It is the only device, the only tool, that I'm certain could command enough power to put a stop to that monstrosity."

"It comes with a price," advised Ben.

"It does."

"I used it," said Ben. "I had poured out nearly all of my lifeblood and much of it soaked into that staff. The discharge it sent was incredible, but it almost killed me. It would have killed me if Lady Towaal and Amelie hadn't immediately healed me."

"Inefficient usage," said Jasper.

They paused on the slope, a dozen paces from Rakkash's ranger camp.

"If it was used more efficiently, you think it wouldn't be as big of a risk?" inquired Ben.

Jasper met his gaze, cold certainty radiating from his eyes. "I think when we face that monster, we use everything we can. We cannot hold back and hope to win."

Ben frowned. "What are you suggesting?"

"Whoever activates the staff should not hold back."

"Wait!" exclaimed Ben. "You're saying that someone should intentionally sacrifice themselves?"

Ben looked to Towaal for support, but the former Sanctuary

mage was looking everywhere but toward him. Ben looked back at Jasper, and the older mage merely returned his gaze.

"No," said Ben. "We'll do what we need to do, but we don't need to do that. Go back and work on the staff. See if you can find a better way to activate it."

"Ben," said Jasper.

"No," declared Ben. "If I'm the leader of this band, then I make the decision. We figure something else out."

Stone-faced, Jasper turned and moved back to his camp. They'd kept the wyvern fire staff there, certain Jasper could provide better protection for it than Ben and his friends. Jasper was by far the strongest amongst them, and he could vouch for every member of his party.

Ben glanced at Towaal as they made their way down the slope to Rakkash's rangers and the men from Kirksbane. "Well?"

She shrugged. "He is right. The demon-king represents as much of a threat as the rest of the creatures combined. If what they saw through far-seeing was accurate, no mundane weapons will bring that creature down. It could strike Whitehall or Irrefort and fly away unscathed. What are they going to do, hope to hit it with a catapult? We have to kill it somehow, no matter the cost. Ben, no matter the cost."

"Jasper is our strongest and most knowledgeable asset," argued Ben. "He cannot sacrifice himself to destroy the thing. Maybe his mages could form a chain and pass the staff down the line when they attack it? All of them would lose a little blood, but no one has to give it all."

"Maybe," allowed Towaal. "That's less efficient, though. Handing the weapon back and forth in the middle of a battle introduces risk. Someone could drop it, for example. Even with no fumbles, there'd be a delay as each new mage took over. How will the demon-king make use of that break?"

Ben didn't respond.

They made it to the outskirts of the soldier's camp. Most of the men were awake, huddled around early morning camp fires. Ben heard chopping in the distance and thought he should ask Rakkash for some of their firewood. There were no trees on the hill, but if the rangers were collecting it anyway in the forest, he may as well use it to make some kaf.

They found the commander moving amongst his men, offering quiet jokes, answering questions about supplies, and mostly keeping himself visible.

"One more day?" asked Rakkash when they drew close.

"We just got done speaking with the mages. Nothing has changed. One more day," confirmed Ben. "They say it's probable we'll see some of the smaller, faster creatures first. Then, it will be tomorrow evening by the time the bulk of the group arrives."

"Night, huh," remarked Rakkash. "I don't suppose anyone thinks they'll stop and let us rest?"

Ben smirked back at him. He glanced several hundred paces away where the ranger's men were hidden in the woods.

"Collect as much fuel as you can today," suggested Ben. "It's going to be a long, dark night tomorrow. We could set fires out in the field to give us a little visibility. At the least, it may mark distance for the archers."

"Do we have a plan beyond that?" inquired Rakkash.

Ben looked around them and then nodded.

"It's important we protect the mages," started Ben. "Your job will be to keep the demons off their backs. The mages can attack from a distance, and we'll need their might when things get hairy. Your rangers and the Kirksbane watch will form a ring, spears and swordsmen in front, archers behind them, ready to drop their bows and draw steel if needed. The blademasters will be placed amongst your men like anchors. They'll be devastating, I hope, but we can't let them get overwhelmed by the sheer size and weight of the demon swarm. My companions as well as some folks arriving this morning will function as a flying company. We'll go where the line is in trouble."

"We'll keep an eye out for the new arrivals," said Rakkash, his eyes scanning the hilltop, already imagining where he needed to place his men.

Ben trusted the ranger's instincts and let him think on it. The line would need to be close enough to the crown of the hill to form a full circle, but not so close that they were standing on top of each other. They would need to flex as the demons attacked. Too far out, though, and men could get stranded from their fellows.

"What do these new friends of yours look like?" asked Rakkash. With a smile, the commander added, "Hopefully no one confuses them with a demon."

"They, ah, they'll come a different way. You won't see them arrive."

Rakkash looked at him, confused.

"Magic," said Towaal.

The commander of the rangers grunted.

"I said there wouldn't be many of us," reminded Ben, "but we pack a punch. These new arrivals are like no one you've ever met."

"I hope so," said Rakkash.

"Set wood for the fires but warn your men not to count on them lasting," suggested Ben. "At Northport during the first battle, the demons were smart enough to knock over the fires in the field. I assume they'll do the same here. It can still help, though. When the demons are close enough to knock over a burning log, they're close enough to hit with an arrow."

"You were at Northport?" inquired Rakkash, surprise evident in his voice.

"When the first big swarm hit," confirmed Ben.

Rakkash glanced at Towaal. "We heard there was some pretty powerful magic that happened. It's good you're with us."

"Just wait until tomorrow," murmured Towaal. "Northport was a warm up."

Leaving a pale-looking Rakkash behind them, they returned to the top of the hill and found Lloyd and his fellow blademasters working through a series of sword forms. It reminded Ben of the Ohms but lacked the elegance between the transitions. Lloyd paused when he saw Ben and Towaal approach.

"We warm up this way every morning. Half a bell, at least," explained Lloyd. "It seems to have a bit more urgency to it today."

Ben nodded. "I told Rakkash your men would space themselves out to strengthen his line. You can anchor his forces, and I think it's best to keep your blades spread out. Make it so the demons can't overwhelm any single point in the line."

Lloyd nodded and then suggested, "What if we worked in pairs? While Rakkash has some of the best soldiers in Alcott, they're not as quick as we are. If we are in pairs, we can watch each other's backs. I think we'll be more effective that way. It's less coverage on your line, but it will be stronger anchors. The breaks will be in the middle, and a flying company could address that."

"It makes sense," said Ben, glancing at Towaal out of the corner of his eye.

She nodded.

Ben added, "I'll be in the flying company along with some other arrivals who will get here today. I think they'll be sufficient to plug any gaps. You and a few trusted men should hang back with us as well, though, in case you see something that your men need to respond to."

Lloyd nodded and did not comment. Unlike Rakkash, he was apparently counting on forces he did not understand to save them. He knew that against the demon-king, even his blademasters would be insufficient.

Ben and Towaal headed toward the tumbled stone wall of the watchtower, and Towaal remarked, "Well done. He had a good suggestion, and accepting it showed you respected his input. You cannot earn loyalty if you do not have respect first."

"I appreciate the tutoring, but do you think this is the right time?" complained Ben. "We have a battle tomorrow that I'm told will be unlike anything Alcott has ever seen. Shouldn't we be worrying about that right now?"

"The soldiers will be worried about that," said Towaal. "A leader needs to worry about what happens after. If we win tomorrow and dispose of these demons once and for all, what then?"

"What do you mean?" asked Ben.

"The Alliance and Coalition are still preparing for war. The Veil and Lady Avril are still sharpening knives in the shadows. What will be done about them?"

Ben paused before climbing over the fallen rock wall.

"You've gained a force that is small but incredibly powerful," continued Towaal. "Depending on what Jasper's group is really capable of, this might be the most effective fighting force on the continent. Will you use them to address the other conflicts once this one is done?"

"They're just following me now because someone has to deal with the demons," responded Ben. "I assume if they are able, they will return to their lords when this is finished."

"If you assume they will, then they will," retorted Towaal.

Ben hauled himself onto the rocks. "I see what you're doing," he said over his shoulder. He caught Towaal's sly smile. Then, he turned and hopped into their camp.

PREM and a young-looking man were squatting in a corner. Rhys was lounging to the side, watching them, sipping a mug of kaf that Ben hoped he'd borrowed from somewhere instead of stolen. Amelie was nowhere to be seen. Prem looked up when Ben's boots thumped into the soil.

"Vree here was sent early to let us know my father is coming," said Prem.

"What can you tell us?" Ben asked the newcomer.

"Fifty swordsmen, seven mages," stated the man. He stood and picked up a sharp-tipped spear. Twirling it, he started marking the dirt.

"Ten of the swordsmen are what you'd consider a blademaster," he said, making ten quick slashes in the soft ground. "The rest are skilled and battle-hardened. Every one of them spent time outside of the rift. The mages are as talented as those of your Sanctuary, maybe a bit more so. We wanted to send more, but after the battle… well, many are not capable of fighting again anytime soon, and the best of our mages were in that cave when it collapsed."

"And Adrick Morgan?" asked Ben.

Vree smiled. "And Adrick Morgan. He will come across this afternoon. Prem tells me you have something special in mind for him?"

"We do," agreed Ben. "There is some risk involved."

"The Lightblade will do it," assured Vree. "After you left, there was a rather robust debate amongst the guardians. In the end, Adrick was convinced that there is no point in guarding secrets to protect the world while we sit back and watch it fall under to darkness from our forest. If we're unwilling to step out and defend people's lives, well, then we're just hiding."

Ben smiled. "I'd like to spread the guardians into groups of a dozen, with two of the most skilled warriors in each group. They'll be stationed near the base of this watchtower, and we'll use them as flying companies to bolster the line in any places the demons are in danger of breaking through. We'll add a small contingent of blademasters as well. Overall, our goal is to protect the mages. It's critical they are fresh and ready when the time comes."

Vree inclined his head. "We're here to fight. I don't think Adrick will have any objections to your plan."

"You'll have a fight," agreed Ben. He looked around. "Amelie?"

"She's with Jasper's group," said Rhys. "Trying to pry some secrets out of them, I'd guess."

"We should get the mages together when Adrick's force arrives," said Ben, thinking out loud. "Lady Towaal, can you organize a meeting? I think it'd benefit everyone to discuss capabilities and how we can work together."

"Let Amelie do it," suggested Towaal.

Ben raised an eyebrow.

"I'm known as a mage from the Sanctuary," explained Towaal. "Amelie trained there briefly, but she is not seen as a true part of the place. She's unbiased and will be a better bridge between the groups."

"Will they listen to her?" wondered Ben.

"They're listening to you," guffawed Rhys.

Ben coughed. Embarrassedly, he pleaded, "Don't tell her I asked that."

"Asked what?" queried Amelie. She was pulling herself over the wall.

"Ah, nothing," said Ben, a flush building in his face.

She eyed him suspiciously but didn't probe further.

THE NEXT MORNING, dawn found Ben sitting atop the watchtower. The stone wall below was broken and fallen, but the structure of the tower itself still stood strong, though the windows had rotted out, and the roof was long gone. The view from the top was incredible. Ben could see leagues up and down the Venmoor River. To the south, he spied dark clouds over the city that gave the river its name, and he knew that by mid-morning, to the north, he'd be able to see the first of the demons infiltrating the broad, open turf beside the river.

Jasper said that many of the creatures were passing through the forest further to the west, but there were too many of them for the crowded confines of the thick undergrowth. The majority of the demon army was in the open, rolling across the landscape like a wave of death. Small villages, merchants, family farms, everything in their path was consumed and trampled. There was nothing but torn earth and death behind them.

Ben anguished about not being able to help the people in the path of the demons, but it was too late. There was no way to make it to the villages along the river in time to warn them. Jasper had done what he could on the way south, and anyone who hadn't fled was on their own now.

Later in the day, they would station a pair of rangers atop the tower, but this early in the morning, it was just Ben. He had his longsword drawn and resting across his thighs. He'd told himself he would give it one last lick with his whetstone to smooth out any remaining nicks, but he'd done the same the day before. The blade was in as good of shape as he could make it.

No, he simply hadn't been able to sleep, so he'd climbed to the highest accessible point to see the sun shouldering its way over the horizon, shoving the darkness back, and filling the world with light. Bright orange, yellow, and red crept into view like a giant ball of flame. Maybe it was flame, for all he knew. The mages might know something like that, what sort of strange magic powered the sun.

"Beautiful sunrise," remarked Amelie.

Ben turned and saw her ascending the weather-worn stone stairs.

"It is," he agreed. "Hard to believe it's going to be such a terrible day."

She didn't respond to that. He was right. Even if they won,

they knew they'd lose companions. Instead, Amelie settled down beside him, their shoulders and knees barely touching.

"How did it go with the mages last night?" asked Ben.

"They're..." Amelie paused, evidently searching for the right words. "They're a diverse bunch. Secretive, unwilling to work together, used to always getting their way."

"So, as expected?" jested Ben.

"As expected," agreed Amelie. "We have a plan, though, of sorts. It's so difficult though, to try to set an agenda when there are so many unknowns. Will the demons even come for us, or will they pass by in search of easier meat? Will they have a plan like some of the swarms we've faced, or are they driven by pure hunger and will come in a rush?"

"The fog of war," said Rhys.

The rogue was lounging several steps below the top of the tower.

"Were you eavesdropping on us?" asked Ben, annoyed.

Rhys grinned at him. "Not for very long. I saw Amelie coming up here, so I thought I'd join you. I was just making sure I wasn't interrupting another, ah, private moment between you two."

"Another?" asked Amelie, a flush creeping into her face to match the ruddy glow of the sun rise.

Rhys winked and then climbed the rest of the way up.

"The fog of war," continued the rogue. "That's the term for the confusion you're talking about. You can plan, you can plot, but once the battle starts, it's chaos. You'll only be able to see what is in front of you, and you have to trust that your lieutenants know what they are doing."

"Lieutenants?" asked Ben.

"Rakkash, Lloyd, Jasper, and the others," explained Rhys. "You can plan with them now, but once the battle begins, we're all on our own, fighting in our little clear space amongst the fog."

Ben frowned.

"Planning isn't useless," continued Rhys, "but what I'm trying to say is, the unknown is what we should expect. It's even worse since we're facing demons, but no leader can hope to anticipate every movement, every action of their opponent. All they can do is hope that they've prepared their force as best they're able, and that they have capable commanders under them who can react appropriately."

Ben glanced down at his sword. In the dark Venmoor steel, a lone mountain peak was etched in bright silver. The top of it rose, narrow and tall. Its base was wide, though, surrounded by several sharp-peaked foothills. He frowned, not for the first time wondering who had crafted the blade and what purpose the etching hinted at.

"Come on down to the camp," suggested Rhys. "I stole some kaf from the Sanctuary mages again. From the smell of the crushed beans, it's high-quality stuff. Too good to waste on those tea-drinkers."

"You stole from the Sanctuary mages?" asked Amelie with a groan.

The rogue shrugged. "They should have set a watch last night. Besides, we're all on the same side now, right? Surely they'd want to share their kaf."

"Surely," replied Ben, scrambling to his feet and then offering a hand to pull Amelie up.

A BELL LATER, the sun was chasing away the shadows inside the courtyard of the watchtower, and the companions stood in a loose circle while Jasper faced Adrick.

"I cannot free you once you are inside," admitted the mage. "I have spent several bells searching the armor, but there is no obvious release."

"The previous owner managed to get out of it, didn't they?" asked Adrick.

Jasper shrugged. "Yes, or maybe it was never used."

The swordsman's lips twitched. "It's worth the risk. We'll need every advantage we can get today."

The mage nodded, and he stepped forward to assist the Lightblade strap on the armor. Prem joined him, and the two of them began to piece each section of plate onto Adrick's muscular form.

"I know it's a lot to ask," said Ben, "but can you stay in hiding until the battle begins? We should have sufficient forces to repel the initial wave. We'll need you when the bulk of the demons arrive. In case the demon-king is tactically minded, I don't want to tip our entire hand until it's necessary."

"Even in the armor, he still won't be much good against the demon-king," warned Jasper.

"I don't know. You should have seen him against the wyverns," responded Ben.

Adrick met Ben's eyes and drew a deep breath. Jasper fastened the shining, silver breastplate around his chest, and his daughter lowered the helm over his eyes. Bright, flawless steel stared back at Ben.

"Can you see anything in there?" wondered Ben.

The steel shimmered, and Adrick's eyes came into view as if the faceplate of the armor was a smoke-filled glass window.

"I can," answered Adrick's smooth voice. It sounded hollow, coming from within the steel helmet.

"Try moving around some," suggested Jasper. "Get the hang of it. Then, you can wait in the shadows when the demons arrive."

Adrick moved one arm and then the other. The steel moved silk-quiet, upsetting Ben's expectations and jarring his senses. It was unreal, watching the metal plates rub together soundlessly. The swordsman moved a leg, bent slightly, and then leapt, soaring a dozen paces into the air and landing atop a still-standing section of the watchtower wall. The steel banged against the rock, giving Ben some level of comfort that the stuff was actually hard enough to stop a demon claw.

Adrick's armored head swiveled. He looked out at the men below them and then back at Ben and his friends. Shouts rose up from outside as men noticed the bright armored shape standing in the morning sun. Adrick jumped down outside the walls, and Ben lost sight of him. He could hear where he was going by the startled gasps and shouts from outside. The swordsman was circling the watchtower, moving faster than a running horse, judging by the noise as people saw him. In a few short moments, Adrick came bounding back over the fallen walls of the watchtower. The silver steel of his faceplate turned cloudy again, and Ben saw the normally stoic swordsman wore a gigantic smile.

"This," he murmured, "is unlike anything I have experienced before. It's like raw energy is flowing through my veins, into my muscles, into my lungs. I feel like I could run and fight for days in this."

"I suspect that's what it was made for," remarked Jasper.

Prem moved to her father's side, proffering his translucent blade. Adrick's gauntleted hand closed around the hilt, and the weapon flared with blue light. The mirror-smooth armor reflected the light, filling the courtyard with a cool, blue glow.

"The Lightblade," whispered Jasper, realization and respect evident on his face.

Ben studied the mage, wondering what he knew of Adrick, what anyone knew of him since the swordsman hadn't left the woods in centuries.

"It's a bad day to be a demon," said Rhys. There wasn't a trace of sarcasm in the rogue's voice.

Ben glanced at his friend. It took a lot to shock Rhys, but apparently a man holding a brightly glowing blue sword and wearing full mage-wrought plate armor, who could easily jump over a two-man-height tall wall was enough.

"Well," said Ben after a long moment, "I suppose the rest of us should get ready too."

THE SUN WAS HIGH OVERHEAD, and beads of sweat ran down Ben's back. He wanted to blame it on the heat, but the late summer warmth was cooled by a consistent breeze off the river. It wasn't the heat that had him sweating. It was nerves. He consciously released his fingers from around the hilt of his sword and shook his hand, cursing himself for letting his grip get so tight.

"Once it starts," said Rhys, "your nerves will settle."

"Will they?" snapped Ben.

Rhys shrugged. "They will, or they won't. It won't really matter, though, will it? You'll be busy fighting or dying."

"Soon," mumbled Amelie.

Ben fought to keep his hand off the hilt of his sword. He glanced to his left where the mages were huddled. A bit over two dozen of them now, including Jasper's group, the Sanctuary mages, and the guardians who'd come with Adrick. Amelie had twisted their arms until they all agreed to follow Jasper's commands, an impressive feat since she'd apparently avoided explaining who exactly he was. Respecting Hadra's warning about spies, they'd also held back the details of the wyvern fire staff, merely telling the assembled mages that there was a powerful weapon they could deploy when the time was right.

Ben guessed the guardians had been around long enough that they could get a sense of Jasper. He wasn't a First Mage, but he was the closest thing there was. The Sanctuary mages fought hard until Amelie finally brow-beat Hadra into agreement, and the mage had turned and brow-beat her companions.

Now, Jasper was standing at their center, speaking quietly. Ben knew he intended to reserve himself for when the demon-king arrived. Most of his group would be held back as well. The guardians and the Sanctuary's mages would act first, deploying their magic strategically. They would wait until they could strike a solid group of demons, causing as much collateral damage as possible. If they could strike an arch-demon, they would. They wouldn't target any individual demons, no matter the temptation. The swordsmen would handle those.

Below them, a ring of Venmoor's rangers, supported by blade-masters and the Kirksbane contingent, surrounded the hill. They had space to fall back, which Ben hated to admit, but he was sure they'd need.

To the right of Ben, Rhys was speaking to a handful of blade-masters and guardians. They would form the flying companies and respond to breaches in the ranger's line until the soldiers could regroup. Forty of them, most of the best blades in the force. Ben and Rhys would hold them back as long as possible, but soon, they'd be in the thick of it. Those men and women were too skilled to keep from the fight. They just had to make sure that when they joined the battle, it was at the hottest point, where the defenders needed it the most.

That morning, the entire force had assembled, and Ben had spoken to them about what they were fighting for, why they were risking their lives. The rift in the Wilds, the one the Purple had formed, and the one in the guardian's woods. They were all closed now. The gateways between the worlds were vanishing, and with it, the occurrence of new demons on Alcott would stop as well. Most of the arms men, and even the Sanctuary's mages, were unfamiliar with the rifts, but they understood Ben when he told them they could end the threat forever. It wasn't just Kirksbane they protected, or even Venmoor and the City. It was all of Alcott. The entire world. If they won the day, they could end the demon threat once and for all.

"It would be nice if we had artillery like in Northport or the battle for the rift in the woods," remarked Ben.

"We have mages," mentioned Amelie, "and Adrick Morgan."

"And Adrick," he responded. He glanced back at the watch-tower where the man had retreated into hiding.

The swordsman was the answer to when the flying companies

were no longer sufficient. With his lightblade and impenetrable armor, he'd be nearly unstoppable. He wanted to be on the front line from the beginning, but Jasper rightly warned, these demons would be more intelligent and cunning than any swarm they'd faced previously. The creatures may understand what the true threats were and respond to them. If Adrick showed himself early, the arch-demons and their king might elect to bury the man in bodies.

Instead, they'd wait until chaos prevailed, and the formations were broken. Then, Adrick with his incredible speed and strength, could move through like a deadly wind. He'd target the arch-demons or locations where the defenders had failed. At least, that's what they were hoping would happen.

"What is that?" asked Amelie.

Ben turned to follow her gaze. He couldn't see anything, but he heard a distant, rumbling thunder. Shouts rang out from below, and the men shifted, everyone making last adjustments to their equipment or offering final curses for the dark forces that would descend upon them. Ben glanced to the top of the watch-tower where two of the sharpest-eyed rangers hid. Those men would be the first to actually see the demons.

They'd erected a tarp over the top of the tower and covered it with fallen timber and rubble. It was the best disguise they could come up with, but Ben worried it wouldn't be effective enough. Some demons could fly, and if they decided they wanted to perch on the tower, those two men would be hard pressed to stop them.

"There!" barked a call from up high.

Ben looked back to the north and waited. Beside the river, a quarter league of lush green grass bridged the land between the water and the thick forest. Like flies buzzing across a cow pasture, Ben began to see dark specks clouding the air.

"Scouts?" wondered Rhys.

Ben shrugged.

The specks drew closer until it became obvious it was

demons swooping in graceful arcs. Forty, fifty of them, it was hard to tell. Behind the first bunch, more dots of darkness appeared. Individuals crawled across the green grass like ants. The distance belied how quickly the shapes were moving, and before long, the movement resolved into the loping bounds of demons. Hundreds of them filled the length of open lawn.

"They don't appear to be marching in any sort of coordinated fashion," remarked Rhys.

"That will come," said Jasper. "These will be a combination of very immature demons and those that are bordering on the rise to arch-demons. The young ones may be too weak to be worthy of inclusion in one of the arch-demon's swarms. The others will be looking to get a jump on their peers, to feast and gain strength, so they too can ascend to the point where they form their own swarm."

"You know a lot about these demons," said Ben.

"We spent the last several months traveling the north, battling them, studying them," said Jasper. "We learned a lot of new information. Before that, I've battled these things off and on for centuries. This first wave will be over-eager and easy to deal with for your arms men. The next wave is what we need to worry about. The arch-demons, and maybe even the king, will be directing their minions. Only then will we find out how intelligent these creatures can be."

"There are still hundreds of demons out there. I think that's plenty to worry about," reminded Amelie.

Jasper winked. "Maybe easy isn't the right term, but compared to what is coming…"

"I'm going to check in with Rakkash," said Ben.

Jasper waved him off and went back to his cabal of mages.

Ben jogged down the slope to find the commander of the rangers walking along his line of men, offering words of encouragement, and trying not to gape at the approaching demons.

"This first wave will largely be on you," said Ben. "The mages will hold back until the balance of the force arrives. We want to save their magic until they can blast masses of the creatures, instead of one here and there."

"We'll be ready," Rakkash said. Ben caught the quiver of uncertainty in his voice.

"The flying company will be right behind you," offered Ben. "We don't need to hold it back yet. Once things pick up, we'll have to be more careful with where we send them, and the pressure is going to increase."

Rakkash nodded and then rushed off to scold one of his men who had shoved a companion. The commander of the rangers chided the two, and Ben could see tension was high amongst all the men. They were taking it out through any outlet they had. Just another quarter bell, thought Ben, and it would start.

THAT QUARTER BELL PASSED TENSELY. No one liked to watch as hundreds of demons descended upon their position. They still could not see the bulk of the demon army, but the black specks continued to materialize on the horizon. First as dozens then hundreds and by the time they got close, Ben thought there may be close to one thousand of the creatures scattered across three or four leagues of open field.

A shout went up, and an arrow left the bow. A ranger had fired at one of the flying demons which swooped in close. The arrow fell short, not even getting halfway to the creature. As that archer was being taken to task for wasting an arrow and firing before the demons were in range, another arrow flew up, narrowly missing a second one of the beasts.

"Well," said Rhys. "It's a pretty day for it. Will you join the flying companies, or, ah, stand here with Amelie and command things?"

Ben snorted and turned to Amelie.

"I'll stand with the mages," she suggested.

"I'll go with Rhys then," said Ben. He gripped her arm and gave her a kiss. "Be safe."

"I-I… You stay safe," she quivered, liquid filling the corners of her eyes as she left the rest unsaid. She turned to Rhys. "Watch his back."

"Do I get a kiss?" asked the rogue.

"You can get my boot against your ass," declared Amelie before squeezing Ben's hand and turning to join the mages.

"A little humor helps break the tension before a battle," claimed Rhys. "If people are fixated on a concern, it becomes all they can think of. When you break that focus, you allow their minds to open, and they're fully aware of their surroundings. They can consider what they need to do, instead of just worrying about what is coming."

"Oh, is that why you do it?" asked Ben. "I never knew it was all part of a grand strategy."

Rhys winked and then produced a silver flask.

"Not for me. Not today," said Ben.

"Suit yourself," responded Rhys before tucking the flask back into his belt.

"When this is over," said Ben, "I'll drink the whole damn thing."

ANGRY SHRIEKS PROCEEDED the first dozen demons before they smashed into the line of Rakkash's men. Like Jasper had claimed, they were small and over-eager. The rangers had gained extensive experience facing the creatures in the hills around Venmoor and reacted efficiently. Arrows were fired at close range to wound and slow the attackers. Then, spears were thrust forward to catch them and pin them. Finally, a man would rush forward with a sword or axe to finish the demon.

Up and down the line, Ben saw the flash of steel and heard cries of enraged pain from the demons. The men worked silently and methodically, only calling out when the wooden haft of a spear snapped, or a man took an injury. Then, the sergeants moving behind the line would instruct a swap, and a fresh body or fresh weapon would be put into position.

The system was working well, Ben saw. The watchmen from Kirksbane carried long polearms, which were perfect for stabbing the charging demons before they got close. It left ample room for Venmoor's rangers to step up and hack into them. Additional polearms were hovering, ready to provide the rangers cover if they needed it.

For the time being, Ben and the flying companies held back, waiting to see stress in the line before they committed to a position. Ben knew once they engaged, it'd be difficult to pull back. Rakkash's men were more than capable of handling the first few dozen demons. The advantage of the flying companies was flexibility, and they needed to maintain it as long as possible, so Ben watched patiently.

Three-dozen demons had been put down before the first man lost his life. From one hundred paces away, Ben saw the man go down screaming, his hands covering his face where claws had gouged deeply. They'd caught his neck too, and in moments, the man's lifeblood pumped out onto the grass. It could have been the man involved in the shoving incident earlier. It was near there, but Ben chided himself for wondering. Whoever the fallen man was, he'd stood bravely against a field of darkness. He'd done what he could to protect Venmoor and all of Alcott. He'd been the first hero to make the ultimate sacrifice.

The line closed seamlessly around the fallen man, and his body was dragged clear. A score of the young men and boys from Kirksbane were assisting with removing the injured and dead. No one thought it would be long before they were pressed into combat. In this battle, there would be no triage for the wounded.

None of the mages would spare energy for healing. No, in this fight, it was to the death. Everything they had would be spent fighting the demons, and only after the last of the dark beasts was felled would they have the chance to worry about their losses.

"There," murmured Rhys.

The line had bulged in, rangers scrambling to find footing as half a dozen demons stormed into them, but even as Rhys spoke, a pair of Venmoor's blademasters swept closer and sliced through the demons. The line reformed, and the blademasters strode back to where they'd been standing a score of paces down the line.

"They're good," remarked Prem.

Ben looked to the girl. She wore no armor and was dressed in simple clothing that wouldn't have been out of place on youngster from Farview, but he'd seen her use those long knives before. He suspected she could hold her own against any of the blademasters.

"How's your father doing?" asked Ben.

"Figuring out how to pee," she answered.

Ben blinked.

"Didn't think of that, did you?"

"I-I, ah…" Ben stammered, searching for a response.

Rhys placed a hand on Ben's shoulder and assured him, "There are things the leader doesn't need to solve. Adrick Morgan is a grown man. Really grown. He's literally hundreds of years old. He can figure out how to take a leak on his own."

"There are other things for you to worry about," agreed Prem. "Like that."

She pointed, and Ben's heart sank. Far to the north, a dark wave covered the green grass. Scattered clumps of individual demons and small swarms had turned into an unending mass a quarter-league wide and no end in sight.

"Are you sure you don't want a drink?" asked Rhys.

"I'm sure I do want one," responded Ben. He drew his sword. "I don't think we've got time to properly enjoy it."

He took a step, heading down toward the line where he saw another point of stress.

"Let someone else take that," advised Rhys. "You stay here and direct the men. We have a few moments at least until the fog of war descends. Use it and maintain organization while you can."

"I'll go," said Prem.

She turned and gestured to a few guardians who stood near them. They trotted down the slope. Ben watched as they reached the line and paused at the rear of the rangers. A man stumbled back, opening a gap, and Prem shot through.

Her knives held low, the small guardian whirled like a dervish, razor-sharp steel flashing in and out of the black bodies of the demons. Her companions followed her, taking her flanks and spreading out. Within moments, two dozen paces of space were cleared in front of the rangers. A score of demons lay dead on the grass and the ones behind them veered away from Prem and her men. Their job accomplished, they retreated, slipping back through the reformed line.

Ben directed another small group to the other side of the hill as Prem returned.

"Are you sure we shouldn't join the line?" one of her men asked.

Ben shook his head. "When the arch-demons get here, some of them are likely to be intelligent enough to see the strong points in our defense. If our best blades are all engaged, then there is nothing to stop them from bursting through the weak points and making a charge toward the mages. Without the mages…"

The man nodded. "It hurts to watch from the back, but I understand."

Ben turned, and to keep himself from breaking his own advice and charging down the hill, he started orchestrating the flying companies. The pressure against the line was still light, but there was little risk early of them getting caught in an engagement they couldn't break away from. He used the flexible force as best he was able, trying to conserve lives on the line for when the battle really started. He was so focused on watching the line that he nearly missed the growing scream behind him.

"The tower!" cried a panicked voice.

Ben spun and immediately saw the watchtower wasn't the issue. It was the demon that swooped by, clearing the stones by two paces and then dropping directly toward Ben and the other members of the flying companies.

Against regular soldiers, the demon's momentum may have scored it a kill. Against a group of blademasters and guardians, the thing was eviscerated mid-air. Its body, trailing a fan of purple blood and sickeningly white entrails, crashed into the grass and skidded to a stop.

"Damnit," muttered Ben. He glanced at a man beside him. "From now on, you're in charge of watching the sky. When you get tired of it, make sure someone else takes over for you."

The man wordlessly pointed behind Ben.

Cursing, Ben turned and raised his blade. A trio of demons had flown over the ranger's line and were headed right for Ben and his friends. Beside Ben, Rhys drew his blade and let the runes flare to life.

"Let's hope they're not smart enough to realize you're commanding this band," said Rhys. "There have to be a hundred of those flying bastards, and I don't want to spend all day chopping 'em out of the sky."

"Better us than the rangers on the line," remarked Prem.

She flung a long knife at one of the incoming demons, and Rhys leapt at another. The third came straight at Ben. He waited patiently until it was almost on top of him. Then, he stepped calmly to the side and angled his longsword into the creature's ribcage. The demon's momentum embedded his sword deep into it, piercing its heart. Ben turned, letting the creature fly past, and he yanked his weapon clear. The three demons crashed down together, all dead.

Rhys shook his sword to fling the purple blood off and remarked to Prem, "If you'd missed, you'd be down to one long knife. Not a smart move in the midst of a battle."

"I don't miss," claimed the girl, scampering over to draw her weapon out of the dead demon's throat, "and I always carry backup."

Rhys opened his mouth, but Ben cut him off. "Save it for the demons."

"A little humor, remember?" asked Rhys.

Ben rolled his eyes and then pointed with his sword. "Take a couple of men down and meet that arch-demon. I don't know if the rangers have faced many of them, and I'm certain the Kirksbane watch hasn't. I don't want the first one to knock a hole in the line. Show them how to kill one of those things."

Grumbling, Rhys pointed at three guardians and waved for them to follow.

"He's incorrigible, isn't he?" asked Prem.

"He is," admitted Ben.

"What was he doing before he came to travel with you?" she asked.

Ben coughed and then glanced at her out of the corner of his eyes. He saw her question was entirely earnest.

"He, ah… You don't want to know."

Another screeching of incoming demons drew their attention, and Ben watched as a pair of blademasters jumped in the air, spinning and slashing wicked wounds into the flying creatures. Below them on the slope, the demons began to pile up, pressuring the line from all sides. A league away, the mass of the creatures was advancing. Thousands of them, Ben guessed.

"Take over here," Ben barked to a nearby blademaster.

He trotted over to the mages. They were standing or sitting, calmly watching the battle unfold around them.

"How much closer before you can hit them?" asked Ben, gesturing to the demon front.

"Another half bell," said Hadra. "The Sanctuary will strike first, seeking to blast some holes in that grouping. If we can spread them out a little, they'll put less pressure on the swordsmen. Then, when they regroup, we'll hit them again."

One of Jasper's mages spoke up. "We have some surprises planned for when they get close. We spent all morning laying traps out in that field. Beyond that, we'll start targeting any archdemons foolish enough to draw near."

"Good," said Ben. He eyed the solid wall of demons again. "The rangers cannot hold up for more than a moment against that full force. The sheer weight of the creatures alone could roll right over them."

"Don't worry. We'll thin them out before they get to the line," promised Amelie.

Ben met her eyes and saw her determination. "It sounds like you've all got it in order. I'd better get back to the swordsmen."

"No sign of the king," called Jasper as Ben turned.

Ben paused. "What does it mean?"

"Nothing good," answered the mage.

He was holding the wyvern fire staff. Ben couldn't tear his eyes away from it.

"Don't worry," said Jasper. "I'll act when you tell me to."

Ben nodded and turned to go back to the flying company. He paused. The day was still sparkling bright, afternoon sun shining down across their formations with only wisps of clouds and the black bodies of the demons filling the expansive, deep blue sky. Strangely, though, a fog was forming on the river.

"What is that?" he wondered. He turned back to the mages. "Are you doing something?"

Several of the mages stood and began cursing, staring at the river in confusion. Jasper and his companions huddled together, speaking quickly in a language Ben didn't understand and shooting concerned glances at the fog.

"What is it?" asked Ben, looking around the group for anyone who could answer.

"The river is boiling," explained Lady Towaal somberly.

"Boiling?" queried Ben. "I don't understand. How is that possible?

"Exactly," said Towaal grimly. "How is that possible, and who could do it?"

Jasper looked up, a well of uncertainty evident in his eyes. "The heat it would take to boil an entire river…"

Ben had a limited amount of knowledge about magic, but knew an awfully lot about boiling water. It had been his job before he'd become an adventurer. "The heat it would take to boil that river would be equivalent to, I don't know, ten thousand campfires. Twenty thousand?"

Jasper studied the river. The steam was coming off in clouds now, obscuring the water below. The entire length, from several leagues north to behind the watchtower, was engulfed in a roiling boil.

"If the wind blows west, the battlefield will be obscured," remarked one of Jasper's mages. "Maybe they plan to blunt our magic by stealing our visibility?"

"Demons hate water," responded the elderly mage. "I can't imagine they like steam much better. They wouldn't purposefully engulf their force in it, I don't think."

"Did you say you'd planted traps in the field?" asked Ben. "Just in the field and nowhere else?"

"We did," answered another of the mages.

"If the water boils off, the riverbed would be an unprotected road that avoids everything we laid out," whispered Jasper.

"We counted on the water to protect our backside," added Ben. "In fact, I think we only stationed one man back there, just in case."

"If he still lives," remarked Towaal. "Those flying demons…"

"Damn!" cried Ben. He started running toward the flying company. At the rate the steam was rising, he guessed it would only be half a bell before the riverbed was as dry as an oven-warmed pan. He made it back to the flying company and yelled for one of the guardians to run around behind the watchtower and report anything unusual.

"Like what?" asked the man.

Ben pointed to the cloud of steam rising off the river.

"Oh, damn," mumbled the guardian before turning and dashing off.

Ben looked back to the battle below. The demons were constantly hitting the line now, but the rangers and the blade-masters were holding up. Beyond them, the field was filled with black shapes.

"Have they stopped?" asked a voice from behind.

Ben frowned, studying the field. In the distance, the army of demons had never advanced closer than half a league. They were still there, bunched up, waiting.

"No," Ben answered, realization stabbing into him. "They're going to turn and come a different way."

Suddenly, a man called a warning, and a storm of demons descended upon them. Nearly every one of the flying creatures seemed to drop from the sky in a direct line to Ben and the men standing around him. Blademasters and guardians, all incredible fighters, but none of them were prepared to be inundated with a hundred demons all at once.

The flying variety were not as strong as some of their shorter, denser brethren, but they were tall, and the sharp claws at the tips of their long arms were just as lethal. One smacked into Ben's back, and he stumbled forward, putting a hand on the grass to stop himself from falling face first. The stumble saved his life as a second demon swept a hand right where his neck would have been.

Shifting his weight, Ben turned and rammed his shoulder into the first demon's mid-section. Its claws clutched his back, and he felt his skin pierced in half a dozen places, but none of the wounds were serious. He could still fight. He used his momentum to shove the creature away from him, launching it like a small child.

Without pause, he spun and swung his sword as if he was swinging a bat in a game of yard ball. The second demon was caught mid-attack, and Ben's steel sheered through its torso, crunching bone, slicing through organs, and sending a blast of blood and gore flying into the air.

Around him, chaos ruled.

Men, surprised by the attack, had gone down, but others who hadn't been caught in the initial surge were on their feet and fighting back. Blademasters whirled and slashed. Guardians nearby had formed a six-man circle. Back to back, they kept the demons away.

Ben, on the other hand, was in the center of a different type of circle. Around him, five of the creatures advanced. Standing still and waiting for them to close was a death sentence. Instead, he charged. Howling a wordless battle cry, Ben ran straight at one of the creatures. Its mouth opened as the demon let out its own battle cry. Ben kept going.

He used the extended reach of his sword to thrust at it and caught the thing in the face. The tip of his longsword punched into the demon's eye and gouged out a good chunk of its skull. Viscera sprayed freely, and Ben continued his charge, running over the body before spinning to face his pursuers.

One down, four to go. Now, though, he'd broken out of the circle, and the four of them tangled trying to advance on him. There was a limit to how well demons could coordinate an attack. Ben took advantage and jumped closer, flicking his longsword and grinning as the tip of the blade caught one of them in the neck, slicing a finger-length into the flesh.

A clawed hand grasped at him, and Ben turned his blade, cutting a laceration along the creature's arm. He danced back, setting his feet for another attack.

Then, Lloyd was beside him, and together, they rushed at the two remaining demons, the blademaster's weapon moving like a buzzing dragonfly. Faster than Ben was able to follow, the silvered steel whipped back and forth. In two blinks of the eye, the demons were dead.

"Looks like you do know a bit about what you're doing," remarked Lloyd.

"You're even faster than your brother," muttered Ben.

Lloyd winked at him and then charged back into the battle, falling on the backs of a swarm of the creatures who'd been pressing the circle of guardians.

"Ben," shouted Rhys.

The rogue was pointing to the side of the watchtower where a man was standing, mouth agape. The man who'd been sent to check the backside of the watchtower, realized Ben.

"Go," instructed Rhys. "We'll get this under control."

The rogue casually lopped the head off a nearby demon and went stalking into the crowd, looking for more.

Ben saw the initial shock of the attack was wearing off, and the incredible skill of the blademasters and guardians was rapidly turning the tide against the demon's superior numbers. Half a dozen men lay dead on the grass, though, and several more sported painful-looking injuries. It took a hundred demons and a surprise attack to do it, but these were Ben's elite warriors, the ones he couldn't afford to lose.

He ran to the man by the watchtower and called, "What did you find?"

The man shook his head, confused. "The water is down, my lord. It's boiling off like it's my mamma's kettle left too long on the fire. I don't understand, sir. What is happening?"

Grim-faced, Ben glanced back at the field of demons. He was

certain that it wasn't just his imagination. They were moving toward the riverbank now. His forces were going to get flanked by a few thousand demons.

"Go get the mages," Ben commanded. "Tell them what you saw."

The man nodded and started to trot off, when suddenly, a grey-clad figure stepped out of the shadows of the watchtower and slid a dagger into his side. The blade sank deep, plunging between the man's ribs.

Cursing, Ben raised his sword and barely ducked in time as another figure swung at him from behind. Skipping away, Ben spun to face the two attackers. His heart sank. They both carried long knives, held low and steady. Experienced, skilled assassins. The Veil was making her move.

"Assassins!" yelled Ben at the top of his lungs, knowing the guardians were nearby, but they would be busy cleaning up the remainder of the flying demons. They wouldn't be able to hear him over the din of battle. The assassins had picked their time carefully.

"Where is it?" hissed one of them.

"Where is what?"

"The staff," barked the other assassin. "Tell us, and we'll let you live."

"He's got it," said Ben, looking over the first man's shoulder.

Both assassins turned, but quickly caught themselves, and snapped their heads back to Ben. It was enough and gave him the opportunity he needed. These men were professionals, and given time, Ben was sure they'd find an opening in his defense. He had to even the odds. The moment the first man's head had started to turn, Ben lunged, his sword springing up like a bolt off a ballista.

The assassin was shockingly fast, but Ben's blade was already a hand-length from his chest when he got a knife up to deflect it. The shorter weapon didn't have the leverage to push aside the sword, and Ben rammed his steel into the man's body, the blade punching through clothing with ease.

The second assassin sprang at Ben, but Ben was ready. He took a risk and let go of his longsword. He stepped into the man's attack. Ben brushed the man's two knives to either side and, borrowing a page from Milo's book, swung his head forward, the crown of his skull smashing against the assassin's nose.

A flash of blinding pain was worth it when Ben heard a sickening crunch and strangled gasp from the man. Without thought, Ben dropped down and spun into one of the Ohm's positions, sweeping his leg forward and smacking the assassin's feet out from under him.

The man dropped to the ground, too much a professional to lose his weapons, but for a moment, he was stunned. Ben scrambled on top of him and slammed his knees down on each of the man's arms, pinning him.

The assassin thrashed wildly, trying to bring his legs up and wrap them around Ben's neck, but Ben ducked forward and maintained his leverage. He reached down and yanked the assassin's mask off, revealing a ruined, blood smeared face. It was one of Renfro's thugs. He recognized the man from the tavern they'd been in prior to finding Captain Fishbone.

"Who are you?" shouted Ben.

The assassin didn't respond. There wasn't time to question the man, and he couldn't just leave him there. Ben drew his hunting knife from his belt and plunged it into the assassin's neck, angling the blade so it penetrated underneath the man's jaw and slid into his brain stem.

The assassin held Ben's gaze as the steel sank into him, only losing eye contact when the light flickered out of his. A brief shimmer of yellow sparkled along the sides of the man's face, passing in front of his ears and down his neck. Before Ben's shocked eyes, the skin of his face seemed to melt away, revealing that beneath the image of Renfro's thug was a non-descript man.

Ben stared at him, confused. He had a thin face with thick black eyebrows and full lips. He looked nothing like Renfro's man or anyone Ben had ever seen.

Someone had disguised him. Someone who had intimate knowledge of Renfro's people.

Cursing, Ben jumped off the man. He stumbled and started to run, bending on the move to snatch his longsword off the ground. He ran past the flying company, which was just then finishing up the last few injured demons.

Rhys, evidently seeing Ben's panic, ran after him.

The mages were clustered together in a half-circle, watching Jasper as he pointed to the wall of the watchtower, faint shimmers showing on the stone. Now that the battle was joined, he'd collected the wyvern fire staff from his camp. He was holding it in one hand and tapping the wall with the other.

Ben, running at a full sprint, raised his sword above his head.

Hadra looked up as Ben charged closer. Her eyes grew wide, and she staggered back. "What are you doing?" she screeched.

Ben paid her no mind. Instead, he ran straight at the runaway mage, Sincell. He brought his sword down in a deadly arc, the dark steel whistling through the air. Sincell, seeing Ben, lunged at Jasper, a hand outstretched to strike the mage in the back.

Ben reached her first, and his sword slashed into her neck, shearing through bone and flesh, decapitating her cleanly. Her head flew free, and her palm slapped against Jasper, but whatever spell she'd triggered fizzled into a puff of acrid smoke. Her head thumped onto the soft ground, and her body fell next to it.

Open-mouthed, everyone stared at Ben.

"Are you crazy!" screamed Hadra.

Ben, bending over with his hands on his knees, merely pointed down at Sincell's head, or what had been Sincell's head. Now, it was some woman he didn't recognize.

"Lady Addin," whispered one of the Hadra's mages, confusion clouding her voice.

"The Veil's attendant," remarked Towaal, her gaze rising to meet Ben's. "What happened?"

"Assassins," said Ben, "made to look like Renfro's people, the ones we met in that tavern the night we left."

Towaal nodded curtly. She turned to study the rest of the assembled mages, paying particular attention to those from the Sanctuary.

The girl, Elle, stepped forward and grabbed one of the Sanctuary mage's heads, pulling the woman down to her level. The Sanctuary mage squawked a protest, but no one moved to intervene. The young girl studied the older mage and then let her go. Hadra was next, and the woman's jaw clenched as the girl's hands grasped her head. Ben was sure she was struggling to hold back a complaint, but then another of the Sanctuary mages raised her hand.

Jasper's sword whipped out of the sheath and plunged into her chest before the woman could gather her power. Like the others, her face melted and revealed another unknown woman.

"Lady Eggesh," remarked Towaal calmly. "She arrived just this morning. Evidently, the Veil knows exactly where we are and what we took. Hadra, is there anyone else in your party that wasn't part of our original meeting? If the Veil knew of Sincell and her connections in the underworld, she likely knows about your companions as well. Who else joined late?"

"What you took?" asked Hadra. "I... No, no. The rest of us left together."

The mage opened her mouth to speak again, but shouts from down the hill drew everyone's attention. The line was buckling, and the rangers were falling back. Men from the flying company were starting to react, but they had just recovered from their own attack.

Ben turned to Hadra and the remaining Sanctuary mages. "I think it's time to make yourselves useful."

Hadra pursed her lips but didn't argue. The girl Elle walked close to them, looking in each mage's eyes. Then, she turned to Ben and nodded. Hadra opened her mouth and then snapped it shut, clearly frustrated. She wouldn't meet Ben's eyes or look at the two fallen mages, who, moments before, she thought were her trusted friends. Instead, she gestured to her companions, and they started walking quickly down the hill, hands raised, energies swirling around their fists.

"Well, that was exciting!" exclaimed Rhys, breaking the silent tension in the group.

Jasper snorted and then glanced at Ben. "I was explaining how much energy I thought it would take to boil that river."

"How much?" asked Ben.

"More than any of us have," responded Jasper. "There's only one thing I think may be strong enough to pull something like that off."

"The demon-king," responded Ben.

Jasper nodded. "We haven't seen it, but it's close. It's aware of what is happening."

"We have to find another way, Jasper," declared Ben.

Jasper's grip tightened on the staff.

"Give it to me," said Ben.

"No, Ben!" exclaimed Amelie.

"You might be able to draw a tenth of the power that I can," stated Jasper. "You don't have the training, the centuries spent strengthening your will, the knowledge of how a device like this functions. No one but me understands how to activate each of the runes on this weapon. Ben, what you did before was a fraction of what this staff is capable of. From what your friends described, I don't think what you did will kill the demon-king."

Ben stared at the mage, his mind churning.

"Ben," cried Amelie, "you cannot do this."

"I will not use it until you give the order," assured Jasper. "But if it is used, it should be by me. It's foolish and wasteful to do otherwise."

"We'll find another way," declared Ben.

A concussive boom rocked them out of their argument, and everyone looked to see what Hadra and her mages were doing. Smoke filled the air, and in front of the line of rangers there was a wide-open space filled with soft brown earth and small fires that quickly flickered out. Another blast rocked the ground, and Ben watched in amazement as fifty paces of demons were rolled up in a wave of fire, earth, and wind.

"Damn," muttered Ben.

"Not all mages in the Sanctuary are capable of something like this," mentioned Towaal, a tremble of concern in her voice. "In fact, I wouldn't have thought any of them could enact that level of destruction and remain standing afterward. I certainly couldn't."

Another blast and a third of the ranger's line was free of demons. Hundreds of them swarmed around the outskirts of the blast area, evidently afraid to venture too close. Ben watched the Sanctuary mages. They had linked hands and were facing out toward the field.

A fourth blast tore out, bigger than the previous three. Charred bodies and demon flesh blew before it. The mages lost their grips on each other, and one fell to her knees. Another flopped on her back. Hadra, standing in the center, wobbled but maintained her footing. Hundreds of demons had been incinerated, but the mages would have little to add until they had time to recover.

"Well, that was rather effective," said Amelie.

"Shockingly so," agreed Lady Towaal.

"Wait until we get involved," rumbled the giant from Jasper's contingent. The man leaned casually on his massive crossbow.

Ben frowned, looking from the demons to the big man.

"What can you do with that thing?" asked Ben, his eyes dipping to the crossbow.

The big man smiled and brushed his black hair back from his

eyes. It fell in a loose wave along the shaved sides of his head. He hefted his huge weapon and responded, "With this, I kill stuff. A lot of stuff."

Ben grinned and then pointed to a thick knot of demons down the slope from them. The creatures had flooded away from where the Sanctuary mages had blasted them, and they had formed into a tightly packed group of several hundred. If they struck the line of rangers, they'd burst through.

To the cheers and shouts of encouragement from his fellow mages, the black-haired giant stomped down the hill, drawing a wrist-thick crossbow bolt from his quiver.

"Really?" asked Ben. "What can he do with that?"

"Just watch," responded Jasper.

Ben turned to look and nearly fell back in surprise at the violent thump that sounded when the crossbow released. The quarrel shot out and flew over the heads of the rangers, plowing into the front ranks of the demons. Then, it kept going. The black iron head of the weapon punched through one demon after another, blowing huge holes in their bodies and continuing through the entire pack, lancing through a score of the creatures. Ben watched in awe as the gore-covered quarrel punched out the back of the last demon and fell to the turf.

"Wow," murmured Amelie.

The crossbow thumped again, and another streak of death flew toward the creatures.

"How long can he keep that up?" asked Amelie.

"He's probably got a dozen of those things ready to go," said Jasper. "I'm guessing the demons disperse before he uses them all up."

"Do you think on the demon-king...?" asked Ben.

"That'd be like you getting stabbed with a sewing needle," responded Jasper. "We can try if no other options are on the table, but don't think we haven't talked this over. A lucky shot might do some damage, but it'd have to be lucky. If the demon-king has any sort of talent, which we think it does since it sensed the far-seeing, it will easily be able to quash the effectiveness of those crossbow bolts. We can't count on Earnest John bringing down the demon-king."

Ben frowned and turned back to the battlefield. The demons were milling about, afraid to come closer. In the distance, he could see arch-demons moving in, ready to put some courage or an even greater fear into their smaller brethren.

In less than a quarter bell, the demons decided the torn patches of turf were no longer a threat, and they advanced and pressed the line again. The battle wore on, and before he realized it, Ben saw the day had passed. The sun was dropping below the western horizon. Darkness was falling, and the bonfires they'd laid out would be worthless. Once the river finished boiling off, the demons would have a broad, flat road away from the traps and lights. The advantage would be tilted decisively away from Ben and his friends.

Except, they held two advantages they hadn't yet shown. Adrick Morgan in his armor and the wyvern fire staff. Ben shook his head, cursing to himself. They couldn't use the staff. It was too dangerous. Adrick would have to be enough.

"The demons are accessing the riverbed!" shouted Lloyd. The blademaster was standing atop one of the walls of the crumbled watchtower, hand over his eyes to shield them from the evening sun.

Ben stopped below him. "Call down to Adrick."

The swordsman, evidently hearing his name, climbed up beside Lloyd. The silver steel of his helmet turned and he studied the battle.

"This appears to be going remarkably well," he said.

"Look to the river," suggested Ben.

"Oh," responded Adrick. "I see."

He jumped down off the wall, landing lightly, his plate armor barely creaking.

Ben glanced over the battlefield, assessing the situation. The bulk of the demons were filing down into the riverbed a quarter league away. The rest of them were pressing against the line of rangers, keeping them engaged. The mages were rested for the most part, but Ben was loathe to spend their energy before the demon-king made an appearance. Finally, the Veil had made a play, which failed, but was it the last card she had up her sleeve?

Ben grimaced. He couldn't worry about that now. Instead, he had to figure out a way to blunt the river of demons flowing down to them. They had to stop and frustrate the creatures enough to draw out the master.

"Adrick, I need you and all of your guardians with me. Lloyd, fetch every blademaster you can work free. The rangers and Kirksbane's watchmen will be on their own with what's out in the field. The mages can support them if necessary. We're going to stop this river."

Lloyd grunted, but Adrick merely inclined his helmeted head and then clanged a fist against the stone wall to draw the attention of the nearby guardians. "Everyone, on me. We're going with Ben. Gather the rest of our force."

Several men nodded amongst the pack and lopped off. Sergeants or whatever their equivalent was in the village, guessed Ben. Lloyd was busy directing his men as well.

Ben strode off, looking for Amelie to explain his plan.

"Do you want me to go with you?" she asked.

He shook his head. "No, I think it's best you stay here. Keep the mages working together if you can. Listen to Jasper, though. He's got a head for tactics."

Amelie smirked at him. "I know I'm no general."

"Neither am I," muttered Ben.

"You're doing well so far," assured Amelie. She leaned close. "I'll see you in the morning."

Ben smiled. "I hope so."

15

DOWN IN THE MUD

BEN LED THE COLUMN OF BLADEMASTERS AND GUARDIANS DOWN the backside of the watchtower hill. It was a short but steep hike to the riverbank. They paused there, looking uncertainly at the ground. In most places, it looked dry and broken like shattered pieces of glass. In low-lying spots, it was still damp and muddy, the last remaining moisture slow to evaporate.

"Whatever heated the water is gone now," commented Adrick.

"Are you sure?" asked Ben. He could feel warmth radiating off the dried mud, but it wasn't the intense heat needed to boil that much water.

The swordsman shrugged his armored shoulders and then leapt a dozen paces to land on the riverbed. His steel booted feet thumped on a patch of dry dirt.

"Pretty sure," he remarked.

"They couldn't have boiled the entire river," muttered Rhys, tentatively stepping off the grassy bank. "This thing extends for a thousand leagues from Northport to the South Sea."

Ben could hear the concern in his friend's voice. "What are you thinking?"

"Where's the rest of the water?" asked Rhys. "There are

hundreds of leagues of the stuff north of here, all flowing south. Did they vaporize all of it? Is there a dam up there somewhere..."

"Or a wall of water rushing down to us," speculated Lloyd.

"You can swim, can't you?" asked Adrick.

"Sure," answered Lloyd. "If it comes to that, but I'm not the one wearing full plate."

Adrick's steel face looked back at them blankly.

"We can't tell if you're smiling in there," said Ben.

"Just waiting," said the swordsman. "Come on. We have demons to kill."

One hundred and fifty men and women filed down into the empty riverbed and turned north, marching to meet twenty times their number in demons.

"You sure this is a good idea?" asked Rhys.

"A bit late now, isn't it?" replied Ben.

Rhys shrugged. "Better late than never."

"I'm good for fifty of the bastards," crowed Lloyd from behind them. "Ransk, how many are you going to take?"

"If you can do fifty," shouted a voice, "I suppose I can do at least fifty-one."

Behind Ben, the group jostled and jeered, each one upping another about how many of the creatures they'd cut down or how many they had in the past. Every man and woman behind him, Ben realized, was an expert. Most had seen combat, and they knew what was coming. They must be scared, but not a single one of them had balked at what needed to be done. They'd seen the demon army now. They knew that if they didn't stop it, countless lives would be lost all over Alcott. They were a small group, but they were the best blades on the continent.

Up on the hill behind them was the most powerful mage on the continent, surrounded by two dozen of his peers. If the arms men could stall the demon column or force them onto the fields, the mages would wreak devastation. If they could punch back hard enough, they may draw out the demon-king. They could end the swarm once and for all. They had to.

"You know we can't stop this many of them, right?" whispered Adrick to Ben.

Ben grimaced. "Got any other ideas?"

"No, I do not."

"Then, let's do the best we can."

Ben gripped his longsword and tried to ignore the sensation of the ground shaking beneath his feet, shaking from thousands of claws digging into the dried river mud, coming closer.

The last of the sun fell away and stars sparkled in the black curtain of night. The moon was high, lighting the world in a silver glow. The men and women behind Ben fell silent. Ahead of them, they saw a wave of blackness that was deeper than the night. From bank to bank, the river was filled with demons.

"Force them out of the riverbed, and there's a chance the mage's traps can do some good," called Rhys. "Keep 'em bunched up, and the mages can rain fire down on them."

Ben knew they wouldn't. They'd been ordered not to. Somewhere out there was the demon-king, and they had to be ready for him.

"You lead the way," Ben said to Adrick. "We'll fan out behind you."

The swordsman didn't respond. Instead, he drew his weapon, and the blade flared bright blue, casting bizarre shadows across his polished plate armor.

"Try to keep up."

Howls, screams, and cries of enraged hunger filled the night air. Ben felt like running, charging at the demons with teeth bared and a battle cry on his lips, but Adrick kept a steady pace. Marching not running. Not wasting a precious sliver of energy.

The demons weren't so disciplined. They broke and ran, smaller, faster ones outpacing their heavier peers. The small ones would be easy to deal with. It was when the squat, denser creatures arrived in a wave that they would have a problem.

Ben swallowed. In the moonlight, it was difficult to pick out individual demons at a distance, but he could easily see the silhouettes that stood out above the crowd. The arch-demons. Already, he could spot dozens of them. He was certain there were more further back in the swarm.

"Whatever you do," advised Rhys, "don't fall down."

The rogue's sword blazed silver. Runes sparkled in an arcane language, bathing Ben, Adrick, and Rhys in a light that mirrored the moon. Smoke boiled off the weapon, drifting peacefully past the rogue as he strode forward.

No other words were possible. The demons were three hundred paces away and their screams drowned out all other sound. Slender, black shapes bounded at them, zipping out of the dark like invisible missiles.

Adrick saw the first one coming, and his glowing blue blade swept up and sheared the creature in two. The swordsman kept walking, stepping casually over the body, staying focused on what was ahead.

Ben stepped a pace to the man's right, and Rhys moved to the left. Behind them, their company wordlessly fell into place, forming a wedge they hoped would drive into the heart of the demon army. If they could force the creatures out of the riverbed and onto the field where the mage's traps could go off, they had a chance.

Ben laughed to himself. They didn't have a chance. There were too many of the beasts and not enough of the men. All they could hope to do was cause enough damage to bring out the demon-king. Or maybe they could leave few enough of the demons alive that Jasper and his mages could clean them up.

A crackling, ruddy orange glow lit the sky, and Ben realized Jasper wasn't waiting. He wasn't conserving the other mage's energy like he was supposed to be doing. Above them, moving rapidly through the air, was a wagon-sized ball of flame.

"Damnit!" shouted Ben.

"Fog of war, hitting them when they're bunched together," yelled Rhys in response. "Trust your lieutenants. They know how much strength they have better than you do."

Ben grunted and swept his sword up. A young demon, immature, no more than three or four stone, caught the blade in the torso, the steel sliding deep. Ben kicked it off and kept marching.

The fireball landed in the center of the advancing wave of blackness and exploded with a whoosh. By the orange flames, Ben could see demons thrown into the air, pin-wheeling across the sky to crash down amongst their brethren. The screams of rage turned to screams of pain as the fire scorched the helpless creatures. There were too many of them to run away from the heat, so those trapped in the middle simply burned.

Adrick broke into a run, flashing across the last hundred paces to the front of the demon swarm.

Ben struggled to keep up, swinging wildly at creatures that sprang at him out of the darkness. The first to meet him were smaller demons, weak ones, but at night, they had an advantage. They were fast, and he could barely see them. They were much quicker than the muscular creatures he was used to facing.

One of the demons slipped by him with only a raking slash from the tip of his longsword. Ben glanced over his shoulder, worried he'd just let one of the creatures into their wedge, but behind the backs of his companions. Prem was following close behind, and the svelte girl plunged both her knives into the creature.

"Don't worry!" she shouted. "I've got your back."

Ben could barely hear her over the growls and screams of the demons. He didn't attempt a response. Instead, he churned forward, trying to keep up with the girl's father. Demons swooped at him, just shapes backlit by the still-burning flames of the magical attack.

One thing he could see through the press of bodies was Adrick. The man moved like lightning, flickering back and forth, the blue glow of his blade scything through the black mass of the demons. He was carving chunks out of their front with the ease Ben had slicing a loaf of stale bread. Adrick was impervious to the attacks of the smaller creatures and moving twice as fast as they were capable of. The demons could do nothing to stop him. At least, the smaller ones could not.

"Arch-demons closing on Adrick!" called Rhys over the tumult.

Ben followed the rogue's lead, and they fought their way closer to the swordsman. Even in his armor, a direct blow from an arch-demon could injure or kill him. If they could take the man's back, he could focus on what was in front and cut down scores of the creatures without fear.

Smashing the hilt of his longsword into a creature in front of him, Ben scrambled over fallen, twitching bodies to get closer to Adrick. Beside him, a guardian was tangled with a man-sized demon, the creature circling the man with its powerful arms and drawing him in, sharp-toothed mouth opened wide to clamp down on the man's neck. Ben tried to thrust his blade into the demon, but the swirl of battle pulled him away. He was bumped into by a cold, heavy body of a demon and stumbled to the side, struggling to keep his footing. In the dark, crowded battle, a fall could be just as fatal as a demon's claw.

Ben finally burst into a clear area around Rhys and Adrick. Their two mage-wrought blades burned brightly, painting the faces of the demons surrounding them in stark shades of blue and white. Turning, Ben backed up, so they formed the points of a triangle. Well, they would have, if Adrick stopped breaking out of formation and plunging like a dagger into the massed demons.

Each time he did, half a dozen of the creatures lay dead in the mud.

The minions lost their interest in the plate-armored warrior, knowing he meant certain death, but the arch-demons were closing fast. A dozen of them, towering above the lesser creatures, encircled Ben, Rhys, and Adrick.

Ben's leg was caught by a grasping hand and he fell to one knee. He looked behind him and saw a wounded demon dragging itself forward, its arm stretched out to clutch at him. A silver blur flashed through Ben's vision, and the demon's wrist was severed. Rhys reached a hand down and hauled Ben up without looking. Ben paused, stabbed his longsword into the demon's face, and then turned back to the battle.

Another eruption of orange fire lit the night sky.

"They're using too much energy," growled Ben.

"It's pointless to conserve power if we can't draw the king," barked Rhys.

Ben dodged to the side and twirled his longsword over his head before bringing it down in a powerful sweep that severed the head of a demon that had been charging toward the rogue's back.

"They've got a better view of this battle than we do," yelled Rhys.

Ben grunted and then ran forward to confront three demons that were looming over a fallen blademaster. The man was scrambling across the mud, looking frantically for his sword. Ben swung hard, catching one demon in the face and drawing the attention of the other two. They closed fast, and Ben dropped low, lashing his sword across both their legs, cutting deep lacerations and spilling the creatures onto the mud beside him.

Adrick flew by in front of Ben, his glowing blue blade shearing through demons like stalks of wheat. Right behind him, three arch-demons pounded closer, solely focused on the armored man.

345

Ben began the chase, running after the huge demons running after Adrick. The swordsman must have heard them coming because he dodged to the side and then came streaking back, flying underneath one of the creature's outstretched arms and severing its thick leg.

The demon's angry cry drowned out all other sounds, covering the pounding of Ben's running footsteps as he closed on another of the arch-demons. The thing was trying to track Adrick. It missed Ben coming behind it until his longsword punched into its back, seeking the creature's spine. Ben couldn't reach any higher than that, but he didn't need to. His blade found the thick bone and slid between a gap in the vertebrae.

The arch-demon roared and tried to turn, but instead, it slumped impotently to the ground. It pounded its fists against the mud of the riverbank and tried to crawl after Ben, but he was able to yank his longsword free and circle it. From behind, he darted in close, delivering another blow to its neck.

Rhys came running and jumped onto the demon's corpse, vaulting off of it and flying above Ben's head. The rogue's blade trailed sparkling silver smoke as he swung it at the third arch-demon. The creature never saw him and had no chance to react before the mage-wrought steel cleaved into its head.

Ben charged into a pack of demons that had been hanging back from confronting them. He was quickly joined by a blade-master and a guardian. Together, the three of them chopped into the mass of muscled flesh, snarling teeth, and sharp claws. They fell into a rhythm, alternating strokes and striking the tightly packed creatures in front of them with every blow.

To the right, another blademaster stepped onto their line, and they marched forward, a wall of steel flashing in the moonlit night. More and more swords came to stand with them, and soon, a score of warriors were pushing the demons back, forcing them out of the riverbed. Hundreds of the creatures were being driven before them, pushing their fellows along in a panic to avoid the sharp steel, wielded by the best blades in Alcott. A handful of arch-demons roared and raged, but they had no effect on the swarm that fled before the men.

One by one, the demons were shoved out of the river and onto the lush grass bank. First individuals then dozens then hundreds. The traps set by the mages went off like a storehouse packed full of fireworks. Ben was blown back, stumbling from the impact. His ears rang from the noise, but he couldn't hear anything anyway over the shrieks of the dying demons. He watched in awe as two hundred of the creatures were incinerated by a gigantic blast, and a ray of hope crept into him.

Men were still standing, and hundreds of demons had been cut down during the course of the assault. Ben turned and looked, seeing the huge bodies of dead arch-demons littering the riverbed. The light of Adrick's sword showed the man was still going strong, leaving death in his wake. Rhys was traveling behind him, cleaning up what he left or picking off the demons who skirted by Adrick on the fringes.

Unable to leave the riverbed, the demons were bunching up, falling back. Ben grinned. Close together, they'd be a perfect target for the mages. They might just win this fight.

"They're going to use their weight to overwhelm us," warned Lloyd.

Ben turned to the blademaster. He hadn't seen the man standing beside him. "What do you mean? This is working!"

"They can't match our skill. Even the arch-demons can do nothing against the armored man. In a fair fight, he could slay hundreds of them."

Ben frowned, not understanding Lloyd's concern.

"They can't take him down individually, but they're bunching up to charge. Look! They'll crush him under their bodies. He's in the midst of the swarm. He can't see what they're doing."

They watched as Adrick pressed further north, leaving swaths of dead beasts underfoot. Several hundred paces north of them, the demons were forming a thick knot. Hundreds of them.

"Damnit," muttered Ben. "We can't let him get caught."

"We'd better hurry," declared Lloyd.

Ben took off running, the blademaster behind him. Adrick was an experienced warrior, and he would know not to get isolated, but in the chaos of battle, he may not have a choice. Ben could already see that bands of demons were fanning out. They would surround Adrick and pin him in place until the wave arrived. He'd be overwhelmed by the sheer mass of demons.

As Ben and Lloyd ran, they took swipes at the creatures they could reach, but they didn't have time to stop and confront every one of the beasts. They had to get to Adrick before it was too late.

Lloyd's sword was a blur. He and Ben carved their way closer to the armored guardian. They passed Rhys, who was leading a band of a dozen against two huge arch-demons.

"We're getting Adrick. Then, we need to fall back!" shouted Ben.

Rhys blinked at him, unhearing. Ben pointed north, and the rogue nodded. Ben chased after Lloyd, watching in awe as the man flowed between two attacking demons. He lashed out at both of them, felling them before they could come within a hand-length of him.

When they got close to Adrick, Ben was further amazed to see the guardian slam a gauntleted fist into the face of a demon, crunching the thing's skull and sending it flying away.

"We're falling back to regroup!" cried Ben.

"We're pushing them back. We have to keep up the pressure!" responded Adrick.

Ben shook his head. "They're bunching up just two hundred paces north of here. Even in that armor, you won't be able to do anything if a hundred demons jump on your back. We have to stay mobile."

Adrick waved a hand to acknowledge him and started to

work his way backward. The demons, sensing retreat, surged after him, and the swordsman took advantage of them coming close, chopping down a dozen before the creatures pulled back again.

The riverbed to the south of them was largely clear, and Ben did a quick count of the men who were left standing. He couldn't see them all in the moonlight, but it looked like a good two-thirds of the force had survived. Rhys was rallying most of them near him. Ben, Adrick, and Lloyd joined them. Fifty paces around, it was clear of living demons. The creatures were circling restlessly, though, waiting for an opportunity to pounce.

"We're fighting them to a stalemate," remarked Lloyd. "Could be worse."

"I was kind of hoping we wouldn't all have to die to finish this fight," said Ben.

"We need a different plan, then," counseled Rhys. "There are just too many of them for us to kill them all. When we first hit them and broke the formation, we had a chance. With them bunched, we'll kill a few, but then, they'll roll over us like a tidal wave. They're adjusting their tactics, and we need to adjust too. We could send a runner for the mages, see if they can blast this riverbed from one end to the other. Maybe Jasper can use that staff to fill the whole damn thing with fire. I know you don't want that, Ben, but we have to consider our options here. The men are getting tired and injured. It may be a draw so far, but I don't think it's going to end that way. They've figured us out, and the arch-demons are keeping them tightly formed. Look!"

Fifty paces north of them, the demons began to assemble, stretching from one bank to the other, shoulder to shoulder. Arch-demons strode amongst their minions, organizing them.

Ben grimaced, and then smiled. "Have the mages fill the riverbed."

"Yeah," agreed Rhys, "with fire."

Ben shook his head, the smile stretching further. "Not fire, water."

"You're right! There's got to be water somewhere north of here!" exclaimed Lloyd. "They couldn't have boiled the entire river, right?"

"Adrick," instructed Ben, "send three fast men to the watchtower. Have them instruct the mages to far-see the river and figure out what happened to the water north of here. If the demons dammed it, maybe the mages can release it. A small amount of energy could bring a lot of water rushing down. Demons hate water, and I doubt they can swim. If I were to guess, a wall of water would kill almost all of them."

Adrick turned and barked orders to his men.

"How will we know if Jasper is successful?" wondered Adrick.

"Tell him to send up a blue light," said Ben. "That will be our signal to run."

With their final instruction, Adrick's runners turned and scampered off, heading toward the watchtower.

"If the demons know that water is coming, they could break east," worried Rhys. "They'd be loose with a clear shot through Sineook Valley and to Whitehall from there."

"If they go east, we can harry them all the way through Sineook Valley," said Ben. "We can carve off chunks of them in a running battle and whittle them down. At Whitehall, Argren's built an army. If we contact him, he can march, and we'll trap the demons between our two forces."

Rhys nodded grimly.

"Our best bet," suggested Adrick, "is to keep them occupied without getting into a full engagement. We can stall them while the mages figure something out."

"Let's do it," said Ben.

Around him, tired warriors prepared to make a feint toward the creatures and hopefully slow their advance. A hundred men and women still faced thousands of demons.

With a resounding roar, the demons started their advance. They were sticking close together, packed in a tight formation that would bowl over the men with their bodies. Ben began to walk, the blademasters and the guardians following behind him.

"Just hit them and pull back!" called Ben. "Don't get tangled up, or you'll be left behind."

High above, another ball of swirling orange flame soared toward the demons.

"Making use of the demons being close together," said Rhys. "Smart. If Jasper and the mages can blast a few hundred of them, that could make the difference for us. This may work, Ben."

But as Rhys finished, Ben saw they weren't going to get so lucky. The ball of fire splashed against an invisible barrier. Fire hung suspended above them, sizzling and popping, and then flickering out.

"Damn," muttered Rhys.

"They have magic!" exclaimed a man behind Ben. "The king must be close."

Ben stopped. If the demons could command magic and send an attack at the men, it would be devastating. Some of the men might be able to harden their will, but the majority of them wouldn't even understand the concept. Those who could protect themselves from magic would be distracted and unable to focus on the thousands of demons marching toward them with sharp claws and teeth. It would be a slaughter.

"Fall back!" yelled Ben. "Fall back to the base of the watchtower. We can use the height there to slow them. The mages can provide us cover and maybe fling some rocks at them or something. With the height of the hill, it will be easier to stand against the demons' bulk. We can still keep them in the river."

The men, perhaps not eager to stand toe-to-toe with thousands of demons again, began a coordinated withdrawal. To their credit, they didn't turn tail and run, but they didn't tarry either. Groups would stand and watch while others scrambled back one hundred paces at a time. Then, they'd turn and cover for their peers. Seeing the men retreating, the demons picked up their speed.

"If they get excited enough to break formation, we can take some of them," called Lloyd.

Another fireball soared overhead, smaller than the previous ones. Either the mage who was throwing it had tired, or they were unwilling to spend too much energy if the attack was going to fizzle.

Ben held his breath. Then, his heart sank. Like the one before, the fire splashed harmlessly well over the demon's heads. It lit their formation in a terrible orange glow, and Ben swallowed. They'd estimated up to three thousand demons, but despite the huge number they'd already killed, there seemed to still be an endless stream of the things. The river was full of them, and Ben saw no end in sight.

"Damn, there's a lot of those bastards," muttered a man.

Ben nodded. Whoever had spoken was right.

"Hurry up!" yelled Ben to a group who were just now coming back. "If we don't get to where the mages can help us, this is going to get ugly."

"Going to get?" wondered Rhys.

Ben ignored him and retreated as soon as the straggling group reached his position.

A quarter bell of harried running got them to the base of the watchtower and the men began to scramble up the slick slope of the riverbank. The grass was wet. Ben tried to imagine it was merely dew and not blood. The men slipped and slid, struggling to gain elevation.

The demons were closing, five hundred paces away. Their hunger drove them, and the more immature ones broke, racing ahead of the army. Forty men still stood on the mud of the riverbed, backs turned, scrambling to get out. Fireballs rained down from above, but they disintegrated short of the demons, just like the others.

"The mages can't help," muttered Ben. He was standing at the rear of the men, facing the demons.

"You can't help against that either," said Adrick, placing a gauntleted hand on Ben's shoulder.

"Don't do it," warned Ben.

"I'm the only one who can," responded the swordsman.

"We need you."

"When everyone is clear," stated Adrick, "I'll retreat. You want to help me, get yourself and the men out of this riverbed quickly. In this armor, I can get up that hill faster than any of these demons. Get the others to safety, and I'll be right behind you!"

Ben grunted and spun, rushing to help push another man higher. Above, soldiers had formed a chain of linked men. The guardians and blademasters were using them as a ladder, scrambling up, booted feet slipping on the grass.

After the last of the guardians was hauled up, Ben jumped and caught the wrists of a stout ranger. The man yanked on Ben, jerking his arms in the sockets but pulling him clear of the riverbed. Hands reached down, and tugged them up, higher and higher. When they reached the top, Ben turned and gasped.

Adrick's sword blazed with pulsating energy. The silver of his armor reflected it like a lamp and illuminated the demon horde charging after him.

The racing demons had retreated back into the pack when he'd run at them, but now, the entire force was charging. No amount of skill could stand up to so many of them. The man had magically enhanced speed from his armor, but he'd inevitably slow when he started up the bank. The demons were right on his heels and no one was left to help him!

"He has no chance," Ben heard one of the rangers murmur under his breath.

Ben took a step forward, but he knew there was nothing he

could do. Suddenly, he felt jostled from behind, and bodies pushed their way through the watching crowd.

"Jasper!" cried Ben.

The old mage looked back and winked. Beside him was the big man, Earnest John, and several other warrior mages. Their weapons glowed menacingly with powerful runes.

"They can block our magic from afar. Let's see what they can do up close."

Jasper's sword burst into flame, and his friends spread out, each one of them clutching mage-wrought weapons. They slid down the hill and jumped into the riverbed.

The demons recoiled, and Jasper and his companions advanced. Ben's jaw dropped open. The huge mage with the battle axe started burning yellow. The man was a living lantern. Jasper's sword and off-hand blazed brightly. The nearly naked, blue-masked woman lashed out, punching with her bare fist and sending a wave of crackling energy into the marching demons. Behind the wave, the silver-haired man danced forward, his longswords free and ready.

"Ben!" called Amelie.

He turned and saw her grasping the wyvern fire staff and her rapier.

"Are you using that thing?" he asked, looking at the blade.

She snorted. "I was coming to check on you. I guess you're not hurt if you have time to worry about that."

"Not badly," allowed Ben. His body was covered in cuts and scrapes, and he had a few stinging lacerations on his back he knew would need attention, but it was nothing that was going to slow him.

They both looked down. From above, it was difficult to see what was going on in the distance. They could see blue and yellow lights, but the scene was obscured by swarming demons.

"We need to help them," said Ben.

Amelie placed a hand on his shoulder. "They're on their own. There's nothing we can do without going down there, Ben."

He started pacing and glanced around the corner of the watchtower, down where the rangers held their line. The men had moved back nearly to the crown of the hill and there were fewer of them than he'd seen earlier, but they appeared to be holding strong.

"How are things up here?" asked Ben.

Amelie frowned. "We've been trying to find where the water was stopped, but we've been blocked somehow. All we see is smoke."

"If we can't release that water, and we can't hit these things with magic, we're in trouble," responded Ben. "There has to be some way we can do something."

Amelie held up the wyvern fire staff.

"No," said Ben. "Whoever uses it will be sacrificing themselves, and we don't know if the wyvern fire can even get through whatever barrier the demons put up."

He looked back at the riverbed. It may have been his imagination, but he thought the lights were making their way back to the watchtower.

"How far does the smoke extend?" asked Ben.

Amelie frowned. "Maybe a quarter league across, but it's thickest over the river itself."

"There is water further north but not pooling around like it's been dammed?" questioned Ben.

Amelie shrugged. "It looks completely normal to the north, but we can't penetrate the smoke, no matter how close we look. The water just vanishes at that point in the river."

"The water is going somewhere," declared Ben.

Amelie looked at him, confused.

"We need to get Jasper!" exclaimed Ben.

"You can't go down there," protested Amelie. "He'll come back."

Ben clenched his fists. "Where is Elle, that little girl in his party?"

Amelie took him around the watchtower and pointed toward the group of mages. Ben ran to them and pushed into their circle, demanding, "What if the river isn't stopped? What if it's being sent somewhere?"

The mages all turned to stare at him.

"The demons in the Wilds drew power from the Rift, and we know they come from another world. The guardians have said they are able to travel the node gates, that they're more attuned to those openings than we are. What if the demon-king managed to create its own rift and was diverting the river into it?"

"That makes sense!" gasped one of the guardian's mages. "The dark forces do have the ability to travel the nodes, and their realm is full of heat. That might explain how they were able to draw sufficient energy to boil the length of river!"

The mages all began speaking at once, offering wild theories and speculation.

"If we assume this is correct," shouted Towaal, trying to assert some order, "what do we do about it?"

"We have to stop the king," said Elle. "But if they've formed a rift, we have to destroy it. It'd be one of the last gateways between our worlds."

Everyone paused and looked to Ben.

"I-I, ah," he stammered. "This is a bit out of my pond."

"How would you even close a natural rift?" wondered one of Jasper's mages.

"The guardians closed one," said Amelie.

"That took incredible preparation, though," stated one of the guardian's mages. "It also took the best of us. A dozen of them had to sacrifice themselves to do it. I'm afraid we do not have the strength to do it again. Not alone."

Elle pulled her cloak tight and looked to her companions. "We might be able to combine our strength and do this, but what of the demon-king? That creature will still be formidable."

"And how would we get to the rift?" muttered another of the guardians, waving a hand down the slope where a massive army of demons stood between them and upriver.

"Can you call on the power of the First Mages?" Amelie asked the guardians. "They have strength still, right? Surely, we can figure out a way to use it. What's the point of that power if it isn't used this moment?"

"It doesn't work like that," responded one of the mages.

Ben frowned, his mind swirling.

Shouts rose up from beside the watchtower, and a heavy rumbling filled the air. The huge, square blocks of the watchtower were being pushed down the steep hill, crushing demons as they rolled. Jasper came striding up to the group. Blood was smeared all along the left side of his face, and he walked with a limp, but the man was still upright.

"We're throwing stones on top of them, but it will only slow the creatures. It may also make it easier for them to climb up and get us, but we're running out of ideas." He looked to Amelie, and his gaze locked onto the wyvern fire staff. "We need to act while we still have strength."

"Contact Gunther," said Ben.

Jasper looked back at him, not understanding. Amelie's jaw dropped open.

"Through a thought meld," insisted Ben. "Can you try to contact him?"

"The man has vanished," stated the leader of the guardian's mages. "It's like he disappeared from this world. We-we tracked him in the past, but he's beyond our reach now. There's no way to contact him."

"He did vanish from this world," responded Ben, "when we closed the rift to the demon world in the Purple's fortress. Jasper, we think the demons may have opened a rift somehow to divert the river. If it's going to their world, we may have a doorway open to find Gunther."

Understanding dawned on Jasper's face. The screech of demons and the crashing of stones shook the air, but Ben held the mage's gaze.

"To establish a natural thought meld," argued the guardian, "you would have to know someone for, I don't know, centuries! No one has even seen the First Mage in that long."

"I'll try," said Jasper calmly. He closed his eyes, and everyone watched.

The guardians studied him suspiciously, but they didn't interfere.

Rhys came running up, glanced around at the mages, and then suggested, "Ah, the demons are coming up the slope now, you know, in case anyone wants to help do something about that."

Ben yanked out his longsword and instructed Towaal. "Your turn."

Grim-faced, the mage followed him back around the remaining rubble of the watchtower. Amelie and a handful of the guardians followed.

"What if he can't contact Gunther?" worried Amelie.

"We'll need to think of a way to close that rift," stated Ben. "If we can do that, then the water will flow back down the riverbed and solve a great deal of our demon problem. It may also finally draw out the demon-king."

"You're right," said Towaal. "Killing a few of its minions isn't going to interest that monster enough to expose itself. We have to show we're winning the battle."

At the base of the watchtower, Jasper's mages were rolling heavy blocks of stone down the slope. Blademasters and guardians stood clustered behind them, ready to charge forward when the demons made the top of the hill. Adrick Morgan was resting on his knees, his sword barely flickering, laid across his thighs.

"Are you okay?" asked Ben.

The blank steel face turned, but before he could respond, a demon crested the hill and bellowed. It was immediately met and felled by a blademaster, but more of the creatures came behind, churning over the huge stone blocks that had been tumbled down from the watchtower.

Ben raced into action, lunging at one of the beasts the moment its head appeared. The tip of his longsword smashed into the creature's face, and it toppled back, but was thrown aside as two dozen of its fellows came right behind. Ben took another in the throat and then stepped back, careful not to get over- whelmed by the press of bodies. Blademasters and guardians joined his side, and together, they formed a wall of steel.

Behind Ben, he felt the crackle of energy. A blaze of lightning blasted between him and a man to his side, catching a demon in front of them and then cascading down the hill, frying the monsters one by one. Packed as closely together as they were, the energy flowed easily amongst them, shocking and killing three dozen in the space of a few heartbeats. The light flickered out, and they had a moment of reprieve as most of the creatures on the hill were now dead.

Ben stepped to the edge and looked down. In the moonlight, he could see demons flowing like the water of the river, stretching north and vanishing in the distance.

Streams of them were heading south, past the watchtower. They could climb that side and flank Ben and his companions, coming around the watchtower to where the mages were.

"We're going to get surrounded," shouted Ben.

Lloyd appeared by his side. The man's left arm was hanging limply, strips of torn flesh visible in the moonlight.

"We could send some of the rangers," he offered, though his tone betrayed how futile he thought that'd be.

The advantage of the mages had been nullified when the demons avoided the traps in the field and came down the riverbed. Packed closely together, the mages might have had a chance to cause severe damage, but the shield hanging over the demons protected them from that as well. If the men were surrounded, their skill with their blades would no longer matter. They couldn't back up, swap for rested men, or have a route to retreat. They'd be finished.

Towaal took Ben's other side. "Jasper has the strength to stop this with the staff."

"And what of the demon-king?" asked Ben. "How will we stop it if we use the staff for the minions?"

The mage's face was a mask of frustration. "If the minions overrun us, it won't matter, will it? One mage could use the staff now, and another on the demon-king if it arrives."

"If," growled Ben. "If we use the staff now, what are the chances the demon-king will come? It can sense far-seeing. It may be cunning enough to avoid us entirely after we use wyvern fire."

Towaal shrugged helplessly.

"Is that what you'd do?" asked Ben. "Direct Jasper to use the wyvern fire?"

"You're the leader, Ben," stated Towaal.

He frowned, glancing down at the demons that were starting to come back up the hill.

"We wait," he declared. "We have to save the staff for the king."

Ben watched as the demons scrambled over their fallen peers and made the bottom of the watchtower hill. In moments, they'd be at the top.

"Lloyd, take your blademasters and as many rangers as you can gather. Circle around to the south side of the watchtower and prepare to meet the demons there. Adrick, you and I are holding this position with Jasper's mages."

Lloyd's eyes showed he didn't entirely agree, but there was no time for a debate. The man waved to his men and turned to go.

Adrick rose to his feet unsteadily, the guardians forming into a line along the top of the hill.

"Are you okay?" Ben asked the swordsman.

"I can fight," responded the man.

"What are you thinking?" hissed Amelie. "We're spreading thin, Ben."

"Either Jasper can reach Gunther and do something about this river, or he cannot. If he can, we can save the staff for the demon-king. If he cannot, then he'll use it on these creatures. As long as Jasper still has strength, we have the choice. We protect him as long as we have breath to do so and give him as much time as we're able. Then, at the end, he can act one way or the other."

Amelie opened her mouth to respond, but a demon bounded up the hill and landed right in front of her. Ben swung his longsword and caught it across the face, gouging an ugly track through its muscle and bone. Amelie's rapier pierced its side and stabbed deep.

"Now's the time to use it if you're saving any energy," called Ben.

"Watch this," said Amelie. She yanked her blade from the demon's body and threw it into the air.

Ben watched the rapier fly end-over-end above the demons climbing the hill. In the blink of an eye, the blade glowed orange and then white hot. It exploded. Tiny shards of burning metal flew at the demons below as if shot from a crossbow.

Ben watched in awe as the hot bits of steel smacked into demons and then continued their momentum, bursting out the other sides of the creatures. The bits of metal were small, but they were flung with incredible velocity. They shredded dozens of demons like overcooked meat. Amelie had taken the attack she'd used against Eldred's men and amplified it three-fold. Smoke curled up from the singed flesh, and the front of the demons staggered back from the impact of the attack.

Beside Ben, Adrick whistled. "Well done," acknowledged the man.

"Are you talking about the attack, or how cooked those demons are?" jested Ben.

Adrick's head turned, and Ben found himself looking at the blank steel of the man's helmet.

"I told you," complained Ben. "We can't see you. It's a bit disconcerting not knowing if you're laughing at my joke or not."

"My father doesn't know how to laugh," claimed Prem, stumbling up to them. Her clothing was covered in red and purple blood. Her tunic was stuck to her like it was glued. She was limping heavily but still stood straight. She looked at Amelie. "What happened to your sword?"

Adrick wordlessly pointed down the slope, where scores of demons were making their way back up.

"Later," said Ben.

He spun his longsword and settled his feet on the dew-damp grass. Amelie retreated. With only a belt-knife, there was no reason she should stay close to the fighting.

"I'll find out what I can from Jasper," she called to Ben.

"Let him know what I said," Ben shouted back.

A demon came flying at them, gliding silently on nearly developed wings. Adrick casually swung his sword, letting the blade fill with the cool blue glow. The light cleaved through the creature and neatly sliced it in two.

More were coming, and Ben found himself hard-pressed to stop the vicious attack. The light, fast demons had attacked first and been slaughtered. The creatures they faced now were thick, muscular monsters. The larger ones had the strength of two men, and any slip that allowed them to get a claw on you would be fatal.

Ben weaved back and forth, cutting the creatures down and pushing their bodies back down the slope. There were always more, though, and the men had little room to back up. The remains of the watchtower were behind them, and beyond that were the mages, with another swarm of demons closing from the other angle. Now, it was kill or be killed. There was nowhere to run to, no quarter.

Tired, stinging from a dozen cuts, sore from a score of bruises, and thirsty, Ben fell into a battle haze. His arms churned, swinging his sword with blademaster-like precision, each cut made with minimal effort, minimal thought. He acted on instinct and counted on it to keep him alive. He used senses that were beyond the five he was familiar with. He was aware of the demons, aware of where they were, and where they'd move. He was one with them, joined in battle.

He was aware that Rhys was a dozen paces south of him and Adrick three dozen north. Prem was slinking around the base of the tower, sprinting into the fray whenever she saw an opening and then falling back when her knives would be insufficient.

Like a slowly rising sun, awareness crept through Ben, settling into the back of his mind. He sensed that below them, something was moving. Not the demon-king, but something else. Something dangerous.

He turned and fought his way to Adrick, bobbing and weaving as demons reached for him, thrusting and slashing his way through their thick bodies.

"Something's below!" Ben called to the swordsman.

Adrick spun in a circle, his blade flaring bright and whipping through five demons that had surrounded him. "What do you mean?" asked the man.

"We need light below," responded Ben.

Adrick grunted and absorbed a blow to his shoulder. It didn't even scratch his plate armor, but the force of the strike rocked him.

Ben leapt to the man's side, cleanly stabbing the tip of his longsword into the attacking creature's eye and then twirling to sever the arm of another.

"Use your sword to provide some light."

Adrick paused, and Ben lashed out at a creature that was charging the man.

In the back of his mind, Ben realized that the demons were coming faster at Adrick than anyone else. Something was directing them to the man. Ben thought he knew what.

"This armor is giving me strength I'd never have on my own," responded Adrick, "but the sword is draining me. Using its power takes energy, and I only have so much to give."

"It's necessary," said Ben, understanding that the man was propped up by shear will, but that he wasn't yet exhausted. Ben could feel he was saving up for the end.

Adrick grunted and raised his weapon. Suddenly, the blade flared bright like a small, blue sun. The swordsman held it high, and below them, row after row, wave after wave of demon was revealed, stretching far past the last of Adrick's light.

Ben saw what he was looking for. A pair of tall, slender demons, nearly lost amongst the pressing horde. He'd been looking for... something, and they were it.

"We have to get down there," he said quietly.

Adrick let the light dim and sliced his blade cleanly through two demons who'd arrived close together.

He growled, "Down in the riverbed, again? Please, tell me why."

"I saw their mages," said Ben, spitting the words between breaths as he lunged at snarling faces and parried grasping claws. "There are only two. They're the ones protecting the horde from magical attacks."

Adrick didn't respond for several moments. Finally, he asked, "You are sure?"

"I am sure. Adrick, if we kill them..."

They didn't discuss how Ben would know that, or what would happen if his strange intuition was wrong. The path was clear to him, the solution obvious.

"Follow me," said Adrick, evidently sensing Ben's conviction. "Stay close. I'll get you as far as I can."

Without word to the other men, the plate-armored swordsman plunged over the edge of the hill like a bright, silver knife. He sliced down, parting the demons like flesh under a sharp blade. Ben scrambled after him, struggling to keep up with Adrick's magically enhanced speed. He heard the cries of the men behind them, but Ben didn't have time to explain what they were doing. He didn't have time for anything other than fighting for his life. The attack was madness.

The descent down the slope was completely uncontrolled. Dew, demon blood, the blood of men, it all made the grass as slick as an ice-covered hill. There was no stopping their momentum once they started, and the demons that would have stood in their way all parted in front of Adrick's charge.

The creatures didn't expect the assault and didn't have time to react before the swordsman was cutting through them, his bright blue blade merely a whirl of color in the black of night.

Ben tried to run after the man but after a few steps gave up and jumped. He landed on his seat and slid down the slope. He bumped into corpses and rocks with his feet and scrambled over them, only to continue his controlled tumble.

At the bottom of the hill, Adrick made a final leap and soared into the air, coming down into the riverbed like a meteorite. He landed on a handful of the dark creatures, crushing them with the force of his jump and the weight of his plate armor. His forward momentum carried him too far, though, and the man went rolling into the legs of another bunch of beasts, knocking them over like lawn bowling pins. He was down, and the demons howled with bloodlust around him. They closed, all pounding on the armored man, burying him with their bodies.

None of them were paying attention when Ben came flying down behind, landing near where Adrick had and rolling quickly to his feet. He didn't have the preternatural strength and speed

Adrick's armor imbued him or the centuries of experience, but Ben knew what to do about a score of demons with their backs turned.

He fell on them, hammering his sword down, slashing through flesh, shattering bone. All around them, the demons cried out. It seemed the entire riverbed was closing in, the black bodies like water that had been pushed away by a heavy rock and was now rushing back in. Frantically, Ben chopped and hacked, his instincts driving him, his mind struggling to hold back the incredible panic of being alone in the center of two thousand demons.

Then, a light flashed in the center of the pile of creatures in front of him, and Adrick's blade carved the pile in two. The demons screamed, writhed, and then burst outward.

Ben ducked as heavy bodies and pieces of bodies were thrown, bearing flickering blue flames and trailing glowing smoke. Rushing forward, Ben reached down and gripped Adrick's gauntleted hand, hauling the swordsman to his feet. All around them, demons swirled, afraid to come too near the swordsman's lightblade. Ben knew it wouldn't last.

"The arch-demons are coming," remarked Adrick. "They'll drive the rest of these at us."

"We've still got a hundred paces to go to where I saw the mages," said Ben.

Suddenly, the wall of creatures behind them bulged, but the demons weren't charging. Instead, they were spinning in fear of something approaching from behind. They were lit in stark relief from a blaze of silver.

"Rhys!" cried Ben.

Without thinking, he attacked. The haze of battle consumed him. Demons came at him, and he cut them down. Demons fled, and he cut them down. In a blink, Rhys plowed through the last of them and stumbled into the clear space that Adrick was maintaining.

"What are you doing?" shouted the rogue, his face painted with streaks of purple blood from the demons. He didn't look pleased to be there.

"I saw their mages," stated Ben. "A hundred paces due east."

"I'm nearly spent," called Adrick, still moving half again as fast as Ben had ever moved and wreaking carnage amongst the demons. "I can get us closer, but I don't know if I can get us back out."

"This is a suicide mission?" cried Rhys. "When I came down here, I thought you'd have a plan."

"You told me the end was near," yelled Ben, ducking to avoid a thin creature that had sprung at him like an over-eager puppy. "In the desert, didn't you say you were ready to die?"

"I didn't mean literally right now!" shouted Rhys. "But since I'm already here, let's do it."

Without needing instructions, Adrick charged into the tightly packed mass of demons with Ben clinging to his heels and Rhys bringing up the rear.

Without the exceptional power of the two mage-wrought blades, there was no chance they could fight through the press. The demons were afraid, and even the most rabid of them didn't want to be on the front line when one of the glowing blades swooped near. A pocket formed around them, with only a handful of the creatures brave enough to venture close. They were cut down quickly, and step by step, Adrick led them deeper into the riverbed.

"Where are we going, Ben?" he called.

"Twenty paces northeast," panted Ben.

His blood was churning, his mind was swirling, and he couldn't gather his thoughts. They were slippery like soap-covered hands, but through the haze, the path remained clear. There was only one route. One way. One thing they could do. A moment later, he found his instinct had been correct.

"Harden your will!" screamed Rhys.

Adrick stepped in front of them, his light-filled sword held diagonally across his body. Sulphurous smoke blasted over them and before Ben's mind could process it, incredible heat. His will hardened, locked in stasis. That was until Adrick's armored body smashed into him, and they both went flying back to land on Rhys.

The breath whooshed out of Ben, and the night went black for a moment. The first thing he heard when he returned was Rhys growling unspeakable curses.

"Adrick?" asked Ben weakly. He could feel the weight of the man's armor crushing him down onto Rhys, but the man wasn't moving.

"Hold on," responded the swordsman. It sounded like through tightly-grit teeth. "That hurt a bit."

"You should try it from down here," grumbled Rhys.

Suddenly, the weight lifted, and Ben was hauled to his feet.

Around them, the dry riverbed was bathed in the soft glow of the moon. Ben blinked. Nearby, it was clear of demons except for two of them. Standing on the other side of Adrick were two tall, slender creatures. While thin, they were corded with hard muscle. A pair of thin horns swept back from their heads, protecting their skulls and ending in sharp points. They looked at Ben and his companions with curiosity.

"They just pulped three or four hundred of their buddies trying to hit us," said Rhys, clambering to his feet. "Keep your walls up. Do not waver."

"This will not be pleasant," agreed Adrick.

In front of them, the demons raised their arms to the sides. From clawed hands, pace-long blades grew from their wrists, extending the length of Ben's sword, swirling with virulent power, and pulsating a menacing purple.

"Oh, hell," mumbled Rhys. "I should have had that drink."

"You were planning on dying, right? You go first," Adrick suggested to the rogue.

"I've got this," stated Ben.

He stepped around Adrick and began to walk toward the two demons. All around them, the rest of the creatures howled madly but stayed away. After what these two had unleashed, Ben didn't blame them. He took a dozen steps before Adrick and Rhys joined him.

"Keep your will hardened," said Adrick.

"And don't get hit by one of those, well, whatever the hell it is they've got," added Rhys.

"Thanks," responded Ben dryly. "You guys are a big help."

He was speaking without thought, falling back on conversational norms learned throughout his life and the banter refined during his time with Rhys. Like his movement, it happened naturally. His consciousness floated above, watching, focused ahead. Surrounded by an army, facing two creatures whose power they could only guess at, there was only one thing to do. It was clear. His next move was obvious.

He charged.

16

WATER AND FIRE

PIERCING CRIES SPLIT THE NIGHT AS THE TWO DEMON-MAGES elicited terrible calls. Ben felt his blood lift, like it was trying to tear itself out of his skin. On the run, he held firm, held stasis, clamped down on the intrusion into his body, and forced it out. He could feel it, though, a presence on his skin, sliding over him, looking for weakness, looking for a way to tear him apart. He wouldn't give them time to do it. In heartbeats, he closed the distance to the awful creatures.

They were ready. Ben, in front, earned their interest. One made a curt gesture, and the mud under Ben buckled, catching his foot and pitching him forward. The other creature swung, its single-bladed claw swishing toward Ben's head. The thing glinted in the moonlight, and along its length, it crawled with purple light that made Ben's skin twitch.

He only had a moment, and in it, he thought he was dead. Then, he was flung violently to the side, and Adrick stepped into his place. The claw clashed against the warrior's side. Purple and yellow sparks exploded, temporarily blinding Ben.

He hit the ground and rolled. A sharp line of pain scored his ribs, and he kept rolling, narrowly avoiding another strike as the second demon-mage ran after him, stomping with clawed feet. Without considering the wisdom of the maneuver, Ben replicated a trick he'd tried on Lord Jason so many months ago, and he rolled back the other way.

The demon jumped, clearing him and slashing down with one arm. Its long, single claw streaked toward Ben's face. The razor-thin tip passed a breath away from his lips, and then the creature passed over him. It landed lightly and looked back, tilting its head slightly to one side.

Ben scrambled to his feet and held his longsword up, his thoughts torn between the calm assurance of the battle fog and the uncomfortable feeling that he was pretty sure there was nothing he could do to defeat a monster like this.

Rhys came to stand beside him. "Any ideas?" asked the rogue.

Ben, his voice catching, responded, "Give me that flask. You kill this thing."

"Why not?" asked Rhys.

Ben stared in shock as the rogue stabbed the tip of his longsword into the mud.

"I…" Ben babbled.

The demon continued to observe them, clearly unconcerned but curious.

Rhys reached into his cloak. Then, fast as a thought, the rogue's hand flashed back out, and one of his long knives flew toward the demon's face. The heavy steel weapon streaked through the night and then stopped half a hand away from the demon-mage. Like it hit a wall, the knife just stopped and fell.

"Oh," muttered Rhys, gripping his longsword and yanking it free of the mud.

Behind them, Ben could hear the other creature colliding with Adrick. He spared a glance back and swallowed hard. The side of Adrick's mage-wrought plate was dented and scored. The demon-mage had done what hundreds of its peers could not. It had damaged Adrick's armor. The next strike might be enough to get through it. Worse, Ben wasn't wearing mage-wrought plate armor, and the demon-mage in front of him was no longer content to observe.

"Pay attention," shouted Rhys as he darted to the side, parrying a slash from the creature.

Ben tried to leap forward and strike while it was occupied with Rhys, but the thing spun to face him. Ben had to jump back, narrowly avoiding getting cut in two. He sidestepped, working a circle around the monster, forcing it to put its back to him or Rhys.

It faced Ben and scampered close, both claws waving madly.

Ben fell into a defensive form, one he'd learned to use against a man with two blades, but no man moved as fast as this demon. No man had its strength. The battle haze still infused Ben, but even that was not enough. His instincts were failing him. In the space of two breaths, Ben had three stinging cuts on his arms and legs. He could feel a tremor of virulent power seeking to tear into him through the lacerations in his skin. A slightly larger wound may leave him crippled.

The demon-mage attacked again, and by pure luck, Ben kept the claws away from his head and torso. He dodged right, and the thing struck to left. If the coin had fallen the other way, he'd be dead.

Rhys struck from behind, stabbing his glowing silver longsword at the demon-mage's back. The tip of the blade skittered away, catching nothing but night air. The creature twisted, and Rhys ducked, rolling on one shoulder and popping right back up.

"It's got some sort of magical barrier around it!" he called.

Ben lashed out while the demon was still recovering from its spin, and his sword nicked the creature's arm, drawing a thin line of purple blood.

The demon snarled at them.

"How did you do that?" shouted Rhys, crab-walking away from the demon.

"Is your long knife mage-wrought like your sword?" shouted Ben.

"These things are bloody impossible," cried Adrick from a score of paces away where he was furiously defending himself and flailing backward.

"They've armored themselves against magic somehow," shouted Rhys in response. "They're impervious to our weapons."

"What?" screeched Adrick.

A painful crunch sounded, and Ben heard the man tumble across the mud again, but Ben didn't have time to look. It was taking everything he had to stay a step ahead of the demon-mage facing him and Rhys.

"It's not impervious to my sword," said Ben. "It's simple steel."

"We need to distract it!" said Rhys.

Ben was wondering how when Adrick's silver armor flashed by. The swordsman smashed into the side of the demon-mage with one lowered shoulder. His mage-wrought armor slammed against the magical barrier, but the force of the blow against the magic sent the demon flying. Both Adrick and the creature crashed to the ground, the man scrambling, sliding along the invisible barrier and trying to stay on top of the demon and pin it to the earth.

Ben rushed forward, and Rhys leapt to distract Adrick's demon-mage. On the ground, the creature didn't have the leverage to stick its claws into Adrick, but they scraped against the side of his plate, sawing through the steel. Adrick was thrown clear, and Ben struck an instant later, slamming his longsword down into the demon-mage's chest.

The steel blade punched deep, finding the monster's heart. The demon-mage twitched violently once and then fell limp. Ben yanked his long sword out and staggered back.

The second creature wailed, a long, sharp, piercing cry that sent Ben staggering to his knees. Blinking tears, he pivoted on his knee and flung his longsword at the demon, hoping to catch it unaware. The demon-mage reacted with uncanny speed and batted away the weapon.

"Oh, damn," muttered Ben. "That was stupid."

The demon-mage charged.

Ben's hand closed around the hilt of his hunting knife, and he crouched low. Closing faster than he thought possible, the creature raised its claws, rage radiating from its eyes. Ben sprang forward, throwing up one arm to brush aside a stabbing claw and whipping his knife out with the other.

Searing pain shot through his body as the sharp claw sliced through his flesh and dug into the bone of his forearm. It spasmed as a jolt of energy leapt from the claw into his body. He could feel his muscles twitching, being ripped apart by the violent power. The other claw swung wide, though, and Ben, holding his knife low, stabbed it into the demon's abdomen.

The creature gripped Ben's shoulder with its clawed hand, the one that had missed him, and tossed Ben as easily as he'd throw a child's toy. He went flying into the air, struggling to hold onto the hilt of his hunting knife. The blade sliced along the demon's midsection as Ben was thrown clear, tearing a huge hole in the creature's abdomen.

As his feet lifted off the ground, he lost his grip on his knife, but the creature's claw was jerked out of his arm, and relief washed over him as the connection to the surging purple energy was severed. With a painful grunt, Ben landed on dry mud. He'd thrown his sword away, and somewhere between him and the creature was his hunting knife.

The demon-mage stepped closer to him and then looked down, appearing confused. Spilling out of its torn-open gut was a disgusting pile of tangled white entrails.

"Nice work," remarked Rhys.

The demon wavered, swaying on its clawed feet. Slowly, it fell to the side.

"We still have the other two thousand to worry about," said Rhys grimly. His tone didn't hide his assumption that they were about to die. He glanced at Ben's bloody arm. "You all right?"

"Could be worse," grunted Ben through gritted teeth.

Stumbling, Adrick made his way to them and then slumped to his knees. The mage-wrought plate armor was barely hanging from him, the breastplate dented and scored. The cuisse, covering his legs, had been nearly torn off from the battering by the demon. Ben could see the leather straps that still clung to Adrick. They were soaked in blood.

"Well," said the swordsman, "maybe it was a suicide mission, but it worked. We got the bastards."

"Don't count us out yet," said Ben.

Rhys snorted. He had his longsword up and was facing the swirling wall of demons that surrounded them. Thousands of the creatures. Perhaps stunned by the death of their mages, they had not yet charged, but they would. At least, they would if they didn't have something else to worry about.

Grinning, Ben stood. He calmly collected his long sword and slid it into his scabbard. He started looking for the knife he'd lost when the demon threw him.

"Giving up?" chided Rhys.

"No," answered Ben, "just preparing for a swim."

The rogue's eyes widened, and he looked up. A single blue orb hung suspended in the sky above them. The signal that the water upstream was released. Barely audible over the snarls and screeches of the demons was a growing roar. Somewhere to the north of them, a wall of water was rushing down the empty riverbed.

"Should we be getting out of here?" asked Adrick.

"Those demons don't look like they're in the mood to let us leave," remarked Ben.

The creatures were starting to tighten the circle around the three companions. Step by step, they were gaining confidence that the men were nearly beaten. Arch-demons were snarling and howling, Ben guessed encouraging the lesser creatures to attack. If the beasts charged, Ben was sure they would be beaten. Time was almost up, though.

"If we're going to have to swim, cut this off me," pleaded Adrick.

Rhys kneeled down and slid a long knife along the exposed leather straps, cutting the swordsman out of his breastplate, his leggings, and the rest of the battered plate armor.

Ben gripped the helmet and helped the man yank it off his head.

"It's a shame to see such a beautiful artifact destroyed," said Adrick wistfully.

"It served its purpose," responded Ben.

A single demon broke from the pack and charged them.

"This might get worse before it gets better," said Rhys, standing and striding forward to meet the creature, but none of the other demons had a chance to attack.

The crashing sound of the river returning was growing to the point even the demons couldn't ignore it. They started to turn and panic. Scores of them began to scramble up the sides of the bank, but any that left the riverbed were rained on by mage-fire. The mages must have witnessed what happened and were keeping the creatures pinned in the path of the water. Unfortunately, Ben and his friends were stuck there as well.

"Time to get wet," said Rhys. He turned, watching for the approaching wall of water.

"Stay on top if you can," advised Adrick. "It's going to be carrying a thousand demons with it when it hits us. Those things aren't going to be happy about being in the water, and they'll sink like rocks, but before they sink, they could tear us to shreds."

Ben nodded, then looked over the heads of the demons and

nearly threw up. A wall of water was rushing toward them, and on the front of that wall, all he could see were the thrashing shapes of demon's bodies. Hundreds, a thousand, he had no idea. All around them, the creatures were racing, trying to put distance between themselves and the water. Ben knew it was futile. That water would keep coming and then keep going until it emptied out into the South Sea. The banks were bound by mage fire. There was nowhere to go. So, he held his breath and gripped the hilt of his sword.

Around the three men, the air shimmered. Ben's jaw dropped open and the wall over water, carrying demons, rocks, and other debris slammed into an invisible barrier half a dozen paces in front of him. The sound crashed into his ears, bringing tears to his eyes, and the tempest swirled around them.

"The mages!" exclaimed Adrick. "They must have seen us."

The wall suddenly flexed, the torrent of water slipping a pace closer to them, rushing an arm-length above their heads, pressing against the invisible barrier.

"I don't think it's going to hold…" declared Rhys.

They dropped to their knees and ducked their heads, the black storm cutting off all visibility. The initial deluge was by, the worst of the danger passed, but overhead, an entire river of water pressed against around them.

"See you on the other side," said Rhys, and then the barrier collapsed.

Ben was inundated, thrown back, flipped, spun, and churned like a leaf in a rapid. There was nothing he could do but pull his arms and legs tight against his body and try to ignore the painful rake of claws and the heavy bodies that battered against him. The demons were confused and angry. He doubted they could even see him, but they lashed out any way they could. Unseen or not, the claws still hurt.

Ben kicked, guessing which way was up, bumping against demons and getting spun around the other direction. The sound of water filled his ears. He didn't bother opening his eyes. At night, underneath a river, and surrounded by the black shapes of the creatures, there would be nothing to see.

His lungs burned, and precious air bubbled out of his nose. A clawed hand wrapped around his ankle, but he kicked free. His chest ached, tempting him to suck in, but all he'd find would be water. He kicked harder, shedding his boots and unclasping his cloak. His body screamed at him, desperate for air.

He felt demons thrashing near his feet, and hoping they were sinking to the bottom, he kicked away from them. His bare feet churned through the water, and he scooped handfuls of the cold liquid with his hands and propelled himself forward.

Finally, he broke the surface. Gasping, panting, he kicked his feet frantically. The current was fast and the river still turbulent, but his head was bobbing in the air as he thrashed his legs, treading water. He drew in deep breaths between hacking and coughing up river water. His heart pounded, and his head swam, but he was kept afloat by the glorious realization that he would live, probably.

The river was racing, pushing him further and further downstream. He saw the bank rushing by and cursed himself. The battle was still continuing north of him, and with every breath, he was moving further and further away. Some of the demons would have made it out of the riverbed, and the demon-king was still lurking out of sight.

He started to swim, his longsword and clothing dragging at him, but he was unwilling to lose either of those. He'd already ditched his cloak and boots. If he survived, he didn't want to hike back to the battle naked and unarmed.

His left arm was numb from the cool water. It dulled the agony where the demon-mage's blade had bit him. The relief from the pain was welcome, but he began to worry he was going to bleed out before he made it to shore. The cut had been to the bone, and his arm trembled with every excruciating stroke.

On the black surface of the river, he didn't see any demons. As Adrick said, they must sink like rocks. Spitting water and struggling, Ben kept his head down and swam for the western bank, giving up trying to track his progress or assess where he was. He swam and nothing else until his hand slapped down on thick grass. The current by the bank wasn't nearly as strong as in the center, and he planted his feet, grabbing handfuls of the grass to drag himself out of the water.

He flopped down like a dead fish, his mouth opening and closing, sucking in lungfuls of air. It was several long moments before he regained enough strength to raise his head and look around. He was on the riverbank, thirty paces from the broad dirt road they'd followed north. There were no demons, and he didn't see Adrick or Rhys. Just him, the river, the grass, and the road. He groaned and rolled onto his back.

After a moment, he drew his hunting knife out of the sheath and started sawing on his shirt, cutting the sleeves off. He wrapped the fabric around the deep cut on his arm. Holding one end in his teeth, he tied a knot and jerked it tight. The pressure felt good, but his entire arm throbbed still. He felt woozy. He guessed it had been half a bell since he'd been injured, and he'd lost a lot of blood in that time. He needed to eat, drink, and rest. Muttering under his breath, Ben sat up and then staggered to his feet. There would be no rest, not yet.

The only sounds were crickets and night birds. The wind rustled the grass around him, and he shivered. He was soaking wet and barefoot. He sighed. Better get moving. He padded across the grass and felt the hard, cold dirt of the road underneath his feet.

Two bells later, his throat was bone dry, and his feet were raw and sore from stepping on small, sharp rocks that were invisible at night. He was thirty. So thirsty.

Ben glanced at the river again, watching the slow current bubble by him. Shaking himself, he thought about how many demons had been washed through that little stretch and how their foul blood and dead bodies were probably still tainting the water.

Behind him, he heard a strange sound. In the moonlight, he saw a lone man hiking along the road. Ben paused, waiting.

Looking like a drowned cat, Rhys marched closer. The rogue's boots squelched with each step, and his long hair was plastered around his head and over his face like a wet mop. His sword belt looked to be gone, but he still held his longsword on his shoulder, one hand gripping the hilt and the other hand holding a silver flask.

"I saved you a bit," declared the rogue, coming to a stop beside Ben.

"I'm surprised," said Ben, accepting the flask.

"Me too," admitted Rhys. He sighed and shifted his longsword. "I have blisters from walking in these wet boots that I'm afraid may never heal."

"I lost my boots in the river," stated Ben. He turned up the flask and let the fiery spirits fill his mouth. It wasn't the water his body was craving, but it tasted pretty damn good.

"Adrick?" asked Rhys.

"I didn't see either one of you after the water hit us. He could be somewhere up the road or somewhere far down it." Ben winced, not wanting to vocalize the other obvious possibility. Adrick may not have made it. Instead, he asked, "How far do you think we have to go?"

"A league, maybe a hair more," answered Rhys. "We should be to the outskirts of the battle in half that, assuming it's still going on."

Ben took another pull from the flask and then handed it back. "We'd best get moving then."

~

THE FIRST THING Ben saw was the single tower sticking up from the hill. In the pre-dawn twilight, it was a black finger standing against a grey sky.

"I don't hear much fighting," remarked Rhys. "That's either good or really bad."

"They should have had plenty of strength left to mop up the remaining demons," said Ben. "Either they did it, or the demon-king found them."

They started passing the bodies of demons interspaced with the corpses of men. It was the column of creatures that had broken off, trying to flank them. Ben was glad to see it was mostly black shapes, but there were plenty of rangers down and even a few of the blademasters. He didn't see Lloyd, but he wasn't going to step off the road and go looking. He wasn't far from lying down and joining the corpses. He was drained of blood, and the hike back to the hill had used up nearly everything he had. His head was swimming, and he felt feverish.

"Just a bit longer," mumbled Rhys.

The rogue's head was hanging, and his boots were scrapping the dirt road with each step. He didn't have a deep cut like Ben, but he'd aged decades in the last year, and it was clearly weighing on him. No one had the stamina to do what they'd done the night before.

The sound of pounding feet drew Ben's head up and he saw a man slipping and scrambling closer to them.

"Lord Ben?" asked the man.

Ben coughed. "I'm no lord."

In the pre-dawn gloom, Ben saw it was one of Rakkash's

rangers. He looked a bit worse for wear. His clothing and armor were torn, rivulets of dried blood stained one hip.

"You're alive!" exclaimed the ranger. "We've been waiting for you, hoping you'd return."

"What happened here?" asked Ben, raising his head to scan the battle-torn terrain.

"Of course, of course you'd want to know," stammered the man. He filled them in as they hiked the last couple of hundred paces up the hill to the watchtower.

According to the man, the mages had all suddenly scrambled out of their huddle, yelling that the river broke and was going to come rushing down. The ranger wasn't sure how it happened, but he was clear that the mages insisted they keep as many demons in the riverbed as possible. They'd seen Ben, Rhys, and Adrick down below, but no one could get close enough to help.

The mages started using their magic. They blew the ranks of demons back from the line of rangers and then started laying down fire to keep the creatures in the riverbed. Within moments, the water came down, and thousands of the creatures were swept away, along with Ben and his companions.

Several hundred demons were still in the field and surrounding the watchtower, but the men had been heartened when the majority of the force was wiped away with no effort. They rallied and made quick work of the remaining beasts. Some of the demons fled, but they'd killed nearly all of them. Word around the campsite was that it had been at least three thousand of the monsters in total.

"How many did we lose?" asked Ben.

The ranger's face fell, his excitement at the victory tempered when he thought about the cost.

"Almost all of the mages survived," he replied. "Over half the blademasters and the forest people. A bit less than half of us made it. Only a third of the Kirksbane watch. No one's found Rakkash."

Ben grimaced. Over half the arms men gone.

"The demon army is done," stated Rhys. "Ben, we won."

Ben shook his head. "What of the king? If it is still out there, then this isn't over."

"Let's ask them," suggested Rhys, nodding toward the mage's camp.

Ben heard a shout and turned to see Amelie charging toward him, her eyes red and puffy, her clothing ripped and ragged. She lived, though, and was still strong. She tackled him in a running hug, and he flopped down weakly. Amelie, lying on top of him, gasped and apologized for knocking him over, evidently surprised at how weak he was.

"He needs healing," said Rhys quietly.

"Of course, of course," murmured Amelie, her eyes darting to find the myriad of cuts and scrapes on Ben's body and then settling on the blood-soaked sleeve of his shirt that he'd fashioned into a bandage around his forearm.

The small girl Elle appeared and knelt beside Ben. "May I?"

Amelie nodded, and the girl placed hands on him.

17

NOT YET DAWN

THE SUN WAS HIGH OVERHEAD WHEN BEN WOKE. HIS THROAT WAS bone dry and he was famished. He struggled to sit, and his head spun. Someone had erected a tarp overhead, which he guessed had saved him from a rather bad sunburn. Around him, injured men and women slumbered. They'd been healed to the extent the mages were willing to spare their energy, but healing only went so far. The body had work to do. Some of the recovery had to happen naturally.

After a quick count, Ben frowned. There were two dozen wounded under the tarp. A chill settled on him when he wondered if there was another area they were keeping the injured or if this was it. Was it possible that every other injury had resulted in death?

Shuddering, he crawled out from under the tarp, taking care to not wake any of the sleeping people beside him. He knew they would need all the rest they could get. He did too, but not as much as he needed food and water.

The sun blinded him, and he blinked, trying to gain his bearings. The first thing he saw was the field to the north of them. He swallowed, trying to stop from retching. The grass was covered in dead demons and more dead people than he wanted to admit he saw. For hundreds of paces in every direction, the dead lay like a carpet around the hill of the watchtower.

"We sent a runner to Kirksbane," said a voice. "We don't have the strength to clean up this mess. Hopefully, Kirksbane can send wagons, fuel for the fires, shovels for the burial mound, strong backs to dig it…"

Ben turned to see Jasper standing beside him. The ancient mage looked as he always did, surprisingly fit and with wisdom shining in his eyes.

"We have much to discuss," continued Jasper, "but you should eat. Come, we have a soup on the boil. You should drink as much water as you can hold down as well. I'm told you lost a significant amount of blood, and your body needs food and water to replace it. We need you back at full strength, soon."

Ben followed the man to the mage's camp and settled down near the fire. The day was bright and warm, but a breeze off the river chilled him. He was glad of the fire. Jasper and his contingent as well as the Sanctuary mages were there.

"Towaal and Amelie are assisting in the search for survivors," explained Jasper. "Not that they are having much luck. It's worth the effort, I suppose, if they find even one man. The arms men appreciate their help. Keeping faith with those men is a worthy goal in of itself."

Ben nodded and couldn't help but ask, "The demon-king?"

Jasper shook his head. "Your instinct was right. The demons didn't dam the river, they'd diverted it. It was flowing through a rift that opened up to their world. From the other side of the rift, they directed heat which boiled off the water that was already in the riverbed. It was brilliant, actually, but with the rift open, I was able to reach Gunther."

Ben blew on a spoonful of hot soup and tried to stop himself from wolfing it down. The first bite had scalded his tongue, but his stomach was crying for sustenance.

"When I found Gunther, he came quickly," continued Jasper. "The communication was hurried, as you can imagine, but I believe he was traveling along the node lines somehow. He'd been there, in their world, apparently working to close another rift. It seems he was searching for a way back so he could close it on that side and not get stuck. He didn't take time to explain fully before the rift on the river vanished. I lost contact with Gunther after that."

"Is he," Ben frowned, searching for the right words, "still able to return somehow?"

"Yes," answered Jasper. "Before the rift vanished and I lost him, he told me he had one last thing to do, then he'd be back. He wanted us to prepare."

"Prepare?" wondered Ben. "What do we need to prepare for? I don't understand."

"The demon-king doesn't seem to be anywhere around here, which leads me to suspect it's there, on the other side. It is a guess only, but I think Gunther moved the demon-king's rift instead of closing it, and that it what he'll use to return. If that is the case, then I think it's best we assume the demon-king is coming right behind him."

Ben groaned. "We still need to deal with the demon-king."

"If the First Mage cannot stop this demon, then how will we?" exclaimed one of the guardian's mages who had been listening to the conversation.

"You're right," said Ben. "None of our mages have the strength of Gunther or a weapon like his hammer. There's something we do have, something he knows about. He was there when we took the staff from the Purple. If he's asked us to prepare..."

Jasper nodded affirmation. "That was my thought as well."

Ben closed his eyes and breathed deeply. "How long do we have?"

"Not long, I don't think," responded the mage.

"We have to figure out a way to use it safely," declared Ben. "Maybe when Gunther arrives, he'll know what to do."

"Did he talk to you about using the staff?" asked Jasper curiously.

"He said it would be dangerous, even for him," admitted Ben. "He didn't tell us anything beyond that. He wanted it destroyed."

Jasper met Ben's eyes. "So, we're in the same pickle we were before we faced the demon army. The demon-king is a threat like no other. We have a powerful weapon, but it's deadly to use."

Quietly, Ben looked away and went back to his soup, unwilling to have the conversation with Jasper about the staff. He knew the man's arguments, and he knew they couldn't risk letting the demon-king roam freely. He also couldn't make the decision to sacrifice a man he considered a friend.

Jasper left him alone to his thoughts.

Ben had finished a third bowl of hearty soup and drank two water skins when Amelie arrived back at the camp. Her face was grim, and the party she led didn't have any injured with them.

"I'm glad to see you're up," she remarked, exhaustion lacing her voice. She took a place beside Ben. "That cut on your arm was brutal. It didn't look like a demon claw, Elle said. What did you find down there?"

He grinned at her. "We figured out how they were erecting that protective barrier overhead. The demons had mages."

"We?" asked Amelie. "Who's we, and how did you know about them?"

Ben frowned.

"They said you and Adrick were the ones who first went down the slope. Had he faced these demon-mages before?"

Ben sat down his bowl of soup before responding slowly. "No. It was me. The thing is, now that you're talking about it, I'm not really sure how I knew about them. I-I just did."

"You just knew there were demon-mages down in the

riverbed and knew where to find them?" interjected Jasper, leaning forward.

Ben shrugged embarrassedly. "Yeah, I was pretty sure. I mean, I don't know. Adrick flared the light from his sword, and we saw them. How I knew what to look for... I don't know. There was a lot going on."

"You were sure enough that you and Adrick charged into the middle of two thousand demons?" probed Jasper.

"They were there!" exclaimed Ben. "I was right."

Jasper scratched the silver stubble on his chin.

"Where is Adrick?" asked Ben, suddenly realizing he hadn't seen the man back at the camp yet.

"He has not returned," responded Jasper, frowning. "The guardians have sent a patrol south to look for him. If he was able to exit the river, they will find him. Tell me more about this intuition of yours?"

Ben sighed. "I don't know. It just, well, during the battle, I started to feel woozy but clear at the same time."

"What do you mean?" asked Amelie.

"It's hard to explain," responded Ben. "I just knew what to do, where to go. I didn't know what the demon-mages were, but I knew we had to stop them. I knew where to find them. It just came to me. The path was clear, and it was obvious there was only one thing to do."

Amelie looked to Jasper for explanation, but the ancient mage's face was closed with thought.

They waited, until finally Jasper said, "There are many types of energy in this world. Many have physical manifestations. Heat, wind, physical forces. Even you, Ben, know some of how we manipulate these sources of energy. Mages and scholars understand these physical things well. Others, like life itself, we do not understand well. We've managed to harness it, though, in some limited circumstances. Healing for example. It is not well understood how the body heals itself, but throughout time, mages have been able to identify that it does happen. We have found ways to boost that process. There are other energies which are even less understood, things we can only speculate on."

He stopped and looked at Ben directly.

Ben scratched his head.

"Are you saying Ben is a mage!" exclaimed Amelie.

Jasper shook his head. "I am saying there are many things we do not understand, many ways we feel and manipulate energy which are outside of our abilities to control or even comprehend. I'm saying I do not understand this."

"What should I do?" asked Ben.

"Pay attention to your instincts," suggested Jasper. "Not just what they are telling you to do, but how you feel when it happens. Is there anything you do differently to make these urges stronger? Study yourself and your actions."

Ben shrugged. "I've always felt that way, I guess. Whenever we're in a battle, it's like clarity just comes over me. I thought it was battle fever, my body responding to the stress."

"Interesting," murmured Jasper. "Maybe that's all it is."

Ben could see the man didn't think so.

Suddenly, shouts from the edge of the camp drew their attention. They were in a strange language, but the guardian mages all turned at once.

"Adrick," explained one of them.

Ben, Amelie, and the guardians scrambled to their feet and rushed to the side of hill. Ben had hoped Adrick survived the river, but he knew in the back of his mind there was a chance he didn't. The water, the demons, there was more than a mere chance someone may not survive all of that.

When they saw him, it wasn't clear at first if Adrick had survived. Two guardians carried the swordsman between them. As they drew closer, the people on the hill could hear them calling.

"What are they saying?" asked one man.

"Get a mage!" shouted Amelie. "He's alive. He needs healing."

Ben turned, but the small girl Elle was already rushing forward. Prem was right beside her.

"He'll be okay," claimed Amelie as they passed.

Ben didn't think she knew that, but maybe it was what Prem needed to hear. He started down the hill, but behind him, there was a flash of blinding light.

Ben and Amelie spun to look out over the field. It was still littered with the bodies of the dead. One hundred paces past where the rangers had first formed their line, right on top of the road that ran north, was a giant, blazing portal. Its edges crackled with lightning, and its center hissed with charge. Smoke and the flicker of static energy faded, and Ben found they were staring out at a blasted land. It was dark, covered in soot. If there was a sun, it was hidden beneath thick, boiling clouds. The only thing discernible through the clouds of soot were glowing fires in the distance. Barely visible, a small figure darted through the open gate. A small figure with a big hammer.

"Gunther!" shouted Ben. He started running.

Atop the hill, it was if a giant kicked an anthill. Mages were grabbing devices, forming into loose groups, and steeling themselves for what may be coming behind the First Mage. The guardians were torn, some of them starting toward Adrick, some of them rushing to Gunther.

The guardians down the slope, closest to Gunther, dropped to their knees and pressed their foreheads to the ground. The big mage waved at them wildly, and while Ben couldn't hear what he was saying, he'd traveled with Gunther long enough that he thought he had a good idea what the man would say.

Ben couldn't help himself from grinning when the giant mage snagged one of the kneeling men by the scruff of his neck. He dragged him up and shoved him, propelling the poor man away from the gate. Ben's grin vanished when a terrific roar burst from the opening behind Gunther. The mage kept running, and everyone else near him turned and ran as well.

Ben and Amelie rushed to stand with the mages at the crest of the hill. They were clustered around Jasper, preparing themselves as best they were able. Ben eyed the wyvern fire staff in the ancient mage's hands and shook his head angrily. There had to be another way. Gunther would know.

"When he gets here," instructed Ben, "ask Gunther about the staff. He was reluctant to handle it before, but now… Now, he has a reason to use it."

"I'm not sure he can do any better than I," remarked Jasper.

Ben didn't answer. The First Mage had to know how to use the thing safely. He had to.

Gunther was still five hundred paces away when the light from the rift was completely obscured.

"That's bad," muttered Rhys from behind them.

Ben didn't turn to look at his friend. He couldn't. Like everyone else, his gaze was fixed squarely on what was emerging from the rift.

"The traps are in place?" asked Ben weakly.

"Everything we laid down for the army of demons is still there," answered Jasper, "plus a few other tricks. I…"

He trailed off. The demon-king stepped out of the rift, ducking low to squeeze through. Malevolence radiated from the creature.

Ben took an involuntary step back when the monster rose to its full height. It towered ten-stories tall. Higher than most of the keeps Ben and his friends had visited, and the thing was wider as well. Its shoulders spread out the width of a small village. Its arms were the size of a sea-faring ship and rippled with taut muscle. Not that it needed the strength, the thing could merely step on a person and crush them as easily as Ben would crush a grape.

"Can you attack it?" asked Ben, unable to keep a terrified tremor from his voice.

"We're trying," growled Jasper, his face locked in concentration. "It's suppressing everything we do. The grip it has on stasis is unbelievable."

Down in the field, the demon-king took a step forward, covering thirty paces with one stride. The earth trembled as its clawed foot slammed down.

One of Jasper's mages raised an arm, and a green, sparkling ball of energy flew from his fist. It soared through the air, arcing toward the demon-king, then sputtered out, and vanished halfway there.

"Anything within three hundred paces of it is not working!" shouted a mage.

Ben saw an explosion down in the field. A line of blasts started, traveling across the width of the space, then stopping abruptly when it neared the demon-king.

Towaal raised her hands and sent a thick bolt of lightning at the creature, but just like the fireball, it crackled and then vanished. Her hands dropped down, and defeat clouded her face.

The mages, realizing the traps they laid were doing nothing, all began to raise their arms and start attacks from afar. Heat, cold, lightning, wind, it all flew off the crest of the hill but vanished when it got close to the demon-king. Frustration was evident on everyone's face, but no one seemed to have a solution.

"It's disrupting our attacks," snarled Jasper. "There's a barrier there, scrambling our will. I can sense it, like a wall of complete stasis. We don't have the power to break through it."

"Does Gunther?" asked Ben.

The big mage was still four hundred paces away, his thick legs churning as he ran. He didn't look like he had any interest in turning and fighting.

The demon-king's gaze found the mage. It opened its mouth, and Ben cringed. He expected a sound like nothing he had ever heard. He was half-expecting to go deaf. Instead, he realized with a sickening feeling that the demon-king wasn't opening its mouth in anger. It was amused. It was laughing. It waved a hand and pure force descended on Gunther and the men and women around him.

The big mage was shoved to his knees, but the dozen people running with him fared much worse. They were squished. There really wasn't a better word for it. Beneath the force of the demon-king, they were crushed into puddles of gore. Even the ground around them was compacted, grass flattened, mud squishing outside of the area of the attack.

Gunther was down, trying to crawl forward, but he still had three hundred paces to go.

Ben swept his sword out of the sheath, but he didn't charge. The thing rose twenty times his height. A sword was useless against a nightmare like that.

"The ground underneath it!" cried one of Jasper's mages. "Try to manipulate that. Maybe we can mire it in mud or burn it."

Several mages attempted, but the demon paid them no mind. Ben could see from afar, nothing they did made a difference. The demon-king took another step, quickly cutting the distance between it and the struggling Gunther.

"He has no chance!" screamed a guardian. The woman started running down the slope.

"Light," said Towaal. "That's what Gunther uses. We can manipulate it outside of the barrier and direct it at the creature. By the time it gets close, it will not have our will focusing it, and we won't be interrupting the creature's field of stasis."

Raising her hands, the mage did something to refract light. Far above them, Ben could see a brilliant beam focusing down on the demon-king. It was the same attack she'd used in Ooswam. Other mages joined her and added their strength to the spell. They gathered more and more sunlight, darkening the rest of the sky, and turning a single beam of light into a brilliant, burning blaze that shone down on the demon-king.

The monster snarled. Then, it raised a village-sized wing, holding it like a parasol overhead. The wing blocked the light from its body, and it shined harmlessly on the creature's black wing. The demon-king took another step closer.

"There is no way Gunther can reach us before it reaches him," cried Amelie. She was clenching her hands, looking on in frustrated terror. Like the other mages, there was nothing she could do.

Ben, his mind swirling, struggled to think of something, anything.

Shouts rose up from all around him as mages attempted to manipulate energy and send it through the demon's barrier. In some cases, it didn't violate the creature's stasis, like the light, and it passed through. In most, it fizzled into nothing. None of it did any damage, though. The demon-king advanced, shrugging off their attacks. In moments, it would be on Gunther.

They needed something with enough force, enough energy, that not even the demon-king could maintain stasis. Sunlight, a breeze, none of that was harming the creature. They had to think of something. They had to do it quickly, or else Gunther would be crushed, and the rest of them would be close behind. If they didn't act, they'd all die.

Grim clarity washed over Ben.

"Jasper," he said.

The ancient mage met his gaze.

Ben drew a deep breath and then released it slowly. "I am sorry."

Jasper smiled and inclined his head. "There is no reason for you to be sorry, Ben. You've done more than could be expected of any man. You brought us together. You've given us leadership and a chance. Now, it's my turn."

The white-haired mage stepped forward, and the other mages

fell silent, watching as the old man raised the wyvern fire staff. His skin split, and blood leaked from his wrists, pouring onto the pale wood, coursing into the tiny patterns carved there, powering the runes. The mouth of the staff began to glow.

The demon-king's head snapped up. Its eyes blazed, looking directly at Jasper.

"Protect him!" shouted Towaal.

The mages swarmed, crossing their arms in front of themselves, erecting barriers around the white-haired man a moment before an enormous funnel of soot and fire blew from around the demon-king, drawn from the rift behind it. The flames swirled, tapering down to a point, focusing on the hilltop.

Ben crouched with Amelie, watching in horror as the fire battered against an invisible shell around them and the two dozen mages. He felt the heat searing his skin, pressing in. The barrier began to shrink, and on the outskirts, mages ignited like torches. Their skin popped and crackled. Bacon on a hot pan. He cringed, but there was nothing he could do. One by one, the mages went up, bursting into flame, and the circle grew smaller.

Ben couldn't see anything outside of the barrier, only flame and soot. Inside, people were huddling closer and closer together, trying to stay within the protective bubble. Grim resignation painted the faces of those furthest out, but to their credit, every one of them held their hands high, maintaining the protection that gave Jasper the precious moments he needed.

Half the mages lost their lives, vanishing in the inferno swirling around them. With each death, the bubble shrank. Ben stood, trying to push his way to the edge to allow more room for the mages. It was critical they survive long enough for Jasper to act, but the bodies were pressed so close together that Ben couldn't get around them without pushing someone else back into danger. He grunted in frustration, watching as another woman on the edge was incinerated.

Ben glanced at Jasper, hoping the man would have time, knowing he was powerless to help.

Then, Jasper raised the staff, and he punched back.

Incredible heat leapt from the wyvern fire staff and flew out into the fire and smoke. The white-haired mage strode forward, following his flame, and in the blink of an eye, the raging inferno vanished from around them. Ben watched in amazement as the tight funnel spiraled back, passing by the demon-king and into the rift behind it. The demon-king itself was contending with a different kind of fire.

A narrow band of flame shot from the mouth the wyvern fire staff. Jasper trained it on the monster, scouring the beast with incredible heat. The demon-king couldn't harden its will against the overpowering heat, and where the flames moved, Ben could see the black flesh bubbled, and purple blood flashed into a charred crust.

Jasper was directing the fire like a butcher carving a hog. He shredded the demon-king's wings when it tried to use them to defend itself, and he lashed the fire across its eyes, blinding it. Then, he bored the flame directly into its chest, melting a hole to its heart.

The demon-king raised its arms, trying to absorb the force of the fire, but Jasper kept going, burning holes through the arms and continuing into its chest. Stumbling back, the creature tried to retreat through the rift, but two of its huge steps away, the rift flickered out. Below them, Gunther had rolled onto his back and was watching the flames scourge the demon-king.

In front of him on the hill, Ben saw Jasper fall to one knee.

The flames continued, scalding hot, but the heat was drawn into a narrow channel, focused on the demon-king. The creature stumbled and fell to its knees, shaking the earth with an enormous boom. It still towered above them, but its massive shape was covered in char, and it struggled to raise its hands, to turn, to do anything to keep the awful fire from burrowing deeper into it.

A moment passed. Then, the creature let out an enormous, pitiful wail. It screeched in terror and anger. Jasper yelled, a cry of pain and elation rising until his voice failed him. The flame intensified in one last, steady blast. Then, the staff fell from his hands, and Jasper collapsed face first onto the grass.

A heartbeat later, the demon-king collapsed as well, falling in a nearly identical pose to the mage who had killed it. The thunderous impact rocked the hill and knocked Ben off his feet. He fell to his hands and knees, his eyes fixed on Jasper's prone body and the fallen demon-king beyond him.

Amelie rushed to Jasper, turning him onto his back, placing her hands on him, and then sitting back, hurt and sorrow on her face like a mask. Elle arrived, pushing her way through the assembled mages and knelt on the other side of him. She didn't touch him. She didn't have to. The man was drained. Every ounce of his blood had been poured out into the staff.

The world was silent. There were no cheers from the survivors, no calls of gratitude. Everyone paused, waiting. They didn't know for what. The demon-king was dead. Its army was dead. The rift it had opened was closed. They'd won. They'd defeated the demons.

And Jasper was dead. Half the mages had died, and over half the arms men in the battle before. They'd won, but the price had been high.

The silence was broken when heavy footsteps proceeded Gunther up the hill. Around him, guardians were swarming, mouths open in awe. The huge mage's face was grim, though, and he stared down at his old friend.

He turned to look at the group before his eyes settled on Ben. "That should have been me. I wish that had been me."

"There wasn't time," croaked Ben. "I tried to make him wait. We tried to think of something else..."

"I understand," said Gunther. "You did what you had to do. Sometimes, that's all there is. That... that creature could not be allowed to roam freely here, no matter the cost. The devastation it would have wreaked would be beyond imagination."

Ben couldn't take his eyes away from Jasper's body.

"This may be hard to hear," rumbled Gunther, "but it was worth it. What Jasper bought with his life was worth it. The rift in the Wilds is closed, along with the one the Purple fashioned in the desert. There was a natural rift west of the City that I felt close, by the guardians I'm guessing since they are here. I closed one east of Irrefort. Now that the rift this monster opened is closed, there is no path, nothing that the dark forces can use to cross. The dark forces cannot come here, not into Alcott at least. Never again will man live in fear of these creatures."

Ben looked up to meet Gunther's gaze.

The big mage placed his hammer down and picked up the wyvern fire staff. It was spotlessly clean. Every drop of Jasper's blood had been burned away, fed into the awful fire which had felled the demon-king. Without word, Gunther brought the staff down onto a raised knee, snapping the wood in two. He tossed the pieces to Ben.

"The power unleashed here today was unprecedented," said the big mage. "In my time, I have neither seen or heard of the like. We cannot allow that to happen again."

"Sir," said one of the guardians. The man took a knee and looked up to Gunther. "We've been working constantly to keep the secrets of your kind safe. What you did today, the rift, the other world, it is astounding. It is more than I ever would have expected us to see. Let us serve you. Let us take you to what we have stored for you. You can use it. The devices, the knowledge, us. You can use it all to make this world right."

Gunther frowned.

"We have devices of immense power," continued the man. "Nothing like the staff, but in your hands, they would make incredible weapons. No one could stand against you. We have texts describing knowledge otherwise lost to this world. Ancient secrets at your disposal. We've collected everything we could from your peers, their knowledge, their power... Nearly unlimited power. You can train us as your disciples, and we will go wherever you command us."

"Disciples?" asked Gunther.

The guardian bowed his head. He didn't see the disgusted snarl on Gunther's face.

"Where are these items stored?" queried the big mage. "In your village west of the City?"

The guardian glanced around nervously, but evidently decided if the First Mage was asking, he should answer. "Yes, safely in our village. No one knows it's location but us, and, well, Lord Ben and his friends. We have a node gate. We can be there in a quarter bell."

Gunther grunted and turned back to Ben. "I ask that you continue your work, Benjamin Ashwood. What you do is important. I understand that now, but I will not assist you. I hope you understand why. That is not the way, it cannot be the way. The time of the First Mages has passed, and the power wielded by us should pass as well. I should have died in Jasper's place."

The big mage gave Ben a hard look, and Ben swallowed uncomfortably.

"That staff, the knowledge and power of the First Mages, it cannot exist in this world," continued Gunther. "It is too dangerous, and in time, it will always be misused. There are those who do not understand that, and they never will. I do not have the time or patience for the debate. You will explain it to them, Ben?"

"I'll do my best," acknowledged Ben.

"Good," said Gunther. "You know where you can find me, but if you ever do, it had better be worth it. Now, I have something to go do."

Without acknowledging the guardians, Gunther strode down the hill, heading south. He passed Adrick on the way, not pausing. The other guardians, confused, scrambled to be near their leader, none of them bold enough to trail Gunther. Ben followed them to Adrick Morgan's side.

"Should we follow him?" asked the guardian who had been speaking earlier.

Adrick blinked, watching the back of the First Mage as he hiked down the road, alone.

"He doesn't want you to follow him," said Ben.

"But he's the First Mage!" exclaimed the man. "The only one left. Our responsibility is to him. The wisdom he has, the teachings he can share with us, we must be with him!"

Adrick struggled to sit, assisted by Elle. He shook his head. Slowly, he said, "Ben is right. If the First Mage does not want us to follow him, then we should not."

"Not follow him! What is he doing then?" pleaded the guardian. "We've spent our lives preparing for this."

Adrick met Ben's eyes.

Ben read the question on his face and answered it. "He's going to your village where I suspect he'll use that hammer to smash your hall. Then, he'll eradicate any knowledge you have of the First Mages. He'll crush any devices you have and burn any written manuscripts. After that, he will leave."

"To where?" choked the man.

"He'll go away," said Ben quietly, "to a place where he can be free. Free from the expectations and responsibilities you'd place on him."

"But-but we need him... The world needs him," stammered the man, tears running down his face. "Why-why would he do this?"

Quietly, Ben answered, "So that we can be free too. Free to live our lives. Free to make our own decisions. Free to save ourselves."

"What do we do?" said the man, falling to his knees. He bowed his head, both hands resting on the turf.

Ben shrugged. "We do the best we can."

There was a long pause as they watched Gunther march away.

"It seems my mission is no longer necessary," said Adrick, breaking the silence. "If we're free to choose, then I will follow you, Ben. After seeing what we faced here, I do not think I can rest comfortably knowing that whether by man or by demon, that kind of evil is possible. As long as you oppose it, you will have me at your side."

Ben grunted, unsure of what to say.

"We will follow you as well," said a ranger. The man was standing in front of a group of his peers. He waved a hand toward the field where a carpet of dead demons stretched for hundreds of paces. "Things like this cannot be. The leaders of this land ignored the threat, and we almost paid a dear price. Venmoor, my city, would not have survived what we battled here. Everyone I know would have died. The Alliance, the Coalition, they did nothing. The Sanctuary knew what was coming and instead of help they sent assassins! You are the one who saved us, Lord Ben, and I will follow you."

"The man's got a point," remarked Lloyd, speaking before Ben could object to the title. The blademaster hitched his belt and glanced back at his companions. "After this, I'd feel awfully silly returning to the college and teaching noble sons how to impress girls with a well-swung blade."

"The Sanctuary is not our place anymore," added Hadra. "We disobeyed the Veil and left against her wishes. We cannot go back there, so we will follow you as well, for now."

Ben looked around the top of the hill, studying the battered group. They said they would follow him, but to where? He couldn't lead these people.

"Ben," said Amelie quietly, "there is still much to do."

His eyes locked on the giant corpse of the demon-king. Smoke drifted off of it, thick and black. The thing was as large as a village, and it was blocking the road. He knew what he had to do. He just didn't want to say it.

Finally, he muttered, "Very well. First things first, let's move camp. It's going to smell here soon, and this many dead demons is certain to bring pestilence. When we've settled, Towaal, I want you and the other mages to far-see the surrounding area. We killed a thousand demons on this field, and countless more were washed downstream, but was that all of them, did any escape? Let's make sure we've finished the job right."

Towaal nodded, a hand rubbing her lips, not quite hiding a smile. Lloyd began barking orders, assembling the rangers, the blademasters, and the Kirksbane watch who looked to be following the rest of the arms men. The blademaster seemed a capable sort, and Ben left him to it.

Adrick struggled to gain his feet, and Ben stooped to haul him up.

"My people," the man started. Then he drew a deep breath before continuing, "Both my people and I will be very lost in this world. We've spent centuries waiting on direction from the First Mage, and when we meet him, he wants nothing to do with us."

"Yeah," agreed Ben, thinking back to his first encounter with Gunther. "He's like that. Come on. We've got work to do."

18

A DEAD KING

ONE WEEK LATER, BEN SAT IN THE COMMON ROOM AT THE CURVE Inn. All around him, the room bustled with activity. Men came and left, plans were discussed, and orders were issued.

In one corner, Lloyd held court with a gaggle of blademasters. The men had been tasked with training and organizing the rangers from Venmoor, the watchmen from Kirksbane, and an influx of new arrivals. When word had gotten out about the giant battle just north of town, it seemed every young man within thirty leagues had come to join the force. Their numbers swelled, but none of the new arrivals had a fraction of the skill of the men and women they replaced.

Luckily, Ben had the squad of expert swordsman from the most elite college of the sword in Alcott. Lloyd and the other blademasters had jumped on the opportunity to help train the newcomers and form effective companies when Ben first suggested it.

In another portion of the room, Amelie and Towaal sat with their heads close together discussing finances and logistics. Men and women were following them now, officially part of their burgeoning army. That meant they expected to be clothed and fed. That meant, somehow, they had to come up with coin for supplies and a way to actually get those supplies into people's hands. Ben's eyes had immediately glazed over the moment the discussion grew serious, but luckily for him, Amelie was willing to step in and handle that role. She'd been training her entire life to run Issen, so managing their small army's material was easy for her.

She was also keeping an eye out on the disparate groups of mages who had joined them. Guardians, men and women from Jasper's group, and runaways from the Sanctuary. They'd all agreed to follow, but none of them actually seemed to be doing it. Ben and Amelie kept them busy far-seeing the surrounding area and healing those they could. He knew that within days, the mages would be looking for more.

Upstairs, Adrick Morgan was slowly recovering from his injuries. The man had been nearly dead, and only the strange girl Elle's healing had saved him. He was able to get onto his feet now without assistance, but they guessed it'd be another week or two before he regained full strength. In the meantime, Ben had the guardians pairing with the more experienced rangers and learning life outside of their forest. The rangers were experienced both in the wilderness and in towns, and the guardians seemed most comfortable around them.

Ben was dealing with a number of reports that had come in and was trying to tie it together with information from the mage's far-seeing. He'd spread a map out across half the table. On it, he was tracking several large swarms of demons that had broken off from the main demon army and were threatening the north. They were nothing like what they'd faced a week ago, but a small village would have no defense against them. Days earlier, Ben decided their next move was to finish off the creatures before moving on to other concerns. While any demon swarm survived, their work was not done. The Veil, Avril, the Alliance, the Coalition, they could be dealt with after. Besides, facing the demons had earned them an army. Maybe finishing the threat would gain more loyalty from the survivors in the north. He hated to think like that, but he had few other choices.

A loud thump drew his attention, and he looked across the table to Rhys. The rogue was leaning back, frowning at a pitcher set in front of him. The man was taking up the other half of their table with his efforts, two empty pitchers and a plate of gnawed-clean rib bones.

"Out of ale again," drawled Rhys.

"It's not even dark outside," reminded Ben. "Is another round really necessary?"

"You're a lot less fun than you used to be," complained Rhys.

"I've got so much to do," responded Ben. "In addition to figuring out how we can efficiently finish these swarms, I have those letters to the nearby lords that Amelie suggested we send, the discussions with that grain merchant up from the City, the banker who fled Northport, the mayor of Kirksbane was talking my ear off all morning... I've barely had time to sit. There's more to do in a day than I can finish in a week!"

"I hear what you mean," agreed Rhys.

Ben frowned at the rogue.

Rhys met his gaze innocently, lifting his mug and taking a sip.

"You're the only one in this group who isn't doing anything," accused Ben. "Can't you find something to keep you busy?"

Rhys looked offended. "I am busy!"

"Doing what?"

"Drinking!" exclaimed Rhys. To prove his point, he turned his mug up the rest of the way and finished it in three quick gulps.

Prem slipped noiselessly into a chair beside the rogue and asked, "You want me to order you another pitcher?"

Rhys favored her with his brightest smile. "That would be lovely."

She stood and walked away, looking for the innkeep Tabor, moving just as silently as when she arrived.

"I don't know what she sees in you," complained Ben.

"Women like a scoundrel," claimed Rhys. "The worse you act, the more attractive you become."

Ben rolled his eyes.

"Seriously," said Rhys, leaning forward, "you should try it on Amelie."

"I don't think so."

"Where did that blond barmaid go, you know, the one Amelie is so fond of?" asked Rhys. "I bet she likes a bit of a rogue."

"Rhys," warned Ben flatly.

They were interrupted when one of the sergeants of the rangers, a man whose name Ben couldn't recall for the life of him, burst into the room. His eyes darted about, and then, he scurried to Ben's table.

"My Lord."

Ben winced.

Not noticing the reaction, the man continued, "Terrible news, sir."

"What is it?" asked Ben, struggling to keep the dread out of his tone.

"King Argren, my lord. He's been assassinated."

Ben sat up straight. "What? When?"

The ranger brushed his hair back from his eyes. "Three weeks past. News made it through Sineook Valley just this morning. Seems someone put a knife in the old man's back. No one saw the assassin, and no one's taken credit. The merchant who brought the news says everyone is assuming it was the Coalition, of course. Who else?"

"King Argren's dead," murmured Ben. "The Alliance, is it over?"

Amelie and Towaal arrived, either having sensed Ben's shock or overhearing the conversation. The room fell silent as others realized the importance of the news.

The ranger shook his head. "No, not from what the merchant said."

"Who's taking the throne?" asked Amelie. "Argren has no natural heirs. His wife is a slip of a thing and has no respect from the court. He married her simply because she's already proven fertile. She isn't even highborn. The other houses will be scrambling. I-I don't even know who would be next in line."

"The general, I'm told," said the ranger. "That new foreign one, the one who was just elevated to high command."

"Saala Ishaam?" queried Lloyd, coming from across the room.

Ben blinked. "Saala Ishaam?"

"Aye," said Lloyd. "He's the new general in Whitehall. He was Lord Gregor of Issen's liegeman for a time. Half a year ago, he uncovered a plot to assassinate Argren and was brought in as the King's personal protection. He's been rising in the ranks since then. I've never met the man, but I'm told he's a blademaster of incredible skill."

Ben's mouth hung open.

"I don't know if it's him or not," said the ranger. "I do know the merchant said that the general's ordered the troops to march, but I guess sail is the right word. They'll be crossing the Blood Bay, headed to Issen."

"What!" cried Ben, springing up and knocking his chair back.

The ranger looked back at him, confused.

"Argren's dead, Saala's general, and he decided to march?" said Towaal, sounding just as confused as the ranger.

"Why would he do it?" asked Amelie.

"There are two ways for a lord to control a population," said Ben, beginning to pace. "That's what Saala told us. You can do good works and earn the respect of your people, or you can unite them in fear."

"You know Saala Ishaam?" wondered Lloyd quietly, but no one answered him.

"The Red Hand," reminded Rhys. "That bald-headed bastard

never forgot his ambitions from before, from the South Continent. He landed in an opportunity he probably never dreamed of,
and he took it."

"We have to talk to him, to stop this!" declared Ben. "With
Argren dead, there's no reason Whitehall should sail to war."

Rhys shook his head sadly. "Ben, there's no reason the lords of
Whitehall would support a general taking the throne unless they
wanted war. There are new lands and profit for them if they win.
If they back down, they'll be seen as cowards, and it's only a
matter of time before the Coalition encroaches or the minor
lords in Sineook and elsewhere think they no longer need to
respect Whitehall. No, Whitehall is set on this road. We show up
there with this force you're assembling, and that will be the end
of it. Instead of a conversation, you'll have a fight."

"No," said Ben. "We have to talk to him. This is senseless. All
this time, we've been struggling to find a plan to stop the conflict.
Now Saala—"

"Ben, Rhys is right," interjected Towaal. "Saala may have given
the orders, but if he did, he did it with the support of the rest of
the lords of Whitehall. What we learned about his past... Ben,
you won't be able to talk him out of this."

"We have to," said Ben.

"You want us to march to Whitehall?" questioned Rhys.

"No," answered Ben, thinking quickly. "The demons are still
out there, still ravaging the north. We must deal with that, and we
must stop Saala. There's only one way. We have to split up."

The room erupted in objections but Ben held up his hand.
"You all agreed to follow me, yes? Was that meant literally, that
you'd always be in my shadow, or did you mean you'd follow my
direction? Working together but apart, we can put a stop to all of
this. We can stop the demons, and the Alliance!"

The room was silent, the men and women shifting and
glancing at each other out of the corners of their eyes.

"Lloyd," instructed Ben, "you and Adrick will take our arms

men north, just like we discussed. You'll clean out the territory between here and Northport and then move east along the high-road. I'll also send you the Sanctuary's mages and Jasper's group. They should be plenty of support even against a large swarm. Without the demon-king, the creatures will be susceptible to magic."

"Amelie," he began, but he paused when he saw the dark look in her eyes. "Ah, you can come with me if you want. It's, uh, it's up to you—"

"Yes," she responded, steel lacing her voice. "I think I will come with you."

"I as well," insisted Towaal. "It's foolish to leave you without a mage, Ben. Besides, I know Saala just as well as anyone. Maybe I can assist."

Ben glanced at Rhys. "You too?"

The rogue merely shrugged.

"Prem," said Ben, "you can discuss it with your father, but I'd like you with us as well. The two of you can commune through thought meld, and we can stay in touch with the bulk of our force."

The girl glanced at Rhys and then replied, "My father will understand. I will go with you."

"Ben," objected Lloyd, "if I go as well—"

"No," responded Ben. "The blademasters and rangers respect you, Lloyd, as they should. You're the best fit to lead them and the other arms men we've picked up. Adrick can manage the guardians and the mages. I trust the two of you to work together and make the right decisions. If needed, we can discuss options through Adrick and Prem's thought meld. Besides, going into Whitehall, we're better off with a smaller group."

Lloyd frowned but didn't object.

Ben looked around the silent room. Blademasters, rangers, mages all met his gaze.

"I'll leave as soon as we're able to get a plan squared away," he said. "Good luck in the north, and know that I would be with you if it wasn't... If it wasn't for what we have to do. If there is any chance to stop the war between the Alliance and the Coalition, we have to take it. The demons would have wrought devastation on Alcott. We can't let our fellow man do the same."

"What happens after we've cleared the demons and head east?" asked Lloyd.

Ben glanced at Amelie and then addressed the room, "We'll meet again in Issen."

19

REVIEWS, ACKNOWLEDGEMENTS, AND NEWSLETTER

I'M AN INDEPENDENT AUTHOR, AND IT'S A TOUGH WORLD OUT there. If you enjoyed the book, please consider making it a little easier on me and leaving a review on Amazon and/or Goodreads. Then go tell your friends.

Special thanks again to James Z for his beta reading services. He shamed me into deleting this beauty:

"They made it around a bend in the river and passed out of view of the Sanctuary two bells before dawn. Fishbone had spent twenty years captaining boats in and out of the private harbor and up the river. Even with a skeleton crew, he could manage it. Even in the thick of a full-blown drunken spiral it turned out. The sails went up as they reached the deep channel, but it was their captain who was three sheets to the wind."

"But it was their captain who was three sheets to the wind"! That may go down as the greatest piece of prose to get axed from a final draft in the history of literature.

As you know by the 5th one, it's really the professionals who bring this together. My cover and social media package were designed by Milos from Deranged Doctor Design (www.derangeddoctordesign.com). Inside the cover, Nicole Zoltack yet again did great work proof-reading (www.nicolezoltack.com). I thought I had mastered the English language, but as her notes describe, I'm a slow learner. Tantor Media is my audiobook publisher. After reading this, I'm certain you'll want to give it a listen as well. The audiobooks will be available on all major outlets within a few months of the digital and print versions. Eric Michael Summerer is the narrator and he does truly amazing work.

Thank you for reading my book,
AC

To STAY UPDATED and find out when Book 6 is due, or to receive **FREE Benjamin Ashwood short stories**, I suggest signing up for my Newsletter. In addition to the short stories, I stick in author interviews, news & events, and whatever else I think may be of interest. One e-mail a month, no SPAM, that's a promise. Website and Newsletter Sign up: https://www.accobble.com/newsletter/

Of course I'm on **Facebook** too: https://www.facebook.com/ACCobble/

If you want the really exclusive, behind the scenes stuff, then **Patreon** is the place to be. There are a variety of ways you can support me, and corresponding rewards where I give back! Find me on **Patreon**: https://www.patreon.com/accobble

16442695R00243

Printed in Great Britain
by Amazon